AMONG THE HUNTED

ALSO BY CAYTLYN BROOKE

Dark Flowers

Wired

CAYTLYN BROOKE

AMONG THE HUNTED

A SKYGLASS NOVEL

bhc
press™

LIVONIA, MICHIGAN

Editor: Chelsea Cambeis
Proofreader: Hannah Ryder

AMONG THE HUNTED

Published by BHC Press

Library of Congress Control Number: 2020936699

ISBN: 978-1-64397-180-3 (Hardcover)
ISBN: 978-1-64397-181-0 (Softcover)
ISBN: 978-1-64397-182-7 (Ebook)

For information, write:
BHC Press
885 Penniman #5505
Plymouth, MI 48170

Visit the publisher:
www.bhcpress.com

To my incredibly, incredibly patient sister.
Thank you for reading these drafts for the better part of a decade.
I hope I made you proud!

AMONG THE HUNTED

1

BEFORE

Kaitaini's neck snapped to the right as her sister's attack knocked her off her feet, sending her body crashing to the snow-covered dirt.

"Come on, Kait. Get up." Jezlem taunted her, circling her like a cat batting at a mouse.

On the outskirts of the training ring, the dozen or so other nymphs in their session winced. They eyed Tahlia, the elder aurai, waiting to see if she would interfere and call off the fight, but she stood still, arms crossed over her chest, her expression unreadable.

Kait grimaced, spitting blood and saliva onto the ground as her fingers turned to fists beneath the cold earth, encapsulating tiny clods of dirt in her grasp. Pushing herself up, she exhaled a ragged breath. They had been sparring for fifteen minutes now, each of them refusing to give in. Her muscles burned, aching for rest, but the look in Jezlem's eyes warned she was far from done with her.

"You look tired." Jezlem sneered. "Don't worry, you'll be flat on your back in no time."

Kait growled and lunged forward. Whipping her arms high overhead, she harnessed the wind and screamed. Opening her palms, she released the dirt, propelling it with startling force at her sister. Jezlem stumbled back, her hands moving to shield her eyes.

"What the hell was that? That's not legal!"

Kait grinned. "It's pankration. Everything's legal."

Jezlem hissed and shook the clinging dirt from her hair. Before she could collect herself, Kait walloped her with another gush of air. The rapid blows smacked Jezlem in the face and gut, wrenching a satisfying wheeze of breath from her as she doubled over.

Kait stacked her fingers atop one another as she gathered the wind between her hands, her magic building in intensity. Jezlem balanced in the dirt on one knee, her face hidden by her wild curls. The golden halo of light enveloping Kait—the physical manifestation of her magic—burned brighter, stronger, sensing her sister's own growing power. Every nymph's halo glowed a unique color to match the feel of her soul. Jezlem's was usually azure, but now it darkened and writhed like an angry river. Kait had to act fast.

Kait launched the swirling vortex of air as hard as she could, then stepped back, carried away at the notion of certain victory. As the vortex neared its target, Jezlem spun out of its trajectory, landing neatly on her feet. In the same motion, she brandished her palms, shooting streaming jets of water at Kait's legs.

Kait cried out in surprise as rogue droplets ricocheted off her skin and soaked the spectators. Still, Tahlia did not speak.

Kait's knees buckled, the pressure blowing her off her feet. She collapsed in the mud, landing on her elbow with a sharp crack, but Jezlem's momentum was just getting started. Twisting her hands, Jezlem lifted Kait off the ground. Water coalesced around Kait in a giant prison. She inhaled a shallow breath, her ethereal connection to the air completely cut off by the rushing waves.

Lungs burning, she writhed within the sphere of water, her kicks and jabs slow and ineffective against the liquid enemy. Her lips parted against her will, fighting to draw breath, and water gushed down her throat, intent on filling every crevice.

"Jez!" Kait screamed, her plea escaping in a stream of bubbles.

She could just make out her sister's silhouette through the pulsing water. Kait couldn't see her clearly, but she knew Jezlem was smiling, taking pleasure in watching her drown. She opened her mouth to cry out again when gravity shifted, slamming her into the earth.

The aquatic prison exploded on impact, dropping Kait facedown in oozing mud. Deep coughs raked her body as her lungs fought to expel the water within. Uneasy applause and Jezlem's snide laughter boomed in her ears, making her face burn red.

Kait leapt to her feet and locked onto her sister, wiping mud from her eyes and lips with exaggerated motions. "You almost killed me!"

Jezlem shrugged, amusement gleaming in her turquoise eyes. "You said everything's legal."

"I obstructed your sight. I didn't try to kill you."

"That wasn't my intention either. You attacked; I defended myself."

"This was supposed to be a pankration spar, not a battle of the elements."

Jezlem scoffed, removing the leather sheaths from her forearms as Tahlia finally abandoned her statuesque pose. Kait gritted her teeth, anticipating an unpleasant conversation from the sour look stretched across her elder's lips.

"Another victory for you, Jezlem. Well done," Tahlia said. "As for you, Kait…" She arched her slender eyebrows and pivoted on her heels, grinding the last of the clinging snow into the soil with her boots. "Where did Kait fail, everyone?"

A young dryad stepped forward, her pale brown eyes steady and unapologetic. "She lost her focus, let her emotions get the best of her. She discarded strategy."

"Precisely." Tahlia's voice was crisp as a January morning. She returned her gaze to Kait, who wiped the trickling blood from her lip. "You could have gotten out of that easily, found a way to use the water against your opponent. You could have accessed the oxygen molecules in the water and forced them to expand."

"With all due respect, Tahlia, drowning makes it difficult to concentrate," Kait replied.

Jezlem rolled her eyes. "If you practiced and took the time to study your element, you'd know how it manifests in both water and earth, and how to use them to your advantage. You can't rely on innate talent. You'll lose every time."

Kait tasted fury. "Don't tell me how to control my element. You're a naiad. Stick to puddles."

Jezlem took a step closer to Kait, her voice serious now. "I'm trying to help you."

"What do you think I'm doing here? I am working on it, okay? I can't help it when you don't fight fair."

"I'm trying to prepare you for what's out there." Jezlem gestured around at an unseen threat. "We can't sit by and lounge around like the nymphs before the Titan War. Their idleness made them vulnerable, and the Titans took advantage of that."

Kait groaned, wringing water out of her black hair. "Not another history lesson, Jez. I know the stories, same as you."

"But you don't put any stock in them. You treat them as cautionary fairy tales. You need to realize there are real consequences when you can't protect yourself."

"From who, Jez? The war is over."

"That's enough," Tahlia said. Her voice was soft but sliced through the tension like a well-oiled guillotine. "Yio, Kendra, it's your turn. As for you ladies, get back in line."

Kait's face burned darker. First, Jezlem destroyed her in the spar, and then she humiliated herself in front of her elder, by acting like a spoiled child. Brushing her hand down the length of her arms, she did her best to wipe the mud away, but the top layer had hardened in the brisk winter air. Only a puff of dust lifted into the sky. A long soak in the bathing pools would be the only way to clean her skin, but the thought of submerging herself in water so soon after Jezlem's "training" made her cringe.

Kait was sick of preparing for an invasion that was never going to happen.

The Immortal Council, made of up a dozen of the most powerful gods, enacted the portal blockade three thousand years ago to ensure immortals could never hunt nymphs again after the Titans were defeated. Created only a century ago, neither Kait nor her sisters had ever been under threat. Kait couldn't conjure the same fear as Jezlem because she had no villainous face to align it with. To her, immortals were colored smoke, a foreign enemy that only existed in a time far outside her own. Striding off the sparring field, Kait left the wooden arena separating the fields from the large apothecary a few hundred yards off in the center of Olean. She directed her feet east, back to the aurai encampment.

"Get back here!" Jezlem called. "Training isn't over."

"It is for me," Kait shot over her shoulder.

Part of Kait knew she should listen, knew she would pay tomorrow, but she couldn't bring herself to turn around. It had always been this way between her and Jez. Sibling rivalry was one thing, but Kait and Jez's relationship went beyond trivial arguments. Luckily, their other sister, Bia, didn't have a competitive nature—unless the challenge consisted of crafting the best healing tonic, but Kait had no talent for medicine anyway.

Compared to the other nymphs, the three sisters were different. Nymphs were not born but created. When the nymph population began to decrease from either disaster or old age, the mother goddess, Gaia, gifted the realm of Olean a new generation. From every drop of her immortal blood, she breathed a new soul into the world and weaved a powerful connection through the spine and sinew of each to one of the three elements: earth, wind, and water. Fire was deemed too dangerous a gift, for it gave voice to greed and destruction.

Yet something unique happened when one fated crimson drop fell from Gaia's flesh and splashed against the earth. Rather than one nymph, three burst forth.

Jezlem, alluring and strong, a naiad, graced with the ability to control and manipulate fresh water. Kait, an aurai, stubborn and impulsive, blessed with the gift of fierce winds. Lastly, Bia, an anthousai, gentle and introverted, imbued with the power of the earth.

The rare creation of the triad hadn't been seen for nearly four thousand years. The Immortal Council welcomed the triplets, honoring them with a powerful prophecy, though Kait carried the heavy burden like a curse upon her dark shoulders. Ever since she could remember, rumors and whispers swirled, promising the triad would herald a dramatic shift in power throughout the seven realms. The last time a triad formed, the three sisters had harnessed their elemental magic and wielded nature as a weapon for the first time—a change that transformed the race of nymphs from helpless prey to a formidable force that threatened the Titans themselves.

After the Titan War, the Olympians rewarded the most courageous of the triplets, Rajhi, with a seat on the Immortal Council, declaring her Queen of Olean and granting her immortality to rule alongside them. With a handful of advisors, Queen Rajhi governed Olean without any interference from Olympus. She raised the spirits the mother goddess gifted her as she saw fit, ensuring all nymphs trained not only in their elemental talents, but were well versed in defensive and offensive techniques should a future enemy threaten their existence. Both of her sisters were slain in the war, but the sacrifice of the triad and Rajhi's reign ensured nymphs would never again be taken advantage of.

For nearly one hundred years, the prophecy that sang of the new triad's impending greatness followed Kait, a lingering shadow, a constant reminder that one day, she would be expected to shine like her predecessors. There was only one problem: there was no greatness buried within Kait, no incredible power waiting for release. She had tried—goddess, had she tried—to unearth it, but beneath her flesh was ordinary blood and bone.

Before they were fifty, Jezlem had mastered her element, able to brew a tidal wave from a single drop of water. As for Bia, from the moment of her creation, the earth hummed beneath her touch. The ability to resurrect life from the most decayed flora had always flown from her fingertips with ease. Now Bia, the youngest of the triplets, was taking her ability further, pursuing the complex talent of healing the physical body.

At present, Bia was studying the different properties of herbs and oils and what tonics could be crafted to bring the body back to life. Kait had come close to going mad listening to Bia's ramblings more than once. If she had to hear the term *soul knitting* one more time… It was Bia's fascination, not Kait's. She didn't have any interest working over dead bodies.

As the oldest of the triplets, Jezlem never forgot her position in the triad or her responsibility to the realm, whereas Kait ran from any opportunity that might showcase it. Maybe one day she'd uncover her purpose, but the constant harping was suffocating, just another reminder that she wasn't special, that her point of the triad wasn't pristine but rather broken and weak.

Shaking the clawing thoughts from her mind, Kait spun her fingers, summoning the wind. She sighed in relief as her flesh melted away and the air embraced her. Shrugging off the glares tickling the back of her neck, she rocketed into the hazy sky. Her anger diffused as she left her corporeal body behind, her flesh evaporating in a haze. Navy blue and fuchsia streaks painted the sky as the sun hovered just above the horizon. Guilt pulled at Kait to return and apologize, but her clashing frustration spurred her up and over the towering pines, far away from her sister.

Cigarette smoke curled around Kait's shoulders, dragging the toxic scent across her bare skin. She wrinkled her nose, frowning as the impurities strangled the air. Her best friend and fellow aurai, Willow, pursed her lips as a group of humans milled behind them, long white sticks hanging from their lips. Everyone was dressed in finery. Young men returned from war wore black-and-white suits starched to perfection and chased women in sparkling red and silver dresses with heads draped in feathers and lace.

It was 1922—a glorious blink in time. The air was void of sirens at last, and a pulsing energy replaced fear. Kait and Willow had begun sneaking off to the mortal realm a few months ago, frequenting an underground speakeasy in Manhattan. Drawn to the beautiful cobblestones, Kait adored the mystery that vibrated within the growing city, especially the hidden clubs constructed behind the old faux brick walls.

A carefree laugh fell from her lips. Jezlem would lose it if she knew where Kait was: in the mortal realm, at a mortal bar. While nymphs frequented the mortal realm daily, doing important work such as ushering in the change of the seasons, taming wild seas, and bringing life back to barren earth, leisure trips were prohibited, and consorting with humans was more than discouraged.

But Kait wasn't there to be responsible.

Beneath their feet, the sidewalk thrummed as Kait's excitement crested. The cold February midnight kept them company as they awaited their turn to descend into the bar. Running her hand through her piled-high locks, Kait adjusted the halter around her neck, shimmying the black sequins over her hips.

"Do you think this is too long?" Kait asked.

Willow scoffed, shaking her beautiful afro blowout with a slight toss. Thin white straps crossed her back, and the silken material of her dress glowed against her umber skin. "Please, any shorter and we'd be invited to a different kind of club."

Kait rolled her eyes. Short was in style. Plus, she loved mimicking the bold young humans and their flirtation with rebellion. "Thanks for coming with me. Sorry for the short notice."

"No worries. I could tell by the look on your face that you needed to get out. I heard Jezlem put you in your place…again."

"Great. I'm glad every nymph in Olean thinks I'm a joke."

"You know nobody thinks that. Tahlia says you're one of the strongest aurais she's ever known."

"True, but she says it sarcastically, regretfully, usually right before she adds how lazy I am and laments how such potential was wasted on a sad sack like me."

Willow brushed her curls behind her ear. "Well, you don't care about reaching your potential. That's why your training is so half-assed."

"Ouch." Kait pressed a hand to her heart, her jaw dropping in feigned offense as the bouncer ushered them inside a dimly lit café.

Several patrons sat sipping black coffee from ceramic mugs. Kait and Willow strode past them to the supply room door. The speakeasy rumbled beneath the cracked tile, raucous trumpets and lively saxophones muted by layers of concrete. The nymphs rose on tiptoe, each leaning in to whisper the secret passcode into the bouncer's ears.

The man's face flushed, and he cleared his throat. Straightening his tie, he opened the door and led the nymphs into the supply room and through stacks of cardboard and dilapidated shelves. Another door loomed at the other end of the room. Several dents marred its steel surface. Kait's pulse quickened at the familiar sight of it, along with the scent of stale tobacco and spilled whiskey that seeped into the narrow room.

Tension built inside her chest, eager for release. Here, she wasn't plagued by prophecies or judgmental looks. Here, she was a body in motion, and she craved that anonymity.

"Enjoy, ladies." The bouncer pulled the heavy door aside, and they stepped across the threshold and descended steep wooden stairs into the club below.

Willow leaned in, shouting to be heard over the lively melody. "Still thinking about Jez?"

Kait shook her head, transfixed by the magical space. Willow's unique apple mint scent was the only detail keeping her tethered to reality. The dim lights tucked into the gentle slope of the curved walls created a cave-like ambiance. Soft piano crescendoed, giving way to growling trombones. Fifty or so couples sashayed and spun around the dance floor like tumbling fireflies. Clear bottles of nectar glistened behind the mahogany bar.

Kait took a deep breath, exhaling every fear and frustration the last few weeks had mounted on her shoulders. Jezlem wasn't there. Tahlia wasn't there. She had five hundred years to devote herself to the realm, but tonight, she was going to dance. Slipping her bronze hand into Willow's, Kait pulled her friend onto the dance floor. Grinding her hips and throwing her hands in the air, she gave in to the music, submerging herself under a flood of rippling notes with no need to come up for air.

⚡ 2 ⚡

The club was a dream, a wonderland. The band pounded the stage as a seething tide of bodies pressed against one another, petting, stroking, and swaying. Between songs, they sipped forbidden liquor, the fire burning any wandering thoughts to ash before they could solidify.

Uncurling like ribbons of smoke, the nymphs broke apart. Kait closed her eyes, giving in to the soulful notes, and let her body take over. Here in the mortal world, she was nobody, just another dancer. She threw back her head and laughed, free from the daily stressors heaped upon her in Olean. Here, she didn't have to be a great warrior, didn't have to fall in line and protect the realm. Here, no one knew who she was, no one expected anything from her, and the only judgement she received was on how fast her hips gyrated.

Tobacco smoke filled the underground club like a noxious cloud. Kait clicked her heels and tossed her hair until her sequined headband shot across the room, getting lost in the shuffle of feet. Hands grazed her backside and playfully pulled her hair. With each touch, she became more lost in the wild frenzy, running as far as she could from her troubling thoughts.

"Well, well," a deep voice whispered in her ear. "Didn't think I'd find a nymph here tonight."

Kait's eyes sprung open, but there was no one in front of her but the same pulsing crowd. No one stood out as the speaker, but she felt a presence, like a magnetic hold pulling her closer. A flash of white moved in the corner of her eye.

"Like you, I'm good at blending in when I want to."

The voice spoke in her ear again, sending chills down Kait's spine. Turning over her left shoulder, her violet eyes alighted on a tall stranger standing behind her.

"You're mistaken, sir. I'm not a…what was it you called me?" Kait asked, eyeing his slender but muscular physique as she turned to face him.

The stranger's eyes twinkled, a crooked grin pulling at his lips. His dark brown hair was combed back, sleek and polished like every other man in the club, but something about him was different. Under the lights, his skin glowed like alabaster pearl, like the underside of a shell. He took a step closer, bending his neck to bring his face close to the slope of Kait's collarbone. Her eyes widened as his lips hovered above her flesh, and he inhaled the natural fragrance of her skin.

"Your scent betrays you, I fear. Honey lavender, is it not?" He pulled back.

"Perfume."

"Ah, what a lovely lie. I detect no chemicals or faux notes. No, you, my dear, are the real thing. And such beauty. I think you would turn Aphrodite herself green with envy. Believe me, I'm an expert at what gets her hot."

Kait froze, taken aback as the stranger twirled them beneath a shadow. Rather than his features becoming cloaked in darkness, his image remained illuminated by a muted glow radiating from his flesh. Realization bloomed in her mind as she recognized his halo.

"You're an immortal."

"Well done."

"But…what are you doing in the mortal world?"

"Same as you," he said. "I've seen you in here several times, you and your friend."

Kait's breath caught in her throat as she followed his gaze through the crowd. Willow was dancing with a human, blissfully ignorant to the fact that she'd caught a god's gaze. Kait turned her attention back to the immortal. She couldn't read him. The elders' warnings flared in her mind.

Gods take what they want.

They had to get out of there. The god's grin widened as his fingers brushed her waist.

Pivoting on her heels, Kait spun away, weaving through and knocking couples aside in a mad dash for Willow. Her fingers itched to call the wind to her aid, but they already weren't supposed to be there. With the mortal world being more of a gray area, Queen Rajhi of Olean turned a blind eye as long as the humans remained ignorant to the existence of their world. Using magic to ditch an immortal would certainly draw unwanted attention and put an end to their unsupervised trips.

"Hey!"

"Watch it!"

"Get out of the way!"

Kait ignored the shouts hurled at her. Frantically, she searched for Willow. Hadn't she been close to the door? A firm hand gripped her upper arm, yanking her backward. She collided against the god's firm chest, and his arms caged her in.

"Relax," he said, his voice husky as his lips traced the curve of her ear. "I'm not going to hurt you." Kait cocked her head, staring up at the handsome immortal. "Your friend is fine. She's right over there."

Kait followed his finger, exhaling a small sigh of relief when she glimpsed Willow in the human's arms, their lips locked together.

The god loosened his grip, the tips of his fingers still holding her as he spun her around to face him. "I'm Hermes."

Kait swallowed, caught between fear and curiosity. Her mind demanded to flee, but her feet remained immobile. After a moment of hesitation, she shook his hand. "Kaitaini. But everyone calls me Kait."

Hermes nodded. "Pleasure to meet you, Kait."

Kait dropped her hand. "What now?"

"Now we talk. If that's okay with you?"

Kait studied his face, looking for signs of deceit. He waited patiently, making no further move to detain her. Ivory skin stretched across a clean-shaven jawline, and his nose bent to the right with a slight crook. It was too dark to see the color of his eyes. He was handsome, but it wasn't enough to dismiss a lifelong distrust of his kind. If she ran again, how far would he chase her? He already admitted to watching them, so what more did he know? What did he want? Kait surrendered to his request, her stomach clenching with nerves.

Hermes grinned and led her off the dance floor to an empty table against the back wall. He pulled a chair out for her before taking a seat himself. "I'm sorry if I frightened you. I couldn't risk you getting away. You're the first nymph I've ever seen."

"How did you know? About me, I mean? I try to be so careful." Kait peered around to ensure her voice didn't carry.

Hermes shrugged, the movement accentuating the lean muscles beneath his fitted blue collared shirt. "Believe me, it wasn't obvious. At first, I was drawn to your beauty. Unlike the humans, your face isn't layered with rouge and lipstick. You're natural."

Kait blushed.

"More than that, it's the way you move. Your steps are fluid and rhythmic, confident. Am I right in guessing you're an aurai?" Hermes arched a brow.

Kait narrowed her eyes. "I thought I was the first you'd seen. Forgetting your lies already?" She poised herself on the edge of her chair, alarms ringing louder in the back of her mind. She was a fool not to escape when she had the chance. Subtly, she scanned the crowd of sweaty faces, searching for Willow. Out of the corner of her eye, she caught the way Hermes slid closer, positioning his shoes on either side of her heels, boxing her in—an aggressive move.

"No, you've got me all wrong," he said. "Everything I know about your kind I learned from a dusty tome. Honest. I was hoping to glean a thing or two from you that those ancient texts can't teach me."

The god's tongue was silver, causing Kait's heart to falter as he stared at her with imploring eyes. She cleared her throat, caught off guard by Hermes's sincerity and the raw power emanating from him. He lacked Zeus's might and Apollo's charm, but his talents went beyond the physical plane. Instead, he snared his prey through twisting words, often pitting people's own wit against them. Like him, Kait was well-read. Part of their training in Olean included learning the characteristics of each god, and none were more clever than Hermes. His show of interest and curiosity was simply that—a show.

"Like what?" Kait's fingers itched to cast. The stagnant air pressed in and around her, trapping her in an invisible cage.

Hermes cocked his head, flashing a dazzling smile of slightly curved teeth. "I don't have a specific question in mind. At the moment, I'm enjoying looking at you."

Kait wrinkled her nose and rose to her feet. She stepped away from the table, but Hermes was faster, latching onto her wrist and spinning her back. His touch was soft, yet deliberate.

"Sorry. I realize how that must have sounded. Please, forgive me. Unlike my numerous relatives, getting laid isn't my first priority. Come on, just five minutes. Let's get to know one another." He released her arm and held up his hands in surrender.

Kait scanned the crowd once more. Willow was oblivious to her plight, swept away by liquor-induced passion. She resumed her seat against her better judgement. "I already know you. Hermes, messenger to the gods. You're a trickster, a patron of thieves. The only question I have for you is, what do you plan on stealing from me?"

Hermes leaned closer, sliding his arm across the polished surface of the table. His sleeve brushed Kait with the faintest touch, but an electric current sizzled between them. "Only your time."

Kait shifted away, drawing her right arm into her chest. "And after, will you take advantage of me?"

Hermes's eyebrows arched. "That's a bit forward, Kait. At least let me buy you a drink first."

Kait frowned, not intimidated by his wiles. "I'm quickly understanding why Olympus was sealed off. I know your game. Gods only want one thing."

"No wonder you ran from me."

"I don't hear you denying it."

Hermes shrugged, tracing his lips with his knuckle. "Lying isn't in my nature. True, the Titans had a penchant for beautiful creatures—nymphs especially—but lucky for you, we slaughtered them all." His mouth twitched, almost daring her to remain seated.

Kait met his challenging gaze. For decades, she had listened to the elders' teachings of Olympus's violent history. She recalled Tahlia's stern voice as she wove frightening tales of how the Titans unleashed hell, attacking the ethereal realms in droves, killing every lesser being who stood against them in their quest for domination. Amidst the killings, the great Titan, Oceanus, indulged in the flesh of a nymph before slitting her throat. From that moment, the secret contained within their halos was revealed. Not only did the glowing energy grant youth and beauty for the longevity of a nymph's five-hundred-year lifespan, but it also yielded an intoxicating high well beyond the power of opium's spell.

The Titans' bloodlust intensified. No longer were they content with slaughter. The great immortals ravaged the realms, forcing the surviving nymphs to the ground while they raped them, over and over again, absorbing their energy into their own. They drained the nymphs of their halos, swept away by the delicious ecstasy coupling yielded.

Once finished, most discarded the used nymphs, snapping their necks or crushing their windpipes with a single squeeze. Others left them in the dirt, immediately on the hunt for another to satisfy their rampant desire. Kait could never figure out who she pitied more: the nymphs they executed or the ones still breathing. Once a nymph's halo was stolen, her magic and elemental connection to the realm evaporated. Gone was her element, gone was her power, gone were her years. She became mortal. Kait thought it'd be better to be a corpse.

"Yes, but the Immortal Council sealed *all* the gods inside to protect us, even the ones who claimed to be heroes," Kait said. "How do I know you're not just a well-mannered descendent intent on my corruption?"

Hermes grinned, his tongue flicking out like a viper. "Are you afraid?"

"No." She hoped he missed the way she trembled. She knew she should get away from him, get back to Olean. But Kait didn't want to leave. There was something enticing about the god. He was as beautiful as a painting, but the longer she looked, the more nuances she noticed. Like the way one eyebrow curved higher than the other and the confident way he bore a thin scar marring his top lip, as if it were a trophy rather than a deformity. If gods were so cruel and vain, why had this one allowed imperfection? Maybe the gods weren't the enemy. Maybe the stories were wrong, embellished through the ages to suit another purpose. "You don't scare me."

"No? I don't inspire even a small sliver of fear?"

Goose bumps prickled along her skin as she inhaled Hermes's warm scent of musk and sandalwood. "Maybe a little," Kait admitted.

"I like that. Your honesty is refreshing. Now it's my turn. How'd you guess I'm an immortal?"

Kait brushed her fingertips along her cheekbone, wondering what his face would feel like under her touch. "Your skin, it shines with an iridescence no amount of shadow can conceal. Though it's duller than I would have imagined. Seems my grandiose imaginings of gods far exceeded reality."

Hermes scoffed. "Again, refreshing. For argument's sake, our halos are not dull. I dim mine to further the illusion of mortality." He unfastened the top button of his shirt. A bright glow the color of nectar radiated off his pale chest. "Layering helps." Hermes closed his shirt. "That's why I avoid clubs in the south."

"How often do you frequent the human realm?"

"Once every few weeks. As you stated, on Olympus, I have the arduous task of messenger. I'm expected to leap to attention the minute another immortal snaps their fingers, but it has its perks. I travel from realm to realm, see all sorts of incredible lands. Plus, I'm privy to all the behind-the-scenes drama."

Kait frowned. "You read the private messages?"

"I don't have to. Body language speaks volumes." Hermes's eyes roamed down Kait's body.

She could feel the heat of his stare, conflicted as to how it made her feel. On the one hand, the attention empowered her, but she was wary of the thoughts behind his gaze.

"What's your story?" he asked, his cool voice in direct opposition to his fiery stare. "Out there, you danced with the ferocity of a storm, like you would explode if you didn't move."

Kait's eyebrows sprung up, stunned for what to say next.

Hermes smirked. "Body language, remember?"

Kait nodded and cleared her throat, gauging how much she should reveal. "Back home, I have to do things a certain way. I crave the freedom this realm offers. I don't have to be anyone here." Her voice faded to a whisper as she looked off into the crowd. Willow was gone.

Hermes listened, absorbing every word. "I know what that feels like. It's nice to disappear for a while."

Kait's gaze flickered to the god. He leaned back in the chair, his body language relaxed, open, and nonthreatening. She furrowed her brow. What did a god know about stress? About impossible expectations? They had everything imaginable and took the rest when it suited them. Yet when she looked in Hermes's eyes, she saw the same burning need to escape that surged within herself.

"Yeah, like you get to be someone else for the night."

Hermes nodded. "It's cool to have someone agree with me, rather than tell me to stop complaining." His lips split in a grand smile, his boyish charm softening Kait's resolve. "I'm glad I caught you." He reached out and touched her hand, lingering for a moment before rising to his feet. "Sounds like we both could use a drink."

Before Kait could reply, he sauntered over to the bar, returning a minute later with two martinis in hand. She accepted one with a shy smile, removing the olive from the surface and popping it behind her teeth.

Hermes lifted his glass, his piercing stare holding Kait's over the rim of his glass. "To rebellion."

"To rebellion," Kait echoed.

3

Jazz exploded through the open door as a server ducked back inside the club. Kait sipped her Mary Pickford, grinning as her tongue tingled.

Hermes ran a hand through his hair. "I'm glad you didn't mind coming outside. I swear, that music follows me back to Olympus. I can't get it out of my head."

"The band does seem louder tonight," Kait agreed. "It's nice out here. We don't have to scream to be heard."

White lights decorated the tiny outdoor patio attached to the back of the building. Because Prohibition was in full swing, the roof and walls were plastered shut with slabs of corrugated metal, but the lights softened the harsh atmosphere.

Today marked one month since she and the god had started seeing each other. The night they met, she never anticipated the chance meeting would blossom into a close friendship. Hermes began as an exciting dance partner, but quickly evolved into a trusted confidant. Before their last few dates, her pulse quickened at the thought of seeing him, and Willow threatened to wring her neck if she changed her outfit more than once.

Sitting across from him now, a small smile warmed her as she watched him swirl his liquor clockwise before taking a sip. Her heart swelled, content to stay there forever, but did she have the same effect on him? They had yet to discuss past relationships. She didn't want to know who he had waiting for him back home. Hermes was her friend, but lately, she found herself imagining the possibility of more. Nothing intimate of course—no one was worth losing her magic and becoming mortal—but she yearned to place her hand in his, to get drunk on the taste of his lips. She set down her drink on the rickety table, her thoughts veering into unexplored territory.

"Are you happy?" she asked.

Hermes's brow furrowed. "Right now?"

"No, I mean on Olympus, as the messenger. Does it bring you happiness even though you'd rather be doing something else?"

Hermes took a sip of his bourbon. "Sure, the work is mind-numbing, but I enjoy the travel aspect. You know my reputation. I have plenty of opportunity to sneak around and inject some chaos. It's fun, but I crave a position that would challenge my intellect or allow me to use my speed for more than just delivering letters."

"Then why don't you?"

Hermes rolled his wrist, swirling the liquor once more. "What else can I do? Roles on Olympus don't change. Besides, I wouldn't know where to start."

Kait chose her next words carefully. "Do you have a wife?"

Hermes scoffed. "Once, though my fling with Aphrodite could hardly be considered marriage. Besides, that's half the problem."

"What is?" Kait leaned forward, pulling at the sequins on her red dress. She tried to remain indifferent, but the thought of Hermes lying beside the most beautiful goddess in existence forced her teeth to grind together.

Hermes sighed, setting down his glass beside hers, tapping the rim with his pinky. "There's no one I relate to on Olympus. Everyone has their responsibilities and partners to spend their immortality with, except for me. I'm not content with stagnation. I want a woman who is wild and unpredictable. That's why I enjoy your company so much. You intrigue me in a way no goddess ever has. You're beautiful, of course, but your defiance encourages my own."

Kait's jaw unclenched, hope blossoming in her chest. "I feel the same way about you."

Hermes placed his hand on hers. Unlike their first encounter, the god's touch now made her feel warm and secure. "Here's an idea: Let's run away. Forget Olean. Forget Olympus. This, right here, is all I want. Knowing I'm going to see your face gets me through my days."

Kait laughed, placing her other hand atop his. She rubbed his smooth skin with her thumb. "That's a charming notion, but where would we go? This realm is the only place we can both enter."

"Then we stay here. Disappear, find a little house, and be happy."

Kait cocked her head, unable to determine how much he was teasing. "You're serious?"

"Why not? You aren't happy in Olean, and I've lived enough lifetimes without you." Hermes's eyes glistened, his emerald irises shining earnestly.

"But my sisters…and Willow. I can't leave her behind. Plus, it'd be like forsaking who I am, what I am." Kait glanced at the back door. Somewhere inside, her friend waited. "I can't turn my back on Olean and live the life of a mortal.

That's not what I want. I don't want to throw away all my training and have to stash my magic away so my neighbors don't see the real me."

Hermes sighed and squeezed her hand, staring off into the corner of the patio where a human couple sat, lips engaged, barely an inch of space between them. "Of course. I was only joking. Thinking out loud." He waved his hand in front of his face, brushing the notion away. His gaze wandered to the couple once more. He licked his lower lip. "I want to try something."

Leaning in, Hermes captured Kait's lips with his own. Caught off guard, she froze for a moment before sinking into the kiss. Energy pulsed between them, like crackling fireworks. She closed her eyes as their tongues danced, leaning into his chest. His lips molded to hers, and together, they moved in perfect synchrony.

Kait drifted away. Her dreams of this paled in comparison. Her body pulsed with desire, but her mind exercised careful control. The consequences of getting carried away were too great. Hermes gripped her upper thigh, his fingers sliding higher as they dove beneath the material of her short dress. Kait's eyes flashed open, and she jerked away, breaking their bond.

"What are you doing?" she whispered, withdrawing her legs from his ardent touch.

"Kait," Hermes said, his voice rough with need. "I'm sorry, I don't know what came over me."

Kait's heart fell. "You're just like the rest of them. Gods only want one thing."

Hermes shook his head and clutched her hands, preventing her from pulling away. "No, don't say that. Forgive me. I got carried away."

Kait was quiet, chewing the inside of her cheek as she mulled over his words, trying to identify if they carried any truth. "It's not like I haven't thought about making love with you, but I can't. I won't sacrifice my magic."

"I'm not asking you to do that. Please, Kait. I...I love you."

Kait startled. "What did you say?"

Hermes's eyes shifted. "I love you." He sat back and dropped his hands away from her, rubbing his knees. "Sorry, I didn't mean to blurt it out like that, but it's the truth. Do you...think you might love me too?" His gaze was honest and hopeful.

Opening her mouth to reply, Kait couldn't form the words he wanted to hear. Her throat was thick with emotion, the strongest being guilt as she watched his hope wither in her silence. She loved spending time with him, loved the way he listened and made her feel invincible, but did all of that equate to love?

Her heart beat erratically while her thoughts grappled for purchase. She had no answer, no way of knowing what love was supposed to look like. She had never experienced anything that resembled the word. And what if she said yes? What if by concurring, she inadvertently granted him permission to take her? Clearly, he desired her body. What if he didn't stop next time?

What if she didn't want him to?

Hermes held his silence, waiting, but Kait couldn't think, couldn't breathe. "I—I have to go."

Wrenching away from the table, she disentangled herself from Hermes and dashed back into the club, leaving him staring after her.

"Add two d-drops of cinnamon oil t-to this mortar," Bia instructed, yanking Kait from her thoughts.

The memory of Hermes peeled away, thrusting her back into the small earthen hut she occupied with her sister. They were working in one of the outer buildings of the infirmary located in the middle of Olean, in a meadow of red and yellow poppy flowers. Even though every nymph had the aptitude for healing, the staff primarily consisted of anthousais or earthen nymphs. Their unique talents for healing diseased roots and floral veins allowed them to easily switch their talents from nurturing nature to nurturing the physical body. As the third triplet of the triad, Bia's healing powers were exceptionally strong, though she often lacked the confidence to execute them.

Kait wrinkled her nose as a damp smell of tossed dirt permeated the air. Hearing only the last half of Bia's instructions, she poured half the bottle of cinnamon oil into the stone bowl. Bia watched over her shoulder and screeched.

"No! What are y-you doing? I s-said two drops!" In her approach, Bia's foot snagged on a raised root, sending her sprawling into the wooden table, knocking it onto its side and sending a dozen half-filled bowls skittering to the floor. "Kait!" Bia's voice was accusatory as she stared openmouthed at her sister. Her hands flapped rigorously at her sides—a physical rendition of her frustration.

"What?" Kait asked. The lingering image of Hermes's crumpled face shattered as she heard the hostility in Bia's tone.

Bia groaned, and her flapping intensified. "I'm trying t-to create an anti-inflammatory tonic, not give these p-poor creatures kidney failure. You said you wanted to h-help."

The scene before Kait was chaos. A mixture of heavy scents flavored the air as the spilled oils dripped off the table's edge, absorbing into the thick moss carpet lining the dirt floor. Mortars and bowls lay shattered on the ground, their contents ruined. Kait registered the agitated wind created by her sister's flailing hands, aware she was on the verge of a panic attack.

"Bia, I'm so sorry. I wasn't thinking. Let me help you clean up. Then we can start over." Kait crouched down, scooping mounds of dirt sprinkled with crushed herbs into her palm.

"No. No. No. I n-need you to leave. If you're not going to t-take this seriously, you need to go."

Abandoning her task, Kait stood, gazing at her sister with pleading eyes. "I'm sorry, Bia. I didn't mean to mess up. I guess I wasn't—"

"Paying a-attention," Bia snapped. She sighed, rubbing her eyes with the back of one hand while the other continued to flap. "What's going on? You have no f-focus. You offered to help me create these medicines for my final apothecary exam, b-but now you're treating it like a joke."

Bia shook her pin-straight scarlet hair and tried to calm her fluttering hands. Kait slunk around the table, staring at the disturbed dirt. She always struggled to comfort Bia, who had a strong aversion to being touched, especially when she was frustrated or nervous. Normally, singing soothed her, but Kait's mind was blank.

Taking a steadying breath, Bia collected herself, flapping her hands in a more even rhythm now. "What's r-really going on?"

"Nothing. Bia, I zoned out for a minute, nothing more."

"I d-disagree. Along with a lack of focus, your m-movements are slow, your eyes are glazed, and I haven't seen you eat anything in nearly a week. T-Tell me."

"There's nothing to tell. I'm fine." Kait smiled, trying to prove her point, but the movement felt foreign.

Bia fixed her with a skeptical look. "You're l-lying."

"Excuse me?"

Bia's hands bounced off her hip bones. She hated confrontation. For a second, guilt plagued Kait for causing such distress.

"Kait, I know you. I know you're s-struggling to mesh your desires with what the realm expects of you, but this behavior goes beyond that. You've lost your joy. You've become a shell of yourself. What's d-done this to you?"

"No one. Nothing. *Nothing* is wrong with me," Kait whispered, but her soft voice was swallowed by the sod-filled walls. "I love being an aurai. It's just…all these decisions about my future. It's become too heavy." Kait stroked a nearby leaf, looking away from Bia's unblinking gaze. "You and Jez have always been so sure of yourselves, blessed with the knowledge of exactly how to contribute to the realm, yet I still don't know what I want to do with my life."

Bia nodded.

"Can you diagnose me? Give me a magic cure?" Kait gestured to the plants and herbs spilling off the narrow shelves and climbing out of window boxes.

Bia frowned. "I'm not a healer; I'm a s-student. And it doesn't work that way. I noticed your trips to the mortal world h-have increased. Have you been exchanging saliva or any other bodily fluids with humans? Did one of them cause this?"

Kait gasped. "Bia! Of course not." She lowered her voice, fearful another nymph passing by the hut would hear. "How do you know I travel to the human realm?"

"I'm a-always listening."

Kait groaned. "Well, cut it out. And nothing happened." Her voice was vinegar, void of the softness she usually reserved for her younger sister.

Bia looked back at Kait, her face expressionless. "I never t-tell; I only listen. But right now, I need you to *tell* me what's w-wrong."

Kait opened her mouth, staring at the floor. "I'm fine."

A pregnant silence ballooned within the space. Kait's palms pulsed with sweat, and the low-ceiled room suddenly felt very claustrophobic. "Are you sure you don't want me to stay and clean this up?"

Bia's hands flapped harder, and she shook her head. "No. Unless you're going to be h-honest with me, you need to leave. It'll be easier to catalogue what was wasted on my own." Bia set to work righting the space. At last, her hands were occupied.

Kait paused near the threshold, drumming her nails along the doorframe. For a moment, she imagined telling Bia about Hermes. About what he did to her, what he said. But it was obvious from her sister's fierce concentration that she'd already been dismissed. Yes, Kait was a mess, but rather than being disappointed in her, she wished her sisters could understand that she wanted more out of life than what the prophecy envisioned.

Kait pushed through the door. It hit the side of the hut with an underwhelming thud. She marched into the frigid afternoon sun, grumbling under her breath. The beads of sweat that dotted her brow inside froze as the wind greeted her. She bit her lip, jogging away from the little structure.

Up until a week ago, she was happy, wasn't she? For the first time in nearly one hundred years, the misery her mundane routine brought about in her was missing. She raced through her tasks and trainings when the sun was high, delighting in the day's descent into twilight, dreaming of what new adventures the night would bring.

Rather than escaping to the mortal realm once or twice a month, the desire to flee Olean burned inside Kait like poison, corrupting her thoughts, carrying her to the Hall of Portals nearly every night before she could consider otherwise.

Kait didn't pretend to wonder what distracted and drove her—he stood about six feet tall with wavy brown hair. Yet, it wasn't Hermes's physical appearance that drew her; it was his depth. Picturing his handsome face caused her stomach to sour. She hadn't told Willow what transpired between them. She hadn't told anyone, too worried what sort of judgment might be cast upon her.

Kait collapsed to her knees, her thin black leggings doing little to soften the blow of the frozen earth. Her chest tightened beneath her golden corset. Bia was right. She wasn't fooling anyone—most importantly, herself. She wasn't fine, far from it in fact. Dreams waited in the wings of her subconscious, pouncing every time she closed her eyes, haunting her with visions of her hasty exit from the patio that night. What was Hermes's crime? Why did she rush away the moment he offered her precisely what she wanted?

For years, she'd searched for love in stranger's beds, empowered when she brought powerful centaurs to their knees or caused satyrs to cry her name. She lived for those stolen nights, when only the stars were privy to her escapades. Kait loved how sex made her feel, the delightful control it awarded her. It was the only way to stay sane when she fumbled through every other aspect of her life.

Casual unions were exciting yet empty. Once the sun awoke, the magic of the night evaporated. She had no one to hold, no one to breathe in. Most nymphs didn't settle down, too dedicated to the realm to form a relationship that existed outside fireflies and stardust. But why couldn't she? Hermes said he loved her. Why should she deny him—or herself—such a chance? She didn't belong in the triad, and there was no reason she had to forsake magic in the mortal realm if she was careful.

Joy swelled in her chest as she raised her face to the sky. Somewhere high above, Hermes raced about Olympus. His words from their first night together echoed within her, bringing to her feet.

To rebellion.

Kait's fingers flexed, and she leapt into the sky. Before gravity could act, the wind cradled her, stealing her away as a fierce wind. She had no idea if he would forgive her, but there was only one way to find out.

⚡ 4 ⚡

Kait battered wooden hangers aside. Like most of the buildings in Olean, the armories were situated inside ancient oak trees. Standing one hundred feet tall and stretching forty feet wide, the massive giants were hollowed out to accommodate elegant staircases that wove up and down, leading to numerous platforms within. Stationed at the point of each cardinal direction in the realm, each clan retained an armory in their own oasis. The one in the south was the largest due to its proximity to the market. It was there that Kait searched for the perfect dress to see Hermes in.

Aside from tactical wear, such as belts, holsters, and vests, the armories boasted a beautiful selection of gowns. With her black hair and bronzed skin, Kait gravitated toward golden hues, happy with how the color made her violet eyes pop.

Flickering candles illuminated the shop, casting dancing shadows along the arched walls. Her fingers leapt from dress to dress, appreciating the varying fabrics. Drawn to an ankle-length silk gown the color of honey, she withdrew it from the rack and held it in front of her body. The length was more conservative than she typically wore, but the plunging waterfall neckline compensated well enough.

The wind rustled, causing the tiny flames decorating the shelves and steps to bend and twist, threatening to extinguish before righting themselves. Kait felt the presence of another aurai and spun around.

"Willow! I'm so glad you're here." Kait rushed over, wrapping her friend in a tight embrace. "I thought you were in Larin?"

Willow pulled away, her hands sliding to Kait's shoulders. "I received a message from Bia. She said you were in trouble."

"She did?" Kait frowned and walked back to the expansive racks in search of matching heels. "I'm sorry. She shouldn't have done that. We had a bit of a disagreement earlier, but I'm fine now."

Willow followed, crossing her arms over her chest. "That's not what I heard. Bia is worried about you, and that's saying something. Unless you're a suffering plant, she won't look twice." Her voice softened, probing for more. "What happened with Hermes the other week?"

Kait slid on a pair of strappy gold heels that wove up her calves, admiring the way they shimmered. Fixing her friend with a shy smile, she pulled her hair back into a smooth updo.

"He told me he loves me."

"What?"

Kait nodded, a bright smile lifting her lips. It was the first time she'd repeated his feelings out loud. "He said he's never met anyone like me and that I dominate his thoughts. He even invited me to run away with him. He imagined a sweet life tucked away in the human realm where we can be together."

Willow's jaw dropped, and her brows jumped. "You told him no, right?"

Kait answered with a sad sigh. "Yes, that's why I've been so off. I can't stop thinking about what I said to him. He took a chance and put himself out there, and what did I do? I left. I ran as fast as I could without giving him an explanation."

Kait grabbed the bottom of her dress, yanking it over her head. Her halo glistened, burning brighter when uninhibited by clothing. Her thoughts drifted to Hermes. Was he at the speakeasy looking for her? Would he let her explain?

"So what's with the dress? Don't tell me you're going to see him."

Kait scoffed at the incredulous inflection in Willow's voice as she slipped the gown over her breasts. "Relax, I'm not going to disappear with him, but he deserves an explanation and…"

Kait paused, shocked by the next words that flowed so naturally through her mind. Why did it take her so long to realize the truth?

"And I'm in love with him too," she whispered. Her admission buoyed her. Never had she felt so light.

Willow inhaled sharply, taking a step closer to Kait. Her full lips were downturned, her eyes grim. Gently, she took hold of Kait's hand. "Please don't be mad, but…I don't think you should see Hermes anymore."

Kait pulled out of her friend's grasp. "What? Why?"

"He's an immortal, Kait. There's a reason gods and nymphs are isolated from one another. You know the stories as well as I. They view us as prey. He's not safe."

"No, the *Titans* viewed us that way. The *Titans* hunted us—the same Titans the gods defeated to protect us."

"I don't trust him."

"Why? He's been nothing but a gentleman to me. Those stories stem from thousands of years ago. The gods are different now."

Willow dropped her head, wringing her hands together. She raised her eyes, pleading. "He's still male, Kait. I know you think he's incredible and special, but it's all an act. I've seen the way he looks at you, the way he touches you. I let it slide because I thought you were using him to let off steam, but now, hearing this confession… Your relationship has become dangerous. Men only want one thing, whether they're human or immortal. I don't want you to get hurt. Or worse."

"I'm not going to sleep with him, Will. I'd never give up my elemental connection to bed an immortal. With Hermes, it's not about sex. We have something far deeper."

"Maybe you view it that way, but what if he doesn't?"

"Hermes would never force himself on me," Kait said through gritted teeth. Her hands curled into fists as she stared at her friend. After a moment of awkward silence, she strode past Willow, disposing of her worn dress in a nearby laundry receptable. "Sorry you wasted your time leaving Larin. I'd head back if I were you." Kait stormed through the curved archway of the armory.

With a swift wave of her hand, a breeze suffocated the firelight, leaving Willow in darkness. Calling the wind to her side, Kait ascended into the sky without a backward glance. Shifting from flesh to air, she melded with the wind and raced toward the Hall of Portals located two miles away in the main square.

Anger drove her as Willow's fears echoed in her mind. Kait shook the disconcerting thoughts away, trying her best to ignore the painful pit in her stomach.

"You came!" Hermes called over the energetic percussion. He wrapped Kait in a warm embrace and spoke into her ear. "I was so worried. I've waited every day, hoping you'd come back, but I wanted to give you space. I'm sorry if I freaked you out last time. Just forget I said anything."

Kait arched onto her tiptoes, brushing her lips along his scruffy jawline. Instantly, his prattling ceased. "No, don't apologize. I'm the one who was out of line. I came tonight to tell you that…I love you too and…I'm interested in seeing where these feelings lead us."

Hermes's eyes widened. "Really? I can't believe this." Hermes bent down and touched his lips to hers. The kiss was gentle at first, but soon, passion ignited between them. Kait's backside brushed the front of the bar as he pressed his body against hers. With a ragged breath, he broke away, smiling his crooked grin while his eyes shone with intensity.

"Come on. Let's get a drink and celebrate. Two sidecars, please, sir!" he called to the bartender.

Kait grinned, slipping her hand through Hermes's elbow. She laid her head on his arm as butterflies took up residence in her stomach. It was incredible to tell him how she really felt, that she loved him—like a rush of adrenaline. Hermes caught the two glasses as the bartender slid them down.

Kait squeezed his arm. "I'm glad you waited for me."

Hermes glanced down at her, withdrawing his hand from his pocket before tracing her waist. "Of course, Kait. I told you last week, you're my everything. I'd do anything to make you happy."

Kait's smiled widened as her fingers threaded around the back of Hermes's head, pulling him closer. She pressed her forehead against his and closed her eyes. "Same. I'd do anything to make up for hurting you."

Hermes kissed her again, his lips lingering against hers. "I'm happy to hear that." His voice was gruff as he inhaled Kait's scent. He passed her a stemmed glass filled with orange liquor and a rim dusted with sugar. "To love!"

"To love!" Kait clinked her glass against his. She tossed back the sweet Cointreau and cognac. The citrusy flavor burst on her tongue, sending unexpected waves of delight through her body. As the cocktail slid easily down her throat, sweet fire snaked its way from Kait's belly to her inner thighs, awakening her desire.

Hermes sighed, setting his empty glass down on the bar. "For how little credit we give humans for being intelligent and sophisticated beings, they sure know how to make a tasty drink."

Kait nodded, too distracted to reply. Her body felt strange, coursing with sudden need. The only thought she could form was of Hermes, of what his hands would feel like grabbing her hips as she sat astride him. Her nose wrinkled in confusion. Where was this bout of lust coming from?

Hermes deep voice shook Kait from her thoughts. She swayed on her feet, nearly colliding with a serving tray littered with empty glasses.

"Whoa, are you all right?" Hermes twirled her momentum into him.

Kait's eyes flickered as she tried to regain her equilibrium. "I'm sorry. I'm not usually clumsy."

"Don't worry. I'm here to catch you." Hermes winked, lowering his lips to hers once more.

Kait kissed him back, getting lost in the taste of him. She pressed her body closer, running her tongue along his teeth.

Hermes paused, tracing her lips. "You sure you're feeling all right?"

"Of course. Why wouldn't I be?"

"Okay, then. Come on. There's someone I want to introduce you to."

Pulling her along, Hermes wove through the crowd until he reached an occupied table on the other side of the mingling humans swarming the bar. He tugged Kait in front of him and followed close behind, his hands resting on her waist. She was acutely aware of the thin space separating them.

"Who are we meeting?" she asked.

Hermes tapped a seated man on the shoulder. At first, he didn't respond, too transfixed by the bottom of his glass.

"Meet any interesting people while I was gone?" Hermes asked, rousing his friend.

The man was clad in all black, and his skin was tanned, as if he toiled under the sun. His eyelids were hooded, his nose hooked. His visage resembled a falcon or hawk. Long blond hair was pulled back behind his head in a low bun—a stark contrast to the crew cuts that all the other men sported. He lifted his glass to his lips, and Kait caught a glimpse of light shining from the cuff of his sleeve. Another immortal.

"Kait, I'd like to introduce you to my best mate, Apollo. Apollo, this is Kaitaini, the aurai I told you about."

Apollo set down his glass and smiled, his square teeth gleaming brightly. He clasped Kait's hand in his large grip. "It's lovely to meet you, Kaitaini. Hermes wasn't lying when he described your beauty. I'm glad we found you tonight."

"Call me Kait. It's nice to meet you too." Kait dropped her hand.

Hermes rested a hand on her hip. "I thought he and your friend Willow might hit it off and the four of us could hang out." Whispering in her ear, he added, "That way you wouldn't have to leave her behind."

Kait's breath caught in her throat. "That's really sweet, Hermes. Thank you." Angling her neck, she kissed him again, amazed at how easily her love for the god seemed to expand. Images of them inside a tidy house with Willow at her side breezed through her mind. What if she could keep Hermes *and* Willow? Was such happiness possible?

"However, I have yet to see her." Hermes scanned the crowd. "Is she in the powder room?"

"No, she couldn't make it tonight, but I'll mention him when I return to Olean."

"Be sure to tell her how rugged and charming I am," Apollo said with a wink.

The scent of Hermes overwhelmed her as he rubbed her back. A wave of intense desire seized Kait, dominating her thoughts. Involuntarily, she backed into the god, fighting the urge to wrap his hands around her waist. Something was wrong. She like was a puppet, unable to deny the sudden pull of her strings. Intense feelings of passion and desire jolted through her like a bolt of lightning, demanding to be satisfied.

"I…ah, will you excuse me for a moment? I need to freshen up. Hermes, can you order me another drink?" Kait asked as she slid away from the gods.

Hermes followed and took her hand, sending shock waves of lust up her arm. Kait blinked and shook her head. What was wrong with her?

"Are you all right? Is there anything I can do to help?" he offered.

Before she could stop it, a delicious image of him fondling her breasts infiltrated her mind, and she answered with a throaty moan.

"Kait?"

Hermes's brows knitted together, oblivious to the physical longing his touch incited. Her name on his tongue made her knees quiver. She had never felt such need.

"No, I'm fine. I'll be right back. I just…need a minute," Kait told him, forcing the words out.

"Okay, hurry back."

His tone sent shivers up her spine. Snaking his other arm up her back, Hermes held her in place. His hands were gentle, but his lips were hungry, dominating hers with an intensity they had yet to breach. Tendrils of lust cascaded down her body, advancing her yearning to a new height. Her hands wove around Hermes neck, and she rose onto her toes, deepening the kiss.

Kait's body ached. It would be too easy to wrap her legs around the god's hips and let him lead her off to a dark corner and ravage her. But that wasn't her, and he was an immortal. She knew the consequences; that's why the feelings frightened her. She was used to being in control, and this strange sensation within her body left her helpless and desperate at the same time.

Kait felt Hermes respond beneath her touch, tasted the growing need on his tongue. If she didn't break away soon, she wouldn't get the chance to. Out of the corner of her eye, she saw a clump of humans staring. They were making a scene.

Ignoring the way her body burned for more, she jerked free and backed into the tight crowd. Hermes licked his bottom lip and pivoted on his heel, weaving back to the table. Over his shoulder, a smirk crossed Apollo's features.

Heading to the back of the club, Kait skirted energetic flappers and dashed by observers, aware of the curious stares and snide whispers following her abrupt departure. She didn't care what the humans thought. She needed to be alone and figure out what was happening to her. A minute later, she reached the back wall, but there was no sign of a bathroom.

"Dammit." She doubted hiding away in a dirty stall would make her feel better anyway. What she really needed was to leave her traitorous body behind and relax into the wind.

Content that she had escaped the humans' attention for the moment, Kait twisted her fingers. The air that replied to her call was stale and smelled of tobacco, but she leapt into its embrace regardless. The moment she shed her physical form, the intense desire evaporated, leaving her thoughts clear at last.

Kait exhaled, swirling above the pulsing lights and raucous trumpeters. She racked her memory for anything out of the ordinary that may have caused such a reaction. Did she catch something? Eat something? The night was early; she only just arrived. One drink couldn't have affected her in such a way. Her tolerance was higher than that.

Something niggled in the back of her mind. The bartender, the sound of glass grating on wood, the way Hermes had turned his body away from her. She knew she was missing something vital, a small detail originally overlooked, but the answer slunk away into the shadows of her mind.

Nausea turned her stomach. Was the god to blame? Hermes was the steadfast messenger of the gods, but he was also a trickster, stealing, lying, and playing off people's emotions for the thrill of it.

The strange expression on Apollo's face as she left flashed before her eyes. Kait climbed higher to hover above the bar, identifying the two immortals seated one hundred feet away from it. They conversed over glasses filled with amber liquor, their camaraderie light and jovial.

Guilt plagued her. Why would Hermes be responsible? It made more sense that something in the drink didn't agree with her.

Something Hermes might have added? Kait thought back to his aggressive kisses. She tried to dismiss her doubts, but her suspicion refused to dissipate, propelling her forward.

⚡ 5 ⚡

Drifting lower, Kait positioned herself a few feet from the gods, high enough that the swirling air wouldn't attract attention, but close enough that she could overhear without strain.

Hermes closed his eyes and tipped the contents of his glass into the back of his throat, then sighed.

Apollo chuckled under his breath, sipping his alcohol with more care. "That was painful to watch. I thought you were going to take her right there. Then, wham, she runs away."

Hermes growled, signaling to the server for another shot. "Rub it in. That's helpful."

Apollo shrugged. "I'm just saying. What'd you give her?"

"A tonic brewed by Aphrodite. She told me if I slipped it into her drink, she'd be moaning my name a minute later."

Apollo whistled. "It certainly looked effective. I can't believe she managed to pull herself off you."

"Neither can I." Hermes smirked. "She'll be back."

"When was the last time you were with a nymph?"

Hermes shook his head and tossed more whiskey into the back of his throat. "A few centuries thanks to that ridiculous portal blockade. I couldn't believe it when I saw her a few weeks ago. It's nearly impossible to happen upon a nymph these days. The last time we were together, I thought I finally had her. She was practically in my lap."

"Let me guess, she didn't drop to her knees?"

"Not even close," Hermes growled. "She took off, the damn tease. This is the first time I've seen her in a week."

"She's got a virtuous head on her shoulders." Apollo chuckled.

"Yeah, *too* virtuous for my taste. But I made up some bullshit—told her I loved her, that kind of garbage. I knew she'd come back."

"Why did you wait around for her?" Apollo asked. "If it were me, I would have saved my energy and taken a goddess the moment I returned to Olympus or even a human down here. They're easy to manipulate."

Hermes swallowed the rest of his drink, tapping the now empty glass against the metal table. "No, there's something about this one. I won't be satisfied until I taste her. Fingers crossed we advance our casual petting to something that offers me some release."

Above, Kait didn't know whether to cry or hurl heavy objects. How dare he? How dare he speak about her like an animal to be mounted? She was a fool—a stupid, headstrong fool to believe a single word he said.

"From the way she was rubbing up on you, I don't think crossing your fingers will be necessary."

Hermes punched Apollo's shoulder. "Right? I guess Aphrodite wasn't messing around when she said the tonic would work."

"Gods, I miss euphoria." Apollo groaned. "You're one lucky bastard."

Hermes grinned, a devilish glint in his eyes. "And I didn't even need the piriol."

The last word transformed Kait's disgust to fear. Even though she had never seen one of the frightening creatures, she had heard about them. A paralyzing coldness gripped her.

After Oceanus raped his first nymph and uncovered the sweet prize of euphoria, the hunt was born. Titans attacked Olean and the lower realms in waves, desperate to capture nymphs and experience the drug-like high sex and the absorption of the halo granted them.

Defending themselves in the only way they knew how, the nymphs transformed, avoiding the Titans as swift currents, shifting soil, and unattainable breezes. Enraged, the immortals created and bred piriols, ferocious animals that closely resembled the saber-toothed tiger. Able to outrun the winged Arion and stronger than the Minotaur, the piriol was also endowed with toxic quills that launched from its back on command. Yet its greatest asset was the ability to detect magic. No longer could nymphs sneak by, camouflaged by their elements. If a piriol's claws and teeth didn't force the nymphs to change back to their physical forms, their quills did.

Coated in a numbing toxin, once a quill pierced the nymph's soul, even in her elemental form, it froze her magic, prohibiting escape. Most of the Titans raped the injured nymphs the moment their flesh became visible, holding them down while they bled out from their wounds. Their pleas did nothing, except urge the immortals to ravish them faster.

Kait stared in disbelief and rage as the two gods laughed. She couldn't tell if Hermes mentioned the piriol for show or if it was a real threat he had the power to carry out.

"Maybe we could share?" Apollo raised an inquisitive brow.

Hermes tossed his head. "No way. She's all mine. Go seduce your own."

Apollo downed the last of his drink. "Wasn't that the plan for her friend? Shame she didn't come along."

Kait couldn't stomach another word. Her heart shattered into a dozen pointed shards at the mention of Willow. The gods were vile monsters. How could they value her and Willow's lives so little? A maelstrom of emotions bombarded her. Hatred, terror, grief, and guilt roiled inside her, fighting to stay contained.

Somewhere amidst the turmoil, Jezlem's voice gripped her.

Don't make a scene.

She was right, as always. If Kait did anything to reveal herself or the realm, the elders—maybe even Queen Rajhi herself—would restrict her travel completely.

Get home.

The thought barely finished before Kait surged forward, soaring over the heads of ignorant humans and plotting gods. She barreled through the front door, kicking up a bitter February wind. The door blew aside with such force it bashed against the brick wall, jarring the hinges.

Panicked shouts erupted from the line of humans waiting to get in as the sudden chill took their breath away. Kait wished to lash out further, to create a wild frenzy to match her anger, but she had to calm down. She had to get back to the portal. Shame ushered her forward. How could she have been so trusting? So stupid?

She pulled up sort, breathing in a familiar aroma—apple mint. Tearing her gaze away from the star-sprinkled night sky, Kait spied Willow standing at the back of the line, worry marring her beautiful face.

Stunned, Kait directed the wind into a narrow alley parallel to the café, stepping out of the air in her physical form once again. She rounded the darkened corner, intending to call her friend over, but a pair of firm hands grabbed her first, stealing her breath as she was pushed back into the dimly lit alley.

"I'm so glad you're all right." Willow sighed against Kait's hair. "I was so worried. I know it's none of my business, but I couldn't let you come alone." She enveloped Kait in a tight hug, her relief tangible. After a moment, she released her grip. Tears leaked out of Kait's eyes as Willow gently touched her cheek. "Kait? What's wrong?"

"You w-were r-right," Kait whimpered. "He was using m-me."

"Oh, Kait. What happened?" Willow's hands dropped to feel Kait's limbs. Her fingertips glided over Kait's skin, checking for bruises or wounds.

"He gave me s-something. Something to m-make me want him."

"Hermes drugged you?"

Kait nodded. Revulsion climbed her throat as she remembered his harsh kisses. The memory was bitter as pure lemon on her tongue.

"What happened after? When did he do this? Thank the goddess your halo is still intact."

"The tonic w-worked. I would have let h-him do whatever he wanted with me, but somehow, I managed to r-run away, and then I heard them talking about me."

"Them?" Willow threw a cautionary glance over her shoulder. Who else was there?"

"Apollo. He came to meet you. They know all about euphoria, even planned to rape both of us tonight. That's why he drugged me. He was sick of waiting. I was a fool to believe he loved me." Kait's voice rose, nearing hysteria as her eyes welled with tears again. "He made me feel so dirty, Willow, so ashamed. I should have listened to you. I'm so sorry."

"Don't." Willow's voice was strong and stern. She guided Kait's face upward, and their eyes locked. Willow shook her head. "Don't you think for one second that this is your fault."

Ragged breaths rattled Kait's chest. "There's more. If the drink didn't work, Hermes was going to… Will, I think he has a piriol."

Willow's grip on Kait's arm tightened as her eyes dilated. "We have to get out of here. Now."

A long whistle echoed off the surrounding bricks as multiple footsteps rang out. Both nymphs inhaled a sharp breath.

"Now, you can't leave yet." Hermes strode into the mouth of the alley with Apollo at his side. "The party is just getting started."

⚡ 6 ⚡

Kait and Willow leapt to their feet, flexing their fingers, summoning the wind to their aid. Hermes was faster. His image flickered, and a breath later, he stood in front of the nymphs, employing his swiftness to catch them off guard.

Kait registered his rapid approach a second too late. Before she had a chance to complete her cast, firm hands gripped her, then clamped a pair of cuffs around her wrists. At her side, Willow readied a fierce maelstrom to blow the gods back, but Hermes's fist slammed into her nose, knocking her off her feet and into Apollo's awaiting arms.

"No!" Kait cried.

Flexing her fingers, she commanded the wind to force Hermes away, but her magic lay dormant. Instead, the cuffs came to life, sizzling as white fire licked her flesh. Kait opened her mouth to scream again, but Hermes's slammed his hand over her mouth, stifling her cry.

"None of that, dear." He sneered. "Do you like those?" he asked, inclining his jaw to her tethered hands. "Borrowed them from a friend. Actually, we borrowed a couple things from him." He laughed, the sound hollow and chilling.

Kait threw her head to the side while attempting to whip her arms over her head, but they remained immobile, imprisoned within the cuffs. With his other hand, Hermes gripped her hair, entangling the loose strands around his knuckles up to the roots.

"Pretty great, huh? They inhibit movement and eliminate the ability to cast magic. He didn't think we'd need them, but I insisted."

"Hurry up. Let's get them farther into the alley." Apollo dragged Willow, who wore a similar pair of electric cuffs imprisoning her hands and ankles, into the darkness.

Hermes complied. He jerked Kait's head skyward, then lifted her against his chest, pushing her forward. The tips of her shoes dragged on the concrete. To the right, the alley yawned, opening like a gaping maw. Thick blackness radiated from its depths. Three brick buildings butted against one another. It was a dead end.

Hermes entered first. Apollo brought up the rear. Kait tossed her head back and forth to break the seal over her lips, but the god held tighter. When they were halfway down the alley, he stopped and spun her around, pinning her against the wall. Apollo mimicked the motion, and Kait flinched as the back of Willow's head collided with the bricks.

"Do the thing, Pol. I bet these aurais have a set of lungs on them."

Apollo slid into view, leveling his fingers with the nymphs' faces. "We need to be quick once I do this. The effect only lasts about ten minutes." He nodded. "Let go."

Hermes removed his hand from Kait's mouth. Golden light beamed from Apollo's fingertips to Kait's lips. Intense heat burned her skin. She went to scream, but her lips failed to separate. Strange magic sealed them together. Kait could only groan, the sound smothered and pitiful.

"Nice, though I was looking forward to hearing her moan my name." Hermes sighed.

Apollo rolled his eyes and cast the same power over Willow. Kait's head swiveled, and she found her own fear mirrored in Willow's tawny gaze.

Hermes grinned, appraising her, no doubt wondering where to start. As he came closer, Kait lashed out with her legs, kicking them in a scissor motion. The top of her right foot caught Hermes in the jaw, while the left connected with his shoulder. He stumbled back. A trickle of golden red ichor flowed from his split lip.

Straightening, he smeared the blood with the back of his hand. He looked wild, savage, a wolf standing over a fresh kill. "Oops, almost forgot."

A quick left hook slammed into Kait's temple, rattling her senses. She fell against the wall, barely managing to remain upright. As her vision came back into focus, she saw Hermes crouched at her feet, securing another set of manacles around her ankles. Acting on instinct, she tried to kick him again, but the cuffs blazed to life just as the others had, biting her skin. A raspy shriek stuck in her throat as her eyes shot venom at the god.

Hermes clicked his tongue. "Come on now, love. Don't look at me like that. You're the one who came back." He chuckled, low and eerie, slipping into the trickster skin he was known for. "I knew you'd come. The way you looked at me with those big, trusting eyes. Are all nymphs as gullible as you?"

Kait seethed with anger and shame.

"I have to admit, your reaction to my confession of love surprised me. Usually, that's the kind of crap women like to hear. Gives them an excuse to open their legs. But then you didn't come back. I nearly went mad stalking the club waiting for you, so I took extra precaution tonight. If you hadn't shown, I would've sent someone in to get you. Lucky for you, we were able to skip that step."

Hermes snaked closer, his strut that of a confident hunter. Kait's heart pounded. She chafed her wrists against the electric bonds as she fought to break free.

"It's been too long since I indulged in euphoria, and I long to taste it with you, my dear," Hermes went on. With deft fingers, he unbuttoned his shirt, revealing the bright halo beneath.

Kait tensed as the wind circled her, batting her arms, her legs, whispering through her hair, urging her to change.

Apollo tossed Willow to the asphalt, smirking as she moaned in pain. His fingertips glowed with the intensity of the sun, burning her friend where she lay until her skin began to bubble. Kait unleashed a muffled scream as she hobbled forward to help. Hermes chuckled, shoving her against the wall.

"It'll be much less painful for your friend if you cooperate," he said. "Pol, hold this one down too."

Apollo sidled up beside Kait, teasing the ends of her hair, brushing it behind her to reveal her breasts. He whistled low as he slipped his other hand around her back, palming the top of her neck. His grip was firm and scorching, holding her in place. In front of her, Hermes tossed his shirt to the damp ground, then unzipped his black jeans and pushed them below his hip bones.

"Come on," he said. "No reason why you can't enjoy this too."

Kait wrinkled her nose, her fingers itching to cast and take off into the sky. Hermes leaned down, inhaling the scent of her. With his thumb, he traced her lips, pushing his erection against her as his other hand rubbed her breasts.

"Come on, I know you want me."

Kait remained silent, her eyes tearing as she watched Willow wither under the intense heat holding her in place.

Hermes gripped Kait's jaw, demanding her attention as he slid the thin straps of her dress off to rest at her elbows. Kait registered the brutal lust in his eyes. She had to move, had to do something to help Willow. Apollo's grip fell lax as he, too, traced the swell of Kait's exposed breasts.

Without warning, she threw her head to the side, smacking Apollo in the teeth with her skull. Using her momentum, she whipped her neck back and smashed her forehead into Hermes's nose. Both immortals stumbled back, reeling from her attack. Blood dripped into Kait's eye, but she exhaled slowly through her nose, concentrating on keeping her balance. Ducking low, she spun on the balls of her feet, ramming her elbows into each of their exposed guts. Crumpling forward, the gods groaned, but she wasn't done. Grasping Apollo's long hair, she pulled as hard as her bonds allowed, earning a satisfied yelp from the sun god. The rays that held Willow hostage snuffed out the moment his focus fell away.

Hermes hissed. He lashed out to tangle his fingers in her hair, but Kait dodged his swipe, hip-checking him into the wall. She couldn't run, but she hobbled on her tiptoes, desperate to reach Willow.

"Kaf!" Hermes cried. He didn't chase her. Instead, he stood, righting his jeans. Apollo snorted, spitting blood onto the street.

A throaty rumble echoed in reply to his call, followed by a loud thump, jostling a nearby metal dumpster. Kait's neck snapped to the left, peering into the thick shadows. Something was coming. Pushing her fear to the back of her mind, Kait focused on Willow. If she could reach her, together they could figure out how to escape.

The air roared around her, fighting for her attention. It was agitated and full of fear, desperate to help her flee, but still, she pressed on. Willow lay a foot away. A fresh laceration above her eyebrow dripped steadily. Her eyes found Kait, pleading for her to run.

"Earlier, when you were eavesdropping, did you hear the part when I mentioned bringing a piriol along? Is that what sent you running? We borrowed it from a friend who has a passionate interest in euphoria. Actually…I'd say we demanded it." Hermes chuckled low in his throat. "You see, he's been indulging in secret for years. But even he couldn't keep his little hobby hidden from me. Blackmail is a wondrous tool, especially when the target has so much to lose."

Apollo licked the blood off his lips. "But the best part of this immortal's games? No one ever noticed. No one even blinked when the nymphs he took didn't return." He sneered. "Do you know why? Because that's the natural order of the realm. You were created to please. Your perfection, your beauty, even your scent was designed to entice immortals to your bed. And now it's time to play your part."

The gods moved as one, closing in. Kait scurried forward, placing herself in front of Willow. Her sealed lips stretched as she growled. They wouldn't touch her.

Another deep vibration sounded, like a rumble of thunder. Kait peered into the darkness behind the immortals. At her feet, Willow whimpered as a massive white silhouette slunk closer.

"That'd be our friend's payment for not telling the Council about his insatiable little habit." Hermes paused, his eyes shining eerily. "Seems not all the piriols were destroyed. One god had the foresight to hide his away in the human realm where no one would think to check. *Evenire*, Kaf. Kait *vult ludere*."

Shadows shifted in the heavy darkness at the back of the alley, giving birth to a terrifying creature. Two mustard-yellow eyes beamed in the blackness as its face emerged. The animal looked like a saber-toothed tiger, only more menacing, with large fangs like ivory daggers and four powerful legs and wide paws, beneath which talons raked the asphalt. The great cat let out a ferocious snarl, arching its muscular back. Kait's eyes were drawn upward. If her mouth hadn't been sealed shut, she would have gaped at the dozen gray quills standing erect along its spine. Lastly, a thick tail twitched back and forth, the tip glowing pale blue.

Kait swallowed roughly, innate fear seizing her muscles as her mind went blank with terror. It was a piriol—a real piriol.

Hermes winked. "We were told they were all destroyed after the Titan War—all save for one, and one was all we needed."

Kait forgot how to breathe, how to think as she stared at the creature's menacing jaws. Willow's weak hands found hers, relaying her own horror at the nightmarish cat lumbering toward them with her trembling touch.

"You may have gotten off a few lucky shots, but let's see how you do against a piriol—a lethal creature specifically designed to track and incapacitate your kind."

Hermes laughed aloud as Kait's stomach knotted. She couldn't fight the piriol and couldn't flee. She closed her eyes, racking her memory for Tahlia's lessons in desperation. Her elder's voice wove through her mind: *Channel your energy. Focus on the wind. Feel every molecule. Feel the air surround your skin. Now, isolate your fingers, your knuckles, your wrists. Give them to the wind.*

A metallic clatter drew her from her thoughts. Kait dropped her gaze to her cuffs, which were now lying on the ground. She raised her arms and sucked in a sharp breath. Her hands were severed at the wrists—no, not severed, but invisible. Her hands were swirling air. Somehow, she'd managed to perform wind isolation—advanced magic she had failed at again and again during training. Power surged through her veins. She was free.

Alarm sprung in the gods' eyes, and they scrambled toward her, but they weren't fast enough.

"Stop her, Kaf!"

The piriol launched forward. As all three converged on the nymphs, Kait vanished, transforming into her element. Summoning all her strength, she wrapped the wind around Willow, heaving her friend off the ground. Relief pulsed through her, empowering her magic.

Below, the piriol's tail burned bright as it snarled with rage. Arching its back, the cat turned, letting loose two quills. With a trajectory like an arrow from Artemis's bow, the quills shot into the sky. One pierced Kait's calf, while the other ripped into her left shoulder.

The pain was blinding and tore the nymphs from the air. They landed together in a bruised heap, their heads bouncing off the ground. Hermes stalked over, the amused sparkle now gone from his eyes.

"Hurts, doesn't it? Piriols were bred to hunt nymphs, remember? The quills deposit toxin into the bloodstream, numbing the area they penetrate while inhibiting metamorphosis," he explained, clearly relishing in the details. "Not only are you injured, but now your magic is useless too, no matter how clever you think you are."

Kait moaned as Hermes gripped the quill buried in her shoulder and twisted it.

"You could have enjoyed it, but now, I'll take you while you bleed out in this filthy alleyway." He shrugged. "Once I absorb your halo and make you mortal, your life will hardly be worth living."

Kait writhed under his touch, cursing behind her muzzle.

"Why don't we save you for last? After all, it'll add a little something extra to have you watch us rape your friend. What is it they say, Apollo? Friends to the end?"

Apollo answered by unzipping his jeans and wrenching Willow off the ground. She tossed her head back and forth, but the same gag stifling Kait was taking its toll. Willow couldn't draw a deep enough breath to fight.

"Who the hell cares?" Apollo spat.

He tore Willow's gown apart, revealing her dark umber skin. Tears welled in her eyes as she tried to break away, but he held her fast. Kait struggled to rise, her knees shaking with the effort, but her leg was numb, and Hermes's grip on her injured shoulder forced her back down. The scene before her spun, the toxin affecting her equilibrium and slowing her heart at the same time.

"Watch, my dear. Here comes the best part."

Silent screams poured from Kait's throat as she watched Apollo force his way inside her friend, listened as he groaned with pleasure and laughed at Willow's broken sobs. She did not know how long he ravaged her, but at last, he sighed.

"Incredible. Better than any high opium ever gave me."

Hermes eyed Willow's bruised and tired body. "Think there's any left?"

Apollo shook his head. "Lucky for us we've got two."

Kait tried to keep her eyes open, but they were swollen from the tears. She heard the gods approach, flinched as Hermes ran his fingers between her legs.

"Your turn," he whispered in her ear.

Hermes kneeled, rolled Kait over, and grabbed her thighs, propping her up. The angle he positioned her body at pressed her face into the ground. The rough asphalt rubbed her cheek raw. Kait wanted to fight back, but by now, the entire lower half of her body was paralyzed by the numbing toxin, and the world spun like a whirling carousel. All she could do was lie there.

Kait sobbed as she heard Hermes shed his jeans once more. His breath turned ragged, indicating he could hardly contain himself. She hoped he took her quickly.

"There they are!" a voice exclaimed.

"Get off her!" another screeched.

Two fierce nymphs descended on the immortals, one commanding brutal winds, while the other hurled chunks of ice.

"Fuck, you've got to be kidding me," Hermes hissed.

"Come on," Apollo called. "We need to get out of here."

"Shit. Give us some cover."

Hermes released Kait's thighs, dropping her onto her stomach. He yanked out the quills punched through her body, removing any evidence of the gods or their deadly hunting companion with him. As the nymphs advanced, Apollo threw up his hands, causing a broken light above them to explode. Glass shattered, falling like sparkling snowflakes, and a burst of intense sunlight erupted, forcing the nymphs to shield their eyes while the gods and the piriol soared into the sky.

Jezlem fell to her kneels at Kait's side. "My goddess, Kait. What did they do to you?" She stroked her bloodied hair. "Tahlia, Kaitaini needs a healer. She's losing so much blood. How's Willow?"

Tahlia whimpered. "She's gone. The monsters killed her."

A hollow wail fell from Kait's lips as Apollo's magic finally broke, her pain audible for the first time. "What? What did you say?" Kait shouted. Forcing her numb body to move, she rolled over onto her other side.

At last, her gaze settled on her friend, and her breath stalled in her throat. Staring blankly back at her was Willow. Her beautiful face was covered in bloody fingernail marks, as if she'd fought to slice her lips open herself. Her vibrant curls were crusted with blood and sweat, and her dim eyes glimmered with the sheen of death. Her emerald-green halo and connection to the realm were gone, leaving her skin a sickly color. Kait screamed, her voice back at full force.

"Shh, shh, you're safe. You're okay," Jezlem whispered, pressing her cheek against the crown of Kait's head.

Kait turned to stone at the suggestion as tears streamed down her cheeks. "Look at what I've done."

Willow had died at the hands of the gods—gods she'd insisted weren't a threat.

She would never forgive herself.

1

NOW

A warm breeze stirred outside the window, but Kait took no pleasure in it. Shoulders squared, she stared at her aurai elder as she described the latest issue plaguing the desert realm of Taryn, half listening as her thoughts orbited a far more urgent matter. Along with Kait, a small group of elite aurais gathered at a polished walnut table in Tahlia's home.

"Strong winds have returned to Taryn, making travel above ground virtually impossible for the Cerastes." Tahlia gestured to the barren desert on a map of the far western border of the ethereal realms.

"Don't they use tunnels to escape the heat? Sand snakes rarely venture to the surface, save for mating," Siorri said.

Tahlia nodded. "Hence why the problem is not yet a priority. However, I will require a volunteer to assess the wind's power and determine if it has caused any damage belowground. Then we can diffuse it before it becomes a larger issue for these creatures."

Tahlia glanced around at the assembled group of aurais. Each one had been handpicked for the task force. All were highly skilled in wind control and manipulation, but their dedication to protecting the realms ran deeper than talent. Every nymph present had something you couldn't learn: courage.

Kait felt the urge to raise her hand. Normally, she leapt at the opportunity to assist, but not today. Another aurai with olive skin and ink-black hair volunteered.

"Thank you, Makani. Be sure to leave at dawn tomorrow. Excellent. That will wrap up tonight's meeting. Thank you all for your participation." Tahlia dismissed the small group, brushing a long strand of honey blond hair out of her eyes.

Kait strode to her elder's side, standing with her hands clasped in front of her.

"Tahlia, may I speak with you a moment?"

Tahlia pointed away from the formal dining room into the cozy living space beyond. Kait moved into the other room and took a seat on a moss-covered papasan chair. A mahogany love seat sat opposite her.

Kait's throat thickened as uncomfortable memories ate at the corners of her mind. She squeezed her clasped fingers to keep from shaking. One hundred years had passed since she lost her friend, but guilt remained her steadfast companion. Even now, Willow's pallid face and bloodied dress wormed into Kait's thoughts. Her chest tightened.

"Here you go," Tahlia said, jerking Kait out of her haunted memories. She handed Kait a mug filled with pale gray hibiscus tea. "Relax. You're always so stiff. Get comfortable."

"I am comfortable."

Tahlia shrugged and settled on the love seat, tucking a yellow throw pillow under her arm. The elder raised her mug to her lips and took a sip. Kait tapped the side of her wooden mug with her nails, anxious to begin.

"There. Now, what was it you wanted to discuss?"

Kait exhaled. "I've heard rumors, whispers that a naiad's halo was taken. Is it true?"

Tahlia's eyes fell to her tea. "Where did you hear that?"

Kait gripped her mug harder until her knuckles turned white. "In the realm of Orlon the other day. I overheard several centaurs speaking with a group of naiads. They spoke of it like a bad dream, but I…I knew better."

Tahlia leaned forward, placing her mug on the low pine table between them and leveling Kait with an intent stare. "What exactly did they say?"

Kait's throat swelled. Surely she'd misheard the nymphs, but why wasn't Tahlia denying it?

"A naiad named Nirina didn't return from an assignment in the mortal realm. They found her body outside a small village in Spain. She was alive, but her connection was severed; her halo was gone."

Tahlia paused, interlacing her slender fingers. "Do you know which naiads spoke of this? Where they gleaned their information?"

Kait shook her head, her eyes glassy as she fought back the intense wave of memories that soured even the brightest of days. She didn't know Nirina, but she didn't have to. A nymph was violated, turned mortal. Willow's dead eyes bore into her, an endless reminder of her mistake. Kait shook her head in answer to Tahlia's question.

"Have you spoken to anyone else about this?"

"No. I came straight to you after I completed my assignment there. Is it...? Is it Hermes again?"

Tahlia released a long breath, settling back against the stiff cushions. "We're not sure. She's not the first one we've found."

"What are you saying? How many others are there?"

Tahlia held up her hand as Kait's stoic trance broke into incredulous anger. "Please, Kait. The other two elemental elders and I are sworn to secrecy by Queen Rajhi. I cannot discuss this any further with you."

"Why not?" Kait jumped to her feet. The warm mug fell from her grasp to the polished wood floor with a hollow rattle. Hot tea sprinkled her bare feet, but Kait's gaze never strayed from her elder's face. "Why are you keeping this from the realm? If another immortal is targeting nymphs for euphoria, everyone is in danger."

"We don't know that yet. Until we can say for certain, we can't make any rash decisions."

"Rash? It's not a rash decision. Call every nymph back from the mortal realm. That's the only common ground they can enter."

Tahlia's gray eyes hardened as Kait's voice rose. "There is important work to be done in the mortal realm. Autumn is upon us in the northern hemisphere and—"

"No. Nothing should be more important than our safety."

"That's enough," Tahlia ordered, rising to her feet as well. "Watch your tone, aurai. Do you think you know better than the queen?"

Kait remained silent as color flooded her cheeks. She had gone too far.

Tahlia gave her a hard look. "Do you think you're the only one with scars? The only one who has lost someone? Just because you had an unfortunate interaction with the gods doesn't mean you can jump to these conclusions. Our decisions—the queen's decisions—affect every nymph in Olean. We need to do what's best for everyone. After Willow, you grew out of your impulsivity, but this brash thinking is exactly what got you into trouble all those years ago."

Kait's jaw dropped as if her elder had slapped her. She took a step away, unable to form words—words to apologize, words to deny what Tahlia said—but her tongue lay still, knotted by the truth. For months after that fateful night, Kait had wallowed in shame and disgust, unable to leave her bed and shoulder the heavy weight of the part she played in Willow's death. Tahlia was the one who picked her back up, collected her broken pieces, and tried to fit them back into the right spaces. Some, like her ability to train and learn the skills of her element, fell easily into place. Others, such as her confidence, joy, and social drive were too shattered to repair.

She didn't deny that Willow's death was her fault, but to hear it stated so plainly by the one person who brought her solace tore what remained of her heart wide open.

Tahlia sighed and stepped through the spilled tea. Her arms enclosed Kait, but they brought her no comfort. Today, they were serpents, constricting what little breath she had.

"I'm sorry," Tahlia whispered. "I never should have said that. What happened to Willow was not your fault. Please forgive me."

Kait remained immobile but slipped the vacant mask she'd adopted years ago into place.

Tahlia registered the change and relaxed her embrace, holding Kait at arm's length. "Until the queen deems it appropriate to share, please keep this information to yourself. And Kait...leave this alone."

"What do you mean?" Kait asked, her voice flat.

"I know the demons you keep buried inside—why your personality changed so drastically after Willow's death, why you volunteer for the most dangerous assignments. It's almost as if you're hoping to get hurt." Tahlia's voice softened. Kait knew her elder was trying to connect with her, but Tahlia didn't understand.

"To die in service to Olean would be a great honor."

Tahlia shook her head. "Guilt is not a valid reason to throw your life away, Kait. You have so much to live for."

Kait's eyes fell to the floor. She was silent for a moment.

"You and I both know I should have died a long time ago."

More disturbing memories of that night fought to swallow her, but she had grown adept at forcing them out before they could take root. Tahlia dropped her arms, the movement drawing a brush of arm along her arms. The unexpected sensation caused Kait to flinch. The silence stretched between them, ballooning with uncomfortable tension. Pivoting on her heels, Kait crossed to the curved front door and pulled it open.

"Thank you for speaking with me," she said over her shoulder.

"You're welcome," Tahlia answered. "But, Kait...please remember to keep this to yourself."

Kait paused a moment but didn't respond. Instead, she exited her elder's home, closing the door behind her with a gentle click.

The sun still warmed the earth, but summer's hold was growing weak. August nights were beginning earlier, diluting the horizon with dark streaks.

Ducking under the loose ivy trickling down the entrance to Tahlia's home, Kait passed beneath a wooden archway at the edge of the property, leaving behind the elder's manicured stone path for the rich dirt roads that connected all of Olean.

Tahlia was wrong. She thought Kait trained until her blisters bled and threw herself into perilous missions because she yearned for death. Kait *was* running, but not to destruction. To die would be too cowardly a way to ease her guilt. No, Kait ran and pushed herself because it was the only way to keep the voices at bay, to stifle Hermes's laughter and Apollo's groans as he raped her friend. If she worked her mind and body to exhaustion, it allowed a few hours rest before her remorse grew teeth again.

As the warm dirt kissed her toes, Kait's thoughts wandered back to the taken naiad. Who had hunted her? Both Hermes and Apollo were brought before the Immortal Council after the attack, and with three eyewitnesses and one corpse to prove their involvement, they had no defense. They were sentenced to confinement on Olympus for five hundred years, and their powers were stripped. It couldn't be one of them, but what of the third-party god they'd mentioned, the one with the piriol?

Kait insisted that the creature existed, even showed the Council her wounds from where the quills pierced her, but they dismissed her claim, confident the whole population had been slaughtered three thousand years ago. She scanned the gently blowing tree line to the golden-edged clouds hovering above. The piriol was still out there, along with the monster who controlled it, biding their time before they snatched another nymph.

Tahlia's quarters were situated on the outskirts of town. Kait was glad she didn't have to make any other stops before returning home. Strolling past the market, she kept her head down and her eyes averted. A large cluster of naiads stood within speaking distance, admiring the latest gowns to debut for the fall season. She wasn't in the mood for small talk.

Veering to the right of the waist-high fence that encircled the market, Kait walked parallel to the coniferous forest lining the town's eastern border. Cheery songbirds greeted her, calling her to fly with them in the trees. She smiled, remaining on the path. The scent of warm lavender cookies with sugar icing the opposite side of the fence threatened to pull her back, but the temptation was squashed the moment she heard the vendors shouting their wares.

"Beautiful chairs, hand-carved from the finest chestnut!"

"Silk and satin, hurry in to see our new colors for fall!"

"Sweet mint cream and blueberry scones, three for the price of one today!"

Sometimes, it was nice to join the crowd and wander from shop to shop. It was easy to disengage from the troubling thoughts as swatches of fabric rippled across her vision and the energetic thrum of a hundred voices merged into a fuzzy cacophony. But not today. Today, she wanted to be by herself.

The warm sunshine filtered through the pines, enhancing the golden halo of light that radiated from her bronze skin.

She could let the breeze carry her back. Usually, Kait favored traveling as the wind. The speed and agility it yielded helped drown everything else out, but the need to walk overwhelmed her. The way her muscles stretched and contracted was cathartic, and she allowed herself the rare indulgence of the sweet scent of the woods.

Kait stopped short when she heard hushed voices carry on the wind. To her left, she spied two nymphs huddled in the narrow gap between shops. Their dark green gowns marked them as anthousais, and the dry grass beneath their bare feet grew lush and thick from their touch. Identical gold leaf pendants were pinned over their left breasts, identifying them as members of the queen's court.

Kait retraced her steps, careful to remain out of sight. Normally, she wouldn't eavesdrop on others' conversations, but there was something about the anthousais' tense posture that caused her stomach to tighten.

"There's been another one," the anthousai with moss-green eyes whispered. "She was found in a small village in southern France early this morning trying to breach the portal back to Olean."

"Just like the others. This is the third nymph in a week. Did she have any injuries? Any indications of sexual abuse?"

"Nothing. She was unharmed like the two before."

The second anthousai pressed her fingers to her temples. "This doesn't make sense. Someone is collecting halos by convincing nymphs without force to abandon the realm. And what's worse, whoever it is knows how to cover their tracks. There aren't many who can erase themselves so completely from the mind while leaving everything else intact."

"Do you think they're after euphoria? Like Hermes and Apollo years ago?"

Kait drew in a startled breath. If there was an immortal hunting nymphs, why wasn't the queen acknowledging it? Why wasn't she alerting the others?

"It certainly is a valid conclusion. Though I can't understand why the nymphs gave in so willingly."

"Have the immortals been questioned?"

"Of course. After Nirina was found in Spain two weeks after Aeryn, the queen summoned a meeting with the Council. The Olympians pledged their innocence, but…"

"But it has to be one of them," the green-eyed anthousai said, her voice full of distrust. "Look at history: Hermes and Apollo were punished for this same offense a century ago, and there has never been a shortage of others punished for violent attacks on lesser beings. I think it's safe to rule out the goddesses, so that leaves only a handful of gods. Each one needs to be questioned. We have to stop this from happening."

"I agree, but it'll never happen. The Council is too powerful, too proud to subjugate themselves to being interrogated by nymphs. All we can do is double our patrols, increase group sizes, and pray no one else falls prey to whatever game this monster is playing."

Both of the advisors sighed, casting off the unpleasant conversation as they stepped out of the shelter of the buildings and melted into the crowd. Kait's heart raced; her chest heaved, trying to draw a deep enough breath.

So another god *was* targeting nymphs. Hunting them down and absorbing their halos, delighting in euphoria. How was this possible? How had he managed to keep his identity secret?

A gentle rustling distracted her from her thoughts as a brilliant red dahlia bloomed at her feet. Another anthousai. Kait's halo burned brighter as it sensed her special connection to the other nymph—a connection that bound the triplets together and enhanced their powers when they were near one another.

"Bia."

Limbs unfolded out of the center of the dahlia, its petals transforming into ivory skin. The spiky folds of the flower shrunk, revealing Bia's slender nose and high cheekbones. Her shoulder-length hair was the last to change. Petals peeled back, giving way to pin-straight locks, the same vibrant color as the flora.

Kait stepped forward, wrapping her sister in a tight embrace. Bia remained stiff in her arms, having been uncomfortable with physical contact since the day of their creation. Kait released her and glanced over her shoulder.

"You were listening too, weren't you?"

Bia stared at Kait's shoulder. "I'm a-always listening."

"Is this true? What they said? Has a god taken up the hunt?"

Bia's hands flapped at her sides as she chewed her bottom lip. "It's h-hard to say. It's not like before. Even your encounter with the immortals wasn't the t-traditional hunt. Before the war, the T-Titans feared no repercussions. A true hunt would incorporate the use of a piriol. This god is c-clever, patient, and elusive."

"Did you know any of the nymphs? I know one was a naiad. Were they all?"

Bia shook her head, drawing a small bead of blood on her lip as her teeth pierced the skin.

"Both Aeryn and Calliya were anthousais. There might b-be a pattern, or it could be random. All I know is the attacks are b-becoming more frequent. Either more than one immortal is behind this, or he's h-hooked on the euphoria. If it's the latter, he's going to start getting s-sloppy as his need grows."

"I need to figure out how he's convincing them," Kait muttered. Tahlia's warning echoed in the back of her mind. She didn't have to broadcast her investigation, but she also couldn't sit idly by twirling her thumbs as more nymphs were taken.

Bia's hands fluttered faster. "I came to find you for a different reason. It might have something to do with this."

"What is it?"

"It's Jez. Something's wrong. She's been acting strange the p-past few days."

"Strange how?"

Bia's hands tapped her thighs, and she squeezed her eyes shut. "She went to the human r-realm last week to assist with droughts along the Nile River. She didn't look different when she returned, b-but she felt odd. She was distracted. Her thoughts were a mile away. Then she was supposed to meet me the other day so I could practice manipulating the body's b-blood flow for my upcoming exam, but she never showed. I tried to locate her by the waterfalls. I was angry she forgot me, but she wasn't there. According t-to her friend Elani, she returned to the human realm. Said she left something behind there."

Kait wrinkled her nose. "Jez doesn't forget anything."

"I know. She l-lied. I sensed her movements. She never went to Africa. She was in San Sebastián, Spain."

The location set off an alarm in the back of Kait's mind. Bia, like many anthousais, was able to tap into the earth's memory. By targeting one nymph's signature imprint, a mental road map materialized, depicting where exactly that individual had left an impression. Aurais were hardest to track because they often traveled above the earth, but Jezlem, being a naiad, would have left plenty of impressions for Bia to track.

Kait's eyebrows shot up. "That's where they found the first two nymphs."

Bia nodded, her wrists flickering every few seconds. "You have to talk to h-her. I just saw her in the market, and the odd feeling radiating off her was worse. Her scent is off too; it's foreign. I tried to s-speak with her, but she brushed me off, claimed she n-needed to get ready."

"Ready for what?"

"She wouldn't tell me."

Kait's head snapped back to the beginning of the fence, her eyes wide with fear. "She's going back to the human realm."

"Do you think it's the s-same immortal?"

"I don't care who it is; they're not going to get our sister. Come on. We have to stop her."

Bia shook her head, her scarlet hair covering her face as her hands grew even more agitated. "I—I can't. You know w-what you two are like together. You're constantly at each other's throats. The y-yelling it—it disturbs me."

"Okay, okay. I'll go alone. Where in the market was she?" Kait asked, keeping her voice calm.

Bia bent down, squeezing her thighs. "In the armory, buying a new d-dress, but she could be anywhere now. The sensors. I'll use the s-sensors to track her movements."

"No, it's okay. I'll find her. I'll keep her safe," Kait promised.

Bia let out a muffled groan and nodded. Kait backed away, her heart aching to stay, while her feet and mind pulled her in the opposite direction. Bia groaned again, the sound loud and guttural. Her fingers twitched, stacking on top of one another as she cast. Her nails lengthened into vines, unfurling in thick green ropes upon the dirt. Bia's hunched form collapsed further. Her sage-green dress splintered into wide leaves as veins spidered up her jaw. Seconds later, she completed the transformation, her roots diving deep into the earth. Kait knew Bia craved the pressure of being held. The earth could give that to her in a way her sisters couldn't.

Kait twisted her fingers. The wind billowed toward her, empowered by Bia's nearby energy. With a running jump, Kait leapt into the wind's arms, her flesh transforming to air in a blink. Jezlem wouldn't have meandered around the market for long, and if she bought a new dress, it meant she had something important planned.

Kait directed the wind to the north, toward the naiad dwelling, praying she wasn't too late.

8

The sun glinted off large pools of water, announcing the border to naiad territory as Kait crested the expansive mountain. Everywhere beyond was covered in crystal-blue water, carved like flowing veins through the green landscape. Olean's water was said to flow from Olympus itself, but this couldn't be confirmed. The tops of the waterfalls were sheathed in thick vapors at the highest point of the nymph realm, and no one could see beyond that.

Funneling toward the earth, Kait passed naiads lounging in the cool pools and others harnessing their element, creating heavy clouds to await the aurais' winds in the morning.

Each quadrant in Olean was like a separate world, offering the ideal oasis for each given element. For the aurais, the land in the east was mostly flat, rolling meadows that led into steep canyons at the realm's easternmost edge—the perfect environment in which to create strong winds and train to control them.

To the west, the anthousais' climate was similar to a temperate rain forest. Their talents enriched the soil and gave birth to the most beautiful flora. Lush gardens and fields of fruits and vegetables spanned two-thirds of their designated space, providing food to the twenty thousand nymphs who occupied Olean.

The south was home to Market Square, Queen Rajhi's residences, and vast coniferous forests. The days were mostly mild, snow in the winter and warm in the summer.

The north was Kait's least favorite quadrant. Being tied to the air, she detested water. It filled the sky and made her winds cumbersome. Experiencing it in her physical form wasn't much better. Water was wet and clung to her like a second skin. Bathing was one thing, but she didn't understand why the naiads required their lands to be practically flooded.

Most naiads slept in caverns below the calm waters, but Kait's destination was above the surface. Swirling through patches of fog, she rounded the base of one of three massive waterfalls, choosing the one farthest to the right. It had been many years since she ventured this far into the naiads' quadrant, but her memory was rewarded as she slipped around the rushing waters to find the hollow cavern the naiads dressed and primped in.

Kait alighted from the air. She brushed lingering spray and mist out of her way and cringed as her bare foot stepped in a shallow puddle. Several naiads jumped when her reflection appeared in the floor-to-ceiling mirrors as she materialized out of thin air. Nymphs of every element were welcome in each of the varying sectors; however, it wasn't common. If the clans needed to gather for pankration or meetings, they all congregated in the center of the realm, a few miles outside the apothecary.

Kait received a dirty look from the naiad closest to her. Her long black hair cascaded down the length of her back, and her blue eyes narrowed to thin slits. It appeared her lipstick application went awry during Kait's sudden appearance.

"Sorry to intrude like this. I was wondering if you've seen Jezlem around?"

The naiad pursed her lips, making a show of wiping away the red stain above her upper lip. "She's in the back. You better hurry though; she's leaving any second."

"Thank you." Kait wove through a tunnel carved of black stone, the surface of which twinkled above her, like crushed diamonds lighting the way. "Jez? Jezlem, are you back here?"

Emerging from the tunnel, she found herself in another pocket full of mirrors and tiny tables cluttered with shell combs, floral pins, headbands encrusted with jewels. At the echo of her name, Jezlem spun away from a mirror, a comb clasped in her teeth as her hands wrestled her long blond curls into place atop her head.

"Kait? What are you doing here?" Jezlem's words were barely discernable through the comb.

Kait shot a sly glance around at the other naiads. Some looked at her curiously, but most ignored her. "I need to talk to you."

Jezlem shook her head, and her curls threatened to tumble out of her precarious hold. After securing them with a pin, she withdrew the comb from her teeth and stuck it into the back of her updo. The alabaster pearl finish gleamed under the bright lights.

"I can't talk right now. I have somewhere I need to be," Jezlem said, dismissing Kait just as she'd apparently dismissed Bia.

"That's what I need to talk to you about." Kait dropped to a whisper. "You're not safe."

"Okay, Kait, I really don't have time for this. I'm late enough as it is."

Jezlem grabbed a dazzling silver purse to complement the navy gown she wore. Gossamer fabric wrapped around her torso, and a glittering pendant lodged between her breasts. The fabric continued up into a thick strap that flowed over her left shoulder. Her other shoulder was bare and exposed. The gown clung to her tiny waist, falling in an asymmetrical pattern across her knees.

"That's a fancy dress." Kait trailed Jezlem out of the cavern to the backside of the waterfall. A gentle breeze blew, carrying with it a tainted scent. Jezlem usually smelled of grapefruit and lemongrass, but there was an odd flavor leaking from her pores—the foreign scent Bia had mentioned. Kait inhaled, tasting tart cherry on her tongue.

Jezlem threw an exasperated look over her shoulder and darted through the fine mist. Kait gritted her teeth, left with no choice but to follow. On the other side, she stacked her fingers. An obedient breeze rolled down her body, evaporating the water droplets that clung to her skin.

"Where are you going, Jez?"

"Why does it matter?" Jezlem leapt from stone to stone as she made her way to the large tributary that fed the rest of Olean with fresh water.

"Because it's dangerous. The human realm isn't safe."

"Who says I'm going to the human realm?"

Kait propelled herself forward, riding a strong current to catch up. Reaching out, she grabbed Jezlem's hand, halting her momentum. "I know you're going to see an immortal."

Jezlem's aqua eyes flashed wide before a carefully constructed mask slipped into place. "What? Wherever did you come up with such a thing?"

Kait ignored her questions. "What are you thinking, Jez?" She didn't recognize her sister. Gone was her stoic gaze, caution, and calculated grace. In Jezlem's place pranced a bubbly stranger, giddy as she twirled in and out of the light's touch. Kait's voice rose with ire, drawing curious stares from the nearby naiads in the pool. "How can you even entertain such an idea?"

Jezlem swallowed. "Not here." She tugged Kait behind her and guided her toward a small alcove away from prying eyes.

A thin strip of sand bordered the edge of the pool tucked behind the waterfall's façade. It was remote and quiet, and offered the nymphs a place to speak without being overheard.

Kait leapt right back in. "Don't you remember my mistake? Have you forgotten what those bastards did to Willow?"

Jezlem put up her hands. "I know. I know how this looks, but let me explain."

Kait crossed her arms, waiting.

"He's different, Kait."

Kait scoffed, pressing her fingertips to her temples. "You can't be serious. After all the lectures you gave me when I told you the same thing. Don't you remember our fight after you and Tahlia brought me back from that alley? Do you remember what you called me? Ignorant. You berated me, asked me how I could have ever believed his lies. All immortals use, all immortals take. Yet when it happens to you, it's different. How can you be so hypocritical?"

"Please, please," Jezlem whispered. "Let me explain."

Kait set her lips in a firm line, anger frothing behind her teeth. Jezlem dug her toes into the wet sand, pausing to see if Kait would interrupt. When she remained silent, she spoke.

"It happened so fast. One minute, I'm circumnavigating the current, and the next, I'm in his arms. I fell and hit my head on a rock. Adrianne was downstream and didn't see. The blow knocked me unconscious. When I woke up, he was holding me, pressing his robes to the gash in my head. He gave me some water to drink and supported me until Adrianne found us."

"Who?" Kait stressed. "Who was it?"

Jezlem shook her head. "None of the greats. He's a lowly god. He took us out for dinner at a local eatery. Have you ever tried kushari?"

Kait ignored the question. "What's his name?"

"Basil. He was doing research on the humans along the Nile, masquerading as one to learn more about the Egyptian gods they worship. Conversion is his goal; however, he isn't hopeful."

Kait frowned, disliking the admiration in her sister's tone. "When was this?"

"Nine days ago."

"And how many times have you seen him?"

"Relax, Kait. He's harmless."

"How many times?"

"Tonight makes our fourth meeting." She lowered her voice. "Look, don't make this into one of your quests. Not every immortal is like Hermes. I'm a big girl. I know what I'm doing. Now, if you will excuse me…"

Jezlem wiggled her fingers, twisting them in an intricate formation as she stepped into the languid ripples reaching for her. The water enveloped her, welcoming her back like a forlorn child craving its mother. It splashed playfully around Jezlem's calves, responding to her cheerful mood.

Kait's heart dropped as the pool washed over her sister's feet, erasing her flesh as she began to transform. She needed to stop her before she raced away to the Hall of Portals.

"Aeryn, Nirina, and Calliya."

Jezlem turned, fixing Kait with a hard look. "Are they supposed to mean something to me?"

"Three nymphs whose halos were taken by a rogue immortal in the last five weeks, victimized by some mysterious god they couldn't name."

Jezlem's brow furrowed. "How do you know this?"

"I heard two members of Queen Rajhi's court speaking earlier today, and a group of naiads were discussing Nirina when I was in Orlon. Calliya was found in Lourdes. The other two turned up in northern Spain. All three of their halos had been absorbed. They were left vulnerable and mortal in the human realm. Bia tracked you the last time you left. The sensors placed you in San Sebastián. That's quite a coincidence." Kait narrowed her eyes as Jezlem swallowed roughly. "Can I ask where you're meeting him tonight?"

Jezlem licked her lips, her gaze unblinking. "Luz-Saint-Sauveur, France. He said the African sun was too harsh and suggested we head north."

"I'm not well versed in the finer points of mortal geography, but I think it's safe to assume he has other plans in mind for your date."

"No. No, Basil would never—he couldn't—" Jezlem shook her head. "He's so kind and gentle. He would never hurt me."

"Look at the facts, Jez. Three nymphs—*three*—have lost their connection to the realm. None of them had any injuries or recalled being raped, so what is this god saying to them? Why are they lying with him willingly?"

Jezlem was silent, but the water betrayed her blank features. The once calm pool boiled with agitation. Frothing waves slammed against the beach.

Kait glanced at her sister, whose golden complexion had turned sickly yellow. "You know, don't you? What did he say? What did he promise if you slept with him?"

Fat tears raced down Jezlem's cheeks, but she didn't brush them away. "He wasn't so vulgar as to come right out and say that, but he mentioned something else…"

Kait grasped her sister's hand, grimacing as the cold waves crashed against her knees. "What? What did he say, Jez?"

A strangled sob stuck in Jezlem's throat. She pressed the heels of her hands to her eyes. "It's hard to recall, like a memory of a dream. We were discussing our future, trying to gauge how long we could keep seeing one another without interference from the Council. He's my ideal partner, Kait. He's smart, sensitive, thoughtful…but he's an immortal. I can't believe how quickly I fell for him. I was crying at the thought of losing him, and…" Jezlem exhaled a shaky breath.

"What, Jez? What did he say to comfort you?"

"He said that if we weren't different, we could be together. He told me he knew a way, a way to…change me. Said it had been done before, with the queen." Jez bit her trembling lip. "He promised…"

Kait looked into the sky, focusing on the top of the waterfall, willing Olympus to appear. "Immortality," she whispered.

"That way the Council wouldn't deny our union." Jezlem chucked her silver clutch into the thin trees, then gripped her hair with angry fingers. She started pulling, yanking, ripping out the pins and delicate comb until her curls sprung madly from her skull like Medusa's serpents. "He played me for such a fool. How did he do this to me?"

Kait took a step forward and placed her hand on her sister's back. "If this is the same immortal that assisted Hermes and Apollo one hundred years ago, then he's had centuries of practice." Kait leaned closer, sniffing Jezlem's hair. The same cherry scent was tangled in her locks. "Did Basil ever give you anything to drink? Hermes slipped me a tonic straight from Aphrodite. The one I drank affected me physically. It ignited my desire the moment it touched my tongue."

Jezlem nodded. "I didn't think anything of it… When we dined in the human realm at mortal restaurants, he volunteered to get them from the bar so we wouldn't have to wait. I'm such an idiot."

Kait didn't argue. "I can't be sure, but I think whatever he gave you is still in your bloodstream. Maybe a type of tonic that creates feelings of affection. That's why you keep going back to him, why your scent is off. Mixed with the offer of immortality, he's brewed the perfect concoction to convince nymphs to sleep with him."

Jezlem growled, spitting venom. "And I fell for it, every word." She slumped down, collapsing onto her backside. "The worst part is how happy he made me feel. I thought it was real. I thought I'd finally found my perfect match." She kicked the sand.

Kait sunk down as well, hugging her knees to her chest.

Jezlem cocked her head. "Go ahead, say it. Say I told you so. All these years you've petitioned the queen to cease working in the mortal world for this precise purpose. We called you—I called you—paranoid and neurotic. After the Council punished Hermes and Apollo, I thought the consequences were too great for another god to seek euphoria. And if one tried, I thought I was too smart to be tricked. I'm sorry." Jezlem nearly choked on the last words, but even though she didn't move to hug or embrace Kait, her gaze was earnest.

Kait answered her apology with a weak smile. They'd always fought to outdo one another, which bred an unhealthy rivalry between them at times. It pushed them to train harder, but it also drove a thick stake between them and discouraged any signs of vulnerability on either side. This competitiveness combined with Bia's nervous tendencies meant the triad wasn't as emotionally bonded as it should have been. Still, a willingness to protect one another burned brightly within them all.

Kait stretched her legs across the sand. "We need to report him to the Council."

"No." Jezlem shook her head. "We don't have any proof. If we take this before the Council with only a simple accusation, Basil will disappear."

"So what do we do? I'm not letting him get away. He won't stop."

Jezlem threaded her fingers together and raised them behind her head. "We set a trap of our own. If we can get a vial of that tonic, it'll prove our story."

Kait bit her lip, the hair on her hairs prickling with uncertainty. Her gut revolted at the idea of getting close to another immortal—of returning to the human realm in general. It went against all her self-imposed rules. "But what if he figures it out?"

Jezlem twisted her fingers. A fierce waterspout crested atop the pool. All the water needed was a blast of wind to create a biting hurricane. "Please, I need you. Together, our magic is strong enough to beat him."

Kait met Jezlem's pleading gaze. Her heart pumped viciously; her stomach clenched. She couldn't face another immortal. The moment she saw him, the memories would swarm and break down the carefully constructed wall she'd thrust them behind. She wasn't ready, wasn't strong, but she recognized the determination in her sister's features. If Kait didn't accompany her, she'd go alone, with nothing and no one to protect her.

"What if he fights back?" Kait asked.

The waterspout collapsed with a deafening boom, and the pool overflowed, licking their calves. Jezlem smiled and cocked her head. "Then we fight harder."

⚡ 9 ⚡

"Kait, where are you?" Jezlem asked, scanning the thin poplar trees.
I'm here.

Kait spiraled around the narrow tree trunks, instructing the wind to carry her voice to Jezlem. Her words whispered along the breeze, tickling the inside of Jezlem's ear like a thought inside her own mind.

Lure him away from the café into the valley. I'll be ready as soon as you give the order.

Jezlem exhaled. "Okay. I better get going. He'll be suspicious if I delay any longer."

Kait wrapped a comforting wind around her, blowing her loose curls off her shoulders.

"Thanks, Kait. And thanks for being here with me."

Jezlem strode through the tall trees, her steps echoing as she reached the cobblestones. Kait danced through the narrow limbs, shaking free numerous green leaves as she paced the canopy. Below, Jezlem's figure grew smaller as she approached the café. Kait told her she would remain at the tree line, but the uneasy feeling gripping her gut pushed her forward. She shadowed her sister as inconspicuously as possible. It would do no good to sabotage their plan by alerting the immortal to her presence. Arching upward, she directed the wind above the outdoor café for a better view, where she wouldn't risk being discovered. She brushed the hanging sign that read *Le Navarre.*

Jezlem sidled up to a wicker table, extending her hand to the seated gentleman. Kait moved to get a better look at the immortal, causing the sign to creak. Thankfully, neither acknowledged the sound as the god took Jezlem's fingers and kissed the back of her hand. Kait grimaced. The wind kicked up in response to her fear.

Jezlem sat down, positioning herself in the setting sun's rays to hide her halo. Her eyes flickered from side to side, but she pasted on a cheerful smile, holding the immortal's full attention captive.

Kait took a breath to steady the breeze and studied the god. As Jezlem had stated, he was different. He certainly didn't have the same allure Hermes and the great gods possessed. A mop of dull brown hair hung to his ears, the ends sticking up in one patch. A navy, long-sleeved shirt covered his torso despite the warm temperature, no doubt to stifle his own halo's glow. Kait wouldn't describe him as handsome, but he had a nice face with soulful brown eyes. Yet she knew the kind of monster that lurked beneath his skin. She swallowed her revulsion.

"I'm sorry I'm late," Jezlem said breathlessly. "I admit, I almost didn't come."

Basil leaned forward, a wrinkle forming between his eyebrows. "What's wrong? Are you all right?"

His concern sounded genuine, but Kait knew better.

"I'm not sure. I haven't been feeling well."

Basil frowned. "Do you feel okay now? Can I order you a glass of wine or maybe a cup of tea?"

"No, no. I think that will upset my stomach more. Do you think we can go for a walk? Movement seems to help."

"Of course." The immortal tucked a bill under his half-drunk glass and pushed back his chair, coming around to offer Jezlem assistance.

"Thanks, but I'm okay." She smiled, lacing her fingers through his. To keep him close.

Kait rushed ahead, soaring past the poplar trees to a natural valley carved into the landscape. The Pyrenees mountains loomed a few miles away, casting the valley in early darkness as it blocked out the sun. Large, mossy boulders rose like giants, lulled into a state of slumber by a shallow brook trickling off the mountain.

As planned, Kait hovered above one of the flat boulders with her back to the town. If the immortal attempted to run, she'd already be on his flank. She settled into position, her heart beating steadily. The plan would work. It had to.

A twig snapped somewhere in the dark. Kait rose, scanning the shadows, but nothing stood out. Another snap—this one louder than before. She moved to investigate, but Jezlem's ringing voice interrupted her search, and she hastily returned to her post.

"Thanks. The fresh air is helping. Too bad we're not on a beach though," Jezlem said as they descended into the valley.

Basil chuckled. "I can't deny that I wouldn't mind seeing you in a bikini."

"Maybe when I kick whatever sickness this is."

Jezlem led Basil into the middle of the depression, stopping to face him when the hills grew steep on either side. Kait tensed, waiting for her to give the order. She kept her eyes trained on her sister's feet where she teetered on river rocks near the coursing stream a dozen inches away.

Basil craned his neck, peering at the few emerging stars. "This is a nice spot. Perfect, actually."

"It is." Jezlem leaned in, running her palms over his stomach, and sighed. "You know, I remember seeing a little bottle in your hand the other night. Didn't you tip the contents into my wine at one point?" Her tone was light, silly almost.

"Just something to enrich the flavor." Basil ran his lips along her jawline.

"It had a funny aftertaste though. Almost like…deception." Jezlem jerked out of Basil's arms and spun in a tight circle, placing herself out of reach. She held up a maroon glass vial. "This is it, right? The special ingredient you've been drugging me with since we met?" Jezlem backed up, only a few inches from the water now.

Basil put up his hands. "Whoa, Jezzie. Calm down. What is this about?"

"Don't call me that, you snake. I know who you are. I know your sick game."

She unstopped the vial, then angled the bottle down, letting one drop leak out. Ready, Kait caught the liquid in the wind, drawing it closer. The familiar scent of cherry cocooned around her. A perfect match.

Kait influenced the breeze, relaying the confirmation to Jezlem in a gentle hush. Casting the poisonous vapors away, she readied the wind for attack.

A treacherous smile transformed Basil's innocent features. "But do you *really* know me?"

Jezlem wrinkled her brow, replacing the rubber top on the vial before depositing it into the pocket of her dress. "I thought I did. I thought you were kind and sweet, where the rest of the gods are selfish. I thought I might love you."

Basil scoffed. "Shame about that, huh? Usually it works far better. How'd you figure it out, I wonder?" He strolled closer, tilting his head.

"The tonic corrupted my scent. They could smell it on me."

"They? Oh, your special little sisters?" Basil said. "That's right. The three of you are supposed to be all-powerful. At least, I think that's what you were rambling about. I wasn't paying attention. I'd like to meet them—see if they're as easy as you."

Jezlem gritted her teeth, taking a wide step back. Her heels splashed into the shallow stream. The meandering current caught the edge of her gown, pulling the fabric to give the illusion that the water stemmed from the naiad rather than the mountain.

Recognizing the signal, Kait rocketed into the night sky, creating strong winds to unfurl along the top of the valley. She started to advance but she stopped short, transfixed by Basil's permuting features.

"The truth is, you have no idea who I am," he said.

Clouds gathered up above as a flash of lightning illuminated the sky. Basil laughed a deep throaty chuckle as he shook his head back and forth. At first, the changes were subtle. His unkept brown hair lightened, the ends curling into blond waves that ended just above his ears. Another blaze of lightning sparked and highlighted the deep blue color of his irises. His pudgy cheeks thinned, revealing high cheekbones and a chiseled jawline. At the same time, his worn shirt disappeared, leaving him bare-chested with a navy-and-gold-trimmed robe covering his shoulders. Yet the most startling change was his attitude. Gone was the timid god. In his place stood a glorious immortal, armed with obvious and stunning arrogance.

Jezlem's jaw dropped, her charged palms lowering involuntarily. "Who are you?"

The new immortal grinned, his eyes gleaming in another flash of lightning. "I am Zeus, king of the gods, and you, my dear, have something I need." Zeus's voice purred, a deep tenor that both terrified and entranced Kait.

Jezlem snapped out of her shock, throwing up her hands once more. "You're not getting the vial back. You can't manipulate your way out of this."

"I don't care about the vial. So I slipped you a little love spell. Do you really think the Council will find that a punishable offense? Besides, I *am* the Council." Zeus laughed.

"They will when they realize you used it to drug three nymphs. All of whom have been reduced to mortals because of your greed."

Zeus's eyes glazed, looking hungry. "It's not greed that propels me, but euphoria. In the past, I've been able to curtail my addiction, but lately, it's become…unmanageable. Yes, I drugged you and the others, but only so that you would enjoy our lovemaking. Believe me, without it, things get messy." He stressed the last word, a perfect rendition of a snake.

"Did you promise the other nymphs immortality too? Is that why they were eager to lie with you?"

Zeus raised his eyebrow. "Does sweeten the deal, don't you think?" He took a step closer as thunder boomed overhead. "But don't fret, I'll still enjoy myself.

Plus, given our remote location, you can scream all you want. No one will hear a thing."

Jezlem stacked her fingers and shot a geyser of water at Zeus's chest. The god leaned to the right, dodging the powerful blow.

"I understand the desire to keep your halo. Really, I do. You don't want to go down without a fight," Zeus said. "But we both know how this ends. If you give in now, I promise to make it pleasurable, but if you continue to fight, I'm going to grow angry, and then I'll take you as hard and as rough as I damn well please."

Jezlem heaved two more pulsating spheres of water at Zeus. One of them skimmed the top of his head. He smiled, but his eyes were hard and unyielding as flint.

"Last chance, naiad. You're all alone. No one is coming to save you."

Kait materialized out of the wind, levitating high overhead. "Want to bet?"

Slamming her hands together, Kait forced the wind to erupt from a docile breeze to a titanic energy. She cast the air from her palms, kicking Zeus off his feet. The god backflipped into the sky, landing easily on his feet.

"You must be one of Jezzie's baby sisters," Zeus called over his shoulder. "That was a fun trick. This could have been a real showdown. Pity I brought a friend as well."

Out of the thick shadows, a giant feline emerged. Long white fur covered in deep blue swirls reflected silver in the waxing moonlight. Sharp fangs lined the cat's lips, and a blanket of venomous quills adorned its back. They were dormant now, but Kait knew how fast that could change. Holding still, she watched as the cat's tail twitched back and forth, the tip glowing a bright blue. Snarling, the animal threw its head to the right, fixing its mustard-yellow eyes on Kait as it sensed her magic.

Kait's body went rigid, phantom pain stemming from her shoulder and calf from decades-old wounds. The piriol from the alley.

Hermes had bragged that he blackmailed another god for the chance to use the creature. All this time, Zeus—who led the Council and Olympus with a heart of gold—was the immortal responsible, the immortal concealing the living piriol to further his obsession with euphoria.

The piriol licked its fangs, growling low in its throat, aligning itself with Kait. Its massive paws spread to support its weight, digging ten long claws into the moist dirt beneath it. Zeus narrowed his eyes, glancing between Kait and the creature.

"You know, I think Kaf here remembers you. Normally, he's shy in front of strangers, until I let him off the proverbial chain. Then he becomes quite friendly." He paused, assessing Kait. "You wouldn't happen to be Hermes's little whore, would you? Shame the poor bastard got caught without enjoying the crime first. Serves him right for blackmailing me."

Kait shivered, unable to remain impassive.

"Kaf?" Jezlem repeated, her voice high.

"Yes, my piriol, darling. Do try to keep up. You see, I can't exactly keep him with me on Olympus, so he stays with a…friend of mine in the area. He loves it here. Lots of wilderness to explore. Because of the love tonic obtained through a hefty bribe to the goddess Aphrodite, Kaf hasn't been necessary with my last few conquests. But what luck you aim to fight, because he's itching to hunt."

The god's eyes glimmered, his bloodlust palpable.

"I must admit, I'm intrigued that he knows your sister." Zeus crossed his arms over his chest, tapping his chin with a finger as he turned his back to Jezlem. His eyes glimmered darkly.

"It was you," Kait said. "You approved our testimony and allowed us to speak before the Council. You persecuted Hermes."

"Would you rather I hadn't? Do you wish I would've sent him back to finish with you instead? What a naughty girl."

Kait's cheeks flared red as the winds surged, pummeling Zeus in the chest. The god doubled over and let out a whoosh of air. The piriol hissed, its quills leaping to attention.

"Easy, Kaf. The aurai was just having a bit of fun." Zeus waved his hand as he caught his breath. "Maybe after I'm done with your sister, I'll have you as well. Finish what Hermes started all those years ago."

Behind Zeus, Jezlem raised her palms, her fingers flexing as power radiated through them. "You're not going to touch us." Her words were ice.

Zeus chuckled, brushing his navy cloak in a wide arc behind him. "You'll find I can do whatever I please. You're a nymph, created to satisfy my needs, and I'm only interested in one thing. The sooner you get that through your head, the easier this will be."

Jezlem curled her fingers one by one. The water at her feet rose, gurgling with anticipation. "I told you, you will not touch us." She opened her hands, and the water roared, exploding in multiple geysers.

Throwing up his hands, Zeus diverted the blasts, sending them crashing against the nearby hillside, but Jezlem was ready with more. A cresting tidal wave loomed over and swept him off his feet, depositing him a dozen yards downstream. The god vomited water from his lungs, then snickered, climbing to his feet.

"Clever," he barked. "I underestimated how strong you are."

Jezlem remained silent.

"I know you probably think you'll escape, that you'll beat me, but I promise you, I always get what I want. I will have you. I didn't waste all that time to let you go without a taste."

Revulsion overwhelmed Kaitaini. She saw the confidence in his eyes, believed every word he said. "Then I hope you're ready to kill, because the only way you're going to touch my sister is by stepping over my dead corpse." Before Kait finished speaking, a tornado of wind attacked, wielding heavy river rocks and fallen tree limbs.

Zeus's gaze widened. He didn't have time to shield himself, and a large, jagged rock caught him in the temple just before the wind carried him out of the small valley. The wind funneled down, slamming him back into the earth. The god crouched on his hands and knees, bellowing in frustration. Lightning crackled from his palms and surged through the air toward Kait.

She threw up her hands, creating a swirling blockade. The lightning struck, ricocheted off the barrier, and collided with a nearby tree. Instantly, the heat set the dry bark ablaze.

"Kaf! Disable the aurai, but keep her alive!" Zeus commanded.

The piriol snarled, biting the air. With a resounding roar, it launched its quills at Kait. New ones grew back the moment the others released. Once the last one slid out, the cat leapt off the rock.

The quills split the air, puncturing gaps in Kait's shield. Melting into the wind, she vanished from sight, but that wasn't enough to trick the piriol. The blue light at the end of its tail brightened as the cat sensed a directional shift of ethereal magic. Its tongue licked the air, tasting her scent.

"Kait!"

Jezlem launched water at the piriol, weaving her hands in an intricate pattern as it lapped at the cat's heels. But the piriol was too fast, intent upon its prey. The markings in its fur sizzled, seemingly increasing its speed. Kaitaini only had a few seconds head start.

Holding her hands in front of her stomach, Jezlem's fingers stiffened into claws as she rotated her hands faster and faster. The shallow stream hardened into slick ice, sending the animal crashing into a moss-covered boulder.

Kait halted her flight, backtracking when she heard the piriol's injured cry. Jezlem stood in the middle of the frozen stream with a triumphant smile on her lips. A surge of hope swelled within Kait. She was stronger than the last time she faced a god, and with the additional power her sister's halo yielded, they stood a fair chance of winning this fight. She scanned the valley for Zeus. Her breath caught when she spied his dark silhouette behind Jezlem.

"Jez! Watch out!" Kait cried, but her warning came too late.

Cuffs of white fire sizzled around Jezlem's neck and wrists. Kait gasped. She remembered those bonds, had nightmares about them.

"Well, that was fun," Zeus growled.

His fingers knotted in Jezlem's wild curls. He ripped her head back to expose her neck. With his other hand, he foraged around in the folds of her dress, withdrawing the vial. He grinned, and in a puff of acrid smoke, their evidence disappeared.

"In case you had any ideas of tattling on me." Zeus sighed, long and dramatic. "I pictured this evening going so much better. I would have wooed you, treasured your body, made you beg for my touch. But you forced my hand, and although I'll be satisfied, I doubt you'll be able to say the same."

Tears leaked from Jezlem's eyes, running into the shallow curves of her ears.

"Please," she whispered, but the fiery manacle around her neck cut into her throat, silencing her.

"What was that, my dear? I didn't catch it." Zeus laughed. "Soon, Kaf will finish your sister and I'll be free to indulge my carnal desires."

"Don't."

"Oh, I intend to do so much more than that."

A blast of icy wind billowed around Zeus, pushing him across the ice.

"Get away from her!" Kait shouted.

This time, the god was ready and fired a bolt of lightning that spidered out and reached for Kait. She was unable to maneuver quickly enough, and the lightning seized Kait, ripping her body from the air and wrenching it to the ground. She gasped, expelling all the air in her lungs as her chest slammed against a sharp rock.

She struggled to push herself up, but heavy paws landed on her back, forcing her into the dirt. Before she could react, the cat's fangs closed around her throat, pinning her in place. Kait stopped fighting and lay still. One bite from the piriol and her spine would be severed.

"That's a good girl," Zeus said. "That was quite a fight. You must love your sister very much. It's a shame you couldn't save her."

"Zeus, don't do this," Jezlem begged.

"Shh, shh, my dear. There will be time for you to say my name in just a bit, but first, I think we should send your sister away. She doesn't need to see what I'm going to do to you."

Kait's fingers tried to cast, but the piriol's heavy body pressed harder, preventing her from completing the correct motions. She swallowed and felt the cat's teeth pierce her skin.

Jez. She had to get to her. She promised she would keep her safe.

Blood trickled down her neck as her eyes rotated in their sockets, trying to locate Zeus from her position the ground. She couldn't let this happen again. She had to stop him.

"Let this serve as a warning to you, nymph. Don't interfere in my affairs again," Zeus told her. "Let her go, Kaf, but give her another souvenir."

The piriol obeyed and closed its jaws, sinking its fangs into Kait's neck. Blinding pain sliced through her. Once it tasted her warm blood, it released its hold and stepped back, licking the stained fur around its teeth.

Kait choked, pressing her palms to the flowing wounds. The pain was overwhelming. She struggled to stay conscious, but her vision grew cloudy as she found her body's instinctual response to shut down. Her dark lavender eyes found Jezlem's, her mouth forming a frightened O.

"Goodbye for now, nymph. I'll take you when you're not so...messy."

With his free hand, Zeus raised his arm and brought it back down to his side with an echoing slap. The rocky terrain Kait was sprawled on cracked and split, crumbling away from the rest of the forest floor.

"Wait..." Kait gasped, reaching toward her sister, but she was too weak and the pain blossoming behind her eyes was too bright. An impending sinkhole trembled beneath her legs, threatening to open up and swallow her whole.

"No!" Jezlem screamed. The electric bonds sizzled against her windpipe, drawing blood as they constricted tighter.

Zeus smiled and spun back to face his prize. Wrapping his fingers even tighter around her hair, he tilted Jezlem's chin higher, forcing her to gaze at the brilliant stars above. Her bonds extinguished, but his hands were ready to replace them. He pulled Jezlem's body against his and nibbled her ear.

"Look at the stars, darling. I want you to imagine all the places I could have taken you."

Kait opened her mouth, trying and failing to scream. Why wasn't Jez fighting him?

Silent tears rolled down Jezlem's cheeks, but she kept her eyes open as Zeus pawed at her body.

Dropping her hands away from the incisions, Kait raised her palms, both arms shaking from the effort and blood loss. The edge of her sight darkened—a sign that her body was too weak to keep fighting, but she refused to stop. She'd already lost Willow. She couldn't let him take Jez away from her too.

Kait's fingers bent to cast, but she felt as if they were made of straw, brittle and stiff. Her magic stuttered, jerking the winds left and right, but they were void of strength and stamina. She had to focus. Had to stop him.

Kait tried again, groaning as fresh blood trickled down her chest. Her hands shook even harder; her fingers twisted into gnarled hooks. Zeus glanced away from Jezlem, offering Kait a quick wave.

A hissing sounded below Kait as rocks and dirt fell away and the earth opened its jaws. Before she could transform into her element, the ground sucked her in.

The stars watched as she fell with grim eyes, their brilliance mocking her. The last sound Kait heard was Zeus sighing as he forced his way inside her sister. His groan echoed as he absorbed Jezlem's ethereal connection, as he tasted the beginnings of euphoria.

Kait screamed as the world fell away.

⚡ 10 ⚡

Aterrifying scream sawed through Kait's dreamless sleep. Her body reacted, launching off the ground into a fighting stance. The enemy was long gone, but his destruction lingered. Sand and pebbles clung to her face, imprinted deeply into her flesh. Wincing, she brushed most of it off. Another scream greeted the rising sun.

Jezlem.

"Please, no," Kait whispered.

She took a step, then fell to her knees as her cramped legs gave out beneath her. A puff of dirt lifted into the air around her face, and her throat burned. Reaching up, she felt four perfect scars along her skin—a forever reminder that she was too late.

"Jez, I'm coming."

Kait leapt into the wind and sprinted through the trees, following the flowing river. She was still in the human realm, but Zeus's magic had thrown her far from the valley. It didn't take long for the water to split. A narrow stream diverted from the main path, descending downhill. She followed it.

At first, she thought she had traversed the river wrong; the valley looked too different. Trees littered the sloping hills, their exposed roots reaching for her like mangled fingers. Deep scars were carved into the grass, remnants of magic and talons. When she'd arrived last night, the landscape was tranquil, but the bright morning sun revealed it for what it was—a horrendous battleground.

A painful scream accompanied the birdsong in the surrounding trees. Soaring into the wreckage, Kait let Jezlem's cries guide her.

Beneath a dead oak tree lay her sister, heartbroken sobs falling from her lips. Her beautiful dress was destroyed. Only a few strips of cloth remained along her stomach. Kait flew around a boulder and jumped out of the air to land at Jezlem's side. Fresh blood puddled by her mouth, while dried cuts zigzagged across her skin. She looked like she had fallen off a cliff.

"Jez. Jez, I'm here. Shh." Kait stroked her sister's matted hair.

With a shudder, she realized Jezlem's halo was gone. The turquoise glow that used to encapsulate her had vanished. Her skin now shown with a sickly yellow hue, as if she were infected.

"Jezlem, it's all right. He's gone."

Kait tried to soothe her sister, but she doubted Jezlem could hear over the guttural screams pouring from her mouth.

Minutes went by until at last Jezlem's screams quieted to whimpers. Shakily, she pushed herself onto her hands, staring at the dilapidated forest surrounding them. Jezlem bit her lower lip and glanced down at her tattered dress. Kait felt her body tense.

"Where were you?" Jezlem hissed.

Kait crouched in front of her sister. "What?"

"I said, where were you? How could you leave me like that?"

Kait's mouth opened, then closed. She shook her head. "I was right here. I was right here the whole time trying to get to you, but Zeus's piriol pinned me down, and then Zeus dropped me into the dark. I couldn't get out." She fought back tears. "But I never stopped fighting."

Jezlem's icy gaze froze Kait. "You didn't stop? Zeus didn't stop either! He took me again and again and again, and now look at me! He took everything from me! My magic, my tie to the naiads, my life! I can't even return with you to Olean."

Kait fell backward at her sister's outrage. "Jez, I'm sorry. It wasn't supposed to happen this way. If we'd went to the Council—"

"They never would have believed us, especially because Basil doesn't even *exist*. It was Zeus. It wouldn't have helped."

"I'm sorry, Jez. I wasn't—"

"Were you hoping he'd take me the whole time?"

"Of course not! Jez, how could you say that? I love you."

Kait placed a gentle hand on her sister's leg, but Jezlem jerked it away.

"Don't," she barked. "I don't want your pity. Just go back to Olean and tell them what happened."

"I'm not going to leave you."

"You need to go."

"I'm not leaving you. How will you get home?"

"I can't go home, remember? The realm won't appear for me now that I'm *human*." Jezlem tucked a limp curl behind her ear. "Go."

Kait remained where she was. "Jezlem, please. Let me help you."

Jezlem raised her red-rimmed eyes. "Kait. Go away. I can't...I can't be around you right now. Please," she added, her voice softening.

Kait drew her hand back and stood. She opened her mouth to argue, but then saw the pleading look in Jezlem's eyes.

"I won't let him get away with this," Kait said. Her breath quickened as an idea took hold. "I'm going to make sure he never ruins another life. I swear to you. I will hunt him down, make him regret what he's done, and do everything in my power to save the nymphs of Olean."

Kait leaned down and placed a lingering kiss on Jezlem's forehead, ignoring the way she flinched. "I'll alert Tahlia. She'll tell the other elders, the queen, the Council. Bia and I will find you after. I promise. Please, stay safe. I love you."

Kait let her vow hang in the air and spun on her bare heels. Dirt and rocks crunched beneath her weight as she sprinted toward the edge of the valley. Her long legs crossed the short distance in seconds. There was no hesitation as she neared the end. With a quick breath, she leapt into the air, throwing her body into the blue sky. Her arms fanned out and flew overhead as the wind swallowed her.

Kait's physical form vanished, her body becoming the warm breeze. Transforming was easier than breathing—a part of her. She exhaled her own sorrow and agony, relaxed into the familiar cradle the air provided, and set her gaze on the heavens above. It was time to find Zeus.

11

Kait rapped a fist on the soft bark door. The harsh sound reverberated through the trees.

"Tahlia! Tahlia, it's Kait. Please! I need to speak with you!"

Silence greeted her barrage. She cursed and spun around, threading her fingers through her hair. An idea bloomed. If Tahlia wasn't available, she'd find another elder who was. She twisted her fingers, and the wind rushed to her call, gathering around her, eager and restless. Kait ascended into the air, her flesh evaporating like colored smoke as the breeze ushered her soul to the north of Olean.

Regret pulled at her as the manicured forests gave way to the flooded swamps and wetlands of the naiads. Was it only yesterday that she flew this same circuit? Years seemed to have elapsed since she left Jezlem in the mortal world. If only they had gone to the Council, exposed Basil, and let the gods seek him out and punish him. It would have been difficult, now knowing who he really was, but at least Kait would still have her sister.

Her stomach churned as she looked down at the interweaving blue and green waters. It seemed empty, wrong, knowing that Jezlem would never again influence the currents or spar in the fields. What would happen to Jez? What would happen to Bia? Or her? No one ever mentioned the consequences to the triad if such a tragedy occurred. Was the prophecy now void, or would the realm expect even more from the remaining two sisters? Was it possible for the Council to reinstate Jezlem's connection, similar to how they granted the queen immortality?

Kait didn't have an answer to any of the questions bombarding her. Better to take it one step at a time before she drowned under everything else. She raced on. Scanning the large pools, she realized she didn't know where the naiad elder's residence was. With the way her luck had been leaning, she was going to get wet.

Transforming to her physical form, Kait touched down on a sandy shore amidst a large group of young naiads. They all stood in the pool, the water licking their hips. Their hands hovered above the surface as they cast their magic. Some frowned and completed the spell pattern with steadfast concentration, while delight colored other students' faces as a flourish of bubbles formed, rising higher and higher into the sunny sky.

Kait approached the nearest naiad, wincing as the cold water teased the back of her knees.

"Excuse me. I'm wondering where I can find Vivien?"

The naiad ceased her casting, observing Kait with wonder. "You're an aurai."

"Yes. Where can I find Vivien?"

"I'm not sure, but maybe Maya can tell you." She gestured to a naiad standing in the center of the class, her long blond braid skimming the water's surface, creating growing ripples with each turn of her head. "I'll be right back."

The young naiad collapsed in a quiet splash, trading her flesh for water. Kait followed her movements and was surprised when she reappeared beside Maya faster than anticipated. The two naiads conversed for a few seconds before Maya glanced over her shoulder, spying Kait for the first time.

"Keep practicing, class. I'll be a moment," she instructed.

She spun around in a quick circle and melted into the pool, only to reconstruct a second later in front of Kait. Several stray droplets coursed down her torso from a navy bikini top that hugged her chest.

"Hello, I'm Maya. Beck told me you're looking for Vivien?"

"Yes." Kait nodded. "I must find her right away."

A frown transformed Maya's curious stare. "Unfortunately, she's not here. All the elders were called to a meeting with Queen Rajhi. Is everything all right? It's not every day an aurai seeks a naiad elder."

Kait bit her lip. Her presence was an anomaly. If nymphs of a different element wished to congregate, they did so in the heart of Olean, at the apothecary, the training fields, or the library. For her to venture so far into the naiad quadrant indicated something serious had occurred, but she hadn't had much of a choice.

"Yes, everything's fine. Sorry to pull you away from your class. Thank you for your time." Kait swiftly vacated the pool, relieved to be out of the water's clinging embrace. It felt like hands, swirling, pulling, searching for something she should've had, searching for Jezlem. Her right foot disappeared as she bled into the wind, but Maya's haunting next words made her falter.

"You're Jezlem's sister, right? Is she okay? We missed her at breakfast this morning."

Kait's throat grew thick. No, Jez wasn't okay. Zeus had seen to that.

Without answering, she urged the rest of her body to vanish into the sky.

"I need to see Queen Rajhi." Kait's frustration leaked out of her in a torrent of tears. "Please, this is an emergency."

She was standing just outside the queen's antechamber in a long, narrow hallway. Thin, tightly spaced trees lined the polished marble floors. The afternoon sunshine filtered down through the overhanging branches. The palace was beautiful, fashioned to blur the lines of nature so that visitors couldn't tell whether they were outside or inside an actual structure. It was enchanting, but impenetrable as well.

One of the queen's guards shook her head, the tips of her chestnut ponytail brushing her folded forearms. "As I've repeatedly stated, Queen Rajhi is in an important meeting and cannot be disturbed."

"But this is about the immortal hunting nymphs for euphoria. There's been another attack!"

The guard's eyes widened at Kait's words. One of her hands flashed out, grabbing Kait by the elbow. She steered her against the wall. Curling bark scratched Kait's skin.

"How do you know of this?" the guard hissed under her breath.

"Because I was there. I saw him take her. I know who it is."

The guard glanced at the ornate green doors behind her, flashing the right side of her head. The hair there was shaved close, fading into longer locks just past her ear. Carved into the side was a sharp triangle with a thin white line etched across the top point. The guard was an aurai like her.

"Come with me." She dragged Kait by her arm.

Without pausing to knock, the aurai threw open the doors, surprising one of the queen's advisors standing on the other side. She spun around, hands already beginning to cast to fend off the intrusion. Jagged icicles formed at their feet in a quick barrier.

The guard held up her empty hand. "There's no need for that."

The advisor dropped her arms to her sides. Thunderclouds were tame compared to the ire in her eyes. "Then what is the meaning of this unprompted entrance, Aella? How dare you intrude while the queen is in session?"

"Save me the lecture. This nymph must speak with the queen. Now."

The advisor raised her chin, looking down her nose at the pair. "She most certainly may. Make an appointment on the way out, and she can come back in a month or two."

"I don't have time for your games and protocol, Doris. Move or I'll make you."

A stiff breeze kicked up to complement the aurai's threat. Kait didn't hesitate. Shifting out of the guard's grasp, she metamorphosed into air and billowed around the corner before either of them realized she was gone.

"Hey! Get back here!"

Shouts crescendoed behind her, but Kait kept moving, sensing multiple bodies charging after. In the high-ceiled inner room, she found all three elemental elders seated at a circular oak table, their heads inclined toward Queen Rajhi.

Kait stalled for a moment, overcome with a mixture of awe and involuntary distrust. The queen was beyond beautiful. Her hair fell in thick black waves to her waist. Gold jewels were woven across her forehead, ears, and nose. Her dark olive complexion was stunning, but her skin glimmered with the same alabaster sheen of the immortals. Kait's stomach clenched, but this was the queen. She wasn't like the gods.

Kait funneled down to the floor and to one knee as the wind peeled away, exposing her to the assembled group. Shock registered on all their faces.

"Kaitaini!" Tahlia leapt to her feet. "What are you doing here?"

Doris and Aella rushed in seconds later, the advisor looking stricken as a satisfied smirk pulled at the guard's lips.

"I'm sorry to disturb you, Your Grace." Kait rose from her bow. "But I have information about the immortal attacks."

Tahlia disappeared to colored vapor, rematerializing directly in front of Kait. Her gray eyes were stone, unyielding and enraged. "I thought I told you to leave this alone."

Kait returned her elder's stare. "I'm sorry, but Jezlem—he took her."

"What?" Vivien pushed her chair back and stood. "What's happened to Jezlem?"

"I apologize, Your Majesty," Doris fumbled. "I tried to stop her."

A chorus of voices swelled as everyone fought to be heard. Kait remained where she stood, standing tall as Tahlia's voice growled in her ear. She ignored her elder and instead leveled her gaze with the queen's.

"Please," Kait whispered, but the queen heard.

"Enough," Queen Rajhi ordered.

The room fell silent. Kait felt the weight of half a dozen stares on her back. Queen Rajhi stood, placing her fingertips on the shining surface of the table.

Three gold rings adorned her fingers, each with a different inlaid gem: diamond, emerald, and sapphire. Warmth flooded Kait as she realized each element was represented.

A maroon-and-gold sari draped across the queen's chest, and numerous bangles jingled musically on her wrists. Queen Rajhi turned her head from left to right.

"Resume your seats, my friends. I, for one, am very curious as to what has brought her here."

As one, the elders resumed their seats. Doris and Aella stood with their hands clasped in front of them. Kait looked around uncomfortably, unsure where to go. The queen pulled out an empty chair beside her own.

"Come sit over here, my dear."

Kait waited for the queen to resume her seat before taking her own. She swallowed roughly, suddenly tongue-tied. Thankfully, the queen spoke first.

"Now, dear. What information do you have regarding the immortal? What is it you have seen?"

Kait took a deep breath and wrung her hands together, uncomfortable being the center of attention after so many years trying to blend into shadows. She pictured Jezlem lying in the crumpled heap Zeus left her in, remembered her broken screams.

"Yesterday, my sister Jezlem went to the human realm to meet an immortal. She pledged he was different, thought the love story he whispered was real. I tried to convince her to come to you, to warn the Council, but she wanted to confront him on her own."

"Who, my dear? Who is the immortal hunting our nymphs?"

"Zeus." Kait nearly choked on the name. "Zeus is the predator."

"Zeus?" numerous voices questioned.

"But it can't be. Zeus is one of the most powerful gods, the leader of the Council," Gemma, the anthousai elder, said.

"Someone would have seen him. He's too well known," Vivien added.

Kait shook her head. "We didn't realize at first. He altered his features, posing as a lower god named Basil. Messy brown hair, dull eyes, slightly hunched posture—the exact opposite of his true identity. Zeus didn't reveal the truth until he knew he'd won."

"What happened? Why didn't Jezlem report this with you?" Vivien's voice rose an octave.

"Zeus raped her, right before my eyes. He absorbed her halo like all the others." Kait crossed her arms over her torso. Fresh pain caused her to double over. Saying it out loud made the fact that her sister was separated from the realm even more concrete.

The rapid questions quieted as each nymph was left stunned. After several long moments, Queen Rajhi spoke. "Why didn't he take you as well? He's been seducing nymphs for weeks and attacked your sister for euphoria. Why didn't he indulge in yours too?"

Kait's jaw fell agape at the queen's accusatory tone. Did she actually think she helped Zeus destroy her own sister?

"Your Grace," Tahlia interjected. "Kait had nothing to do with this."

Rajhi held up her palm, her features neutral as she stared at Kait. "I would like to hear her explanation."

Kait shook her head, tears welling over the rims of her eyelids. Gone was the table; gone was the queen. All she saw were Zeus's fingers gripping Jezlem's hips, the electric bonds sizzling into her skin, the desperation in her eyes.

"He had a piriol," Kait said. "He said he kept it hidden near the Pyrenees mountains in the human realm, far outside the Council's jurisdiction. He didn't employ the creature before because the hunt has been too simple. He's been using a potion from Aphrodite to corrupt the nymphs' minds and plant feelings of strong affection for him."

"Do you have any evidence of this potion?" Queen Rajhi asked.

Again, Kait tossed her head. "We did, but it was shattered in the fight."

"And this piriol you claim Zeus keeps, why did he unleash it on you?"

"He asked Jezlem to meet him in a small town at the base of the mountains. When he realized she would not submit to him willingly, he called his piriol to join the fight. He said the animal stays with a friend close by."

"If I recall, you claimed to have survived an attack from a piriol a little over a century ago as well. Am I remembering that correctly?"

"Yes, Your Majesty. Zeus lent the piriol in exchange for Hermes's agreement to keep the god's hunt and the piriol's existence a secret."

The queen's eyebrows arched skeptically. "That's certainly a convenient arrangement. And unlike last time, do you have any proof of the piriol?"

Fire coursed through Kait's veins, enticing a brisk wind to kick up around the edge of the room. Why was the queen treating her as if she were on trial? Why wasn't she organizing a team to find and issue aid to her sister?

"Yes, I do, just like I did one hundred years ago."

Kait ripped her bloodied dress away and revealed the twisted flesh that marked where the first quill had drilled through her shoulder blade, before displaying an identical mark on her calf. Then, arching her neck, she ran her fingers along the fresh puncture marks left by the creature's fangs.

"The piriol remembered me. This time, it used its teeth instead of quills. Zeus instructed it to pin me down while he raped Jezlem. I did everything I could to protect her, but in the end, I wasn't strong enough. I came here to tell you I've found the monster. Now it's our turn to hunt him."

Silence radiated at Kait's powerful declaration. None of the elders moved, waiting with bated breath for the queen's reaction.

Queen Rajhi stood, head high, amber golden-flecked eyes shining brightly. "I applaud your bravery and your sister's sacrifice, but what you're asking me to do is impossible."

"What do you mean?"

"You're asking me to go to war with Olympus. To accuse the most powerful god in the heavens of illicit activities."

"*Illicit activities?* He raped my sister and three other nymphs. He stole each of their halos for a rush of euphoria and banished them to a mortal life. How can you condone that?"

"Kait, watch your tongue," Tahlia warned.

The stirring wind grew angry, whipping the assembled elders' hair and cloaks back and forth.

Aella withdrew a leather cord. "Settle down, aurai, or I will detain you."

"So their lives meant nothing to you? You're our queen. You're supposed to protect us from the immortals, protect us from being hunted and used. You don't deserve that throne."

Tahlia sucked in a breath. "Kaitaini!"

Hot tears pulsed down Kait's cheeks. She couldn't stop herself. One hundred years of repressed guilt, frustration, fear, and anger boiled to the surface, and combined with losing Jez, Zeus's escape, and the queen's indifference, she could no longer hide behind a static mask.

"Contrary to what you may think, my only interest is keeping the nymphs of Olean safe," Queen Rajhi said, her tone clipped and void of emotion. "Challenging Zeus head-on would curse every creature in the seven realms. Gods would be forced to choose sides, and our fragile alliance would shatter as those immortals who wish to return to the days of lower-being enslavement would fight to overpower our true allies. I understand your frustration, but we cannot bring these accusations to the rest of the Council without solid evidence. You don't have the tonic Zeus supposedly slipped to the nymphs, the marks on your body could have been sustained from any number of creatures, and you're the only one who Zeus revealed himself to—a grieving nymph who's been chasing vengeance for the last century for the death of her friend at the hands of another rouge immortal."

Kait balled her hands into fists. "This is not about Willow! This is not about Hermes! Zeus is seeking euphoria and hunting nymphs down to get it."

Kait's palms burst open, her fingers calling a terrifying storm to match her rage, but Aella wrestled her hands behind her back, securing them together with the strong leather cord to prevent any further magic.

The guard held her tightly and whispered in her ear. "Calm down. Calm down. You need to listen and stop fighting."

Queen Rajhi continued, her face conveying endless patience or more likely, apathy. "That's how you will come across to a jury: a wild, volatile nymph set on revenge, striking at whichever immortal she can. As you learned one hundred years ago, the Council believes they eradicated all the piriols from Olympus. Your wounds will do nothing to change their minds. The fact of the matter is, you have no proof and endless reasons to blindly accuse. You want to help the nymphs of Olean? Listen to your elder and leave this alone."

"Please, Your Grace. My sister. I can't leave her there. She has nothing." Kait sobbed in the guard's firm hold.

The queen spoke over her. "In the meantime, double patrols, ensure every group working in the mortal world has a minimum of four nymphs. Doris, gather the soldiers and send out spies to monitor the portal between Olympus and the human realm. Track anyone matching the description of Zeus or his alter ego. At the first sight of him, call every nymph back to Olean until he retreats to Olympus. As for the lost nymphs, send a team to assist each one. Make sure they have access to food and water and administer any medical attention they may need. Unfortunately, after that, they're on their own."

The queen interlaced her fingers, eyeing every nymph in the room with a heavy glance.

"Elders, you may speak with your charges, but keep the details vague. Let them know we are aware of the situation and are monitoring it. Every nymph must do their part. Be cautious, be aware, and be smart. We do this calmly. We do this swiftly. Keep Olean safe."

The three elders nodded in unison and exited their seats, keeping their eyes to the ground. Tahlia paused near the rounded corner, placing her hand on the wall to await the queen's sentencing for Kait's impudence.

"As for you, aurai. Though I admire your determination, never again make the mistake of accusing me of not caring for my realm and my children. You will not speak of this to anyone, including your other sister. I am also placing you under lockdown for your indiscretion. To ensure you heed my orders, you are prohibited from leaving Olean for three months. If I hear any rumor that you have uttered a word about Zeus or euphoria, I will strip you of your ethereal connection myself. Do you understand, dear?"

The queen's voice was honey, but her expression was carved from marble.

"Yes, Your Majesty." Kait stared at the elaborate robes covering her feet. "I'm sorry."

"Aella, release her to Tahlia and escort them back to the aurai quadrant."

The guard inclined her head and released Kait's wrists once they reached her elder. Kait's shoulders slumped in humiliation and defeat. She thought she could help, thought she was doing the right thing. Tahlia placed her hand on Kait's lower back, but she drew no comfort from her touch. Zeus was going to get away with another attack, and Jezlem would be left wondering why neither of her sisters sought her out to make sure she was okay. The fire that tore through Kait moments ago was slowly replaced by cold steel. If they refused to make Zeus pay for what he did, she would do it instead.

⚡ 12 ⚡

Three full moons had elapsed since Queen Rajhi forbid Kait from leaving Olean. For three months, nightmares saturated her dreams, replaying that awful night Jezlem was taken. She had no idea where her sister was or what had happened after she left her at the base of the Pyrenees mountains. Allowed one slight concession, Kait was able to tell Bia what happened, but with the knowledge came a similar sentence for the youngest sister.

So many times, Kait wandered to the platform that held the Hall of Portals, monitoring the last one on the left that she had slipped through to the human realm so easily before. Tirelessly, she kept watch, attempting to work up the courage to ask one of the returning scouts if they had seen Zeus or more importantly, her sister. Yet every time she edged close enough to be heard, the queen's warning echoed in her mind. Her heart ached for Jezlem, but if the queen followed through on her threat and severed her tie to the realm, Kait would never be able to destroy Zeus.

Over the last twelve weeks, Kait heard nothing regarding the rogue immortal or lost nymphs. Either Zeus had caught wind of her accusation and was lying low or he had resumed the hunt and everyone was being careful to keep their mutterings away from her. Like all news that spread through Olean, it wasn't long before her tantrum before the queen leaked. Almost overnight, her status of self-identified loner transformed into social pariah. Even though she was free to go anywhere within Olean, she might as well have been imprisoned in the dark depths below the queen's palace for all the interaction she had with the other nymphs. No one spoke to her, looked at her, or even passed within her vicinity. Thankfully, Bia, an unfortunate casualty dragged down by her uncontrollable sister, was spared this treatment.

Because of her poisonous reputation, Kait tried spending more time with Bia, hopeful that they might grow closer in their shared quarantine, but her optimism was dashed early on. After the news of Jezlem's attack, Bia retreated even further inside herself. The only certainties she could count on were her medicines and the rich soil. Kait couldn't blame her; she could barely look at her own reflection without being overwhelmed by shame and regret.

A gentle breeze rocked Kait back and forth as she lounged in her hammock, suspended high in the strong branches of a red maple tree. The other aurais had abandoned their sleeping nooks a week into Kait's sentence, moving to a new maple a few miles away. At first, she didn't mind. The solitude allowed her a better chance to grieve, but lately, she craved attention and eavesdropped on others' conversations. It was soothing to be included for a moment, even if she had to pretend.

"Kaitaini," a sharp voice called.

Peering over the edge of the hemp woven hammock, Kait spotted Tahlia standing at the base of the tree with Queen Rajhi a few feet behind her. Excitement buoyed her out of her slouched state. Today was the day. Today, she would finally be free to find Jezlem.

Melting into the wind, Kait spiraled down to the leaf-strewn forest floor. Autumn was in full swing, both the trees and the earth a swirling pattern of red and gold hues. The air deposited her in front of the stern pair, and déjà vu assailed her as she sunk into a deep bow.

"You may rise," Queen Rajhi said. Her voice was different than the last time they spoke, soft and gentle as a lullaby.

Kait complied but continued to keep her eyes on the bright carpet underfoot.

"You have been an ideal charge these last few months. I appreciate your responsibility and the effort you have demonstrated to reform your attitude. I come today to revoke your punishment. You are now free to travel to the other realms."

"Thank you, Your Grace." Kait lifted her head. "How is Jezlem?" She awaited the queen's next words with a hammering heart.

"Your sister is okay. She is learning to live as a mortal, safe from the gods. She is in the state of Florida, living on the coast at the ocean's fingertips. However, I caution you from visiting at this moment."

Kait swallowed her disappointment, struggling to complete the motion. "May I ask why?"

Queen Rajhi stepped forward, gliding soundlessly across the dried leaves. "Becoming mortal has been a huge adjustment for your sister. We have been monitoring her and all the lost nymphs to ensure they're all right, but if you meet with her, I fear she will regress and her progress to join the mortals will flounder.

I'm not forbidding you from ever seeing her, but I'm asking you to have compassion and give her a little more time. It would be more appropriate to visit once she is settled and confident in her new self."

"Are all the lost nymphs together?"

"No. We have them separated throughout the human realm, much for the same reason I've asked you to refrain from visiting Jezlem. If they are not forced to branch out and adapt, they will never survive."

Kait took several deep breaths. What the queen asked made sense. She remembered the way Jez flinched away from her, unable to stand being reminded of what she'd lost.

"Does Bia know?"

Tahlia answered. "Yes, your sister was informed of the delicate situation last week."

Kait nodded, biting her lower lip. "I understand. I miss her, but I don't wish to cause her more pain. Thank you for your guidance." She bowed again, blinking back a stray tear. "Have there been any more attacks? Any sign of Zeus or another immortal? I... No one has spoken to me since it all happened." Embarrassment colored her cheeks.

Tahlia looked away, her lips set in a tight line. Queen Rajhi clasped her hands in front of her. The gold filigree lining her emerald sari sparkled in the sun's rays that peeked through the still clinging leaves.

"No. There have been no more attacks or seductions. My scouts have kept a vigilant eye on the portals from Olympus to the human realm and haven't seen one immortal cross over. I'm not dismissing what you experienced; however, there is no evidence that Zeus played any part in your sister's taking."

The queen's amber eyes were piercing, saying more than her quiet words. Kait held her tongue, accepting the final decision with an affirmative bob of her head.

"Now, you are free to go. Please use this newfound freedom to better the realm and assist your elder and fellow nymphs any way you can." The queen spun gracefully on her toes and strode back toward the perimeter of the aurai quadrant. Three guards appeared in the corner of Kait's eye, startling her. They moved as one and surrounded the queen in a tight bubble.

Once the group was out of earshot, Tahlia faced Kait.

"I'm sorry for all this. Throughout your sentence, I petitioned numerous times for your release. I told her you were overwrought with grief over the loss of your sister. As you know, my request was denied. You were to be an example, to keep the rumors of another hunt from sparking."

"Thank you, Tahlia. I'm sorry if my behavior caused you any embarrassment." Kait exhaled, rolling her shoulders back. "But I know what I saw. Zeus is behind this, and he isn't finished."

Tahlia lowered her voice, even though the meadow surrounding them was empty. "I believe you." She smiled. "I know you, Kait. You are steadfast and true. Over these last few decades, I've watched you blossom into an incredible aurai, proving the strength of your magic again and again, but your heart is even more powerful. I fear the queen is making a grave mistake in not trusting you, but she won't be told otherwise."

Kait frowned. "What are you saying?"

Tahlia licked her lips. "As your elder, I'm telling you that you must respect the queen's decision not to pursue evidence against Zeus, but as your friend, I urge you to do whatever you must to gain closure. In the queen's chambers, I saw a fire in you that I thought had been doused by Willow's death. I don't want you to lose yourself again. I want you to live, Kait. You're one of the triad, prophesized to bring greatness to the realms. What if this is your opportunity?"

Tahlia reached out, interlacing her fingers with Kait's. Her words hung in the space between them.

"Is this a trick?" Kait asked, scanning the nearby trees for more of the queen's guards.

"No, my dear. Though I will advise, if you're going after him, do it sooner rather than later. As you said, Jezlem will not be the last of these attacks. If you can find any evidence against him before he strikes again, bring it to me. This time, the queen will heed your warning."

Kait closed the distance separating them and wrapped her elder in a tight hug. "I don't know what to say. Thank you."

Tahlia returned her embrace, squeezing her shoulders. She pulled back a moment later and held Kait's gaze. "Be smart and be safe. If there is another nymph you trust to assist you, take her. If not, keep your mission to yourself." Tahlia leaned in, offering her one last hug. "Good luck."

The landscape was nearly unrecognizable. Kait wandered through the valley where Zeus attacked them, where she'd been left with no choice but to leave her sister behind. The remote French town at the base of the Pyrenees mountains was the only place she could think of that might hold a clue as to where Zeus went. The trees that had been so full and green a few months ago were now barren and skeletal as they danced in the slight breeze. Shivers that had nothing to do with the cold decorated her bare arms. She hadn't forgotten the threat of the piriol, but perhaps the naked trees, brittle twigs, and lack of cover would inhibit its prowling, or at least allow her to notice in time.

Kait dragged her boots through the withered grass. Scraps of navy fabric caught her eye, trampled into the earth by curious paws and heavy rains. Kait pushed the broken image of Jezlem away before it could form. She needed to concentrate, and tears would disrupt her search. Meandering closer to the giant mountains, she adjusted her black vest, comforted by the small knife tucked in the waistband of her jeans. She didn't anticipate running into any humans this far from town, but it would be easier to parry any questions if she played the part of a casual hiker.

Pausing her stride, Kait raised her arms, twisting her fingers to cast a simple charm. She didn't have the aptitude for sensing like the anthousais, but the wind could still uncover secrets. She kept a wary eye on the tree line for the piriol as the air kicked up dead leaves and natural debris, searching for anything that might help her prove the immortal had been there.

Her head swiveled as she completed her sweep. A light blue glow flickered a few hundred feet away. Curious, but cautious too, Kait ceased the spell and instead redirected the wind to slither beneath her soles, carrying her soundlessly forward a few inches off the ground. She ducked behind a gnarled tree trunk. Trepidation evolved into confusion when she saw a beautiful dark-skinned nymph sobbing into her hands.

Her lace gown puddled on the damp ground, the fabric as delicate as spider's silk. Musical notes rose higher as her tears deepened and her shoulders shook. Kait left the cover of the tree, overcome with the need to comfort the poor nymph. As she wove closer, a wave of familiarity overwhelmed her. She knew the slope of her body, knew what color her eyes would be.

Her strides lengthened as she abandoned all caution. She raced forward, sliding on the decayed foliage. The crying nymph looked up, startled as Kait landed in front of her.

"Willow?" Kait gasped. Dropping to her knees, she gazed at her friend's lovely face. "Am I dreaming or dead?

Willow shook her head, wiping tears off her cheeks. "Neither."

"Then how are you here? Goddess, I've missed you so much." Kait reached out to cradle Willow's hands in hers, but her fingertips hovered, almost afraid to touch her, as if she might shatter the illusion.

"Please, I'm not who you think I am. You shouldn't be here." Gathering her gown, Willow skirted Kait, brushing her arm as she slipped past.

Kait frowned. Willow was not a mirage, but rather tangible and real. "I don't understand. You're dead."

"No." There was a heavy sadness in her voice. "It's a wonderful trick though, isn't it? To see the one you love most? Of course, I view it as more of a curse. While I command everyone's attention, no one cares to see the real me underneath. The lie is more appealing."

"What are you saying?" Kait struggled to follow Willow's dizzying puzzle.

"I'm sorry. I'm not your friend, but an omodian."

"An omodian? But those nymphs haven't existed since before the Titan War."

A grimace transformed Willow's features as she opened her arms wide. "Yet here I am."

The moment the truth fell from Willow's lips, her appearance blurred, as if different parts of her were moving too fast to comprehend clearly. Umber skin diluted to smooth ivory as her tight curls relaxed, lengthening past her elbows. The warm brown color of her hair darkened to raven black as her facial features shifted. The last to change was her eyes. The soulful amber irises bleached to an almost translucent gray.

Willow was gone. In her place stood a stranger. A pale blue halo radiated from her body, but the alabaster sheen of an immortal made Kait's breath catch.

"Who are you?" Apprehension and curiosity warred within Kait. She had never met an immortal nymph besides the queen.

"My name is Layla. Beyond that, I cannot explain. You need to leave this place. It's not safe."

"It's all right. I know about the piriol."

Layla's icy eyes dilated. "How? If you know the creature that stalks these woods, you shouldn't have come." Layla grabbed Kait's shoulders and started pushing her back into the valley.

"Wait, is the piriol still here? I'm looking for Zeus," Kait said. She tried to slow their pace, but Layla was strong.

Layla let out a low hiss, gazing at Kait with obvious distrust. "If you're seeking Zeus, then you are a fool. Leave this place, and if you know what's good for you, you won't come back."

"No, wait, please. I need—"

Above, the scant clouds gathered, darkening with rage. A rumble of thunder announced an approaching storm. Layla's grip tightened, her triangular nails digging into Kait's flesh.

"Oh, my goddess. He's coming. You need to hide. Hide and don't make a sound," the omodian warned. Layla's head snapped back and forth, and she thrust Kait forward into a dark crevice between two stones. "The moment he's gone, get out of here, okay?"

Unfiltered fear shone in Layla's eyes. Without a sound, Kait nodded, wedging her body as far into the makeshift hiding space as possible. Satisfied, Layla spun away, sprinting back to the base of the mountain. Kait could still see Layla's bright white dress as she raced through the trees. Her heart pounded. What was the nymph afraid of?

A flash of blinding light sizzled across her vision. Kait flinched. A light swell of white-gray smoke drifted up from the scorched earth. A tall figure stood in the center of the lightning strike. Short blond hair, navy cloak over exposed muscles, and a furious expression.

Zeus.

Revulsion and anger seized Kait as her hands fought to join the wind. The desire to strike the god nearly tore her in half, but she remembered Layla's words, her true terror. She had regarded Kait like a lamb set for slaughter. Now she understood why.

"What are you doing out here?" Zeus asked.

The nymph Kait met a few minutes earlier transformed. No longer was she weak and vulnerable. Rolling her shoulders back, she smiled, exuding confidence as she greeted Zeus head-on.

"Getting some fresh air." Layla's voice was sharp as a whip. "That mountain is suffocating. Of course, it could be the company I'm forced to keep."

"Believe me, I can't wait to be rid of this place. Being contained like this is driving me insane." Zeus pressed the heels of his palms into both eyes, grunting like a starving dog.

"Perhaps you should return to Olympus. Come up with another disguise and portal in. The nymphs are more concerned with who's coming into the human realm than leaving anyway."

"Don't you think I haven't thought of that?" Zeus sneered, circling her. "I should have killed that aurai when I had the chance. Now the whole realm is watching, waiting for me to expose myself. They're waiting for me to make a mistake so they can gather the information they need to condemn me. I'll be punished, locked away on Olympus for a thousand years for breaching the treaty. I have to stay. If I return, I lose my chance at euphoria. I won't find the release I need with Hera or any other goddess. I need a nymph."

Layla threw up her hands as she angled her body away from his aggressive stance. "It was only a suggestion."

"Spare me your condescension. Why don't you do something useful?" Zeus stepped closer. "Find me a nymph. Bring one to me."

Layla emitted a sarcastic snort in reply. "Sure thing. Do me a favor first. Remove the endless curse you and the rest of the Council used to bound me to this horrendous mountain and the abomination of a man inside. Set me free and see if I ever come back to serve your revolting appetite."

Zeus's hand shot out and smacked Layla across the face. Kait flinched, both from the sound and the unexpected outburst. Layla dropped to the forest floor, cradling her left cheek. Even from a distance, Kait could see the livid red marks of the god's slender fingers marring the nymph's flesh.

"I'm so sick of you." He glowered at her. "And I am not meant to be locked away like a prisoner. I am Zeus. I am a mighty god."

Rubbing her cheek once more, Layla stood, raising her chin in defiance. "A mighty god who might show a bit more appreciation for the people hosting him. We feed you, offer you our ale and spirits, and drop everything for your smallest whim. Yet all you do is whine and complain like a spoiled child."

"Because you don't give me what I *need*. I need euphoria." Zeus ripped off his robe. He stood bare-chested, muscles hard as chiseled stone. "I can't sleep; food doesn't satisfy; not even liquor can distract my longing. My desire was manageable before. No one paid attention when I took two nymphs a year, but this time, when I tasted it again…" He shook his head. "And so I took and took and took again. Now it's gone, and my need is worming into my brain, corrupting my sanity. I *need* a nymph. I *need* euphoria."

Zeus's blue eyes blazed darkly, dangerously. Kait's heart quickened as the wind snuck inside her haven, howling with unease. She wanted to yell, to warn Layla, but fear froze the cry in her throat. Layla's strong stance hunched—an opponent shrinking to the role of prey as she, too, registered the disturbing change in the god.

Shaking her long curtain of hair, Layla backed up several steps, raising her hands in front of her. Kait knew it was an empty gesture. Omodians didn't have an element to wield for protection, and her slim build was no match for Zeus's power.

"We've been over this, remember? You won't find any release with me. They made me immortal, like you, like Hera. It doesn't work."

Layla's voice cracked. Her words bounced off Zeus like pebbles, clattering uselessly to the ground. He advanced. He swung his arms casually by his sides, but his burning gaze made his intentions plain.

"I don't care. I'm going to try anyway." He backed her against the tall rocks.

"Please. Please, just wait. Think how Atlas will react when he finds out," Layla pleaded as the backs of her legs bumped against the stone.

"I don't give a damn what Atlas thinks. You may not satisfy my craving, but it will feel good to break something."

Zeus's arm arched again, and he cracked Layla in the same spot as before. The blow slammed her into the rock, sending her eyes rolling into the back of her head. He spun her around, squeezing her arm with a granite hold. A sharp whimper of pain fell from Layla's lips.

"Good, I want to make sure you're still conscious for this. It feels so much better when my prey tries to resist. So go on—fight back, scream. Give me what I need."

He wrenched his waistband down, then shredded Layla's lace dress, exposing her backside beneath. He entered her without warning, thrusting inside with a grand sigh. A choked sob rattled Kait's chest. She refused to sit by and let him destroy another life. Scrambling out of her hiding place, she flexed her fingers, commanding the wind.

Taking a step closer to the mountain, a loud crack echoed as she stepped on a brittle twig. Zeus twisted his neck, his features savage and wild. Kait sucked in a quick breath as their eyes met. She saw the way he looked her up and down, saw the flicker of recognition, saw the way his eyes grew black with desire, saw that she was next.

With a rough push, Zeus shoved Layla into the dirt. In the same motion, he pivoted on his heels, stalking toward Kait naked.

"Kait, right? What excellent timing you have, though you're a bit over-dressed. Come to me."

The wind swirled at Kait's feet. She wanted to help the omodian but doing so would endanger her own survival.

"Come to me!" Zeus bellowed. Lightning flashed from his palms, and he broke into a run.

Kait didn't hesitate. The wind engulfed her, swallowing her flesh and hurtling her soul back to the safety of the portal.

⚡ 13 ⚡

"Kait, p-please," Bia said. "They need me. Fires have r-ravaged the grasslands all throughout Earth's Southern Hemisphere. I must aid them to bring life b-back into the earth."

"No," Kaitaini answered curtly.

"Please." Bia's hands smacked her thighs as she fought to remain calm. Moving from the doorway, she kneeled in front of Kait, waiting.

Kait didn't react and kept her eyes on her book.

Gnawing on her bottom lip, Bia shook her scarlet hair back and forth. "You can't keep me l-locked away forever, Kait. This—this is my life. I-I decide what I do with it. The anthousais need me. Earth is dying. I can't s-sit here any longer."

Kait ignored her sister's plea, having lost count of how times they had discussed the situation.

The sound of Bia's flapping hands paused as she reached up and snapped the book shut, then tossed it to the moss carpet of the library. The small but cozy quarters were carved into the trunk of a towering oak tree.

"It's been three w-weeks since you saw Zeus, yet still no other nymphs have b-been taken."

Kait glanced away from Bia's pleading eyes, drumming the tips of her fingers along the wooden arms of the chair. "Just because they haven't doesn't mean he isn't out there. I told you I saw him violate another nymph and stop halfway through to charge me. Something happened to him. He isn't stable."

"So tell the queen and let her d-deal with it."

"You know I can't. I don't have any proof. They want tangible evidence, not testimony."

The moment Kait returned from the Pyrenees, she relayed the horrifying event to Bia. When Tahlia first mentioned confiding in a trusted source, she didn't consider burdening her sister. But after what she witnessed, the tale spilled out. She relayed the ragged state of the god to Tahlia as well, but they needed something more concrete than Zeus's empty wishes for euphoria before they alerted the queen again.

"Trust me, Bia, he's out there, plotting, waiting for us to let our guard down. I can't stop every nymph from putting themselves in danger, but at least I can keep you safe."

Bia slapped her thigh with one hand; the other formed a fist, and she pressed into her temple. "So what am I s-supposed to do for the rest of my life? Live in fear? Never h-help outside Olean again? What about Jez? We haven't seen her in months."

Kait remained quiet and pursed her lips. They were two hundred years old, but Bia behaved like a forlorn teenager. "You will live, Bia. Olean is our sanctuary. There is plenty to do here to keep you occupied. As for Jezlem—when it's safe, we will find her. I promise you won't remain here forever."

"And why is that? In ten years, Zeus will finally f-forget about euphoria and move on?"

"No. I'm going to kill him."

Bia rocked back and forth, groaning. Kait slid to the floor and drew her into her arms, applying the pressure her sister craved. Slowly, she stood, bringing Bia with her to sit on the wooden love seat behind them.

"H-How? He's an immortal. He can't die."

"I'm well aware of what he is, but even immortals can be destroyed. The body is just a vessel. If I can shatter it far enough beyond repair, Zeus's soul will be forced to flee to the Underworld."

Bia shook her head. "But Hades is his brother. He'll craft him a new body, and Zeus will come back with a v-vengeance."

Kait pursed her lips. "If he hasn't learned to stay away from nymphs by that point, I'll kill him again and again until the message sinks in."

"And how d-do you plan on doing that? Especially when you're babysitting me night and day."

Kait leaned over and scooped up the leather-bound book, tapping its cover. "Research. I'm hoping these old books speak of a spell or power that can be used to defeat the immortals—or better yet, take away their immortality."

Frowning, Bia picked up a different book from the accumulated pile on the stump coffee table and fanned through the yellowed pages. "But if there really is such a s-spell, wouldn't the immortals have it guarded in the vaults of Olympus? I doubt the answer is scribbled in one of these m-margins." She huffed, dropping the book back into place.

Kait's violet eyes scanned several more lines of slanted, cramped writing. "Maybe that's exactly where they hid it," she replied with a mischievous grin. "In an ancient little book covered in dust that everyone forgot about."

Bia wrinkled her nose and crossed her arms, not convinced.

"Kaitaini! Kaitaini!" a frantic voice cried.

Before she could blink, Kait was on her feet, the book forgotten. "By the goddess, Tressa, what's wrong?"

Before Tressa's legs could even fully materialize out of the wind, she reported, "I was just sent word by a scout patrolling the far eastern portal to the human realm. In the Thar Desert in northwestern India, an aurai was spotted struggling through the sands."

"What is s-she doing there?" Bia asked.

"We don't know. Tahlia would never sanction a mission into a climate that harsh. We assume she's dehydrated and delirious."

"Why did you come to me with this information? Why didn't you enter the human realm and save her?" Kait asked. Fury caused her words to sizzle.

Tressa flinched at Kait's harsh tone. "We tried, but we can't reach her. She seems to have enclosed herself in a self-made tornado. None of the aurais on patrol were strong enough to breach it," she explained, bowing her head.

"Did you try as one?"

Tressa brushed her cropped auburn hair off her sweaty forehead. "Yes. The winds are too powerful. I thought you might be able to assist us."

"Say no more." Kait raced out the door and into the sunshine.

Bia fell into step beside her. "I'm c-coming with you."

"No." Kait shook her head. "You're staying here where it's safe."

"But the aurai may be h-hurt. You need a healer."

"What they need is an experienced aurai to get her out. We'll fix her once we get her back to Olean. You'll just get in the way. Stay here, Bia. I mean it." Kait fixed her with a hard stare.

Bia's eyes fell, and she slowed her pace, hands flapping against her hipbones. Her hesitation allowed Kait to leave her far behind.

Guilt tugged at Kait's chest, but she couldn't bear to lose Bia too. Pushing off the warm grass, she jumped into the air with Tressa at her side, letting the wind usher her away to the main square and the portals beyond.

⚡

Kait stood on the platform, staring at the hot sands of the Thar Desert on the other side of the portal. A saddened whisper wove through her mind as she remembered standing beside Jezlem before their world went to hell. It had been nearly four months since she lost her sister, and because of Zeus's threat, she hadn't been able to seek her out in the human world. Her stomach knotted. She wasn't even sure if she was okay. She cleared her throat, burying her growing guilt back into the familiar corner of her mind. She couldn't afford to be haunted by the past today.

Gathered behind her were Tressa and three other aurais, along with two scouts dressed in sleek black armor that matched their black cropped hair. Everyone wore serious expressions. If they didn't act fast, the stranded nymph would die.

Kait peered farther into the portal, but it was impossible to make out anything concrete.

"And all three of you tried to subdue her winds?" she asked, still unable to believe one aurai could conjure such strong winds by herself.

"Yes," a tight-lipped nymph named Prilla said. Her caramel hair was cut short and stuck out at strange angles around her head. "We could barely break through. There's something else involved here."

Kait inhaled, then blew the air out through her mouth. "All right. I'll go in first to the north. Then, Prilla, you and Krenya follow. Take the east and west posts." She turned to the last aurai, a somber looking youth with piercing green eyes. "Olana, you cross over last and stand guard in the southern corner. Tressa, you wait here. I want to make sure the portal is available so we can get her back to Olean as quickly as possible." She turned back to the others accompanying her. "Wait for my signal, then we aim everything we've got directly at the center, okay?"

"Do you want us to incapacitate the nymph?" Olana asked.

"Yes." Kait nodded. "It's for her own good. If we stun her unconscious, we can more easily rescue her from herself."

The assembled aurais nodded and stepped back, flexing their fingers, readying their magic. Wasting no more time, Kait leapt through the portal, armed with nothing but the wind dancing between her fingertips.

Harsh sand stung her face, burrowing into the corners of her eyes, the curves of her ears. In seconds, she was blind and deaf, hardly able to move her feet as the scorching dunes swallowed her knees. Summoning all her strength, she pointed her palms to the shifting ground and unleashed a torrent of concentrated wind. One shot and she rocketed upward, instantly transforming to blend into the air, and headed toward the northern post.

Down below, she located the exhausted aurai. She kneeled, her head thrown back, neck exposed to the blazing sun. Angry red blisters cut across her skin. How long had she been wandering?

Her eyes were closed, her features serene—a complete juxtaposition to the raging winds spiraling around her. The air howled, pulling, biting, clawing. It felt urgent, like it was trying to tell her something. Prilla was right. This wasn't a case of a lost nymph. She had never felt the wind so wild, as if it were being forced, then contained, unable to break free of this isolated space. Kait frowned. It felt as if someone else was pulling the strings rather than the poor nymph below.

Curious, she soared overhead and tried to tunnel her way straight to the center of the whipping tornado, but her attempt was deflected, as if the nymph were encased in a large box. Stretching herself throughout the wind, Kait tested the barrier for any weak spots or holes, but the magic was airtight. Now she understood why the others' attempts failed.

At the thought of her fellow aurais, Kait glanced around, but she could neither see nor feel the other nymphs' presence. Hadn't they followed her through the portal? She let go of her control, and her soul whirled through the air. The angry winds tossed her back and forth with such fury, she hardly knew which way was up. However, she was sure of one fact: the other aurais were not in the realm. They had left her to fend for herself.

Gritting her teeth, Kait vaulted out of the possessed wind and righted herself. Concern gripped her. Why hadn't the other aurais followed?

The stranded nymph gave a sudden lurch and came to her feet. She seemed to glide atop the burning sands. Kait was amazed to find that the foul winds didn't move with her but stayed in place, spinning closer to the portal's edge. Briefly, the fear of not being able to escape tugged at Kait's mind, but she pushed the worry away. First, she had to save the aurai.

Kait floated above, watching the nymph's progress. After a minute, it was clear what her destination was: a haphazard outcropping of rocks that would serve as a shelter. As the nymph shimmied inside a narrow crevice on the ground, Kait directed the wind downward. She poured into a small gap between two rocks wedged together.

Materializing out of the air, Kait alighted onto a small circle of sand cooled by the long shadows of the jagged rocks. Her body cried out for water as the humidity plagued her physical form. Her throat prickled painfully the moment the air revealed the last of her skin. With fevered eyes, she searched for any sign of the aurai. She had been exposed for too long and was surely on the verge of death.

A huddled figure wrapped in a frayed gray dress lay sprawled on the opposite side of the small alcove. Kait raced over and dropped to her knees, ignoring the way the tiny grains of sand bit her flesh. Not wanting to frighten the nymph, she gently placed her hand on her shoulder, while the other cradled the base of her head.

"Hey, it's all right. I'm here to help you." Kait coughed as the heat licked the inside of her throat.

The nymph didn't respond, and Kait worried she had lost consciousness.

"Hey, stay with me."

She turned the frail nymph onto her back, and a horrified scream rent Kait's throat. Rather than the frail nymph she'd followed into the alcove, a mummified corpse rested in her hands. Her sun-blistered flesh had shrunken away until nothing but shriveled skin remained, pulled taunt across her skull underneath. Her cheeks were sunken, matching the hollow pits where her eyes used to be. Her brown hair was stringy, and large clumps tangled around Kait's fingers, pulling away from the scalp like clinging spider webs.

Kait pushed the decayed skeleton off her lap, scuttling backward in terror. "What black magic is this?" Her back slammed against rough stone, and she slid to the sand.

"Do you like it?" an amused voice asked. "She turned out quite appalling, didn't she?"

Kait whipped her head to the where the voice originated. Her jaw sagged as Zeus stepped into a shaft of sunlight.

"I have to admit, I had my doubts if my little scheme would work, but here you are."

Panic clenched Kait's heart, stealing the breath from her lungs. "The other aurais?" Kait's gaze roamed around the alcove, afraid he had already taken them hostage.

"They won't be joining us," Zeus said. "The moment you crossed into the human realm, I sealed the portal. No one else can enter, and no one can escape." He smiled wolfishly, delighting in his clever trick.

"Sealed the portal? How?"

"That's none of your concern. All you need to know is you won't be leaving this barren wasteland." Zeus took a step closer. He shook his head and rolled his shoulders, shifting about like a stallion eager to race. "I've hit rock bottom because of you. Being unable to come and go as I please has put quite a damper on my hunting practices. Therefore, I re-strategized. You don't have nearly the same respect for your own life as you do for others. That's your weakness. That's how I knew you'd end up exactly where I wanted you."

Kait swallowed, curling her fingers into claws. She'd played right into his hands. The thought of a trap never crossed her mind. "Who was she?" Kait asked, jutting her chin toward the skeletal nymph.

"A slave of Hera's. She served her purpose well, but now my beloved seeks another."

"Slaves were outlawed thousands of years ago."

Zeus shrugged. "As was hunting nymphs. You'll find where there's a big enough will, there's a way."

Kait didn't miss the way his eyes slithered up her body. She could feel the weight of his gaze as if he were running his fingers along her skin. "Let me guess: I'm to be a present when you're through with me."

A brilliant smile lit up Zeus's face, showing all his perfect teeth. "The human realm is a dangerous place for a lonely woman. By pledging yourself to Hera, you will be taken care of. Perhaps she will even let you indulge in a few arduous romps with me every now and again."

He reached out to run the back of his fingers along Kait's jaw, but she jerked away. "As I said before, I will never give myself to you, and I would sooner spit on Hera than serve the likes of her." Fire burned in Kait's eyes.

"I was hoping you'd say that. You see, it's satisfying to charm my lovers. I enjoy breaking down their walls, watching as they begin to trust me. The lovemaking is sweet and beautiful, but I prefer a nymph with a little more fire. One that I can straddle and mount and feel her fighting beneath me. Those are moments I dream of—when I am in complete control."

Zeus's eyes smoldered. He shrugged out of his robe, letting it puddle at his feet. His bare chest glistened in the sunlight, further enhanced by the blazing halo of white light encircling him. He wore baggy navy slacks. Kait eyed the elastic waistband. If she didn't move, he would be on top of her in seconds.

Kait inhaled and flexed her fingers, keeping her movements slow. She had only one chance for escape. She pulled her hands out of the sand, her fists full of the tiny grains. Zeus leaned down, inches from her legs.

"Do you want it any way special, nymph?" he growled, his pupils dilating with passion as he inhaled her.

"How about blindfolded?" With an angry cry, she whipped the fistfuls of sand into Zeus's face, then rolled away from his advance.

The god yelled with rage as the harsh grains burrowed into his eyelids, obscuring his vision. "No! Get back here, nymph!"

Sucking in a quick breath, Kait fell into the stirring wind, her flesh evaporating into the air. Pushing the breeze as fast as her body could move, she rode the rising current to the top of the alcove and burst through a narrow opening into the humid sky. Seconds later, the rock formation was miles below, and she exhaled the pent-up breath she'd been holding. There was no time to think, no time to plan. Kait knew Zeus was telling the truth about sealing the portal and didn't want to throw away precious minutes tossing herself against a brick wall. She had to get out of the desert, find the nearest untampered portal, and disappear.

The dry air constricted around Kait, threatening to separate her from the element. Rising higher in the clear blue sky, she slid into a cool jet stream and propelled the wind recklessly forward. Closing her eyes, she took a steadying breath, searching for the magnetic pull of another portal. At first, she couldn't feel anything amongst the swirling winds, but after a few moments, a dull ache bloomed in her chest. She wasn't sure where the portal emptied, but it was her only chance of escape. She refused to give in to Zeus.

As she soared ahead, part of her was relieved the waiting game was over, while the other half worried at how long she would last exposed and vulnerable outside of Olean. Zeus was the master of Olympus, with endless resources, including a piriol. He'd managed to sneak past the queen's scouts to reach the desert. He was either trying a new tactic or his desperation had reached its climax and he no longer cared. If he didn't find her, Kaf would.

Kait fixed her gaze on the low strip of dark mountains hovering on the horizon of the western border and gritted her teeth.

Like it or not, a new hunt had begun.

⚡ 14 ⚡

Sweat rolled down the back of Blake's neck, and he swatted it like an annoying fly. He gritted his teeth and turned up the volume in his earbuds, letting the hard rock drown out his thoughts. If he could keep up his workout routine, maybe he'd have a chance of getting a date to senior prom. Blake's calves burned as he pushed harder up the incline. The circuit through the woods was short but full of endless hills.

Joel, his best friend, was supposed to be out there with him, but the pack a day he smoked interfered with breathing. Blake exhaled as he rounded a large boulder, careful not to slip on the blanket of dull brown leaves as the latest hill sloped downward. Most of the trees were still yellow or red, but it was nearing the middle of October. They'd all be dead soon.

Blake glanced down at his heart monitor. "Halfway."

He jogged a few yards off the trail, taking a quick breather at the edge of a large pond, when something blinked in the corner of his eye. He looked around, sure it had been the fading sun's reflection on the water, but something was off. The golden glow hadn't come from his left, where the pond stretched, but from the right.

Placing his hands on the top of his head, Blake rotated away from the water back to the path, this time seeing nothing but tall grass and a mossy log along the muddy shoreline.

He sighed. "Whatever."

He took several steps before the golden shimmer caught his attention again. It was at the base of the log, shining brighter now that the wind bent the grass. Blake paused his music. He swatted the overgrowth with his palms, his curiosity getting the better of him.

"Probably an old fishing pole left here by some old man who—ah!" Blake fell backward, landing hard on his tailbone.

It was a body.

"Oh my God."

It lay half submerged and facedown in pond scum. Long dark hair suggested it was female. One arm stretched above her head, as though she'd been reaching for something as she died. Blake sucked in a sharp breath. What if she was still alive?

Leaping off the gravel path, Blake charged through the shallow water, kicking waterlogged sticks and a floating mass of collected leaves and dried grass out of his way. Green algae sloshed over the tops of his sneakers, soaking his socks, but he kept going. He reached her a moment later. His hands hovered above her shoulders. But what if she *was* dead? Would her flesh fall apart in his fingers?

He drew a shallow breath. She didn't smell as if her body had started to decay, but he didn't hear any labored breathing either. If she needed help, she needed it now, not next morning when the few cops in town managed to find her.

Gritting his teeth, Blake reached out and tapped the exposed flesh on her upper back. The skin was firm. If she was dead, she hadn't been for long. A nervous prickling started at the back of his neck as he glanced around the empty woods for a possible attacker.

"Hello? Miss, are you all right? Can I help you?"

He waited several seconds, his heart beating so loud he wouldn't be able to hear the girl anyway. "Hello?"

A shrill gasp erupted from the body as the girl arched her head back.

Blake cried out in surprise, falling backward into the muddy water.

"Is he here? Where did he go?" the girl asked, frantically searching the late afternoon sky.

Blake untangled his feet and stood. "Who? Are you okay?"

The girl didn't respond. Instead, she pulled the rest of her body from the cold pond. The same golden light from before shimmered around her. Blake realized it was the girl's skin. He shook his head; fear was making his eyes play tricks on him. His senses came back, and he closed the distance between them, ready to offer the girl his hand.

"Are you hurt?"

He scanned her wet body for any missing limbs or bleeding, but he didn't see anything out of the ordinary. In fact, apart from being covered in mud, she had a great body. Blake averted his gaze as her short dress bunched up around her hips.

"Listen, I'm here to help you," Blake said. "Do you know your name?"

The girl eyed him warily. "Who are you?"

"My name is Blake." He put up his hands in a gesture of surrender. "I was running, and I saw you. What are you doing out here?"

"Where am I?" She stood, doing her best to brush the clinging pond scum from her skin. Fuzzy green algae collected underneath her fingertips, and she grimaced. "Where am I?" she asked again.

Blake continued to stare, suddenly unable to form a coherent thought.

"Hello?"

"Sorry. Do you know you're glowing?" Blake pointed.

She brushed her wet hair off her neck. "Yes. Can you please tell me where I am?"

"Bennington," Blake managed. At her lost expression, he added, "Vermont."

"Vermont," she repeated, scanning the scant clouds.

Blake frowned. Her tone was strange, as if she had never heard of the state before.

"Thanks." The girl piled her damp hair on top of her head and started toward the narrow path in the depressed leaves.

"Wait!" Blake jogged to catch up with her. "Do you need help? I mean, you look like you're in rough shape. Let me take you to the hospital. Did someone do this to you? Should I call the police? Why are you shining?"

The girl ignored him, striding away. Blake's gaze ran from her shoulders to the back of her calves. He matched his stride to hers. "Sorry, I'm not trying to be rude. I just… What's wrong with you?"

"What do you mean?"

"I mean, one second you're lying unconscious in the mud and the next, you're taking off with no injuries."

"Why are you following me?"

Blake's steps faltered. "I'm not. I don't live out here. I told you I was on a run when I found you. What were you doing out there?" He noticed four angry white scars carved into the soft flesh of her neck. "Did someone try to hurt you?"

The girl ignored him again. Her eyes shifted back and forth, and her pace slowed like a deer detecting a hunter. Blake furrowed his brow. He knew that look, had seen it cross his mother's face when his dad came home at night.

"What's your name?" Blake asked, his voice softer now.

"It doesn't matter." Resuming her pace, she veered off the path into the thinning foliage.

"Of course it does. Wait, where are you going? Town is this way." Blake pointed to the path in front of them.

"I'm not going to town. I need to find—something." She bit her lip.

Blake's frown deepened. He could sense her hesitation and see how guarded she was by the way she carried herself—hunched and tight, trying to make herself as small as possible. "Well, if it's a tree, then you're in luck. Forest stretches for miles in every direction save for this one."

The girl narrowed her gaze. "I don't need a tree. I need to find a place to hide. He's close. I'm not sure how long I have before he finds me again."

"He? Who, your boyfriend? Did he leave you out here?" Blake cursed as he caught a branch of thorns across the cheek.

"No."

"Who, then? Are you running from the cops?"

A heavy sigh fell from the girl's lips as her fingertips danced with nervous energy.

"Maybe we should take you to the police station. You know, make sure you're not hurt or anything."

With a shake of her head, the girl's damp bun slid off, and the long tendrils of hair slapped her exposed back like tentacles. She took off sprinting, dodging the trees and loose sticks easily.

"Wait! I might be able to help!" Blake fought to catch up, stumbling when the toe of his sneaker snagged on a clod of dirt and grass. Up ahead, the girl slowed. Balling her hands into fists, she pressed them to her temples and waited for him to catch up.

Blake reached her at last and braced his knees, huffing. He kept several feet between them, unsure what to expect from the stranger. "Why'd you do that?"

"I like to be in motion. Running helps me think. Do you know a place I can stay?" She pinned him with a hard stare.

"Hang on." Blake heaved forward, trying to catch his breath.

"Do you have a place I can stay?" she repeated, clearly annoyed. She wrinkled her nose as Blake spat a wad of saliva onto the fallen leaves. "I thought you were a runner."

Blake waved a hand in front of his face. He used to be able to go eight rounds without getting winded, but that was a couple years ago, before he quit boxing because his mom couldn't afford it anymore. His most recent goal was simply to find his abs again. "Let's just say I'm on my way to being back in shape."

"Oh."

Blake inhaled deeply and pointed his index finger at her. "All right. I have a place you can crash, but first I need you to answer my questions."

She nodded. "Kaitaini."

"What?"

"My name is Kaitaini."

"Katyana. That's pretty."

"No. Ka-ta-nee, but everyone calls me Kait."

"Kait." Blake nodded. "That's definitely easier. Okay, first question: why is your skin glowing?"

Kait frowned, crossing her arms over her chest. "It's complicated. Trust me when I say it doesn't matter."

Blake rested his hands on his hips. "Fine, but no more passes. Why were you out here? What kind of trouble are you in?"

"It's not like that," she said. "I'm… I'm running from a…guy."

Blake narrowed his eyes. He knew she wasn't telling him the whole story. People's voices rose when they lied—a tell he learned from his mom whenever he inquired about the newest bruise dotting her skin. He studied the beautiful girl, read the fear hidden behind her eyes. She didn't trust him, but she didn't have to. All she needed to do was allow him to help her.

"First, we should go to the police station. You can file a report or get a restraining order or something."

Kait shook her head. "I can't. The guy that's after me, he's…he's a really bad person with endless connections. All I need is a place to wash up and take a quick rest, and then I'll be out of your life forever. I promise."

The girl stared at him, waiting. He wanted to ask her one hundred more questions, but he didn't want to overwhelm her. Whatever truth she was omitting, he couldn't ignore the real fear shining in her strange violet eyes.

"All right," Blake agreed. "Come on. We'll get you cleaned up. My house is this way."

⚡ 15 ⚡

Hot water cascaded down Kait's shoulder blades, the scalding liquid warming every inch of her skin. Thick clouds of vapor swirled in front of her, and she amused herself by manipulating the molecules to swirl in lazy patterns.

Humans were blissfully unaware of the ethereal realm, yet there she was, nude, playing in one's shower. What was she doing?

She twisted the metal handle counterclockwise, then wrung out her heavy hair and wrapped a fraying green towel around her chest. Stepping onto the bath mat, she glanced around the small bathroom. Old yellow tile wrapped around the bottom half of the wall, while pink roses dotted the wallpaper. Placing her hands on the chipped corner of the vanity, she stared at her reflection in the steamy mirror. Large pupils, fringed by wet lashes gazed back at her. Kait leaned forward and swiped at the beaded water frosting the glass, smearing her image.

"Just get out of here," Kait said aloud, wrapping the towel tighter. Her eyes swept the floor where she'd tossed her dress, and her nose wrinkled in disgust. Lying in a heap was her gown, or rather what was left of it. The once lovely golden fabric was now a dingy gray, covered in mud and algae. The thought of putting it back on made her stomach turn.

Wringing droplets from her hair, Kait emerged from the hazy bathroom. A tiny shiver tickled her spine as her body registered the drop in temperature in the picture-lined hallway.

"Brad?" she called.

"Yeah? I'm in here," answered a voice from down the hall.

Kait padded atop the plush carpet and pushed open the last door, then leaned against the entryway to the cluttered room. She didn't see the boy at first. Her gaze was bombarded by piles of dirty clothes strewn about the floor, an unmade bed, and colorful posters haphazardly arranged on the walls. A pair of faded red gloves made her pause. They looked well-worn, and judging by several golden statues below, they had been worn well.

"Do you have any clothes I can borrow?" she asked, her eyes finally landing on the back of his head.

Blake spun away from the flashing screen before him. "Oh my God." His eyes bulged as Dorito crumbs tumbled out of his mouth and landed in his lap.

Kaitaini glanced over her shoulder. "What's wrong?"

"Um, nothing. Nothing. Let's just get you some clothes." Blake blushed, dropping his gaze as he tossed a white controller onto an empty chip bag. "And it's Blake."

"What is?"

"My name."

"Oh, sorry." Kait cinched the towel tighter and cocked her head. Soft golden water droplets ran down her neck as they absorbed her halo. She wished she could cast a glamour, anything to seem more "normal," but using magic might alert Zeus to her whereabouts. She couldn't take any chances.

"No problem. You've…had a big day." Blake crossed the messy room and threw open the door, sifting through several shirts hanging askew on their hangers. He selected a white one with slanted writing on it. "Here's a shirt." He tossed it in her direction. "As for pants, I don't think I have anything that will fit you, but I'll check."

Kait slipped the shirt over her head, lowering the towel to her hips. Blake rifled in a drawer but came up empty-handed. His gaze settled on her, and an awkward silence filled the room. She watched, slightly amused as his eyes traveled down her athletic frame, his cheeks burning a dark red.

"On second thought, let's get you a different shirt. White was a very poor choice."

Blake shook his head, grabbing another. This one was black with white "paint" splashed across the front. Kait wasn't sure why the first one was inadequate but stripped out of it nonetheless.

"Oh geez, you're going to change right here?" Blake sucked in a breath and dropped his gaze to the floor, slamming his hands onto his hips.

Kait ignored him, tossing her heavy hair back as she slid the black shirt over her head.

Blake coughed, peeking up at her a minute later. "It's a little big. I'll check if my mom has any old stuff in her closet. You'll probably feel more comfortable in something of hers."

Blake exited into the hallway and rounded the corner. Kait sighed and let her head drop back against the doorway. Exhaustion riddled every bone, and she fought to keep her eyes open.

Blake returned with two dresses in hand. One was light blue with snow-flakes, and the other was a dark brown with gold polka dots. Neither were Kait's first or even second choice, but they were far better than slipping back into her filthy gown.

"Thanks." Kait reached for the brown one.

Blake threw the blue dress onto his bed. "Do you need anything else?"

"No. I'll just take a quick nap on the couch, and then I'll head out. Thank you again. I really appreciate your kindness."

"Sure, sure. My mom won't be home until late, so no one will bother you."

An awkward silence settled between them, and Kait turned to leave.

"Can I ask you one question?" Blake asked. "What happened that forced you to run away? What will happen if you get caught?"

"Well, that's two questions." Kait gave him a small smile and took a deep breath. "I'm being hunted because of one man's greed, and if I'm caught, it will determine my fate. Either I succeed and manage to end his onslaught, or he wins and takes away the only life I've ever known."

The silence stretched.

"Wow," Blake said at last. "That's a heavy burden to shoulder. Do you have anyone to help? Any friends, family?"

Kait's chest constricted at the thought of her sisters. She pressed the heel of her palm into the center of her chest. "Two sisters, but I can't involve them. He's too dangerous."

Blake clenched his jaw. "Nothing says tough guy like preying on defense-less women."

Kait cocked her head, intrigued by his unexpected malice.

Blake took a seat on the edge of the bed, resting his elbows on his knees. "Sorry, I've just had experience with guys like that." He exhaled a long breath and shot her a sideways glance. Kait read the hesitation in his eyes. After a few seconds, he continued. "When I was younger, I almost lost my mom."

The tendons in Blake's hands stood out white against his skin as he squeezed his hands into fists. Kait hovered in place. She knew she should leave—clearly, he was upset—but her curiosity as to the source of his pain fueled her to stay. Side-stepping several empty water bottles, she sat down next to him.

"When I was little, I didn't realize what was going on. I believed my mom when she said she tripped on the stairs or broke a glass. It wasn't until I was elev-en that I figured out my father was actually hurting her."

Kait frowned, remembering the feel of Hermes's knuckles, but tears pricked the back of her eyes when she envisioned Apollo holding Willow down. Watching someone you love suffer was so much worse. She pointed to the faded gloves hanging on the wall. "So you learned to hit back?"

Blake shrugged. "You could say that."

"Where's he now?"

"Gone. That's all that matters to me."

Without thinking, Kait reached out and touched the freckles on his long arm. His skin was warm, and she wondered what it would feel like to be held by them. Lifting her gaze, she took stock of his features. When standing, he was as tall as a god. He had messy dark hair, thin lips, and a light scruff of facial hair lining his jawline. He wasn't beautiful like the gods. Acne scars pocketed his cheeks, and his voice was gruff, but he possessed a rare kindness, and his eyes held a haunting quality that intrigued her. She gestured to the gloves again.

"You don't box anymore?"

"No," Blake said, straightening up. "I quit three years ago when I was fifteen. Money was tight and boxing was expensive, so I gave it up and got a job to help my mom with the bills."

"Are you going to start it up again?"

He shook his head. "Nah, especially with college next year. I need to save everything I have for tuition. Lately though, a few guys at school have been messing with me, calling me fat. I'm tired of dealing with their shit, so I thought I'd get back in shape."

"That must be hard. My older sister picked on me too, so…I get it."

Blake gave her a small smile, his dark green eyes holding hers. Kait felt a slight flutter in her stomach. Even though she used to surround herself with humans when she was younger, she had never sat down and talked to one.

She returned Blake's grin, feeling the flutter strengthen. She had always viewed humans as living trivial lives, meandering through the stages of life without much thought while the nymphs created and tended the beautiful world they inhabited. Yet, here was Blake, a young adult who had already endured more suffering than many of the nymphs she knew. She admired his strength.

Kait cleared her throat and tucked a strand of hair behind her ear, her smile widening as a wave of warmth coursed through her. Who knew she could feel so comfortable with a human, even find common ground to share?

Kait slid off the bed. "I should get out of this towel." She rose to her feet and headed for the door.

"Sorry about the mess. My mom gets on me to clean up. Now I see her point." He shrugged with a nervous chuckle, his earlier anger fading.

Kait reached the doorway and paused at the threshold. She placed her hand on the painted wood and glanced over her shoulder. "Don't worry about it. Thanks for taking me in. To be honest, I didn't expect to find such a kind soul down here."

Blake's lips quirked, but Kait didn't elaborate. "Of course. I'm happy to help."

With her other hand, Kait rubbed the hem of his T-shirt she wore between her thumb and forefinger, inhaling the scent of laundry detergent. "It was nice. You're nice," she said, her words barely a whisper. Her gaze flickered to his. "I'll change out of this and get it back to you. Thanks for the dress," she added, louder. She motioned to the brown material hanging from her fingers.

Blake started to reply, but she ducked out of the room and closed the door with a solid click. On the other side, she pressed a hand to her heart. She remembered this feeling—thought it was lost to her a century ago. After Hermes, she swore she would never again let love make her a fool. And while this wasn't love, it's how it had started before.

Kait awoke a few hours later. She peeked out from beneath the thin throw blanket and gasped as the moonlight crept up the couch, its touch inches away from her exposed ankle. It was late, much later than she had intended to stay.

It won't be long now, little one.

Kait froze. Her eyes flickered around the quiet room, searching the long shadows. "Blake?"

He will find you.

"Blake?" Kait asked again, but she knew she was alone.

The voice wasn't coming from inside the house, but rather inside her mind.

You thought you could outrun him, thought you were clever, the husky female voice continued. *Hiding in the human world won't save you. Once the sun crests over the hills, Zeus will have you. He's on his way now. There is no escape. If you're smart, you'll let him take you. I've already shown him where you're hiding. If you continue to resist, I'll find your sister. I'll find your friends. Everyone you love will be revealed to the gods and their endless lust.*

Kait's head swiveled, trying to find the speaker even though she knew it was pointless.

The woman said she knew where she was. Once the moonlight began to ebb and dawn broke, Zeus would be at the door, and then there truly would be no hope of escape. He'd take her, and she would have no way to protect Bia. She had to leave, had to at least try to get away while the sun still hovered beneath the world.

Before she could finish constructing her plan, the voice laughed, cruelty dripping from her words.

You can't win, little one. The longer you run, the fiercer my vengeance shall be upon your sister. Your choice, nymph.

The voice faded away, along with the oppressive presence swelling in her mind.

Kait tried to swallow the fear thickening in her throat, but she couldn't force the spit on her dry tongue down. Her heart pounded, and her palms pulsed. The need to disappear into the wind poured powerfully from her. Piriol or not, he'd clearly already found her. What use was discretion now?

An intense breeze spiraled around the room, forcing picture frames to bounce in their place on the walls while loose pieces of mail lifted into the air like frightened doves.

Where could she go? She thought the human realm would be safe. She thought she'd have at least a day to gather her thoughts, but there would be no rest. There was no end to Zeus's game, and whoever was watching her now seemed intent on her demise.

Should she give in? Surrender to a life void of magic? It might be better than running for the rest of her life.

The image of Jezlem bruised and beaten, hunched and broken, hit her like a fist to the gut. Without her halo, her sister looked dull and lifeless, her energy and will to fight back decimated. And it was all because of Zeus.

Renewed hatred coursed through Kait, rattling the wooden windows like a hurricane.

No. He would never have her.

Unable to control her emotions any longer, Kait allowed the wind to sweep her away, her body instantly dissolving into its cool embrace.

The blanket fluttered to the floor as the fierce wind barreled through the window, shattering the glass into dozens of jagged shards. Once outside, she glanced east. She had maybe an hour's head start, and she didn't plan on wasting it.

⚡ 16 ⚡

Blake hiked up his backpack straps and fit one earbud into place. Heavy rock music cocooned around him. He had awoken to his mother screaming. When she returned home from working second shift at the hospital, she found the living room a mess and a giant hole busted through the front window. The girl was gone as she promised she would be, but why destroy his house? Had the guy she was running from found her?

Blake had apologized and cleaned up the broken glass and ruined picture frames, then stuffed them in the trash on his way to school. The whole thing left him feeling hollowed out, as if Kait had taken something intangible from him when she fled. Part of him was relieved to return to his mundane life, but deep down, his stomach was in knots. Clearly, she needed help. The fear in her eyes had haunted him all night. He'd vowed to get more information out of her in the morning, but apart from a few shards of glass and a rumpled blanket, it was like she was more a dream than reality.

Blake turned up his music as he neared the old well on the edge of the sleepy town, trying to drown out his nerves. His best and only friend, Joel, was leaning against the corroding bricks, a burning cigarette perched on his bottom lip.

"What's up, man?" Joel flicked his shaggy blond hair out of his eyes.

"Not much. Ready?"

Joel nodded, and Blake retreated back into his thoughts. He'd tried to help Kait, but she ran off before the sun came up. Still, he was unable to staunch the flow of guilt that assailed him.

The two boys fell into step and headed toward the high school about a mile away. In a town as small as Bennington, everything was practically a mile away. Blake considered telling Joel about the girl, but part of him was skeptical it had even happened. What proof did he have? The image of the beautiful stranger wearing nothing but his shirt and a towel popped into his mind.

"You're quiet this morning." Joel coughed, flicking the butt of his cigarette onto a browning lawn.

Blake turned to look at him. "What?"

"I said you're quiet." Joel laughed, pulling another cigarette from behind his ear. "So, what are we doing this weekend?"

Blake scratched the back of his neck as they rounded the corner and began climbing the steep hill to the school. "Same as any other." Blake shrugged. "Video games and junk food at my place?"

"I thought you were over all that crap with this new workout thing you're trying out?" His lighter clicked and sparked, and the sour smell of nicotine polluted the crisp October morning.

Blake pictured the girl lying in the mud. "Oh, yeah. Well, you should have known I'd cave. But maybe I'll go one more time. You know, finish the week strong."

"Sure," Joel said, arching his eyebrows. "Did you get that lab report done?"

"What?"

"Come on, man. What is up with you today? The lab report for Burns's class? You said you were going to finish it yesterday." Joel stopped short. "Dude, tell me you wrote it up." He stared at him, his amber eyes alarmed and threatening.

Blake cursed as their previous conversation came flooding back to him. He'd planned on doing it after his run. On the front steps of the school, he unzipped his backpack and rifled through the few notebooks inside. At the bottom, lying in a crumpled heap, was their shared lab report, the conclusion still blank and mocking him.

"I can fix this. Just give me a few minutes." Blake pulled the report out as the loud squeal of bus tires drowned his plea.

"Seriously, Blake? If I don't turn this in, he's giving me five weeks of Saturday detention." Joel sighed. "Man, thanks a lot." He took one last drag.

"Look, I'm sorry. I met this girl last night, and she needed help. I totally forgot. I'm sorry. But I'll fix it. I'll write it up right now."

Joel pursed his lips. "A girl? What girl?"

Blake threw up his hands, trying to remember the right format for the conclusion. "I met her on my run."

"And she needed help? With what? Tying her shoelace?"

"No, some guy. Just let me finish this and then I'll explain." Blake slung his bag back over his shoulder. "I'll see you in first period."

He ran up the wide concrete steps, leaving Joel behind in a dissipating cloud of smoke. He withdrew his phone from his pocket and glanced at the time. He still had five minutes before the first bell. If he was lucky, he might be able to hole up in the library through homeroom.

Pushing the gathering students out of the way, Blake crashed through the front doors and raced to the library, grateful for the first time that it wasn't sprawling like the one at Champlain. The small lounge was full of hippy sophomores, their organic values washing over him as soon as he stepped inside. Frantically, he scanned the crowded tables for a free flat surface. At this point, he'd take an empty bookshelf, anywhere he could write the last paragraph.

His gaze swept the stirring crowd, and an empty chair facing the window made his heart leap. Jumping over a dozen bags, Blake crossed the circular room and slid into the chair, slamming the wrinkled report onto the table beside Jane, the only girl in his class of twenty-three with spiky black hair.

"Come on. Please let me have just one," Blake mumbled under his breath as he turned his backpack inside out looking for a pen, a pencil, anything. Groaning, he hit the table, making Jane flinch in her seat. "Sorry," he said. "Do you have a pen?"

Looking at him with her slender eyebrows raised, Jane withdrew a pen from the spirals of her notebook and rolled it across the table.

Blake snatched it. "Thanks."

The bell was going to ring any second. He scribbled something down about how the results did not support their theory. The speaker overhead blared to life with a monotonous hum. Students stood and slung their backpacks over their shoulders, shuffling through the exit like the walking dead, but not Blake. His mind was whirling, trying to explain why the experiment didn't work in the eloquent way Burns demanded. He couldn't let Joel down.

"Heads up," Jane whispered as she departed their shared space.

Blake glanced over his shoulder. The elderly librarian, Mrs. Hayes, waddled toward him, a scowl on her face.

"Young man, the bell has rung. You need to get to homeroom."

"I'm almost done," Blake said, then looked back down on his paper.

"One minute. Then I'm getting the hall monitor to escort you where you belong."

Blake ignored her, trying to collect his thoughts.

"What you working on, Blakey?"

A pair of hands yanked the report out from underneath Blake's palm. The unexpected movement jerked the pen, leaving a bold black line across the length of the paper. Blake glanced up. His stomach dropped.

Justin Lowell stood above him, his light gray eyes fixed on Blake like a sniper scope. Justin's stained white T-shirt hung off his skinny frame, bunching up around his waist to expose red boxers. Arching his pierced eyebrow, he surveyed the lab report and twirled his tongue ring with a snort.

"Lookie here, boys." Justin brandished the wrinkled paper for the big linebackers behind him. "Blakey didn't finish his homework. Here, let me help you out."

"Give it back, Justin." Blake gripped the pen hard. He yearned to lash out with an upper cut but was all too familiar with the consequences.

Justin scrutinized the report, his eyes darting over the headings, clearly not taking anything in. "Nah, don't think I will. This looks important, and I'm guessing that if you're scrambling this close to first period to get it done, you need it pretty bad."

"It's just some stupid assignment." Blake looked over his shoulder, hopeful Mrs. Hayes kept her word about grabbing the hall monitor. Unfortunately, the library had completely emptied out.

"Why are there two names on it? Where's your pal Joel?"

"Christ, Justin. What are we, five? Just give me the damn paper." Blake made a grab for it.

Justin jerked the paper backward, a slow smile creeping up his face. "All right, I will. You just tell me how many pieces you want it in." With a quick flick of his wrist, Justin ripped the top right corner off and let it float uselessly to the floor.

"Screw this," Blake growled under his breath. He grabbed a nearby textbook and clocked one of Justin's lackeys in the head, then spun around and hurled the book at the other. The tall boy's eyes widened as the book sailed toward him, then caught him in the nose.

Using his momentum, Blake rolled over the edge of the table and slammed his sneakers on the carpeted floor, inches away from Justin. Three more white flakes of paper littered the floor.

"Wow, really cool moves, Blake." Justin ripped off another piece.

Blake threw out his fist, but Justin dodged it, hammering Blake's shoulder with his own attack. Blake groaned, but Justin was on him again. Using his other fist, Justin blasted him in the gut with a quick jab, then smashed his elbow into Blake's face.

A burst of pain exploded in Blake's head, and a torrent of blood pulsed from his nose. Gritting his teeth, Blake wrapped his arms around Justin's torso and charged him backward, slamming his spine into a table. A puff of air escaped Justin's lips, but he recovered fast, threading his hands around Blake's skull until his thumbs were level with his eyes. Before Justin could squeeze, Blake reared back his head, then thrust it forward, hitting Justin's jaw. The other boy's head snapped up, and Blake punched his exposed throat.

He brought back his fist to hit Justin again when two meaty hands wrapped around his waist and yanked him away. Justin's other sidekick punched Blake as hard as he could in the stomach. Blake sunk to his knees, frowning as droplets of blood covered his jeans. Out of the corner of his eye, Blake saw Justin wipe his mouth on his sleeve. A crimson line of blood trailed from his split lip.

Mrs. Hayes gasped. "What's going on here?" She staggered forward with her wrinkled hand clutching her frail heart.

"That's enough, boys." Coach Brown's deep baritone voice boomed, stopping Justin in his tracks.

"Hey, Coach." Justin grinned, touching the tip of his tongue to his sore lip. "We were just helping Blake finish his homework."

"Can it, Lowell." Coach Brown pointed to the library exit. "Office. Now. Everyone."

The trio of football players shuffled away under their coach's murderous glare. Blake grabbed his torn lab report, closing his fist around the pieces. He sighed as he tried to fit them together. Tape would work—if the sheet wasn't soaked through with blood in four places. Blake shook his head and crammed the destroyed report into his backpack.

"You too, Gibbons."

Blake pinched his nose, sniffing twice. At least the bleeding had stopped. The final bell rang, announcing he was late for homeroom as he made his way to the principal's office. Throw in tardiness on top of his fourth fight of the year— maybe Mr. Burns would accept suspension as a sufficient excuse.

The front door of the school slammed against the brick exterior, ricocheting with a thunderous smash. Blake jogged down the stairs to the silver Honda idling at the curb of the circular lane. Behind him, Justin and his friends snickered. Coach Brown's thick shadow stretched across the sidewalk, a silent threat.

"See you later, Blakey," Justin called with a wave.

Blake didn't respond. He reached the car and slid into the front seat, pulling the door firmly shut behind him, but he could still hear Justin and the goons cackling.

"Sorry," Blake muttered, staring at the windshield.

He placed his backpack on his lap, debating how angry his mother would be if he put in his headphones. She was quiet for a minute, staring at him with both hands folded neatly in her lap.

"Can we go?" Blake clenched his teeth.

Without a word, his mom shifted the car into drive and pulled away from the curb. Blake glanced at the clock, wondering how long she'd wait to start laying into him. The car rolled up to the stop sign at the bottom of the hill.

"I don't understand what's going on with you, Blake." His mom sighed as she pulled into traffic. "First the window and now this?" She paused for a moment. "How long?"

Blake flexed his jaw. "The rest of the week."

She scoffed. "This is no way to start off your senior year. It's only October, and this is your second suspension for fighting. What is it? Why are you behaving this way?"

"It wasn't my fault, Mom." Blake looked over at her for the first time. "It was Justin and his dumb friends. He started it. Would you rather I didn't stand up for myself?"

"I'd rather you didn't get expelled for reckless and dangerous behavior. What did we talk about last time? Walk away, Blake. No matter what that awful kid says, don't let it get to you."

"That's easy for you to say. Just let him make fun of me while everyone watches and laughs behind my back. At least Dad wanted me to be a man and stick up for—"

"Is that the type of man you want to be? Beating people up isn't the answer." Her voice softened, then broke as tears overwhelmed her.

Shame clenched Blake's gut. "I'm sorry," he whispered. The memories he divulged to Kait last night flooded him.

Most of his memories consisted of shadows and raised voices, but fear spiked in his stomach, along with the usual feeling of helplessness whenever he thought of his childhood. Blake found his mother's hand and squeezed her fingers, remembering when they were more black-and-blue than fair and unblemished.

His dad had been gone for years, and though his mother's complexion had healed, he knew her greatest fear—that one day Blake would turn out to be just like him—lingered below the surface of every smile. And he was playing right into it as if on cue.

"I know I'm like a broken record, always preaching to rise above it and avoid giving them the satisfaction of knowing they hurt you," she said. "I know how hard it is, but if you fight like them and hit like them, you're no better. I didn't let you box to learn how to hurt people."

She pulled into the short driveway, engine idling in front of their faded yellow Cape Cod situated at the end of a cul-de-sac.

Blake nodded, rubbing his palms along his jeans. He stared at his mother, marveling at her quiet strength. "Yeah, I know." He sighed when his words came out harsher than he meant. He shook his head and gave his mother a weak smile. "It won't happen again. I promise." He leaned over and kissed her temple, shifting his backpack. "I'm going for a walk, okay?"

His mother frowned. "Okay. I'll see you after work. Stay out of trouble, please." Her eyes pleaded, swimming with ghosts.

He stood in the driveway until she reversed. Because of him, she'd have to work even later to make up the time left in her shift. He lifted his hand in a limp wave as the car traveled back up the quiet road. Their only neighbor, an elderly man named Harold, was checking his mail. He gave Blake a knowing look and lifted two fingers in greeting.

Blake nodded once in his direction and crossed their shallow yard to the plum front door. A frustrated sigh slipped from his lips as his backpack strap slid down his arm. The black bag landed on the lone front step with a thud. Without a thought, he spun around, pointing his feet to the small hill rising behind his house.

Blake didn't want to think about his past. Didn't want to picture the way his father's knuckles bled or the way his mother's voice rose when she lied. For a second, his mind flipped back to the girl, Kait. He had tried to help, but he was clearly still inadequate, always too weak, too small, too dumb. He didn't blame her for disappearing. If only he could do the same.

The sour thought deepened his guilt. After shoving his earbuds in, he chose a random song. He didn't care about the lyrics. All he wanted was something angry and loud. A flurry of drums erupted as he left the overgrown yard behind, knocking aside several low hanging branches as the woods welcomed him.

"What did Burns say yesterday?" Blake asked, punching the buttons on the controller to give his car a burst of nitro.

Joel took a swig of Gatorade and shrugged, frowning as his car bumped against the barrier wall. "Nothing really. Principal Sweeny called me in after you left and gave me the pieces of the report. I showed them to Burns, blood and all. Then he told me to sit down, so I guess I'm free."

"That's cool. Yet you pay him back by ditching today?"

A smirk pulled at the corner of Joel's mouth. "I went for two weeks straight. I'm due for a break. High school is stupid anyway. Wait till we get out of this crummy town. College is where it's at."

Blake didn't reply, concentrating on shooting his car across the finish line, even though he, too, dreamed of the day he would leave Bennington and never come back. He tossed the controller onto the floor and rubbed his eyes, which had started to burn two hours ago. Maybe he needed a break too.

"I'm going for a smoke." Joel rose to his feet. "Want to come?"

Blake nodded, wincing as he stretched his cramped legs.

They meandered downstairs, threw on light jackets, and exited through the kitchen door. Joel's lighter clicked to life, and the usual cloud of nicotine billowed from his lips the moment the door shut.

"So how long do you think your mom is going to stay pissed for?" He took another drag.

Blake shrugged, digging his hands into his pockets as he took a seat on the only metal lawn chair on the weed-covered patio. "I don't know. Another day? I stayed up late last night to do all the schoolwork they gave me for the suspension and tried apologizing again, but she didn't want to hear it. She thinks I'll end up like my dad." Blake sighed, wrinkling his nose from the smell of Joel's cigarette.

"Yikes." Joel flicked ash onto the crumbling pavers. There was a long pause before he continued. "Have you heard from him at all?"

Blake sucked in a cool breath, the bitter flavor of nicotine dancing on his tongue. "No, but it doesn't matter. I wouldn't talk to him anyway. Not after everything."

Joel nodded, taking a slow drag.

Blake cleared his throat. "It feels good out here. Want to walk for a bit?" He jerked his thumb over his shoulder toward the trees.

Joel exhaled. "Yeah, I'm not doing anything else."

He dropped the used cigarette into a deep crevice alongside the pavers, the short orange butt sticking out between the unruly weeds. He began pulling out another one. Blake put up his hand.

"If you're going to come with me, don't smoke. I want to enjoy the fresh air, not your toxic tobacco cloud."

Joel rolled his eyes, but let the unlit cigarette fall back into the pack. "Fine, you health-conscious, freak. I won't smoke in your precious woods, but if you start eating gluten-free, we're going to have a real problem." He punched Blake in the arm.

The two friends left the patio and scrubby backyard behind in exchange for towering trees that closed their street off from the main road. The midafternoon sun was crisp and bright as it reflected off the falling leaves. Blake was enjoying himself, but after twenty minutes of roaming the sloping hills, Joel started hacking.

"Why are we doing this?" Joel coughed, tossing his unkempt blond hair out of his eyes.

"A little exercise won't kill you."

"This isn't exercise. This is a death march. Are we even walking toward anything? Denny's, maybe?"

"Are you serious? How are you passing gym?"

"Oh, that's easy. I swiped an inhaler from the nurse's office last semester. Guardi thinks I have asthma." Joel gave him a proud smirk.

Blake shook his head and squinted as a bright light made him turn away. He shielded his eyes with his hand and realized they were at the small pond he used as the turnaround point for his runs. Before he could stop himself, his eyes swept to the right where he found the girl, but it was empty, save for the rotting tree and long grass.

Joel wheezed, and Blake directed him to a small log several yards away from the water's edge. Blake picked up a few rocks and pitched them into the still water, watching the ripples fan out from where he stood.

"Where are we?" Joel asked, looking around for the first time.

"I don't know if this place has a name. I found it on a run. It's actually where I met that girl the other day." Blake threw in a handful of rocks and sand. They made a tinkling sound as they punched through the surface.

"Great, is she a runner too?"

"No. It was weird. At first, I thought she was dead." Blake threw the next rock hard. "I found her right there." He gestured to the moss-covered log.

Joel wrinkled his nose. "Here? But this place is a swamp. Why was she out here?"

"I don't know. I tried asking, but she was vague. She said she was running from someone. Anyway, she came back to my house, got cleaned up, broke my window, then disappeared."

"She went back to your house?"

"Yeah, she was filthy and needed help. I let her shower and gave her one of my mom's old dresses."

"She showered at your place?" Joel repeated, arching his eyebrows. "Did you—"

"What? Spy on her through the crack in the door? No, you idiot; I'm not a creep," Blake said, throwing a rock at Joel's feet. "She came to my room in her towel though. Damn, she was something."

"I'd like to see her." Joel fiddled with his pack of cigarettes. "But what was she doing out here in the mud? Hot girls don't do that."

Blake shook his head. "Like I said, she was running from someone—at least according to her. I don't know if she was hiding or what, but when I woke her up, she was really disoriented."

"And then she broke your window?"

"Yeah. Busted the living room window wide open while I was asleep. Glass was everywhere, and the room was a mess. Like a tornado hit it or something. Whoever she was, her life was somehow more screwed up than mine."

The same protective feeling Blake felt when he found her overcame him. He thought back to the story she told about her sister, about never being good enough, and felt bad about describing her in such a way. She wasn't weird. In fact, Blake found he almost longed to see and speak to her again.

Joel whistled low. "Wow. You're lucky she didn't do anything to you or your mom. How old was she?"

"Our age, maybe a year older."

"Did she tell you her name?"

Blake remembered the annoyed look on her face when he pronounced her name wrong. "Kaitaini."

A large splash erupted a few feet away. Both boys flinched as a small wave lapped against the muddy shore. An eerie feeling settled over Blake, like he was being watched.

He stepped back from the shoreline. "Let's get out of here."

Another splash, this one even closer, disrupted the water again.

"Yeah, that's a good idea," Joel agreed, stumbling to his feet.

The boys jogged up the small incline, eager to put as much distance between them and the water as possible. The wind surged, rustling the remaining leaves on the thinning trees. A chorus of whispers made Blake's skin prickle. He could have sworn he heard his name.

⚡ 17 ⚡

The rest of the week passed uneventfully. As predicted, his mom's anger over his suspension ebbed, and on Sunday night, they shared a bowl of popcorn while watching a new rom-com. It certainly wasn't his choice, but he didn't argue.

Blake turned his head, watching his mom out of the corner of his eye. Happy tears leaked out of her eyes as the characters said goodbye. He groaned internally and stuffed another handful of popcorn into his mouth. Cheesy, dramatic music started to ring, piercing the melancholy scene.

Blake, a soft voice whispered.

Blake stopped crunching and strained his ears. He leaned a little closer to the screen. Wasn't the guy's named Wyatt?

She'll come back to you, the voice said, so quiet Blake could hardly make out the words.

Blake turned to his mother. "What?"

"Wyatt can't leave his sick dad, but Maria has to go to school." Her eyes never left the screen.

"Oh, thanks." Blake settled back against the couch. He pulled out his phone. It wasn't even nine. Maybe too much screen time this week was messing with his head.

"I'm going to get a drink. Do you want anything?"

His mom shook her head, scooping up more popcorn with a smile. Blake unfolded himself from the couch and padded into the kitchen. He poured a glass of milk and set it on the counter. A small movement flashed outside the window. The sun had set, casting the yard in a deep blue glow. The sporadic call of the wind chimes colliding every few seconds was the only sound, apart from the movie in the other room. The same feeling he had the other day caused goose bumps to rise along his arms. Someone was watching him.

Blake stood in front of the window, resting both hands on the edge of the sink. Nothing looked wrong or out of place. A scrawny tree stood next to the patio, where a light breeze ruffled the cover of the grill. Wrapping his hand around his glass, Blake shrugged and began to turn away.

Death will be swift if you aid her again.

A sharp, grinding sound erupted outside. Blake spun back around. A black shadow pressed against the window, its long, spider-like fingers trying to shred the screen.

"What the hell!" he cried, stumbling back.

His glass slipped from his hand, shattering the second it hit the tile floor.

A frightening chuckle filtered into Blake's ears, causing his heart to accelerate. The voice was all around him, inside him. Distantly, Blake heard a heavy thud, followed by thundering feet.

I'll be watching.

Blake fell to the floor, crying out in pain as a large shard of glass pierced his palm. He had to get it out. Something was in his mind. Blake squeezed his eyes shut and felt two powerful hands dig into his shoulders, shaking him. The maniacal laughter continued, feeding off his fear.

Blake, Blake.

The rough voice barked loudly, setting his teeth on edge.

"Blake! Blake, open your eyes!"

Blake's eyes flashed open to see his mother sitting in front of him, her brown eyes wild with fright.

"Mom?"

"Oh, thank God." She sighed. She ceased the shaking and pulled him close. "What happened? Are you okay?"

"I dropped my glass." Blake raised his bleeding hand.

He glanced down and saw he was sitting in a puddle of milk. The blood from his wound swirled with it, turning it a sickly shade of pink.

"Let me see." His mom took his hand and cradled it in her lap. "Why were you screaming?"

Blake glanced at the window and flinched. The shadow was still fighting to break through the screen. "That!" he cried, pointing with his other hand.

His mom craned her neck, and her eyes widened in surprise. "What?" She stood up, milk running down the tops of her feet. She flicked on the patio light, and her shoulders drooped. "It's just the grill cover. The wind must have blown it off, and it got snagged on the windowsill."

She pressed her hand to her chest and ducked outside, yanking the black cover away from the window. Sure enough, *GrillMaster* was emblazoned on the side in white lettering. But what about the voice? The talons? Something was there, warning him to stay away. But to stay away from what?

The kitchen door closed with a bang.

"Let's get you cleaned up. How bad is your hand?" She looked at the wound again in the light. "It's not deep. I don't think it needs stitches. If the bleeding doesn't stop, we'll take you in, okay?"

Blake nodded, his eyes wandering back to the window.

"Honey, can you grab the paper towels?"

"What?"

"Get the paper towels, please," his mom repeated, but then grabbed them off the counter herself. "Are you sure you're all right? Is something else bothering you?"

Blake shook his head. He was being stupid, irrational. Mysterious shadow creatures weren't a thing. "Yeah—I mean no." Blake flexed his wounded hand. The bleeding had stopped, but sticky blood covered his arm from fingertip to elbow. "I'm going to take a shower. I'm sorry I ruined movie night."

His mom stood, her jeans soaked with bloody milk. She wrapped her arms around him and kissed his cheek. "Don't worry about it, baby. Things happen, and we all need a little rescuing now and then." She smiled, running her hand through his black hair. "I'm glad you still need me. You've grown up so much, gotten so tough. I like being your hero." She kissed his cheek once more. "Go take a nice shower and relax. You're back to school tomorrow and…"

"No fighting."

His mother nodded and placed her hands on her hips. "That's right."

Blake turned toward the stairs. "Thanks, Mom."

Twenty minutes later, he was showered, bandaged, and lying in bed. His mind whirled, trying to piece together the strange events of the night. There had been a voice, a voice warning of danger if he interfered again. Whoever had sent the message wanted to be sure he understood the consequences if he didn't listen. Blake thought back to Kait. She'd told him she was running from a guy.

Blake wrinkled his nose. None of it made any sense. Was he going crazy? He didn't know much about hearing voices, but he was pretty sure it wasn't a good sign. He exhaled and rolled onto his side, pulling the blankets up like a little kid afraid of monsters stalking him in the night.

"May I have lavender tea?" Kait asked the waiter, handing him the menu.

The young man stood silently in front of her, gawking. At last, he responded. "The tea, of course. Excellent choice, Miss…?" The waiter let his words hang, fishing for her name.

"Lynn," Kait replied, hoping it was a suitable human name.

"Perfect." He grinned. "I'll be right back with that."

She swiped a long black curl out of her face and tapped the edge of the fork on the sleek wooden table, enjoying the warmth of the sun. She had requested a patio seat on purpose and sat directly in the sunlight to mask her halo, but she didn't exactly blend in.

All around her, people stared. She had forgotten the power of beauty. In Olean, beauty didn't stand out. Talents and skills were the attributes that were highly coveted. Kait frowned, wishing she could show them what lurked beneath her pretty face. Blake, at least, had seen past it.

Kait stopped the thought before it could gather more ground, but it wasn't the first time her mind had wandered to the sweet boy. She pictured his careful smile, the freckles dotting his arms. She couldn't involve him.

Dispelling her musings, Kait reached forward and tore a piece of pumpernickel bread off the roll situated in the middle of the table and looked out over the bustling street of Greenwich Village. The café was tucked between two old-world brownstones, helpless to defend against the bright green ivy slowly invading the canvas roof of the restaurant. She smiled as nature attempted to reclaim the earth, and her heart ached thinking of Bia. It had been a little over a week since she left with Tressa. She prayed her sister was staying safe.

Ripping off another piece of bread, Kait lowered her gaze to the endless parade of people walking by, taken aback as dozens of eyes lingered in her direction. Her throat constricted, and she tossed the uneaten slice onto the serving dish. She thought a big city like New York would make it easier to hide, but the constant attention only heightened her paranoia.

The tips of her fingers itched, anxious to cast so the wind could cloak her, but Zeus was waiting for her to slip. She was amazed she had traveled from Vermont to the city without detection. Already under intense scrutiny, she couldn't risk alerting Zeus and his piriol to her new whereabouts by using more magic. Kait's chest tightened. She yearned to return to Olean.

A portal hovered above a crooked willow tree just down the street, open and inviting. Yet Kait was cautious. Why was this portal accessible when all the others had been shut tight? It felt like a trap.

Instead of leaping at her chance to go home, she'd found the café a safe proximity away and settled in to wait, half hoping to catch a glimpse of the woman aiding Zeus. Then she'd have two gods to accuse in front of the Council. On the other hand, she may have succeeded in dodging the immortals. Regardless of whether the woman showed or not, she was diving through the portal after her tea.

Picking at her discarded bread, she watched a little girl seated a few tables away. She couldn't have been more than four years old, but the wonder in her eyes made Kait pause. Amidst her thoughts, the sun had shifted, showcasing her illuminated halo. Her eyes widened with fear, but the little girl only smiled, content to keep her discovery to herself.

Kait grinned and offered a little wave in return before she adjusted her seat to follow the arching sun. She aligned her body with the golden rays, hiding her halo once more. Glancing up from under her lashes, she winked in the girl's direction.

A clattering caused her to break eye contact as the waiter arrived with her tea. The delicate china cup danced precariously on the matching saucer as he navigated through the tightly spaced patrons. Reaching up, Kait took the saucer before it landed in her lap.

"Thanks," she said, setting it down on her table.

"Sure—I mean, of course," the waiter stammered. "Is there anything else you'd like? Anything I can get you?"

"No, I'm fine."

"Right. If you change your mind, I'll be watching you." He gave her a charming smile as he backed away.

Kait held his gaze, his last words like a punch to the stomach. Eyes, so many eyes on her, watching. Goose bumps scattered across her arms, and a cool flush made her shoulders twitch. Sticking her spoon into her tea, she pushed her suspicions away. She was being paranoid. He didn't know anything. She was safe.

The metal clinked against the sides each time the spoon hit, creating a disarming melody amidst the noisy restaurant and loud street. Kait's thoughts meandered as she scanned the nearby humans. Her gaze lingered on one man: dark hair, green eyes, a dimple on one side.

The spoon clattered, falling off the saucer and scattering light brown stains across the tablecloth. With surprise and confusion, Kait frowned at the face that swam behind her eyes. She left Blake and Vermont far behind, so why was she looking for his features in all the strangers?

"Miss Lynn?" the waiter said, wrenching her back to the present.

"Yes?" she asked, working hard to keep the annoyance out of her voice.

The waiter set down a chocolate pastry in front of her. The sweet pastry dripped in warm fudge.

"I didn't order that."

"No, it's from a guy inside." He scoffed as if to discredit the suitor.

"A guy?"

She uncrossed her legs and sat up straight, her brown dress grazing the ground with the movement. Kait stared into the dimly lit restaurant. The treat wasn't an invitation; it was a threat.

At last, a group of friends parted, calling goodbye as they separated. Behind them sat a solitary man dressed in an expensive navy suit jacket, his golden cuff links winking at her. Kait's breath caught in her throat as her eyes traveled up the well-dressed man. He had a chiseled jawbone, flawless skin, and menacing blue eyes that bore into her. A small candle wavered in front of him, highlighting the amusement carved into his features.

Zeus.

"I need to leave. May I have the check? Never mind, I'll pay cash. Here." Kait rushed to open her clutch. She thrust several bills into the waiter's hand and pushed back in her chair, bumping the patron behind her. "Sorry, I—"

A cold hand gripped her wrist.

"Darling, I'm so glad I caught you." Zeus's deep voice reverberated up her spine as her heart knocked against her chest. "Come, sit down. Enjoy your treat before we leave."

Kait's jaw trembled as she stared into the blinding sun. He knew she was there the whole time.

"Darling." Zeus's voice was firm as he pulled her arm down, forcing her to turn and look at him. He was dazzling in the suit, but he leered at her like a wolf that had cornered a sheep at last.

Kait resumed her seat, feeling like a caged moth throwing itself against a glass jar.

"Hello, Zeus."

⚡ 18 ⚡

"**W**ipe that horrified look off your face," Zeus growled under his breath as he flashed a confident smile at the retreating waiter. "Smile."

Kait complied, her lips stretching nervously. She looked around at the crowded restaurant, searching for anyone or anything to cause a distraction. Apart from the few people engaged in conversation, the majority of the diners' eyes were glued to their flashing screens. There was no one to read the plea in her gaze.

Zeus sat opposite her, tapping the ceramic saucer with a butter knife to re-capture her full attention. "So, are you happy to see me?" He slung his left arm over the back of the polished chair, at ease.

Kait cleared her throat and tucked a stray curl behind her ear. "How did you find me?"

Zeus shrugged. "You're actually quite skilled at evading me. And as thrilling as it would be, I unfortunately can't allow Kaf to wander the human realm in search of you, so I had to ask for help from someone who understands my needs. She has this marvelous tool that allows her to find anyone anywhere, regardless of deflection charms and the like."

Kait's attention narrowed. "Who is it?"

Zeus waved his hand in front of him. "That doesn't matter. Do you mind? This looks delicious." He dipped his fingertip in the dripping chocolate and brought it to his lips, sucking it off with a loud smack. "Yummy. I like it down here. Maybe I'll stay a little longer. It might do me some good to...*study* these humans a little more. Take my mind off things. It's been a long time since I've had the pleasure of their company. Oh, I can start with that one." Zeus arched his eyebrows at a beautiful blond woman several tables away.

"You know that's against the laws," Kait straightened her spine. "Unions be-tween gods and mortals are forbidden. The consequences—"

Zeus sighed. "Oh, let's not bore everyone with those. I only suggested it as a bit of fun. You would be welcome to join us. We could see what you taste like covered in fudge." He smiled, his blue eyes roaming her body.

"No thank you." Kait prickled, turning her head to face the street.

Perhaps she could manipulate the wind and then increase the speed gradually until it was strong enough to carry her away. The humans would think nothing of it.

A cool touch stroked the back of her hand, and a jolt of electricity sizzled her thoughts of escape.

"Don't be jealous," Zeus said. "You're much prettier, but my favorite part is that you're

Untouched—a quality I find insatiably addictive."

"But I'm not, Zeus. I've lain with other men. I'm not pure."

Zeus shook his head, a playful grin brightening his features. "Men? Beasts and half-breeds aren't men. And they're not powerful enough to absorb the energy halos yield. The effect of euphoria will be heavenly, and better yet, with all your prior…experience, we can turn this taking into a real party."

Kait tried to pull her hand away, but Zeus held her firmly, his intense stare darkening. She was reminded of how truly unstable he was beneath his composed manner.

"Do you have any idea how hard it is to be this close to you after all you've done? To touch you without throwing you atop this table and tearing your clothes off?"

Kait shivered. She could feel the power pulsing off the god. If she wasn't careful, he would carry out his fantasy and more.

"I've never wanted a nymph as badly as I crave you. Even the way you breathe arouses me." Zeus took a steadying breath. "But I will control myself. I simply followed you here to talk." As if to prove it, Zeus released her hand and resumed his casual posture.

Kait balked, unsure she heard correctly. "Talk? About what?"

"Well, you see, my dear, it seems you've created a little game."

"What do you mean?" She leaned away, trying to keep as much distance between them as possible in the small space.

Zeus clucked his tongue. "Careful now, aurai. Wouldn't want the locals getting *wind* of an unnatural disturbance."

Kaitaini remained silent, but the edge of the tablecloth continued to flutter.

"Nothing? I thought that was clever." Zeus shrugged with a chuckle. "The game, my dear, back to my marvelous game. It's never been done before, but that's what makes it so interesting. And I have you to thank for that." Zeus grinned and paused, waiting.

"What are you talking about?"

"Your decision to involve the human."

Blake's kind face leapt to her mind again.

"I didn't involve him. I took shelter in his home one night, that's all."

Zeus leaned forward, elbows on the table as he cradled his chin in his hands. "Details. So, here's the deal. You give yourself to me and the boy goes free. If you continue to make me chase you, there is a very favorable chance he is going to die in a very unpleasant manner."

His words were gravelly, a sharp contrast to his smooth hands, which twirled the butter knife around. The sun reflected off the metal with a foreboding crimson shine.

A small lump of guilt formed in Kait's stomach. It was her fault. The moment Blake saw her, she should have hidden in the wind and let him wander back to his normal, safe existence. He didn't deserve this. She had to warn him.

Zeus winked. "Exciting, isn't it?"

Kait pursed her lips. Zeus wasn't going to make it easy.

"You need to decide fast. My patience is wearing thin."

Kait pinched the skin between her eyes. She couldn't let Zeus kill Blake, but she refused to sacrifice herself.

An idea formed. What if she could find a way to hide him in Olean? Never before had a mortal entered the ethereal realm, but if she could convince the elders, show the queen his life was in danger from the gods, maybe they'd make an exception.

A tiny blossom of hope surged within her chest as Kait raised her eyes to Zeus. "Kill the human. He means nothing to me. But know this: I will never surrender to you. I will run until my last breath and laugh as my body dissolves and my soul ascends back to my mother goddess. You will never have me."

Up above, the sunshine vanished, hidden behind a darkening thunder cloud. People seated around them gasped and pointed to the black skies, but Kait's eyes never left the god's murderous gaze.

"You speak confidently for one so young," he said. "Maybe I'll say to hell with it all and just take you right here in front of all these humans. Pin you over the banister and let you taste my desire." The clouds thickened, and the wind whipped hard and fast to match her racing heart.

She glanced up. Lightning crackled above. When she looked back at Zeus, she inhaled sharply. His pupils had dilated to the entire circumference of his iris, leaving his eyes black as night. He grinned, reminding her of a great white shark. A deep rumble of thunder clapped. Several diners shrieked.

"I'm rather fond of that idea," Zeus whispered, swallowing once. He rose to his feet, just inches away now. "Come, the chase is over." Another roar of thunder echoed like a shotgun. Everyone started to stand, trying to carry their plates inside before the clouds unleashed an onslaught of rain. "Now, nymph."

The wind spiraled from every pore in Kait's body, a mini tornado wreaking havoc among the elegant silverware and tea service. If she was going to move, this was her chance. She slid to the edge of her chair as her long black curls danced about her face.

"You can go to hell, Zeus."

The god roared, lunging toward her over the table as a furious bolt of lightning exploded feet from where they sat. Terrified screams rent the air as the mortals raced inside, upturning tables and sending half-finished meals shattering to the bricks beneath their feet.

Zeus was fast, but Kait was ready. The moment he moved, she slipped to the ground, his long fingers just missing the tips of her hair. Without pause, she dove into the awaiting wind and raced past Zeus's feet. He bellowed and picked the table up over his head before throwing it several yards into the street. By the time he realized what she had done, Kait was five hundred feet down the block, racing toward the portal.

She didn't look back. She had no idea how close Zeus was, but she knew the consequences if he caught her. Long translucent tendrils reached for her soul as the ethereal realm welcomed her home.

A swarm of faces greeted Kait as she descended from the air and stepped onto the wooden platform in Olean. A dozen nymphs stood assembled on the planks, waiting to depart for their assigned tasks. Once she regained her physical form, curious stares surrounded her.

"Kait, where have you been?"

"Are you all right?"

"What happened to you?"

The flood of voices enveloped her, but Kait ignored them all. She pushed past two anthousais who were blocking her path, their long black braids adorned with soft white petals.

"Bia?" Kait called out over the gathering crowd. "Has anyone seen my sister?"

Kait maneuvered through the staring eyes and reaching hands, escaping down the tall steps to the soft dirt below. Bia would be in the forest or secluded in the apothecary.

"Kait?"

"Kait, talk to us. We've been searching for you."

"Kait! Thank the goddess," Tressa's panicked voice called over the swell.

The aurai slid through the mass of nymphs and latched onto Kait's arm, holding her in place.

"I don't know what happened. The other aurais couldn't get in. We tried another portal over China, but by the time we arrived, you were gone, and we found…we found…the nymph's remains. We thought you were dead too."

Kait frowned, placing a comforting hand on Tressa's shoulder. "I'm sorry to worry everyone. The sandstorm was a trap. Zeus was waiting for me inside and sealed the portal. That's why no one could get through."

Tressa's eyes widened. "Zeus? But how?"

Kait shook her head. "I'm sorry, but I don't have time to explain. I need to find Bia."

Spinning away, Kait pulled out of Tressa's embrace and melted back into the wind. A few minutes later, she touched down in the western quadrant in a small meadow. There were only a handful of anthousais there, creating gorgeous flora to add pops of color to the endless sea of green, but not the one she sought.

Kait took to the blue sky once more, spiraling toward a new destination. The wind carried her back toward town, veering left before she reached the gossiping group still filling the square. The air peeled back, depositing her on the smooth stones leading to Tahlia's home. She strode through the curved archway and rapped her knuckles on the wooden door.

Muted movement could be heard through the thick bark. The door was wrenched open.

"Kait," Tahlia breathed, her eyes wide. "Where have you been? Tressa reported the portal to northern India was sealed with you inside. What happened to you?"

Kait stepped across the threshold, trying to rein in her nerves. Flickering sconces illuminated the room from above, and the scent of rose enveloped her. She took a deep breath, focusing on a climbing vine hanging from the open window.

"It was a trap. The aurai lost in the sands was a decoy. She was long dead by the time I managed to reach her, and before I could leave, Zeus sealed the portal."

"Zeus? But how? The scouts haven't reported any signs of immortal activity through the realms."

"I'm not sure. I managed to evade him in India and wound up in the American Northeast. I eventually collapsed in a place called Vermont. Every time I closed in on a portal back to the ethereal realm, something was blocking it, forcing me to remain in the mortal world."

"How did you manage to break through now?"

Kait sighed, exhaustion riddling her body. She fought to remain upright. She couldn't remember the last time she'd slept more than an hour or two.

"Zeus found me in New York City at a café full of mortals. There was an open portal a mile away. I'm not sure if he was unaware of its existence or was simply lying in wait for me to try, but there's another immortal working with him. I hoped to identify her, but only Zeus appeared. His desperation has reached a new level. His movements are wild, animalistic. I think his desire is overtaking logic. He no longer seems concerned with getting caught, either that or his precautions are getting sloppy."

Tahlia grasped Kait's hands. "Another immortal? Thank the goddess you escaped. I'll tell the queen at once. She will convene with the Council and agree on the best course of action to stop Zeus before he targets another."

"Except he's already targeting me," Kait whispered.

Tahlia's face fell. "I'm so sorry, Kait. This is my fault. I put you up to this."

Kait shook her head. "No, I wanted to help. It was my own fault for rushing into the mortal world. I didn't think he was that clever."

Tahlia placed a comforting hand on Kait's shoulder. "Well, it's all right now. You're safe here. However, I must petition an audience with Queen Rajhi immediately. This type of aggression is unprecedented, especially from one of the great gods. If Zeus has become as desperate as you claim, every nymph in the mortal world is in grave danger. We must suspend all portal travel and keep everyone within the confines of Olean until he is stopped."

Kait shook her head. "No, I can't stay here. There's a human boy. His name is Blake. Zeus is going to kill him."

"What do you mean? What motivation does he have to commit murder on a mortal?"

"It's my fault. He helped me, gave me shelter for the night. Now Zeus is going to kill him unless I give myself to his desire."

Tahlia's lips pursed. "A human? Kait, you know the laws. We can't expose our world."

"It was just for the night. He doesn't know anything. Please, Tahlia, help me persuade Queen Rajhi to bring him here. Let me keep him safe until I'm able to rid myself of Zeus."

"Absolutely not. No mortal has ever set forth in Olean. What little knowledge they have of us is shrouded in myth and legend. I will not permit the secret of our world to be shattered to save the life of one human. I'm sorry, my dear, but he must die."

Movement slithered in the corner of Kait's eye, but it was only the vine she'd noticed earlier. It seemed to be curling in on itself, no doubt shrinking from the growing tension in the room.

"How can you condone this? He's innocent. His only crime was helping me. We can't leave him for Zeus to pick apart."

"Unfortunately, that's not in your power to decide. I will speak with the queen. For now, we'll send a message throughout the realms calling every nymph to gather here. Once they've come, I'll look to you to remain calm and lead your sisters with a level head. Can I count on your discretion?" Tahlia asked, though it was more a command than a question.

Kait's mouth gaped open. As her elder, Tahlia's was an order she couldn't disregard, but what of Blake? She couldn't believe Tahlia would so easily dismiss his life. She closed her mouth and hung her head, her black hair falling over her face.

"Of course, Tahlia," she whispered, even though the words stung her heart.

Kait left a moment later. Instead of taking comfort from Tahlia's presence, she felt hollow and lost. How could she be so cruel? How could she disregard Blake's innocence?

Slipping outside, Kait headed back to the busy town. The other nymphs' lips moved with hushed words as soon as their eyes alighted on her, but the heavy stares hardly touched Kait as she maneuvered through the crowds. She had to find Bia.

"Have you seen Bia?" Kait asked a group of naiads blocking the archway to the main square.

The naiad in the center tossed her blond hair behind her, fixing Kait with a sneer. "That freak? I doubt she's in town. She's probably hiding, like always."

Kait's eyes clouded with rage, and the nymph named Shalise stepped back.

"Say what you want about me, but if you ever speak ill of my sister again, my winds will personally deliver you to Hades's door. Thanks for the help."

Before Shalise could compose herself, Kait strode away, doubling back the way she had come. Shalise was right about one thing: it was foolish of Kait to search in town. Bia hated crowds and, thankfully, the gossip that grew like weeds in town. It made more sense to check the forest, the meadows, and the apothecary.

Closing her eyes, Kait suspended all thought, relaxing into the swirling breeze ruffling the bottom of her dress. Gone was her flesh, replaced by the twisting wind. She headed for the pine woods first. Bia was fond of sprinkling the towering trees with pine cone blossoms. She swallowed her fear and anger at Tahlia's rejection. Once she let Bia know she was safe, she would escape to the human realm before the queen issued the travel ban. Kait refused to leave Blake unprotected. She only hoped Zeus was bluffing, or she may have failed already.

⚡ 19 ⚡

Kait broke away from the wind, exhausted. She had searched all of Olean, and Bia was nowhere to be found. Part of her wondered if her sister was avoiding her.

Kait curled beneath a pink dogwood tree, finally allowing herself a short break. Lazy petals kissed her hair and slid down her skin. Bia couldn't have left the realm. She knew how dangerous it was with Zeus circling the portals like a hungry shark.

But what if she'd come after Kait anyway?

Kait pounded her fist on the grass, but it was without anger. Of course Bia had followed her. Wouldn't she do the same if Bia never returned? She closed her eyes, cursing herself for not sending word earlier. Bia could be anywhere in the ethereal realm by now.

Pushing off from the cool grass, Kait sat up, her body full of tension. The hair on the back of her neck curled. She wasn't alone in the meadow. Her violet eyes narrowed, scanning the dancing trees in the distance, looking for a lingering shadow or unfamiliar silhouette. The petals blowing gently around her thighs scraped her skin, their soft touch suddenly sharp as needles. She swatted the delicate flowers away and returned her searching gaze to the tree line. A figure stood in front of her.

Kait fell back with fright, catching herself on her palms as a young nymph she didn't recognize stepped forward, raising her hands.

"Sorry. I didn't mean to scare you," the nymph whispered.

Her voice sounded like a bell, a perfect match to her soft features and waist-long brunette hair. Vines and beautiful flowers were woven into the dark strands. The pure white petals of a large lily grazed her round cheeks.

"My name is Haven. I have a message from your sister."

Kait's eyebrows shot up in surprise as she righted herself. "Bia? You have a message from her?"

Haven nodded, taking a seat in the grass and curling her short legs beneath her. Her pale skin was scarred with floral carvings, and several hemp anklets with tiny rose buds sprouting from each adorned her feet. Kait self-consciously rubbed her own skin. When she was younger, she considered getting marks too, enchanted by the fact that they heightened certain skills, but the pain that came along with it always stopped her.

"She came to me this morning," Haven began, brushing her hand along the grass.

"This morning? She's here? In Olean? I've just spent an hour looking for her. Where is she?"

Haven placed a soothing hand on Kait's arm, keeping her in place. "Gone, I'm afraid. She wanted me to tell you she's glad you're safe and not to worry. She'll take care of it."

"What?" Kait's brows lowered. "Take care of what?"

Haven shrugged. "I don't ask questions about the affairs of others. I am simply a vessel in which to pass the love of one sister on to another. It is not my business to pry."

"What are you talking about? Where did Bia go?"

Haven didn't reply. Instead, she cupped her hands and blew a long slow breath into the space. From the air, a vibrant flower bloomed in her palm, its petals unfurling as if reaching for the sun.

"Hey, Haven." Kait blew the flower out of her hands. "Bia. Where is she? Did she say where she was going?"

Haven's calm features wrinkled as the flower twirled away, riding the breeze until the wind dropped it on the grass several yards away. "No. She said you needed help, but she couldn't linger any longer," the anthousai said, her tone souring.

"Where did she go? Does she still think I'm in the human realm?" Kait rose to her feet.

Haven reached out to call a ladybug from the sky. "No. She saw you return."

Kait ground her teeth together, silently cursing the dreamy earthen nymphs for their eternal ease and carefree attitudes. Still, she tried to keep the frustration out of her voice. "She did? Why didn't she come to me?"

Haven lifted her leaf-green eyes to Kait and smiled sweetly. "I don't know. I've been out here all day and was returning home when she ran into me. She told me something big happened in the mortal world, but she didn't have time to explain." Curiosity sparked in Haven's gaze. "Do you know what happened?"

Kait shook her head. "The mortal world? But how would she know about that?"

She bit her thumbnail and tried to imagine her quiet sister.

I'm always listening.

Kait gasped as Bia's words washed over her. "Of course." Bia was nearby when she arrived, maybe even saw her go to Tahlia's. What if Bia had listened to their conversation? The image of the vine pulled at the back of her mind. Her stomach tightened as she cursed herself. Kait had one guess what she overheard.

Kait sprinted across the grass and leapt into the air until the wind cradled her body in its hold. She looked to the sun. It was approaching late afternoon. The queen may have closed the portals by now, but she still had to try.

The maples and birch soon gave way to spruce, pine, and evergreens, their dark colors creating an ominous feeling as Kait skimmed their narrow limbs. She was almost certain where Bia had gone and understood her sister's rush, for Kait would have swiftly prohibited it. She doubted very much that she would be able to stop her now.

⚡

The school bell trilled, announcing the end to another day. Blake slid his backpack onto his shoulder and followed the zombie-like crowd of dazed teenagers shuffling through the doors. He stepped into the dull sunshine, inhaling the crisp October air. It tasted cold.

A hard shove sent Blake stumbling. He caught himself against the concrete wall to the side of the stairs and scowled over his shoulder. Justin Lowell and his friends barked with laughter as they made their way to the football field around back.

"One day," Blake said, shaking his head. Another hard hit jolted him to the right. Without thinking, he pulled his fist back, ready.

"Whoa, whoa. Cool it, man. It's me." Joel leaned back to avoid the blow. "What's up with you?"

Blake shook his head. "Sorry, I thought you were Justin."

"I don't know why you let that guy get to you. He's a Chihuahua."

"Whatever," Blake said, falling into step with his friend.

"Are you amped for tonight? The concert is going to be crazy. I've been waiting for Faded Walls for months!"

Blake grinned. Joel's excitement was contagious. "Yeah, it's going to be sick. I can't believe your cousin got us tickets."

"Guess all those lame frat parties he invited me to were worth it," Joel said. "We can grab a pizza on the way back to my house. We've got time to chill."

They followed the path that looped away from the school down the steep hill, turning left toward the center of town instead of back to their neighborhood. To Blake's right, the woods loomed silent and watchful. He couldn't shake the eerie feeling that someone was watching him. Now, being outside, he felt even more exposed and vulnerable. The sooner they got to Joel's house, the better.

Curling brown and yellow leaves tumbled across the road and crumpled with a loud crunch every step they took. Blake sighed, debating if he should ask Joel if he felt it too. Blake shook his head, quieting the paranoia in the back of his mind. Digging the toe of his shoe into a leaf, he shredded it into decimated flakes, leaving the vein mangled and broken.

A tinkling bell announced their arrival at the fifties style pizza shop a few minutes later. The owner, Bart, nodded in their direction and finished at the sink behind the counter. Flour residue still clung to the hair on his forearms.

"Hey, my two best customers," he said. "What'll it be today?"

Joel slapped the counter. "Hey, Bart. Can we get two pepperonis to go?"

"Aye, you got it. Give Bart ten minutes to whip them up." Bart winked and gestured to the soda fountain at the other end of the counter across from the register.

"Get me a Coke," Joel told Blake. "I'm going to grab a quick smoke."

Blake rolled his eyes. Joel's previous cigarette butt was still smoldering on the sidewalk. With two cups from the condiment station, Blake maneuvered past the growing crowd as families and students poured in for an early dinner. Pressing the paper cup against the black dispenser, he waited until it filled with dark brown bubbles. Blake slid his own cup along the sticky grate next, intent on the root beer, when a cool breeze grazed his neck, followed by a light touch on his arm.

"Sorry about that," a husky voice said.

Blake glanced up, and his breath caught. He was staring at an angel. The woman was in her early thirties, with long, curling golden hair. Below high cheekbones, her lips were bright red and complemented her flawless tan skin. She was gorgeous.

The woman was dressed in a tight short-sleeved black turtleneck that hugged her chest and a clinging red skirt. Toned legs shone beneath, and her feet were wrapped in matching red heels. His eyes roamed back up to her face. Her gray eyes made his heart stutter.

"Uh, no. Sorry. I was in the way." His cheeks warmed as his words tumbled out.

The woman smiled, flashing white teeth, then turned to go. "Enjoy your drink," she said.

Blake watched her slide into an unoccupied booth several feet away from his own and cleared his throat.

Finishing with the sodas, he popped a plastic lid on both and spun around to head back to his table. The woman was staring at him. He swallowed and gave her a quick nod as he walked by, intent on the shaggy blond hair at their usual table along the wall, third booth from the door.

"That was fast." Blake set the drinks down as he took a seat. His eyes wandered back to the woman, but she was no longer looking at him.

"I only smoked half. I left the rest on the windowsill for the walk home." Joel reached for his cup. He took a large sip and grimaced. "Man, this is root beer. I told you to get me Coke."

Blake snatched the drink out of his hand. "I did, you idiot." He pushed the other cup toward Joel. "Did you even look?" He pulled his cup back.

Joel grunted before taking another gulp.

"Geez, you want to slow down a bit? It's not going anywhere."

Joel scoffed, then burped under his breath as he set the half-empty cup down. "Smoking makes me thirsty."

Blake shook his head and raised his cup to his lips, but a strange sizzling sound made him pause. Scrutinizing the soda, he tried to identify the noise. It was louder than the normal carbonated fizz, but only bobbing ice cubes met his gaze. Blake shrugged. He was being paranoid again.

"Are you hot?" Joel ran his hand through his shaggy hair.

Blake pursed his lips. "No, I'm fine. Why?"

Joel yanked off his sweatshirt. "It's so hot in here."

Blake looked around. "Maybe Bart just opened the oven?"

Joel shook his head, pressing his palms to his forehead and cheeks. "No. No, that's not it. I feel like I swallowed my cigarette or something. My body is on fire." Joel slammed his hands on the table, rattling the metal napkin holder and spilling the remnants of his Coke.

"Joel, are you okay?"

"No. My throat, my stomach—they're burning. I need water! Water, please! Water!" Joel coughed into his hands. When he pulled them away, they were wet with scarlet blood.

"What the hell?" Blake yelled, jumping to his feet. "Someone call an ambulance! Bart! We need help over here!" Blake ran to his friend's side, trying to hold him steady as another ferocious cough rattled him. More bright blood dripped between his fingertips, scattering across the table like crushed red peppers.

"Water," Joel croaked as a large bubble of blood popped on his lips.

"Christ! Hang on, hang on!"

Blake pushed concerned and curious observers out of the way as he raced to the soda fountain. He filled two large cups with water, then spun back toward their booth.

"Get out of the way! Move!" Cool water splashed against his fingers as he was jostled side to side.

"What's going on?"

"Is he okay?"

"We're calling 9-1-1!"

"What happened?"

A dozen people were shouting, trying to elbow their way closer to get a better look. Blake knocked them out of the way, desperate to reach Joel. He got stuck a few tables away as a toddler fell down, letting loose a shrieking cry.

"Move!" Blake shouted at the toddler.

In his periphery, a tendril of golden hair twitched. Blake's gaze found the woman. She was still seated at her booth, yet unlike everyone else, her eyes weren't on Joel. She was watching Blake. Her red lips were set in a firm pout, and her gray eyes regarded him with anger. Blake was taken aback by her hostile expression. A small eddy of grease-stained napkins and rumpled straw wrappers coalesced in a small tornado around him.

It should have been you.

⚡ 20 ⚡

While Blake paced across the scuffed tile floor of the waiting room, the doctor interviewed Joel's parents. He couldn't hear what was being discussed, but by the way the doctor kept pursing his lips and Joel's mother sobbed, he gathered they hadn't pinpointed the cause of the bleeding yet.

Joel's parents resumed their seats in the off-white plastic chairs and held one another. Then the police arrived. After speaking with Joel's parents and the medical staff, they questioned Blake, asking him to recount the events of the afternoon again and again.

"Did your friend do any drugs? Is it possible his cigarette was laced with something else?" the detective asked, circling back to the beginning.

Blake rolled his neck and squeezed his eyes shut against the pulsing fluorescent lights. "Like I said, he took it from the same pack he bought yesterday. He isn't on drugs. He didn't meet anyone outside the pizza shop. He didn't even eat anything. All we did was have some soda while we waited for our order."

"You had the soda as well?"

"Yeah, I—" Blake paused, remembering how he had almost taken a sip, but something had stopped him. "No. I filled both cups and sat down. Joel grabbed mine by mistake and then drank his. I was going to drink mine too, but I something made me pause. I remember hearing a weird sound."

"What do you mean, *weird*?"

"Kind of like a hissing."

"Hissing? Hissing how?"

"I don't know, like bacon frying in a pan. I guess the sound of something fizzing makes more sense."

The detective jotted down a few more notes and turned to his partner. "See if you can go back to the pizza shop and find those cups. There might be some residue left." The middle-aged man turned back to Blake. "Was there anyone who stood out to you? Anyone who might've wanted to hurt Joel?"

"Wait, back up, *residue*? Like you think someone poisoned him? Why?"

"That's what I'm asking you. Is there anyone he doesn't get along with at school?"

Blake shook his head. "No. There's this guy who bothers me, but Joel is cool with everyone."

It should have been you.

The woman. How could he have he forgotten her?

"There was this lady," he started. "She bumped into me at the soda station. Sh-She told me to enjoy my drink." Blake ran a hand over his mouth, wide-eyed. "Oh my God."

The pieces that had been bumping into one another in the back of his mind suddenly clicked into place. Her voice. It was the same one he'd heard the other night at home.

"A lady?" the cop said. "What did she look like? Ever see her before?"

"No. She looked like she stepped out of a magazine, tall and blond. She had on a black sweater and red skirt."

"Was she with anyone?"

"Not that I saw. When Joel started choking and everyone started getting frantic, she just sat there, staring at me." Blake left out the part about hearing her voice in his head.

"This is good." The cop nodded, tapping his clipboard. "Thanks, kid. If you think of anything else, give me a call at this number." He handed Blake a stiff card. *Detective Kramer* was stamped above a phone number and an email address.

Blake accepted the card and leaned back against the white wall.

It should have been you.

A shiver crawled up Blake's back, making the hair on the back of his neck bristle.

The poison was meant for him. If Joel hadn't drunk from the wrong cup, Blake would be the one lying in a hospital bed. But why? Why was that woman targeting him? He hadn't done anything to deserve such a hostile attack. And from a stranger?

Blake pressed the heels of his palms into his weary eyes as he stumbled out the front doors of the hospital. He had no idea what time it was. After one in the morning for sure.

Relief spread through him at the sight of the silver car pulling up to the curb. A wintry breeze slid down his throat, billowing across his stomach. He hugged his light jacket tighter around him and opened the passenger door.

"Hi, sweetie." His mother wrapped him in a hug. "How are you doing? How's Joel? I was going to come in and talk to his parents. Are they still here?"

Blake shook his head and rubbed his eyes. "Yeah, but they were speaking with the doctors again when I left. We can come back tomorrow. Joel is stable, but they're keeping him for a few days to run more tests, see if any other symptoms surface."

"I was so worried when I got your text. I thought something had happened at the concert, but this…" She let out a long breath. "I'm so sorry I'm just getting back."

"Mom, it's okay. I'm sorry I made you cancel your trip. Was Aunt Lucy disappointed?"

She pulled out of the parking lot and onto the street. "Of course not. She understands. I can visit her another time." They were both silent. "Are you sure you're okay?"

Blake nodded, playing with the cuff of his jacket. "Yeah, it's just…" He hesitated, unsure how much he wanted to reveal. "It's just scary is all."

His mom reached across the center console and gripped his hand. "I know, baby. But you said Joel is going to be okay, right? You can visit him tomorrow and hang out if he's feeling up to it. Maybe we'll get him a new video game to cheer him up or something?"

Blake smiled. "Yeah."

They pulled into their driveway a few minutes later. Blake gritted his teeth against the gathering wind as he waited for his mom to unlock the front door. Winter was baring its teeth.

Upstairs, he shrugged out of his jeans and shirt, yanked on a pair of ratty navy sweatpants, and collapsed into bed. Images of the afternoon played in his mind like a movie reel: the strange blonde, the weird voices, and the bright red blood as it spilled from between his friend's lips. It was all too much.

Turning to face the wall, Blake burrowed under the covers as the wind howled outside. It was going to be a long night.

Several hours later, Blake slipped into unconsciousness. In his dreams, terrifying monsters taunted him as he watched Joel choke on his own blood. A slithering python wound up his body, its weight crushing his ribs, threatening to snap them into brittle pieces. He stared into the snake's face and saw pale gray eyes leering back at him.

"It should have been you," the snake hissed, its muscled body constricting tighter.

Blake couldn't breathe. The snake was killing him.

"Wake up. I'm here to take you away." The serpent cackled, opening its gaping mouth, ready to swallow him whole. "Hurry. Wake up, wake up. I'm here for you."

Blake's eyes sprung open as his body propelled forward, rigid and alert.

"Let me go!" he cried. His chest heaved; sweat soaked his brow. Slowly, he realized his mistake. There was no danger. It was a dream. "One hell of a nightmare." He sighed. Blake relaxed against his damp pillow and exhaled. Shifting positions, he tried to curl his legs under his body, but the same weight he experienced in his dream persisted. "What the hell?"

"I'm here to t-take you away," a voice whispered from the shadows at the foot of his bed.

Blake followed the soft voice. The woman was in his room.

"Get away from me." Blake launched his pillow toward his feet as he glanced around for a heavier weapon. Save for his alarm clock, nothing was within reach. He threw back the twisted sheets and gasped. From his waist to his ankles, he was covered in wiggling snakes. A strangled cry fell from his lips as fear paralyzed him.

"Listen to me. You're in d-danger."

"Yeah, from you. How did you get in here? What do you want with me?"

With a tight fist, Blake pounded on one of the snake's bodies, bracing himself for the inevitable fangs, but no bite followed his onslaught.

Outside, the sky was beginning to lighten, night and dawn colliding in a hazy blue sea. Blake couldn't find where one snake ended and another began. There were no heads. He didn't know if he was relieved or terrified.

The stranger stepped forward. A dull red glow outlined her petite frame. Her features were cast in shadow, but her hands were white as bone. She raised them, flicking her fingers in an odd motion. In response, the snakelike bonds crawled upward, circling around Blake's chest and neck, only stopping once his mouth was securely gagged.

Blake's heart stuttered. He couldn't move, couldn't speak. The woman had incapacitated him. She moved closer, seeming to glide above the floor, and leaned in until her face was inches only away. The shadows peeled back. Blake was startled to see it wasn't the blond woman from Bart's, but a girl no older than himself. He stopped struggling when she began to whisper.

"I'm s-sorry about this. You were becoming too agitated. My presence here must go undetected. As I said, I'm h-here to take you away. You have nothing to fear from me, but we must leave now." Her light brown eyes were careful not to make eye contact. "Can I trust you to remain silent if I release you?"

Blake nodded, trying to keep his tongue from touching the gag as it continued to wriggle around his head. The girl straightened and flexed her fingers once again. As if by magic, the snakes released their suffocating hold, slithering off his skin and his bed to pool at the girl's feet like trained dogs.

"Thanks." Blake rubbed his jaw. "I hate snakes."

"Snakes?"

Blake pointed to the curling pets at her feet.

The girl tucked her hair behind both ears. "Oh, those are vines. I'm not s-supposed to tell you this, but I think a little breach of secrecy is warranted. I'm an anthousai. I don't have much talent for taming wildlife, just plants."

"A what?" Sleep deprivation was making it difficult to keep up.

"Blessed with the element of earth. Please, we m-must leave. You need to hide before he finds you." The girl's eyes danced feverishly.

Blake rose to his feet. "Before who finds me? What's going on? Who are you?"

The girl was stunning, pale and graceful, wrapped in a knee-length red dress, but beneath her beauty Blake could feel her anxiety.

"My n-name is Bia," the girl answered. "My sister Kait met you several days ago."

"Kaitaini?"

Blake's mind conjured an image of the beautiful girl he'd helped out of the water. Her words wove through his mind, and he remembered the way she'd spoken of her sibling and the rivalry between them. Blake frowned. He didn't get that impression from the girl in front of him. In fact, she was quite endearing with her stutter.

"You're her sister? You don't look alike."

Bia shook her head, glancing at the lightening sky beyond the window. "The concept is very different. Please, we m-must go."

Blake didn't move. "So, if you're sisters, does that make her an afoosi too?"

"Not. She's an aurai, blessed with the ability to c-control the wind."

"Control the what? What are you doing in my room?"

Bia hissed, checking the sky once more as her twitching hands began to flap by her sides. "Please, now is n-not the time for questions. A powerful god wants your life and will stop at nothing until he takes it."

"A what wants my life?"

"You sheltered his nymph. Zeus is d-desperate to claim my sister and isn't above murder if it helps him accomplish his goal. The aurai elder was going to leave you to die, so I came in Kait's stead to protect you."

The mattress wheezed as Blake perched on the edge, getting lost in the girl's strange words. Amidst his confusion, however, he caught one phrase: *leave you to die.*

"I should have been poisoned yesterday," he said.

"What do you mean should h-have?"

"My buddy and I went to a pizza parlor after school. There was a woman there. The cops think she poisoned our drinks. My best friend is in the hospital right now because of her." Blake rubbed his eyes.

"Why do y-you think you were the one she was after?"

"She told me. I heard her voice in my head after it happened. I think it was the same person I heard the other day too."

Wrinkles formed above the girl's eyes. She began to pace the messy floor, hands flapping wildly. "That doesn't make sense. I heard Kait only m-mention Zeus. Are you sure it was a female who threatened you?"

Blake scoffed, picturing the tight sweater and short skirt. "Pretty sure."

"I'm not sure who else is h-hunting you, but you can be sure they are no friend to you."

"So what do I do? Wait for these psychos to try to kill me again? What if next time they succeed?"

"That's w-why I'm here. I'm going to take you somewhere safe. As we speak, Kait is trying to beg the queen for your sanctuary in the only haven from the gods' influence."

Blake pondered her statement, trying to catch her eyes, but she continued to avoid him. She was right. None of this made any sense. Gods? Nymphs? It was as if he had fallen into a chapter of the *Odyssey.*

"Come on. You can't honestly expect me to believe this. A mythical god wants me dead for helping some girl in the woods, and now you want me to run off with you and what, hide in the trees?"

Bia's hands started to flutter once more. She slapped her thighs as her face crumpled. "I d-don't—I don't know. Kait said you needed help. I didn't wait to talk to her. I just came because she needed help. I traced the earth's memory of her to your house using the sensors. I thought you would be grateful."

Heavy tears streamed down Bia's cheeks. Her stutter went into overdrive, her words barely audible over her rapid breathing. Taking a step closer, Blake held up his hands.

"Hey, I'm sorry. I didn't mean to hurt your feelings. That was really nice of you to come…check on me." Blake wanted to say more, but he could see the girl wasn't listening to him. She was too upset. He let out a soft sigh, running a hand through his tousled hair. On the one hand, he wanted to comfort her, but how could her believe her? She was describing a fantasy movie. These things didn't happen in real life…

But the poison, the woman, the voice, the ever-present feeling of being watched, even meeting Kait under such strange circumstances—none of that happened in real life either.

Blake shook his head, too tired to think straight. The girl was becoming increasingly upset. A quiet rustling sound drew his attention upward, and his jaw fell slack as thick green moss bloomed in the middle of his ceiling and expanded to the far corners.

Maybe it was real.

"How long will I have to stay with you?" Blake wondered aloud, speaking before his decision was final.

Bia wiped her eyes, her cries receding. "I'm n-not sure. Until Zeus is eliminated."

"Eliminated? Like destroyed? But he's a god. I didn't think you could kill a god."

The nymph was silent for a moment, her hands fluttering gently now. "You c-can't."

Her words hit Blake like a punch in the gut. "So you're saying he'll hunt me forever? No. I'm sorry, but I can't. I'm not going anywhere. I'm not running away."

Bia took a step closer, her glassy eyes pleading. "It w-wouldn't be cowardly of you. This is about self-preservation."

Blake sighed. "It's not about me. What do you think Zeus will do if I disappear? Someone has already tried to kill me, practically killed my best friend. I can't leave my mom or Joel behind." He shook his head. "No. I'm not going anywhere."

Bia chewed her bottom lip. "I understand. You want to stay and fight. You think you're being noble, but you underestimate h-how cruel he is. Even if you die protecting those you love, there's nothing to stop him from killing them after you're gone."

Blake remained quiet. It didn't matter what Bia said. He couldn't abandon his mom, not after everything she went through to keep his father's fists from finding him. And Joel—what kind of friend would be Blake if he ran off and left him alone?

"Sorry to d-disturb you. Goodnight." The nymph turned toward the window.

Blake blinked, and she was gone. Like a vision from a dream that dematerialized the moment he opened his eyes.

He frowned and lay back down, pulling the twisted sheet up to cover his waist. He strained his ears, listening for the sound of footsteps on the crunching leaves below or the squeak of the back door, but nothing but the wind answered.

He closed his eyes, willing the darkness to take him away, but already dawn was creeping into his room, chasing away the dark. In the light, there were no places to hide, no dreams to distract him from the chaos of reality.

Sighing, Blake threw his arm over his eyes in a hopeless attempt to keep his doubts at bay.

⚡ 21 ⚡

*B*lake sat in the ugly maroon chair beside Joel's hospital bed. "Hey, man. How are you feeling?"

Joel raised his right arm and lifted his middle finger, an oxygen face mask covering his nose and mouth. Blake laughed and tossed him two tickets to another concert coming up the following weekend. It was a different performer, but hopefully it would help Joel feel better.

The door swung open, and a nurse entered, her face obscured by the light blue face mask stretched from ear to ear. She flipped a sheet up on her clipboard. "I'm just going to check your vitals, honey."

Joel gave a small nod, and his dark brown eyes found Blake. He tapped his index and middle finger to the mask over his mouth.

Blake smirked, understanding. "I can imagine the struggle, chain smoker, but this is for your own good. Plus, think what a cool story this will be to get girls."

Joel rolled his eyes. He didn't need any help in that department.

"I talked to the cops," Blake said. "There was a lady I didn't recognize at the pizza shop. I think she did something to your drink. I gave them her description, and they're probably getting close to catching her."

Blake hoped the information would cheer his friend up. If it did, Joel didn't show it. Instead, he just arched his eyebrows as his eyelids fluttered.

Blake reached out to touch his cold hand. "Joel, are you all right?"

The beeping from a nearby monitor blared in Blake's ears, and an uneasy feeling tugged at his gut. Something was wrong. Why was Joel's heartbeat slowing?

He jumped to his feet. "Nurse!"

"Yes, darling?" The nurse seemed distracted as she attended to Joel's IV.

"Something's wrong with him," Blake said, his own heart rate racing.

The nurse sighed. "I know. He's still breathing." She stood up from her bent position. "But this will take care of it."

With a swift tug, the nurse removed her mask, revealing dark red lips set in a pursed bow.

Blake's eyes traveled up, gasping as the same gray eyes of the woman from the pizza shop smiled back at him.

"He's lucky." She inclined her head toward Joel. "He won't feel a thing. Your mother on the other hand—she'll be in agony for days, until I drain all the blood from her pretty neck."

A throaty chuckle rang in Blake's ears. He opened his eyes. Gone were the stark white hospital walls, the slow beeping as his friend died, and the murderous gleam in the woman's eyes.

"It was just a dream." Blake shielded his eyes from the piercing sunlight. "A stupid dream."

Peeking through his fingers, he glanced out the window, a small part of him hoping to glimpse the girl from last night. The dream hadn't changed his mind, but he wished she was still with him. It would have been comforting to know he wasn't completely alone in this—whatever this was.

Without checking the time, Blake rolled out of bed and stumbled into the shared bathroom. He turned on the shower, praying the hot water would clear his head. Blake slid into the stall and closed the foggy glass door behind him. He sighed, arching his neck as the scalding water pounded against his skin.

"Blake!" a voice screamed, shaking him from his daze.

Blake slammed back against the porcelain wall, jostling the metal shelves. He opened the door, straining to hear the voice again.

"Mom?" he called, raising his voice so he could be heard over the water.

A moment of silence passed, and Blake shut the door. The shower filled with steam as the water turned his skin pink.

"Help me, Blake!"

The speaker sounded as if they were in the shower with him, the terror in their cry intense.

Shivers climbed his spine. Hastily, he wrapped a towel around his waist and ducked into the hall.

"Mom? Mom, are you okay?"

The soft carpet muted his footsteps as he crept to the opposite end of the hallway. His wet hair clung to his scalp, slimy and uncomfortable as it grazed the back of his neck. Cold water droplets trickled down his legs, splattering across the light carpet. The feeling of being watched was almost tangible, and he gripped the towel tighter.

Swallowing dryly, he reached his mother's room. The door was slightly ajar, the foot of the bed just visible. A gentle whoosh of air brushed his shoulders, like the tickle of someone's hair. Blake flinched, goose bumps rising along his arms. He bit his lip and began to push the door open while his heart pounded inside his chest.

"Blake!" a shrill voice bellowed from behind.

"Jesus Christ!" Blake yelled, crashing into his mother's room.

A huddled body lay beneath the sheets. His cheeks flared with embarrassment as he realized his mom was still safe and still asleep. Blake ran to his room, threw on whatever clothing his fingers touched first, and was out the back door a minute later.

Striding toward the woods, Blake frantically searched the yard, his heart hammering. He had no idea where to look, no idea if she was still in the area, but he didn't have much choice.

"Bia?" he called uncertainly.

A flock of sparrows shot into the air at his outburst. Blake flinched and called again. "Bia, are you here?"

"Not so l-loud," a soft voice whispered to his left.

Blake spun around, and his jaw dropped as a nearby tree moved. A shower of white petals fluttered from the limbs and mounted together until the petals gave way to flesh. The nymph from last night stepped forward.

Blake rubbed his eyes. Surely, he didn't just see her materialize before him. He took a steadying breath and shook the lingering echo of the haunting voice away. He was a fool to think he could handle this alone.

"I need your help."

"Tahlia! Tahlia, please!" Kait cried, bouncing on the balls of her feet.

Tahlia stood on the platform among the other elders, who had finished sealing the portals leading to and from Olean, an extreme safety precaution to keep any other nymph from falling prey to Zeus.

"Tahlia!" Kait called again, but there was too much noise, too much commotion in the square, and her shouts were lost.

With the orders announced, the assembled nymphs milled about, unsure where to go or what to do. They were cut off, trapped. Kait was shocked no one had fought Tahlia as she carried out the queen's order, but then again, she was an elder, and judging by the stern looks on the other elemental elders' faces, they fully supported the decision. After all, they were only trying to protect the nymphs of Olean, but Bia was still out there.

Kait groaned, shoving several anthousais out of her way.

Tahlia had reached the bottom of the staircase and was speaking with one of the aurais on her task force team. Kait slipped between two nymphs, ignoring the angry looks thrown her way.

"Tahlia," she exhaled. "I need to speak with you right away." Kait grabbed the elder nymph's elbow, steadying herself rather than pulling Tahlia away.

"Kait, I am very busy. It's going to have to wait." She brushed Kait's hand off her arm.

"No, this is important. It's about the portals."

"They will be reopened when the queen deems it appropriate. Relax. We are safe here. You are safe here." Her voice was sweet, but her stare was unyielding.

"But that's just it. We may be safe in here, but the nymphs out there are not." Kait pointed to the platform.

Tahlia narrowed her gaze. "All nymphs were ordered to return to Olean before the portals were sealed. I waited an hour. Everyone who was scattered throughout the realms returned."

"Except for one. Bia fled Olean before the portals were sealed. I think she overheard our conversation about the human. I think she's going to try to save him."

"That's not possible." Tahlia swallowed, her eyes wide.

"I checked the whole realm. She's not here. An anthousai named Haven delivered a message to me that confirmed my suspicions. If Zeus finds her with the portals sealed, she will have nowhere to run."

Clearing her throat, Tahlia scanned the square, which was still crowded with nymphs. "Excuse us, Jule. Make sure we are not disturbed."

The redheaded aurai nodded and spread her fingers. A concentrated wind cocooned around them, the fierce winds distorting their image and masking their voices, allowing them to speak in private. Tahlia gripped Kait by the upper arm and marched her several feet back against a cobblestone wall.

"What would you have me do? I've already set all of this in motion, for *you*."

"Open the portal. Let me find her and bring her back. Then you can seal us in until you deem fit. Please, I can't leave her unprotected, especially when she left because of me."

Tahlia stared at her, her jaw clicking. "You have made a mess of this. When you return, that's it. You resume your place among the aurai and leave the punishment of gods up to the Council. Do I make myself clear?"

Kait nodded.

"Good. Find your sister and get back. Send a sparrow when you are ready, and I will reopen the portal to Olean. But if you fail and Zeus captures you, know that the realm will not come to your aid."

Kait bit the inside of her cheek, but this was her only option. She bowed her head. "Thank you, Tahlia."

"I will open the portal to the human realm for a few seconds. From there, navigate to Vermont as quickly as you can. Stay hidden. You have my prayers for a safe journey."

"Thank you." Kait wrapped her elder in a quick embrace.

Tahlia hugged Kait to her chest and then pushed her away. "Go. You will only have a few seconds to exit."

With one last grateful look, Kait spun in the dark dirt and broke though Jule's barricade. Sensing a breach from within, the magic fell away. She slunk along the underside of the large platform, keeping to the shadows. No one paid her any attention, and she reached the other side undetected. She watched, waiting for the portal to ignite in golden ripples. She only had seconds. Tahlia couldn't risk the other nymphs seeing after her big speech.

Melting into the air, Kait drifted upward through the cracks in the thin slats, positing herself directly in front of the last portal. She glanced at Tahlia, worried the elder may have changed her mind. A low prickle of energy pulled her attention away from the stairs as the portal awoke.

Kait surged forward into the tingling waves. The moment her feet grazed the thick grass, the portal's energy collapsed, withdrawing until there was nothing but empty air behind her.

Kait set her gaze on the faraway hills of the mortal world. She would find Bia, but there was something she had to do first.

⚡ 22 ⚡

"Wait here, okay?" Blake told Bia over his shoulder.
"We agreed on five minutes, r-remember? We've already lingered too long." Bia took a seat in one of the hard plastic chairs in the hallway. Her fluttering hands gripped the edge of the seat, holding on tight, as if she might float away. For all Blake knew, she could.

Bia's eyes scanned the nurses scuttling back and forth and lifted the hood of her red sweatshirt. Changing her clothes had been Blake's idea. He didn't want the beautiful nymph to stand out more than she already did.

Blake drew in a quick breath and rapped his knuckles on the light wood, then pushed the door open. "Knock, knock. Are you decent?"

"I'm buck naked, but come on in," a weak voice called from the other side of a blue curtain.

Blake brushed the curtain aside to find Joel propped up in bed, his eyes heavy-lidded. "Hey, how are you?" He crossed the room and sat down on a bench underneath the window.

Joel pursed his lips. "I've been better."

Blake leaned forward, spreading his feet wide to rest his forearms. "So what did the doctor say? What happened?"

Joel rolled his head from side to side. Blake had never seen him look so weak. "They still aren't sure." He licked his dry lips. "My blood work came back clean. No cancer, no infection."

No poison. Blake wondered if the police had seen him yet.

"Basically, I'm a medical mystery. I feel okay now, just wiped. I could sleep for a week. But man, I could use a smoke," Joel said with a quiet laugh.

Blake's dream curled around his thoughts like a suffocating fog. The hairs on his arms prickled to attention, and his heart rate accelerated. The scenes were identical, and a sense of déjà vu distracted him as Joel rambled on. A sound in the hallway caused Blake to flinch.

"Look, I have to go," Blake said, cutting Joel off. For a moment, a hurt look crossed his friend's face, but Blake put up his hands to explain. "I'm putting you in danger just being here."

Joel cocked his head. "What are you talking about?"

"You don't have cancer or any crazy medical condition," Blake said. "For the past week, I've been hearing a voice, seeing creepy shadows. Yesterday, at Bart's, I saw this woman. She bumped into me at the soda stand and told me to enjoy my drink. Then, the second you took a sip, you started coughing up blood." Blake paused, trying to read his friend's blank expression. "It took me a while to realize it, but she was the same lady that I heard in my head. She put something in my cup, something that you drank by mistake."

The room was silent for a minute as Joel stared at Blake.

"That's a terrible joke. It's not even funny." Joel sighed, settling back into the pillows.

"It's not a joke."

"You're telling me you've been hearing a lady's voice in your head and then she tried to kill you by poisoning your soda? That doesn't make any sense."

Blake rose to his feet. "I know, but it's the truth."

Joel rolled his eyes and pulled the covers up to his chest. "Whatever, man. Just get out. I'm exhausted and need to sleep."

Blake put his hand on his friend's shoulder, giving it a light squeeze. "I'm not making this up. I wanted to take her to the police station, but she refused and vanished the next morning. I tried to forget the whole thing, but then I started hearing a voice, and I think someone's been watching me. After I left last night, a girl appeared in my room and told me she can protect me, that she can help me stop whatever this is. I know it sounds ridiculous, but I have to do something. I just...I needed to tell someone." Blake's fire began to simmer, and his confidence shattered as Joel regarded him with a dumbfounded expression. He sounded insane.

"I don't really know what to say," Joel admitted.

Blake nodded and took a step away from the bed. "I get it. I wouldn't believe me either without proof."

The door opened, and Bia sidled in, coming to stand at the end of the bed. With a graceful flip, she tossed back her hood, revealing satin scarlet hair and hypnotizing amber eyes. "Hello, Joel. I'm sorry this happened to you, but Blake and I r-really must go."

Joel leaned forward, visibly magnetized to the beautiful stranger. "Who are you?"

"Bia." She twisted her fingers in front of her.

"Was she the one in your room last night?" Joel asked.

"Yes," Bia answered curtly. She turned to look at Blake. "Please, we need t-to leave."

"Just give me another minute," Blake said.

Bia narrowed her eyes. "One m-minute."

"Leave?" Joel repeated as she walked out. "What's going on, man?"

Blake frowned, waiting until he heard the soft click as Bia exited. "I'm not supposed to say this, but a god wants me dead. I agreed to lay low for a few days until Bia can gather more information about the woman I saw at Bart's, the one who did this to you."

"Did you say *a god*? What does that mean?"

Blake put up his hands. "It's a really long story."

"Then give me the short version."

Blake glanced over his shoulder, expecting Bia any second. "There isn't time, and you won't believe me anyway."

"Try me."

Blake's lips pressed into a thin line as he contemplated telling Joel the truth he had only learned a few hours ago. What was the worst that could come of it? Joel wasn't going to believe it anyway.

"Fine. The girl I met the other day was a nymph, just like Bia. And she wasn't running from an old boyfriend, but a god—Zeus. Now Zeus is looking to kill me for helping Kaitaini. Bia is her sister, and she's here to take me someplace safe."

Joel stared at him, a glazed look in his eyes. "A nymph? Like, she can turn into a tree?"

"I know it sounds crazy, but it's the truth." Blake looked over his shoulder again, but they were still alone. "I'm sorry to drop all this on you, but I have to go."

"Dude, I'm coming." Joel threw back the thin blanket covering his legs.

Blake was taken aback. "What? No way. You can barely keep your eyes open."

Joel shrugged. "You just said you're going to be lying low. I can chill, rest up, and then help you fight whoever did this to me."

Blake shook his head as his friend began to scour the room for his clothes. "Absolutely not. You're going to get yourself killed. I don't even know what all of this is yet."

Joel groaned. "Come on, Blake. You're always talking about how you want to get out of here and do something noteworthy. This is it, man. Plus, I can't say I'm mad about spending a few days with *her*," he whispered under his breath. "Have you seen my pants?"

Joel spun around the room, the back of his hospital gown flapping open to reveal his butt. A metallic ring scraped the rod as Bia pulled back the curtain.

"We need to leave now. The hallway is clear." She froze as she noticed Joel moving about the room. "What's g-going on?"

Joel jerked upright, leaning an elbow on the bed rail. "Hey, I'm coming along."

Bia's lips parted as she glared at Blake. "You t-told him? Didn't I explain not to do that?"

"I'm sorry. He's my best friend. I just gave him a few details."

Bia's eyes flickered back to Joel. "My mission is to p-protect Blake. Kait didn't mention you."

Blake threw up his hands. "I didn't invite him. He won't listen to me."

"Oh, come on." Joel strode toward Bia. "Afraid you might like my company?"

Bia's fingers blurred, and the same vines that had wrapped around Blake earlier were now curled around Joel's lanky frame. "Let m-me make this perfectly clear," Bia whispered. "I have no interest in y-your games. I came here to help my sister save *Blake*. If you accompany us, know that I will do nothing to protect you from whatever f-follows. Understand?"

Joel's eyes widened with fear, in response to his wiggling bonds or the icy threat in the nymph's voice, Blake wasn't sure.

"Maybe he can help," Blake volunteered, trying to diffuse the tension.

"No," Bia said. The vines retreated, leaving Joel wobbling on his feet. "He's a l-liability. This rescue mission is becoming more complicated than anticipated."

Bia's hands resumed their flapping as she bit her lower lip, chewing on the already raw tissue. He didn't like causing her stress, but he couldn't leave Joel behind.

"Please, Bia. Joel was poisoned because of me. I didn't come here to bring him with us, but he went through hell last night."

Bia exhaled, setting her eyes on Blake's chest. "Fine, but the moment he begins to slow us d-down or jeopardize your safety, we leave him behind. Got it?" Both boys remained silent. "Hurry up. This p-place feels wrong."

Joel combed his shaggy hair with his fingers. "Okay, okay. Just let me find my pants."

Blake spied a folded pile on the back of the padded bench—jeans and dark green shirt. "Here, man. Get dressed and meet us outside." Blake tossed the clothes onto the bed.

Joining Bia in the hallway, Blake leaned against the wall and slipped his hands in his pockets. "What do you mean this place feels wrong?"

Bia wrinkled her nose and crossed her arms over her chest, her fingers tapping. "I've n-never been in an apothecary like this. Your entire world is so sterile and forced. It's suffocating." One hand fluttered against her throat. "I'll feel better once we g-get back outside. Is your friend almost ready?"

"I think so."

"When we leave, you will need to do exactly as I s-say, all right? I need to transport us to the nearest portal back to Olean."

"Sure." He was about to say more when Joel joined them. "Ready?" he asked his friend.

"Yeah, I can't wait to get out of this place." Joel took the lead and started down the hallway.

Blake yanked him back by the collar of his T-shirt. "Keep your head down. You're a patient under care. You can't just leave because you feel like it," he said under his breath as they passed a group of nurses.

"Oh, right." Joel lowered his eyes to the white tiles.

The trio brushed passed the nurses' station situated three rooms down on their left. Blake fixed the nurse behind the desk with a brief smile and a wave. "Thank you."

The nurse glanced up, her eyes smiling. "Have a great day," she called, oblivious to the fact that their party had expanded.

"All right," Bia said. "When we g-get outside, we need to find a deserted area. Then I can transport you to the—-"

"And where do you think you're going?"

The trio turned to see a beautiful woman dressed in traditional blue scrubs staring daggers at them. Blake recognized the voice even before he saw the gold hair and gray eyes.

"I just needed to get out and stretch my legs," Joel replied.

She ignored Joel, stalking across the few yards separating them. "You're not taking them anywhere, nymph. He's mine." The woman pointed a triangular nail at Blake's chest.

"Hera?" Bia gasped. "What are you doing h-here?"

The goddess smiled, and a tremor tweaked Blake's spine. He took an involuntary step forward.

"That's none of your business. Hand over the boy and I'll spare your pathetic existence."

Blake took another step.

Joel put up his hands. "We were just on our way out."

"Do you think I like coming to this wretched realm?" Hera asked, ignoring Joel. "Your kind are a rancid infestation that must be cleansed. Your whore of a sister determined this one's fate." She gestured to Blake. "If you're smart, you'll take that one and run before I change my mind."

Bia stood her ground. "I can't let y-you do that, Hera."

Hera tossed her long curls to the side and sighed. "What a shame."

With the flick of her hands, the hallway exploded. A high-pitched popping sound like gunshots cracked as the windows to several nearby rooms imploded, showering them with jagged glass. Wheelchairs leapt into the air, careening toward them from every direction. The lights from above crackled and shattered in a series of orange sparks.

"Get down!" Bia screamed, throwing up her hands.

Joel and Blake hit the floor, curling their limbs close to avoid the battered tiles. Nurses screamed and ran, desperate for any makeshift protection they could find. From her crouch, Bia threw open her hands. Ferocious vines snaked through the air toward Hera, each tipped with needle-like barbs.

"Is that the best you can do?" Hera smirked, unimpressed.

She raised her arms, and the vines' progress halted. Instead, they waved gently in the air. Hera smiled and brought her hands together in a powerful slap, igniting the vines with white-hot flames. Under the fire's touch, the plants sizzled and disintegrated, leaving a trail of black ash twirling toward the floor. The flames licked and gulped, devouring Bia's magic with frightening speed. Bia tried to separate herself from the vines, but Hera was too quick. Seconds later, the fire reached her, consuming her hands greedily. Bia shrieked, trying to smother the flames with a nearby sheet that lay crumpled at her feet.

Hera laughed as the flames engulfed the dirty linens and lapped at Bia's pant legs. "I was hoping for a better fight." She sighed, rotating her finger in a small circle. The fiery sheet mimicked her action, rising off the floor like an angry cobra ready to strike.

A metallic flash glinted in the corner of Blake's eye. Amongst the spilled carts and shattered glass lay a silver tray. Blake clutched it in his hands and stood, taking advantage of Hera's distracted focus to flank her. He brought the tray over his head, then swung down, straight at Hera's skull, but there was no collision, no impact. The tray and Blake continued through Hera and to the floor. The tray rattled, then bounced up and ricocheted into his face.

Hera glanced away from Bia. The sheet dropped to the floor. "Sorry to disappoint. I should have warned you I don't fight fair." Her hypnotizing eyes flashed dangerously. She rotated at the waist, reaching for Blake, her nails ablaze.

Reacting on instinct, Blake crouched behind the metallic tray just as Hera unleashed her molten fire. The flames roared, eager to taste Blake's skin, but rather than biting into flesh, the fire bounced off the metal shield and seared the air over her right shoulder. Hera shied away from the flames, but not before they singed the skin along her jaw. Holding her burned flesh, Hera screamed and collapsed to the floor.

"Run!" Blake cried, scrambling to his feet. Taking advantage of Hera's momentary lapse, he raced forward, wrenching Joel up by his underarms. "Move! Stay with Bia!"

The small group ran as fast as they could. Bia charged forward, waving a curious orderly out of the way with the flick of her wrist. The large man went flying, the soles of his shoes lifting off the debris-strewn floor.

Up ahead, the front doors loomed.

"Hurry, get out and run to the b-back of the building!" Bia shouted.

Blake and Joel sprinted after Bia, skirting the few stairs and jumping the metal railing. Their feet hit the sidewalk, and they continued running until they reached the edge of the parking lot out back.

"Now what?" Joel leaned against the brick wall to catch his breath.

Bia held up her hands, and Blake winced. Her skin was marred with vicious red burns. The several large blisters were causing her fingers to swell. Her fingertips were scorched an ashy black.

"It'll just t-take me a second." She closed her eyes. Her damaged fingers moved, the intricate patterns slow and clunky. The air before them began to shimmer, like staring through a bubble.

A piercing blast exploded beside Bia's head. All three of them ducked as a shower of bricks and mortar slammed into the ground.

"Look at what you did to my face!" Hera screamed, her once husky voice now shrill and coursing with hatred. "I will carve your eyes from their sockets and feed them to the crows. No one escapes me!"

More bricks blasted outward from the rear of the building as the goddess strode through the rubble.

Blake turned to Bia. They had no weapons and were completely exposed. Hot, red blood pulsed down Bia's temple. A shattered brick lay at her feet.

Blake moved to support her. "Bia, what do we do?"

A look of blinding pain crossed the nymph's delicate features as she squeezed her eyes shut. "Jump," she whispered.

"What? What did she say?" Joel flung a brick in Hera's direction.

A maniacal laugh echoed across the parking lot as Hera deflected it.

"Jump?" Blake repeated.

Bia lifted her arm, extending a shaking finger toward the pavement. A large sinkhole erupted inches from their shoes. Joel's heels were already teetering over the edge.

"What? You're joking!" Joel stared at her with wide eyes as a tornado of bricks and building debris hurtled toward them.

"Jump or d-die." Bia's eyes rolled into the back of her head as she tipped sideways into the dark void at their feet.

Joel's mouth fell open. "Christ. What do we do?"

Blake gritted his teeth. Hera was almost on them. Flames danced in her palms. Her lips curled. "Jump!"

He stepped off the eroding edge, plunging into the endless black.

⚡ 23 ⚡

Kait slumped, resting atop the white sand. Warm waves lapped around her, the gentle roar lulling her into a hazy slumber. The shifting sand pulled and ebbed beneath her. A lazy seagull called above as it circled the beach.

It was Kait's first time at Mākua Beach on the western shore of Oahu, Hawaii. She remembered Hermes speaking of it. Its beauty, tranquility, and seclusion made it an ideal destination for immortals to visit when escaping to the human realm, a fact she was going to hedge her bets on today.

An eerie feeling swept over Kait as the calm waters kissed the shore. Apart from a few scattered humans a few thousand yards away, she was alone. She closed her eyes and tasted the flavorful air. The sun shone bright red behind her eyelids.

The beach was gorgeous. Maybe after all this was over, she would come back and actually enjoy it. This time, she was there as bait. It was the only way she could ensure Zeus wasn't hunting Bia. It was a risk. If Kait was caught, no help would come to her rescue as Tahlia warned.

Drowning her troubling thoughts, Kait pulled up her dress and exhaled, reveling in the way the sunlight kissed her naked skin. Positioning herself out of the water's reach, she lay on her back, wiggling her toes in the hot sand.

"What are you doing here?"

Kait sat up, squinting into the sun. She didn't recognize the lovely creature standing above her. "I'm sorry?"

"You're not supposed to be here. I heard rumor that all nymphs were forced back to Olean. Something big brewing?"

Kait fixed her dress, narrowing her gaze at the young woman. Obviously, she was part of the ethereal realm, but her nature evaded Kait. "Who are you?"

The woman tossed her long blond hair behind her, exposing her almost translucent skin beneath. She smiled, her teeth like a shark.

Kait gasped. "A siren?" Jezlem had told her stories of the fierce water creatures when they were younger, but born with the gift of air, Kait avoided the water, especially the open oceans where sirens were said to haunt.

"I'm Peisinoe. Normally, I don't frequent the shallows, but its mating sea-son for great whites and I'm hungry." Her glassy eyes and unnerving smile rattled Kait. "I caught sight of you on my way in. Being naughty, are we?" she purred.

Kait pushed off the sand to her feet. "No. I have special permission to be here."

Peisinoe's eyes narrowed. "Special permission to lounge on a beach? I don't buy it." A silver bikini hugged her curves. Kait shivered; the siren's allure was strong. Now she understood why mortal men drowned just to be close to them.

Peisinoe licked her bottom lip. "Do you swim? Want to help me hunt?"

She eyed the humans far down the shore, unsure what exactly a siren's prey was. "Sorry. I'm waiting for someone," Kait said, dodging the siren's touch as she reached for her hand.

"Waiting for who?"

"Zeus. Have you seen him?"

"Not lately. What are you doing together? I thought you stayed in your own little circles. Though, you're missing out being sequestered from the gods. Posei-don is delicious. The way he makes me squeal." She giggled with delight. "How's his brother?"

Kait shook her head. "He's a demon. I would never lie with him. He raped my sister. Now my other sister is in danger of the same fate. This is the only way I can keep her from harm."

"By sacrificing yourself?"

"More or less." Kait clenched her teeth.

"Well, seems like you're already hunting, then. I'll leave you to it. I'm going to introduce myself to those fine-looking morsels—I mean, mortals—playing volleyball down there."

Kait grimaced. Part of her wanted to protect the unsuspecting humans, but the other part was terrified of the siren.

Peisinoe snapped her head to the right, scanning the lush jungle a few yards behind them.

Kait followed the siren's gaze. "What?"

"Just the trees. I thought I sa—" She gasped. A solid thunk sounded as a scream whistled from beyond the trees.

"What was that?" Kait's skin crawled with unease.

Frantic movement caught her eye. Several hundred yards down the beach, a human girl emerged from the tree-lined path. She was running—no, sprint-ing—toward Kait. Tears poured from her eyes. Kait glanced behind her but saw no pursuer. That's when she realized the girl was shouting, but Kait couldn't hear her over the crashing waves.

"Peisinoe, do you see this?" Kait pointed. The siren remained silent. She spun around to face her. "Can you hear—oh my goddess!" Tears sprung to her violet eyes.

A sleek, black quill protruded from the base of Peisinoe's throat. Her once lively eyes were clouded and shiny with death. Her skin was the color of a dead fish. A fountain of blood bubbled over the siren's bottom lip, running down her chin and splattering her neck like tribal war paint. Kait fanned her hands. She aimed to help, to lay her down at least, but the other end of the lengthy quill was buried in the sand, forcing her to remain upright.

Kait's head swiveled, trying to locate the beast that shot the quill. It could only be one animal. She had to move.

Several cries erupted in Kait's ears as her adrenaline kicked in, heightening her senses. Down the beach, the few other humans fled, running for cover in the thick jungle. She turned back to the sprinting girl. A gathering sandstorm nipped at her heels. Kait took a step to the right just as another quill sailed through the sky, the poisoned tip biting into the sand inches from her foot. The girl's cries reached her ears.

"Run!" the girl shrieked as a sudden torrent of lethal quills rained down around them, puncturing the picturesque paradise.

Silver claws extended from the swirling sand behind the girl, hooked into her back, and yanked her to the ground. A ferocious growl erupted as the beast tore into her, ending her life. Raising its menacing mustard eyes to Kait, the piriol licked its blood-stained muzzle. Its lips pulled back in a snarl.

"Kaf," Kait breathed. This wasn't the plan. No one was supposed to die. Why would he unleash the piriol in plain sight? Why attack humans? What was Zeus thinking?

The wind roiled around her, tugging and pushing her to change. He was growing even more careless, frantic to claim her.

As if it could hear the wind coaxing her, the piriol hissed, its lips pulling farther back to reveal daggerlike teeth. Kait listened to her element. She leapt into the wind, her flesh disappearing, and directed the salty breeze into the humid jungle encroaching on the white sand. She didn't look back, hurtling herself through the thick foliage, twisting and rolling through the vivid flora. But the piriol wasn't an easy hunter to flee. They never lost a quarry. That's why the gods turned them loose. They were the ultimate weapon.

Kait pushed herself through the heavy air as fast as she could, but there was too much humidity. She could feel the piriol catching up, feel his breath on the wind's tendrils surrounding her, but in the air, at least she stood half a chance. Just a little farther.

Bursting through the dark canopy of leaves, she raced on, her target shining like a beacon, calling her to safety. Death cried out as the piriol killed another unlucky human to cross its path. Their final breaths carried on the wind, whispers filling her mind. Kait mourned their pain, held their anguish, and tasted their sorrow. She was the common thread linking their deaths. She'd killed them all.

Kait pushed the fevered whispers from her thoughts.

She spiraled down beneath the trees' shady leaves. The network of portals that connected the human realm rippled just beyond the next tree. If she could reach it, she might be able to lose the piriol.

The muggy air seemed to hang stagnant, as sticky and immovable as honey. Kait's breaths came out in short gasps as she strove forward, pushing the breeze harder. From far away, another snarl rattled her teeth. A shiver gripped her spine. The air split apart, and a loosed quill found its mark, slicing into her side like a toxic needle. In the same breath, she fell from the sky, the toxin in the quill immobilizing her elemental connection.

Kait wheezed as her chest smashed against the damp earth and all the air in her lungs was forced out between her teeth. She spared a quick look at her side and gritted her teeth, feeling the poison enter her bloodstream. She had to remove it. She didn't know what would happen if enough toxin filled her heart. If only Zeus were kind enough to let her die.

Inhaling sharply, Kait wrapped her hand around the sleek quill and jerked it upward, screaming as it slid out of her flesh. Scarlet blood pulsed from the wound, soaking the thin material of her dress in seconds. She squeezed her eyes shut against the brilliant pain. A throaty growl echoed close by as the pounding of swift feet caused the dirt beneath her palms to tremble. She had to get up.

Pressing her filthy hand to her side to staunch the flow of blood, Kait rose unsteadily to her feet. Sweat pulsed down her face as she stumbled through the unforgiving jungle toward escape. Before her, a giant leaf split in two as another quill rent the air. The smell of blood and dirt made her head swim. The desire to lie down and float away was overwhelming, but she couldn't give up, couldn't let him win. A string of tears fell down Kait's cheeks as she made her feet take a few more steps. She was almost there.

The piriol rasped, right behind her. The heat of his breath grazed her calves. Searing pain engulfed her as the animal raked her skin with its claws, shredding her flesh. She stumbled to the right, but a powerful hit from a large paw sent her sprawling forward instead.

Kait collapsed over a moss-covered rock. Her neck snapped with the momentum. With blurring vision, she turned her head, waiting for the piriol to deliver the final blow when she slipped and fell through the cool air, as if she had leapt from the top of a towering tree.

A pair of solid arms caught her, cradling her petite frame against a muscled torso.

"Right on time, my sweet. Rest now. You'll need all your strength," the deep voice whispered as the pain capsized, claiming her consciousness.

⚡ 24 ⚡

B lake was dead. He was sure of it.
He'd leapt into the giant sinkhole and crushing darkness. The fall wasn't like in the movies, when the hero bravely jumps and falls stylishly for a minute before landing in a cool pose. Instead, Blake kicked off at a funny angle and twisted his ankle, smashing his shoulder against the opposite side of the hole. The gaping maw wasn't wide either. It swallowed Blake easily, but as he fell, the sides of the gullet narrowed. He jolted his leg, his foot, his elbow, and his head as he banged against the rocky soil in the pitch-black until the soles of his shoes reached the ground—or whatever surface was below that.

Now Blake stood there, confined as the dirt walls constricted around his body. A quiet hiss resounded as dirt and sand trailed down the front of his shirt, piling atop his scalp while the earth digested him and eradicated his small pocket of air.

"Help!" Blake shouted, but there was nowhere for the words to go. He'd jumped into his own coffin, buried twenty feet under. "Joel?" An eerie silence followed as the dirt pressed closer. Blake barely had enough room to inhale. "Bia!" he cried, using the last of his air. Could this entire thing have been a trick? Was Bia helping Hera capture him?

He tried to wiggle free, but his arms were pinned to his sides. Blake moved his fingers, but all he felt was shifting dirt pressing tighter and tighter as it filled the remaining gaps. His tomb would be nice and snug. He was an idiot.

He closed his eyes, waiting to suffocate and for death to wrap its scythe around his neck. Tiny clacking sounds whispered in his ears, and something long and wet brushed the small trace of bare skin still exposed on the back of his hand. Bugs. Blake tossed his head from side to side, envisioning thousands of beetles scurrying up and down his neck, burrowing into his ears. His breaths were shallow puffs, blowing the dry dirt back and forth over his lips. Why couldn't death be swift?

Blake yelled as antennas tasted his forehead. A sudden rolling sensation pressed against the soles of his feet, pushing him back up through the displaced earth. Faster and faster the source drilled. Blake closed his eyes and shut his mouth, but dirt still managed to slip onto his tongue and fill his throat.

At last, the pressure of his momentum crested, shooting him through the grassy surface above. He rocketed into the sky and free-fell back to the ground, blind as clods of dirt clung to his face. Blake sucked in as much of the glorious air as he could. He landed with a muted thud, his right arm twisting painfully behind him, but he didn't care. He lay on the ground, inhaling to the point of pain.

A few minutes later, Blake forced himself to roll onto his back. With weak arms, he dusted the clinging dirt from his sweating skin. Above, a fuchsia-streaked sky glowed as the sun completed its descent, painting purple and navy streaks in its wake. He sat up. A shower of sand and earth slid from his hair.

Blake coughed, tasting rocks and wet dirt. He inhaled deeply once more. He was sitting on a grassy knoll overlooking a beach. The shore was deserted, and the waves created a soothing melody as they crashed against the sand. Bia was nowhere in sight, but there was a dark shape slumped at the bottom of the hill. Joel.

"Joel!" Blake jumped to his feet.

He stumbled down the small incline, forgetting about his sore ankle until he stepped on it. Sharp pain caused his leg muscles to seize, but he ignored it, doing his best to hobble.

"Joel? Are you okay?"

Blake flipped his friend onto his back. His stomach lurched as he took in Joel's limp body. He looked like a corpse; his limbs flopped uselessly at his sides. Rich, dark brown dirt covered his pale skin and darkened his blond hair. His shirt was a mess, and Blake held back his revulsion as a centipede scuttled across his torso.

"Come on, man. Breathe," Blake begged, patting Joel's cold cheek. His fingers felt around, searching for a pulse, but they came away empty. "Breathe." Blake pressed down on his friend's chest, starting compressions. "You better wake up, man, because there is no way I'm giving you mouth-to-mouth. Breathe!" Blake continued to press steadily for two minutes. His muscles burned, and his own breathing was ragged with the exertion. "Come on!"

Blake pressed down a few more times, and Joel's eyes fluttered opened. A wheezing sound erupted from his parted lips as he breathed on his own for the first time in minutes. Blake leaned away, sighing in relief as Joel rolled onto his side, coughing grass, dirt, and grit from his mouth. Finally, he lay back and looked at Blake.

"Thanks, man," he whispered. "Two near-death experiences in one weekend. Maybe I'll just quit while I'm ahead." A soft, strained laugh slipped from his lips.

"Here, give me your arm." Blake bent down and helped Joel up, supporting the bulk of his weight as he leaned on him. Hot pain crackled up Blake's leg once more, but he forced it down.

Joel looked out over the ocean. "Where are we?"

Blake spun around in a circle, slipping on the loose sand. "I have no idea. Somewhere with palm trees."

"How did we get here?" Joel's voice was rough, like he'd swallowed a sheet of sandpaper. He stepped out from under Blake's embrace as they reached the edge of the beach.

"Bia, remember? We jumped into the hole and ended up here."

"But where did she go?"

Blake didn't answer as his anger flared. "Come on. We need to find a road and some water." He gestured for Joel to ascend the grassy hill first, not yet trusting his friend to make the climb without falling. A few hundred yards away, houses loomed and streetlights buzzed overhead like annoying mosquitoes. "We're almost there."

"Blake!" a voice yelled.

"Did you hear that?" Blake asked, straining to hear over the crashing waves.

"Hear what?"

"Blake!"

His name fell around them again, but this time it was unmistakable, as was the speaker.

"Bia?"

"Blake! Joel!" Bia said, the relief in her voice palpable. "Thank the goddess. I've b-been looking for you for over an hour!"

Bia climbed up the bluff to meet them, still clothed in the same jeans and red hoodie from the hospital. A large gash split the smooth skin on her forehead, and a trail of dried blood had crusted to her cheek.

"What happened?" Joel stumbled as he tried to balance on the hill.

Blake steadied him, stepping in front of his friend. "Yeah, Bia, what happened?" he asked, his tone hostile. "Why did you tell us to jump? Are you working with Hera? Do you even know Kait? Why did you pretend to help me?" His questions fired like a machine gun, allowing no time for the nymph to answer.

"Blake, what are you talking about?" Joel asked.

"Can't you see? She set us up." He pointed a stiff finger to where Bia stood, the sand covering her bare feet. "She meant for us to die back there, and now she's probably here to finish us off."

Blake glanced around for a sizeable weapon, but nothing except small pieces of dried seaweed and brittle twigs of driftwood met his gaze.

Bia put up her hands, her large eyes pleading. "No, p-please. You don't understand. I didn't mean for you to get stuck. I'm so sorry."

"I don't want to hear it. I can't believe I trusted you." They weren't too far from a cul-de-sac. They could make it.

Joel jerked out of Blake's hold. "Dude, chill out and let her talk."

"Please," Bia said before Blake could refuse. "I came here to protect you. To take you someplace s-safe. I tried transporting us to the outskirts of the portal, but Hera's explosion struck me. I passed out before I could complete the spell. That's why you got s-stuck. It took me forever to find you. As an anthousai, I am connected to the earth. It remembers all who walk upon it. By channeling the sensors in the soil, I can usually locate anyone's past activity easily. Each person leaves their own visible, unique signature, but with you inside the earth, it was harder. I'm amazed you're both alive."

"Yeah, well, so am I," Blake said bitterly. The distress in her voice seemed genuine. Her hands fluttered against her thighs. After what happened, he didn't trust her, but he did believe her. "What now? Where are we?"

Bia frowned. Fresh blood dotted her fingers. "If the magic I cast after I woke worked, we should be near my sister's house in Vero Beach, Florida."

"Another sister? Wait, you have a human sister?"

"It's complicated. Come. We're t-too exposed here. The sensors are pinpointing that blue house as hers." Bia turned toward the third house on the right on the opposite side of the cul-de-sac.

Blake paused for a minute. He had no idea what to think. The whole thing was getting out of hand, bordering on crazy. He should have never agreed to come. He considered grabbing Joel and walking until they found a freeway. Maybe they could hitch a ride back to Vermont.

Blake sighed, pushing Joel in front of him. "Come on. Let's go."

"Do we think we should trust her?" Joel asked, still weak from their ordeal.

Blake scoffed and looked back at the tomb he'd crawled out of. "No, but we don't have much choice at the moment."

Bia rapped three times on the white front door, then stepped down onto the bottom concrete step. Blake and Joel hung back.

"I'm not sure what her reaction will b-be," Bia admitted, a worried expression replacing her pained grimace from before.

Joel paced back and forth in the short driveway. He plunged his hands in his pockets, only to take them back out and crack his knuckles, flex his fingers, and then chew on his thumbnail.

Blake glanced at him. "What's wrong with you? Why are you so jumpy?"

Joel groaned and scratched his neck. "I need a smoke."

"You better get used to it, man. I don't think we'll be stopping at a convenience store anytime soon."

The distant echo of footsteps could be heard moving within the house, and a dark figure stopped at the edge of the front window. The corner of the lacey curtain twitched, but the movement was too fast for Blake to make out any details. A moment later, the front door peeled back. Pale yellow light shone down from somewhere in the house, cloaking the small sliver of the figure in shadow.

"What do you want?" a crisp voice asked.

"Jez? It's me. We need h-help."

Blake could hear the pain in her scratchy plea.

The door flung open, revealing a beautiful blonde clad in white shorts and a teal halter top.

The girl gasped. "Bia? Goddess, what are you doing here?" She sprinted down the few steps to her sister's side. Her large aqua eyes scanned the darkness behind Bia, and she jerked backward, as if stunned. "Who are they?"

Bia didn't spare them a glance. "Let's get inside first." Jezlem didn't move. Her hands were rigid by her sides. "Jez, trust m-me. They're good guys."

"Fine. Come in…all of you."

Joel looked to Blake and fell into step behind him, while Jezlem brought up the rear. Blake stepped into the sparse entryway, wincing from the pain in his ankle as he placed himself against the wall. Joel copied his movements, and Jezlem hurriedly shut the door. She flicked off the overhead light, plunging the tiny hallway into semidarkness. The only light was the soft red glow surrounding Bia.

"This way," Jezlem said before turning her back on them.

"I guess she's satisfied we're not here to murder and pillage," Blake muttered, curious about the sister's suspicious greeting.

"Right?" Joel agreed as the three followed Jezlem through the narrow hallway to the back of the house. "There's nothing even in here to take."

Joel was right. As they weaved from room to room, Blake noted there was no furniture inside any of them. No tables, no chairs, not even a bed. The walls were bare as well.

They turned a sharp corner, entering a living room, and Blake's jaw dropped. It spanned the entire back of the house with floor-to-ceiling windows wrapped around all three walls. Wispy moonlight peeked between the clouds as the last shred of dusk dove beneath the ocean, illuminating a small yard that led directly to the beach beyond. Sky-blue sheer curtains fluttered delicately against the windows; tea light candles provided gentle up-lighting behind them. Dark wood stretched across the floor, and two tattered blue couches faced the water. Blake took a step inside the room and felt his feet roll.

Confused, he glanced down. White sand was sprinkled atop the floorboards. His gaze wondered to the abundance of shells scattered throughout the room: large and small, white and rosy pink. The shells and willowy curtains made it seem as if they were standing on the ocean floor.

Jezlem and Bia took a seat on the love seat, leaving the boys to stand awkwardly on the outskirt of the room.

"Let me see." Jezlem gestured to Bia's head. Bia pushed back her hood and leaned forward so Jezlem could inspect the wound. "Goddess, what happened?"

Bia closed her eyes. "A g-goddess attacked us."

"Us? What do you mean?"

Jezlem wandered over to a small end table. From a basket, she withdrew a white hand towel and plunged a corner into a ceramic dish of water before returning to the couch. Gently, she pressed it against Bia's forehead.

"Hera was t-targeting Blake," Bia said. "I came to protect him, then that one got involved." She nodded at Joel. "As we were leaving, Hera attacked us. A brick hit me. Maybe a pile of b-bricks."

"Hera?" Jezlem said, astounded. "Hera attacked you? And them? In the mortal world? That's not possible."

"Why not?" Blake asked, speaking for the first time.

Jezlem regarded him warily, edging closer to her sister. "Hera is the goddess of women, marriage, birth. She represents virtue and innocence. Why would she gallivant across the mortal world after you?"

Bia tucked her legs beneath her body. "He sheltered Kait."

Jezlem shook her tight curls. "I don't follow."

"Hera said I interfered," Blake said. "I guess Zeus thinks something happened between us, and now he's using me to get to her."

"What was Kait doing in the human realm? Bia, what aren't you telling me?" She turned to her sister, her lips pressed into a firm line. Bia opened her mouth to reply, but Jezlem held up her hand, her eyes going wide. "She went looking for evidence against Zeus to take to the Council, but now, now he's hunting her."

A pregnant silence filled the room.

"I'm s-sorry," Bia finally whispered. "We were trying to escape, and I got hurt, and they almost died." Her words tumbled out. "Kait's trapped in Olean. I just...I didn't know where else to go. I thought we might be able to clean up. I just need a bit of time to fix this." She gestured to her head. "An hour at most and then we'll go."

Jezlem brushed her curls out of her eyes. "I can't help you. You know I can't. I'm worthless without my element," she said, her voice full of despair. "But I might have some information you can use."

Bia shook her head and waved her hands. "It's okay. I d-didn't come to involve you. A glass of water and a minute to catch our breath is all I ask, though I can't tell you how good it is to see you."

Jezlem nodded, her lips breaking into a small smile. "Of course. Stay as long as you want. It's amazing to see you. I was wondering if either of you would ever come look for me..."

Bia's hands fluttered anxiously in front of her as she sawed her bottom lip with her teeth. "We wanted to c-come after your attack. Kait and me both, but the queen forbid it. Plus, we were both placed on lockdown for three months."

Surprise leapt into Jezlem's eyes. "You'll need to fill me in on all the details." She pressed her forehead to Bia's, calming her movements. "For now, I'm just glad you're okay. I love you."

Her voice was soft and gentle, the perfect remedy. Bia visibly relaxed under her sister's words, and Blake got the feeling that Jezlem had years of practice soothing her agitation.

Rising to her feet, Jezlem withdrew the bloodied towel from Bia's wound and folded it in her hands. "I'll go get a fresh one for you. How did you find me, by the way?" The question was casual, but Blake could hear the anxiety layered underneath.

Bia shrugged, brushing her greasy hair over one shoulder. "I can s-still sense you. You might not be part of the ethereal realm anymore, but the earth hasn't forgotten you."

Jezlem nodded, her eyes focusing on something far away. "Right. Bia, why don't you use the shower? It'll be easier to clean the blood out of your hair." She bounced the dirty cloth in her hand. "The bathroom is through there."

"Thank you. I'll b-be quick." Bia disappeared in the direction Jezlem had indicated.

"I could use a shower too," Joel chirped, eyeing Bia's retreating figure hopefully.

"Don't even think about it." Jezlem pointed a finger at him.

Joel put up his hands. "Geez, we come in peace. You nymphs are a suspicious lot."

"I'm not a nymph," Jezlem spat, her words like ice.

"Oh, but I thought…" Joel started to say, but Jezlem was already gone. "What's with her?"

Blake shook his head, as lost as Joel. "Not sure, but I don't think she wants to talk about it."

"Whatever. I'm going to head out back, kick some sand or something until we figure out what the hell is going on."

"Don't wander too far," Blake warned as Joel slid the glass door open.

"Yes, Mom." Joel snickered and let the door roll shut.

Blake rubbed his eyes, alone for the first time since Bia showed up in his room. It felt like a year had gone by. His head snapped up.

Mom.

Blake withdrew his cell phone from his back pocket, imagining the string of angry and scared voicemails that must be overflowing his phone. He clicked the narrow button on the top right-hand side, but nothing happened. He clicked it again and held it down.

"I charged it. How is it dead?"

A black screen continued to stare back at him. That's when he noticed a hair-thin crack running diagonally down the glass and spiderwebbing into baby shards in the bottom left corner.

"Shit."

No doubt word had reached his mother of Joel's departure from the hospital and the bizarre fight he was involved in on their way out. Blake had been terrified of the voice and desperate to find Bia. All he had time to do was scribble a note to his mother explaining that he would be back late and not to worry. Some son he was. He was supposed to protect her. Guilt washed over him as he realized this was the first time she'd crossed his mind since that morning. He had to find a phone.

Blame limped across the room and smacked aside the sheer curtain, scanning the yard and beach for any sign of Joel, but they were both deserted.

He huffed. "Three seconds on his own and he's gone."

Forgetting Joel, Blake retraced his steps back the way he had come when they first arrived. He could ask Jezlem to use hers. Empty room after empty room greeted him until he passed a closed door with steam curling under it. He'd found the bathroom, but where was the kitchen? Had he missed it?

Grinding his teeth, Blake returned to living room and noticed a dark archway tucked to the left. A few feet down, the corner of a white bedspread could be seen. Blake took a step inside the dark bedroom, then stopped. He couldn't go foraging around someone's room.

He tried to clear his head, but worry clutched his gut. What if Hera went after his mom? What if she was hurt? He emerged from the bedroom and glimpsed a warm light surrounding another door. He pushed it open and crossed into a small but tidy kitchen.

Jezlem looked up from the food she was prepping at the island. She was positioning cheese and crackers on a tray, enough for all four of them.

"Can I help you?" she asked, her voice wary.

"Can I borrow your phone?"

Jezlem shook her head. "I don't have one."

"What? How?"

"I don't need one. I don't have anyone to call."

Blake sighed. "Great, that's just…perfect."

"What are you doing here?"

"I was looking for a phone. I thought that was obvious."

"No, I mean, here in my house." Jezlem ignored his sarcasm. "How did you meet Kait?"

Blake stepped over to the counter and leaned back. "By accident. I thought she was dead, some horrific body murdered and dumped in the woods."

Jezlem's eyes bulged, and her jaw dropped. "Zeus?"

"No, no, sorry." He hadn't meant to be that graphic. "She was fine. She'd fallen asleep. She told me she was running from a guy. I let her shower and rest at my house, and then the next morning, she was gone. I didn't put any thought into it until that Hera person started messing with me. Yesterday, she almost killed Joel, and then this morning, she attacked us at the hospital. It's been a rough week."

Jezlem pushed the tray of food to the side of the square island, chewing the inside of her cheek. "It doesn't make sense. I imagine Hera is upset because until Zeus takes Kait, he won't return to her, but to enter the human realm and not only reveal herself, but to publicly engage with you is forbidden. Humans aren't supposed to have knowledge of the ethereal realm."

Blake shrugged. "If she wants a fight, I'm here."

Jezlem scoffed, placing a few more crackers onto the full tray. "Don't be ridiculous. You're a mortal. How do you plan on defeating an immortal goddess?"

Blake opened his mouth and stared at her. "Well, I haven't had time to really think anything through yet."

Jezlem laughed, a pleasant, throaty sound. "Of course not." She turned around to the sink and ran her dirty knife under the steady flow of water. "Hera is obviously aiding Zeus. All his other conquests submitted to him willingly, but she must be losing her patience waiting for him to catch Kait. If your death brings about a swift end to the chase, she will do whatever it takes to ensure that happens."

"So what now? I spend the rest of my life running from some deranged Greek myth? I don't want any of this. I was just trying to be a decent person."

Jezlem laid the clean knife beside the sink and dried her hands, then tossed the towel onto the countertop. "I know it might seem hopeless right now, but we'll figure it out. And you don't need to try to be decent. You're already a good guy, Blake. I can tell." Jezlem gave him a weak smile, which he returned half-heartedly. The pressure to survive and protect his loved ones at the same time was crushing, but at least he didn't have to do it alone.

"Can I ask what happened to you? I don't mean to pry, but I don't know anything about your world."

Jezlem pursed her lips and rubbed her hands together, brushing the clinging crumbs from her fingertips. "I was a naiad, blessed with the ability to manipulate water with a special talent for currents and storms. Zeus...Zeus forced himself on me and absorbed my ethereal connection. He made me human and then abandoned me. The first night was the scariest. I'd frequented the human realm before of course, but this was different. I was alone with no way to defend myself."

"What? That's why he's chasing Kait? To rape her?"

"It's called euphoria. When a god lies with a nymph, they steal our halos. It manifests as a glow of energy around us. No doubt you've noticed Bia's. During the coupling, the god absorbs it, heightening their own power. Apart from the physical pleasure the act yields, the god's experience euphoria on top of that, which is even more addictive."

"Like a shot of heroin?" At Jezlem's quizzical look, Blake said, "Not that I've tried it personally, but we learned about it in health class. It's a really powerful drug that makes everything shine bright for a second."

"Yes, exactly. I don't know how it is for mortals, but euphoria doesn't last very long, and judging by Hera's rash attempt to stop you, Zeus is growing desperate for more."

Blake's anger flared. "But this isn't right! How can he get away with something like this?"

Jezlem sighed. "Our world is ruled by a council of immortals, and Zeus is the leader. He's king of the gods. I used to think the Council would do anything to protect us, but now... I don't understand how they could abandon us. Surely Kait told them what Zeus did to me. They may have sealed all the portals to stop nymphs from entering the human realm, but are they trying to catch Zeus? To stop him? It doesn't seem so."

"Then we have to stop him. He can't get away with this again."

A small chuckle fell from Jezlem's lips. "If only it were that easy."

A solitary tear slid down her cheek, but she brushed it away with the back of her hand. Blake's stomach tightened. He was unsure how to comfort her—if she even wanted comfort from him. He cleared his throat and awkwardly reached out to pat her shoulder but withdrew his fingers before making contact. Instead, he crossed his arms over his chest.

"You're brave," he said.

"Me? No."

"Yes, you are. Look what happened to you. Most people could never move on from a tragic incident like the one you endured, yet here you are, thriving."

Jezlem snorted. "I am not thriving."

Blake glanced around the kitchen and arched his eyebrows. "Looks like it to me."

His thoughts turned to his mom, how depressed and scared she was to ever go anywhere or try anything new in case it angered his father. Plus, going out in public meant creating new lies to explain away her purple bruises. He looked at Jezlem, slightly in awe of what he saw after hearing her past. It had taken his mother years to gather enough courage to live on her own.

"How did you do it?" he asked.

Jezlem shrugged, brushing her unruly curls off her face once more. "The queen sent two of her advisors to help me after my attack, but besides offering me minor medical treatment, there wasn't much they could do. They brought me to Florida and left me with enough food to last a week, but after that, I was on my own. I knew I needed money and a place to live, but with no identity, it was a lot harder than I expected. After inquiring at a few retail stores, I stumbled across a pub just off the beach. The manager didn't care who I was or what I didn't have. All he cared about was my cup size." She arched her eyebrows and rolled her eyes.

Blake felt his cheeks redden as he tried to look anywhere but at her chest.

Jezlem chuckled and placed both palms on the edge of the island. "I took a job waitressing and got paid under the table, which the manager said was a dream. One night, I overhead a group of guys I was serving arguing about trying to find someone to sublet their place to. I had no idea what any of it meant, and when I asked, they offered me the house. And bam, just like that I had a job, money, and a home. Of course after I pay rent and buy a few meals, I'm broke, but I'm proud of myself for getting this far."

"You should be." Blake's mom had worked two jobs to keep a roof over their heads and food on the table after finally leaving his father and the abuse behind. He was too young to understand just how hard she was working then, but now, he wished he could turn back the clock and take some of the burden from her.

Jezlem peered at him. "Why are you so bent on helping Kait? You barely know her."

Blake shrugged. "I've got this thing with injustice."

"You want to be a hero?" She raised an eyebrow at him, and he almost laughed.

"I don't know about a hero… Maybe a shield. I'm not a fan of the strong preying on the weak."

Jezlem stared at him, her expression unreadable. "Thank you," she said at last.

"For what?"

"For being a good person."

Blake scoffed.

"No really. Putting up with my sisters is one thing. Kait is so guarded after what happened, and Bia, well, she has challenges that complicate even simple relationships. On top of that, you didn't hesitate to jump into a foreign world—literally."

"I didn't have much choice."

"Yes, you did, and your choice speaks volumes about your character."

Blake shrugged. "Thanks, but I'm not sure I'm making that much of an impact."

"Trust me, you are. Before all this, Bia never spoke much. She was always more comfortable with plants. Yet, today, she not only traveled through the human realm, but also found you and worked up enough courage to convince you and your friend to come with her. Believe me, you are."

Blake was quiet for a moment. "Bia reminds me of my cousin Harper. She was diagnosed when she was five. I remember my aunt being nervous whenever we played together. It wasn't until I was older that I realized she was a little different—sensitive to certain sounds and materials. How old was she when she started stimming? Bia, I mean."

"Stimming? What are you talking about?"

Blake flapped his hands, imitating Bia whenever she became nervous. "My cousin rocks back forth, but I've heard there are lots of different methods people on the spectrum use to help self-soothe."

"I don't understand. What spectrum?"

"Oh, I'm sorry. She doesn't make eye contact often, and I just thought—with her stutter and the flapping... I thought Bia was autistic."

"Oh," Jezlem replied. "In Olean, we don't have a name for it. Of course, I knew she was different, but I always thought they were just little quirks. That's just who she is." She was thoughtful for a moment. "How does your cousin cope with stress? Bia's gotten better as she's grown older, but Kait and I always struggled to calm her down. She doesn't like being touched or comforted the way others do."

"When we were little, Harper used to throw wild tantrums. Scared the hell out of my aunt." Blake shook his head, then smiled. "She's doing great now though. She still rocks, but over the years, she's learned some deep breathing techniques. Puzzles seem to calm her too. She's a student at Boston College."

"But she's independent?"

"Oh yeah. She's studying to become a court reporter."

"That's wonderful," Jezlem whispered, more to herself than Blake.

A question mulled around in Blake's mind as his thoughts wandered back to what Jezlem said about Kait being guarded. What did she mean? What had happened to Kait?

"Hey, y-you two all right in here?" Bia stood in the threshold wringing her wet hair in a white towel.

Jezlem's head snapped up, the pensive look on her face replaced by a small smile. "Yeah, just talking. I made some food. It's nothing much, but it might help."

"Thanks, Jez. Food w-will help us brainstorm."

Blake cocked his head. "Bia, I know this is a long shot, but do you have a phone I can borrow? Mine is dead."

Bia frowned. "A w-what?"

"Never mind. Is there any way we can go back to Bennington and check on my mom? She's probably freaking out."

Bia's frown deepened. "I'm s-sorry, Blake. I can't risk taking you back there."

"But what if these people hurt her?"

"I d-don't think they will. I think Hera was bluffing. To kill a human would condemn her to Tartarus, the worst part of the Underworld. She wouldn't risk her freedom for you."

Blake sighed. Her words did little to calm his worry. He had seen firsthand what violence Hera was capable of.

"Where's the other one?" Bia asked, scanning the tiny kitchen.

"Oh, man." Blake groaned, remembering Joel. "He went for a walk. I'll go find him."

Blake left the kitchen and found his way back to the airy room that led to the backyard.

He stepped out into the dark night. "Joel!" He turned to the right and saw nothing but empty beach. "Joel!" he yelled again, turning around. To his left, a figure stood a hundred yards away. Blake hobbled along the wet sand, recognizing the shaggy blond hair. He slapped Joel on the shoulder. "Hey, the girls need us back at the house."

Joel pulled his gaze away from the ocean. "Okay."

"You all right?"

"Yeah. I've just been thinking. This whole thing is crazy. Guess I'm still trying to talk myself into believing this is real."

"I know what you mean. I'm having a hard time wrapping my head around it too. Hey, can I use your phone?"

Joel patted his pockets. "I don't have it. I must have left it at the hospital."

"Shit. I can't catch a break. Come on. Let's go."

They turned back to the house when a blazing streak of lighting exploded in the dry sand. The eruption threw both boys off their feet, and they landed with a heavy thud in the receding water. Thick white smoke swirled like curling tongues before them as the silhouette of a tall figure appeared.

A handsome man stepped through the haze. His unbuttoned navy shirt fluttered in the wind, exposing his bare chest chiseled with muscle.

"So, which one of you knows my little Kait?"

⚡ 25 ⚡

Blake and Joel sat in the wet sand, gawking. Slow waves lapped against the shore and soaked their jeans.

"Who are you?" Joel asked, glancing up at the sky like it might hold the answer.

The stranger crossed his arms, and the movement accentuated his ripped chest and toned abs. Blake swallowed. He looked like both an MMA fighter and a Calvin Klein model. He was tall—taller than Blake's six-foot-two frame—with piercing blue eyes, angular features, and golden hair that hung across his forehead, styled to look laid back and casual. Apart from the open button-down, he was clad in light jeans, and his feet were bare.

"I'm Zeus," the man said. "Is one of you Brad?"

Blake pushed himself to his feet, his soggy jeans clinging to him as if he'd just wet his pants. He cleared his throat and threw back his shoulders, trying to extend to his full height, but the guy still towered over him by at least three inches.

"It's Blake." His eyes bulged. "Wait, did you say *Zeus*?"

"Yes."

"You're Zeus?" Blake repeated, looking the god up and down again. "But… you're so young."

He had pictured an old man with a long white beard. This guy barely looked thirty.

"I came to speak to Brad about a certain nymph I currently have chained to my bed, so if you don't mind, I'd prefer to hurry this exchange along. Don't want her getting lonely."

Zeus's blue eyes burned as he spoke. Blake didn't miss the longing in his voice.

"You're lying."

Zeus scoffed. "Why would I lie?"

Surprising fury ripped through Blake's chest, and for a moment, he was taken aback by his reaction, shocked by the intensity. "Where is she?"

"Feisty. I like that in a lover, but this century, I'm afraid I favor females."

"Did you hurt her?"

"Maybe." Zeus grinned, his eyes sparking. "What's it to you?"

Blake clenched his jaw. "Let her go. Call off Hera and leave my friends and family alone."

Zeus uncrossed an arm and wagged a finger. "Oh, I can't do that. I've waited far too long to give her up so easily."

"What's going on here?" Joel asked.

Zeus cocked his head. "You must be the poisoned one. You can't possibly add anything to our conversation, so why don't you take a seat." He waved his hand.

A crackle of electricity coursed from his palm, hitting Joel square in the chest. He fell into a receding wave with a quiet splash. Joel opened his mouth to shout, but dead air surrounded him. Zeus had muted his voice and from what Blake could tell, paralyzed his body.

"Stop it," Blake cried, but before he could move to help his friend, Zeus was in his path.

"Listen closely." Zeus took a step forward, forcing Blake to step back. "I will call off my lovely Hera and allow you to return to your banal existence. You can go home and forget this ever happened."

Blake frowned. "And what about Kait?"

"Her fate doesn't matter." Zeus's eyes shone black and deadly against the night.

"Yes it does. I won't let you rape her."

Zeus scoffed. "Rape? No. I'm not going to rape her. I'm going to ravage every inch of her body until my need of euphoria is satisfied. Then, who knows? Maybe I'll keep her to use at my will."

Rage pushed Blake forward, and before he knew it, his arms were swinging, then wrapping around the god's torso. Yet rather than pulling Zeus to the ground, Blake fell straight through him, as if he were a column of smoke. Cold saltwater splashed across Blake's face, sending a shock through his system as he tumbled into the surf. Catching himself on his hands and knees, he spat out the offensive liquid.

Zeus chuckled, turning around. "I could watch that all day. Shame I must be off."

"Wait! Wait! There must be something I can give you in exchange."

Zeus paused. "In exchange for what? Euphoria? Mortal, there is nothing in all the worlds better than that. Goodbye."

"Wait!" Blake yelled again. "What about a trade? My life for Kait's?"

Zeus waved his hand dismissively. "Please, what would I want with your life? Your life is worth nothing."

"Then what about a game? How about, if I beat you, you let Kait go, unharmed and untouched."

"And more realistically, if I win?" Zeus countered, cocking his head.

Blake shook his head. "I can't stop you from taking her at that point, but you'll have to kill me first."

Lightning crackled above as Zeus flexed his palms. White electricity pulsed angrily.

"And what if I kill you right now? Then I could return to Kait and force her into whatever position I please."

Blake struggled to think on his feet, but he kept talking. "Then your victory wouldn't be as sweet. It'd be too easy. But if I failed and died trying to save her, it would prove your greatness even more." The god hesitated, mulling over Blake's offer. "Unless you're afraid I might win and actually defeat you, then maybe you should go ahead and kill me now."

Blake regarded the god. On the outside, his demeanor was calm and suave, but his eyes were as wild as a rabid wolf's.

Zeus drew in a large breath. "Fine. I will give you three days to find and defeat me. If you magically manage to do that, then I will let Kait go *untouched*, as you say. However, if you don't, then I will make you watch as I ravage her and then kill you both for dessert."

Blake's mouth gaped open, at a loss for what to say. The odds were strongly against him, but how could he refuse? This was his idea, and he couldn't return home and forsake Kait. There was no telling what atrocities this animal would subject her to.

Blake swallowed his fear. "How do I know you'll keep your word and not take her until the end of the third day?"

Zeus shrugged. "You don't. That's what makes it fun." His lips curled. "See you in three days."

Another sizzle of lightning lit the sky, and Zeus disappeared. The stench of smoke permeated the air. Joel sucked in a large breath behind Blake as his temporary paralysis ended.

"What just happened?" Joel shouted, rising to his feet. He reached down to help Blake out of the surf, scanning the navy sky for the god.

Blake stood there, unable to process what he'd just agreed too. "Things just got a whole lot messier."

They started back to the small house in silence. Their footsteps burrowed into the sand, only to be washed away a moment later.

"What's your plan?" Joel asked.

Blake rubbed his eyes. "I have no idea. There isn't a handbook on how to rescue a nymph from a god's clutches. I don't know what I'm supposed to do, but if I don't so something, he's going to rape her, maybe even kill her." He suppressed a shudder.

"But if you fight back, he's going to kill you both anyway," Joel pointed out.

Half a dozen thoughts swirled in Blake's mind, as murky as the dark ocean water. This wasn't his world. Why was he digging himself in deeper?

"Why don't we just go home?" Joel asked. "You barely know that girl, unless there's something you haven't told me."

"I told you everything. I don't think I said more than a dozen words to her."

"Then let's go. We can leave right now. Figure out where the heck we are, call our parents to wire us some cash, and leave. I'm ready to get out of this weird twilight zone."

Blake closed his eyes, and an image of his mother, crouched on the kitchen floor, battered and bruised, assailed him. The memory played out like an old movie reel. He saw himself padding across the tile floor, careful to avoid the broken plates and scattered food. His mother was crying, the sound barely audible. His father hadn't cared if he woke him.

Blake sat down next to her, wrapping his small hands around her arm. He remembered wishing he could grow up faster. That way he would be strong enough to stand up to his dad, to keep him from hurting her. Now he was older and actually had a chance to be brave and do the right thing. How could he leave?

Blake shook his head and kicked a small pile of sand with the lip of his sneaker, sending the fine grains dancing along the breeze. "You can leave if you want, but I'm staying. I'm going to find her."

"Seriously, Blake? You can't do this. You're eighteen years old. He's an immortal god. We need to cut our losses and scram before things get any worse."

"Worse? They're already worse. Zeus has Kait in chains. Do you know what comes next? He's going to rape her, Joel. Beat her and rape her until he gets his high. That's what all this is about. If I don't help her, who will?"

"I don't know… Someone else?"

"Get your head out of your ass, man. Zeus is a predator. I can't leave her to that fate."

"Man." Joel sighed. "Are you sure this is about her?"

"What's that supposed to mean?"

"Come on. Fighting back against Justin and his dumb goons? You'd rather people think you're tough than ignore him like everyone else. Then getting wrapped up in this mess and going up against a literal god for a girl you barely know? I think you like the idea of playing hero." Joel looked uncomfortable but didn't break eye contact. "It's going to get you killed."

Blake stared ahead silently, Joel's words running through his head. He opened his mouth to reply, but he didn't have a good response. His mother's stifled screams echoed in his head, opening up that hollow place inside him that had always been there. Reflexively, his fingertips dug into his palms, forming tight fists. He couldn't protect her then, but he could protect Kait now.

The sliding glass door opened, revealing Bia's concerned face. "Guys, get in here! My sensors t-tripped. Zeus is c-close."

Blake looked away from Joel's gaze. "Coming."

He jogged several strides forward, the pain in his ankle finally lessening. He didn't look back to see if his friend followed. He reached the door a moment later and stepped across the threshold. Hero or not, if Joel was right, Blake had just taken a dare with lethal consequences.

⚡ 26 ⚡

Kait awoke to a dimly lit room, shrinking back as elongated shadows danced and kicked along the walls. Several sconces lined the walls, their orange flames whispering secrets as they watched her.

The room was foreign and unfamiliar. The damp walls glistened in the candlelight like they were painted with stolen stars. Kait arched her neck. The strange walls continued up, encasing the entire room in the same rough texture. There was no sound apart from the seductive flames, and the room was void of scent. A dark alcove peeked around a corner, where the edge of a pedestal sink was visible.

She pushed herself into a sitting position, and a shrill sound rattled in her ears. She froze. Kait felt soft sheets graze her touch and glanced down. She was in a bed with no memory of how she arrived there.

Kait pressed her hand to her head, trying to remember. The beach, the jungle, the piriol, and pain—so much pain. Taking stock of her wounds, she noted her body was filthy, covered in sweat and dried blood. Her waist was pierced with two dime-sized holes from the piriol's quills, along with numerous cuts from her escape. She glanced at the tiny bathroom, desperate to wash up.

Kait shifted her weight to roll off the bed, but her momentum was halted. Her eyes widened in alarm and her pulse quickened as she scanned the length of her bare arms to her hands. Heavy steel cuffs encircled her wrists, the metal humming with electricity. She was chained to the bed. Trapped.

"Finally," a deep baritone voice called. "I was beginning to think you were dead."

Kait whipped her head backward as the speaker glided into view. The rosy glow of the fires touched Zeus's exposed chest, highlighting his strength.

"Morning, darling."

Kait jerked her arms, pulling, yanking, and clanging her chains uselessly. Zeus smirked, amusement dancing in his blue eyes. He crossed his arms over his chest and leaned against the wall.

"By all means, please, knock yourself out. I love watching you sleep. The way your breath blows your curls, the way your breasts heave while you dream— it's so sexy." He took a step closer.

Kait could smell his lust. She needed to be careful. The memory of fiery manacles snaking around her flesh leapt to mind. She'd broken free from Hermes's chains; she could do it again. Her fingers flexed, focusing on the way the air moved around her skin. It would take only a moment to isolate her hands, for the manacles to fall through empty air. But a minute went by and nothing happened. Why wasn't it working?

"Hermes told me about that little trick of yours," Zeus said. "Very clever. I wouldn't bother trying to escape. I changed the properties in the spell. Even if you were a puff of air, the electricity would cling to you, make you drop to the ground like a stone."

Kait kept her expression impassive, focusing her magic once more, but her skin remained tangible and opaque. She attempted a smaller, easier cast, alighting her attention on the nearest torch. She fanned her fingers. Usually, the small action would douse the flame, but it continued to burn, weaving back and forth, taunting her.

Zeus sauntered to the edge of the bed and sat down on the foot of the mattress. His weight caused her body to roll toward him, and the edge of her thigh bumped against his little finger. Panic flared in her chest. He was too close.

Kait grimaced, twisting her legs away from him.

"But now that you're awake, we can have fun," Zeus whispered, running his palm along the sheets.

She furrowed her brow and tried to think back to the last minute before she blacked out. She had been so weak from her wounds. She remembered wondering if she would die in the jungle as she struggled to reach the portal. Somehow, she'd made it. She stumbled through and left the fierce cat behind, but that wasn't all she'd left in her wake.

Vivid memories washed over her. "I was on Makua Beach with a siren when your piriol attacked. You killed her. You killed half a dozen humans."

The lust evaporated from the god's eyes, and he sat up. "No, my dear. That was not my doing. Kaf was following orders. If any humans were killed, you are the responsible party."

Tears welled over her eyelids as she heard the haunting screams, saw the blood splashed across the sand. He was right. If she hadn't led Zeus to Hawaii, hadn't flaunted herself in the open, all those lives wouldn't have been lost. "Their blood may be on my hands, but you're the monster that pulled the trigger."

Before Kait could blink, Zeus closed the distance between them and poised a golden dagger at the base of her throat. "Careful, nymph," he hissed. "I'm already restraining myself, but if you'd like to see the vile monster you think I am, keep going. I promise I won't disappoint." He pressed the tip of the blade into one of the old puncture wounds, drawing a few beads of fresh blood. "No? Didn't think so."

Leaning back, Zeus withdrew the dagger and ran his tongue along the edge. Kait stared, refusing to break eye contact as he sheathed the weapon in his belt. Zeus inhaled a deep breath, his features serene once more as he stood. "I am excited that you could join me, my dear. I must admit, I was starting to worry if we'd ever have this time together."

He padded across the stone floor to a natural table carved out of the wall. He rummaged through the sparse contents, popping several withered grapes from a chipped bowl into his mouth.

Kait shook her head, fuming. It was never her intention to be caught. She only wanted to distract him, to keep him in her sights with Bia so vulnerable. "But I got away. I passed through the portal right after your piriol's quill pulled me from the air."

Red juice dribbled over his lips, turning Kait's stomach.

"Correct," he said. "It was never my intention for Kaf to capture you. Think of him more like a shepherd." At her blank stare, Zeus continued, crunching another grape. "It's your fault for being so predictable. If you had simply left the beach and flown over the water, Kaf would never have been able to follow. But I knew you would flee through the portal. All I had to do was wait on the other side."

Kait remembered the husky voice, the warm hands catching her after she fell. The whole thing had been a trap, and she'd walked right into it.

Disgust roiled in her stomach as the image of the siren's glassy eyes reflected blankly back at her, her vocals cords sliced in half by the piriol's lethal quill. It was her fault. Vomit climbed her throat as her stomach bucked, but before it could spill, Zeus shook his head, clucking his tongue.

"There, there, none of that." He crossed back to the bed. "Death is a part of life. The sooner you understand that, the easier it will be."

He reached out to stroke her cheek with the back of his fingers, but she jerked away.

"Don't touch me," Kait rasped, swallowing her nausea.

Zeus frowned, pretending to pout. "Oh, come now. Don't be like that. I was hoping we could put all this animosity behind us. How about a bath? I'd be happy to wash every inch of your skin until you're glowing again."

"You're despicable," she spat.

She wished she'd thrown up on herself, anything to help keep the monster at bay. Feverishly, she called the wind, pleading for it to accept her into its folds, but nothing happened. Zeus's cuffs were too strong.

"Have it your way, but know this: You're no longer a vixen, little one. You are a mouse, and I am the cat. The only way you leave this room is if that pathetic mortal shows up, but even then, you won't be leaving without a few...scratches."

"What do you mean?"

Zeus crawled back onto the bed, resting just out of her reach.

"Oh, I forgot to mention it." Zeus clapped his hands. "I ran into your little boyfriend and offered him the chance to go home and forget all this." He paused, drawing in an incredulous breath. "The fool turned me down. He said he wants to fight for you. I suppose the violent nature of your future didn't sit well with him."

"What does that mean? He's coming here?"

"Yes. Apparently, there's to be a whole rescue party. I found him with another mortal down in Florida. According to Hera, your anthousai sister escaped her and brought them to Jezlem's new home. I'm glad to see she's settling into mortal life."

Kait's thoughts bounced inside her mind, spinning off in chaotic directions. Were her sisters all right? What was Blake thinking? What other mortal?

Kait could barely finish one thought before another slammed into her skull. If anything happened to her sisters, she'd never forgive herself. She should have gone to find Bia the moment Tahlia unlocked the portal rather than inventing a pointless diversion that ended in her own ruin.

"Easy. Easy, darling." Zeus patted the top of her foot. "I've called off Hera for now. Give your boy a chance."

"He's not mine," Kait said. "What did you say to him?"

"Nothing much. Just established a few ground rules."

"But you don't play by the rules."

Zeus laughed, his voice echoing throughout the room. "Yes, but he doesn't know that."

Kait leaned back against the solitary pillow. Her arms were starting to go numb. Her heart swelled as she pictured Blake, remembered the way he made her insides flutter. She was beyond touched that he wanted to come after her. Maybe he'd felt something too. But the small flame of hope wavered. No matter how hard Blake fought, she knew Zeus would ensure he never won.

A depression in the mattress roused Kait from her wandering thoughts as Zeus closed the distance between them. His face was inches from her own, so close that she could smell his masculine scent. She pushed her body as far back as it would go, and the cold iron posts of the headboard licked the exposed skin on her back. Throwing her hands out, she tried to hit Zeus, but the length of chain was too short. Her prison had been carefully created to allow her zero advantage over the god.

Zeus's hand shot out, his long fingers gripping her lower jaw, holding her head in place.

"No!" Kait cried, but her shout was muffled as Zeus tilted her chin up, the pads of his fingers digging into her cheeks. She wrenched her head back and forth, desperate to escape the god's hold.

Zeus ignored her feeble attempt, bringing his face even closer. Tracing the tip of his nose along her skin, he inhaled her unique scent. "I will have you. Whether you like it or not."

Before Kait could reply, Zeus mashed his lips to her own, his hold intensifying. At last, he broke away and dropped his hand, rising to his feet in a graceful spin. Kait rotated her jaw. She could already feel the bruises.

"Until next time, nymph."

ϟ 27 ϟ

Blake sunk onto the sandy wooden floor of Jezlem's living room. He rested his head against the wall and closed his eyes. He didn't know what time it was, but his body pleaded for rest. All he wanted to do was curl up and doze off for a few hours, but judging from the flurry of activity between Bia and Jezlem, sleep was out of the question.

"I thought you were getting the other one," Jezlem said, glancing up from the coffee table that was laden with curling pieces of paper.

Blake waved his hand. He couldn't blame Joel for leaving. This wasn't his fight, wasn't his world. It wasn't Blake's either, but it was the right thing to do.

Blake shook his head. "He—"

"I'm here," Joel called, sliding the door shut. "And my name is Joel. Not *the other one* or *the sick one* or—what'd that guy just call me? *The poisoned one?*" He settled down beside Blake. "Makes me sound like some weak little king."

Blake glanced at Joel, a small grin pulling up the corner of his mouth. "Thanks, man."

Joel shrugged. "I knew you'd miss me."

"Who c-called you that?" Bia asked. She sat down on the love seat beside Jezlem, then offered the boys the tray of cheese and crackers.

Joel popped a cracker in his mouth. "Said his name was Zeus."

"Zeus? Zeus spoke to y-you?" She looked at Blake.

Blake nodded. "Yeah, I kind of made him a bet."

"A bet?" Jezlem repeated, her voice dubious. "Regarding what exactly?"

"He offered me the chance to go home, but I refused."

Bia cocked her head. "Why?"

"He claims to have Kait, and he wasn't shy about his plans for her. If I had walked away, he would've violated her, maybe even killed her. I wagered that I could defeat him. If I win, he lets her go."

"And if you lose?" Jezlem asked, her words heavy.

Blake swallowed. "He's going to make me watch him rape Kait before he kills us both."

Furious shouts tumbled from the girls' mouths, their gestures wide and sharp.

"What were you thinking?"

"Why d-didn't you come get us? How can I protect you when y-you throw your own life away?"

"You're crazy! You can't defeat him."

"Enough!" Joel yelled.

The girls fell silent. Both radiated fury and disbelief.

"Give him a break. He's doing this to save your sister. To buy her a little more time before that animal takes her. You should be grateful. I told him to walk away, but he stood up to Zeus and didn't back down. Yeah, he's probably going to die, but he's doing more than either of you to recue her."

Bia bowed her head. "I'm s-sorry, Blake. Thank you."

"I'm not going to apologize for what I said. What you did was stupid and reckless, but thank you." Jezlem tossed her hair behind her, clearing her throat. "How much time do you have?"

"He said he would refrain from touching her for three days. If I can find and defeat him by then, she'll be okay."

Jezlem scoffed, crossing her arms over her chest.

"What? You don't think I can do it?"

Jezlem fixed him with her bright eyes. "No. You don't stand a chance."

Blake didn't respond. He'd come to the same conclusion himself.

Joel cleared his throat. "Let's not worry about that right now. First, we need to find her."

Jezlem brushed her wild curls behind her ear and sat on the edge of the couch. Large papers had been strewn about the coffee table in their absence.

"Right, I've drawn a few maps of portals in the ethereal realm and paired them with the geographic locations in this world. I highly doubt he'll hide in the ethereal realm, not after agreeing to play," Jezlem said.

"Why not?"

Jezlem's eyes scoured the twisting lines before her. "Humans can't travel to the ethereal realm. The portals don't activate for them."

"That's why Kait wanted to b-beg the q-queen to allow you in," Bia explained.

Jezlem frowned. "These two? Queen Rajhi would never allow that."

"That's why I brought them here instead."

"What if he kills me the second I get close?" Blake asked, interrupting the sisters.

"That's not going to happen. He wants you to find them. He wants the fight," Jezlem said. "It'll make his conquest of Kait that much sweeter. Especially if he kills you in front of her."

"Blunt and to the point," Joel said with an uneasy chuckle.

Blake frowned in his friend's direction, catching the way his eyes lingered on Jezlem.

"Be warned that Zeus won't make the fight easy. If you aren't ready to die, you should go home." Jezlem's words hung in the air, a threat, another dare, but Kait didn't have that choice.

Neither Blake nor Joel moved.

Then Joel clapped his hands and leaned forward. "So, now that everything is settled, does anyone have a plan for what to do next?"

Jezlem's eyes flashed. "We fight power with power. We bring in another god."

The cracker Blake was swallowing turned to glue in his throat. "Another one? How will that help?"

"I don't see w-what good that will do. The other gods won't ally themselves with us, especially against Zeus," Bia said. "And with the portals blocked, we have no way of contacting the Council. After your attack, Kait petitioned the queen to alert them, but she turned her away. She didn't have any proof he was the immortal involved. Unless something changed after I left, the Council doesn't know about Zeus."

"But she was there, she saw what he did to me, what he did to all the others. How is that not proof enough?" Jezlem asked, enraged.

"That was Kait's argument. That's why she left Olean, to try and collect evidence against him."

"And now he'll destroy another nymph," Jezlem growled. She rifled through the papers, shaking her head. "Fine. Forget about the Council. I've heard rumor of a fallen god who might be of help."

"Fallen? What does that mean?" Joel asked.

"He was kicked out of Olympus and stripped of his immortality for the part he played in the Titan War. We just need to convince him to join us."

"Which g-god?" Bia asked.

"Atlas."

"Atlas? An actual Titan? How? They were all k-killed centuries ago."

Jezlem shook her head. "Not Atlas. He was exiled from the heavens. Imprisoned in the human realm as punishment for his crime."

Bia's hands flapped at her sides. "We c-can't trust him. He's volatile and dangerous and a Titan. Remember what they did to the nymphs?"

Jezlem placed a comforting hand on her sister's shoulder. "I do, but he's also seeking revenge. Zeus is the one who banished him. Let's talk to him and see what he thinks."

"How do you know this?"

Jezlem paused, fiddling with her fingers. "After…everything, I began looking for a way back. I don't want to be mortal, I can't. I feel so lost, so useless. Not even the water can cheer me. For the past few months, I've been suffocating, drowning, trying to figure out how to exist without my magic, but I can't," she admitted, her voice a fragmented whisper. "I'll do anything to get it back and maybe…maybe Atlas has an answer."

Jezlem pointed to a colorful map. Her finger landed on a range of bumps that stretched halfway across like a jagged wound. "I did some research and found traces of ethereal activity here. It might not be Atlas, but it's worth a shot. Before I lost my connection, Kait told me that Zeus's other victims were found scattered throughout towns in northern Spain and southern France. It's not a lot to go on, but I think it's a solid start."

"Okay, so where is he?" Joel leaned over the map. "The Pierens?"

"The *Pyrenees*. It's a mountain range on the border of France and Spain." A small divot flexed between her eyebrows.

Bia placed a comforting hand on her back. "Are you going to be okay going back there so soon?"

"Is that where…?" Blake bit his lip.

Jezlem frowned, then nodded. "Zeus took me at the base of those mountains, outside a town called Luz-Saint-Sauveur in France." Jezlem paused as Blake raised his eyebrows. "I'll be fine. I have to be. This is the only way we can keep Kait from suffering the same fate."

"If you're sure, but how are we supposed to get there?"

Jezlem's lips twitched, and her teal eyes slid to Bia.

Joel and Blake threw up their hands.

"No way!" Joel cried. "We almost died last time. There's no way I'm doing that again."

Jezlem growled low in her throat. "Look, we don't have the time or resources to get there any other way. You do this our way or not at all."

The boys paused, glancing at one another. A shiver tickled down Blake's spine as goose bumps multiplied on his skin. The first time, they were trapped in relatively loose dirt, sand being their only obstacle to climb through. Now they were headed for the mountains. What happened if he got trapped underneath a boulder or the mountain itself? Granted, suffocation worked the same way, no matter what material he was buried in.

Blake exhaled. "Fine, but if I die down there——-"

"Relax," Bia said. "You'll b-be fine. I'm not hurt this time. You'll barely notice the transition."

"Fine. When are we doing this?"

"Now." Jezlem rose from the couch. "I'll grab some old clothes the previous tenants left behind."

"For what?" Joel looked down at his stiff black shirt. The saltwater had dried, leaving a wavy white line stretching from his shoulder to his stomach.

"It's the mountains. Going to be a little colder than it is here." She disappeared, returning a few minutes later with a large armful of long-sleeved coats, sweaters, and jeans. "I think the last renters liked to ski."

Blake grabbed a thick olive-green sweater and a dark pair of jeans, along with a coat filled with down. "Where should I?" He pointed to the clothes.

"Bathroom is that way." Jezlem tilted her head.

"Be quick," Bia added. "We need to get m-moving."

"How about I change here?" Joel winked in Jezlem's direction. "In the interest of saving time and all."

Both girls shook their heads and waved him away.

Blake sighed as he shut the bathroom door, finally alone. He stepped in front of the bathroom mirror, unimpressed with the reflection that stared back. The saltwater caused his hair to curl in places, and sand covered the light hair on his arms. He shrugged out of his soiled shirt and jeans, frowning at the soft flab hanging over his belt. An image of Zeus's taut abs and biceps jumped into his head.

"This is crazy. I'm never going to save her," he whispered to his sad reflection. At least this time, he would die trying.

Blake pulled on the clean clothes and opened the door, leaving his small flame of hope in a pitiful pile on the cold tile.

⚡ 28 ⚡

The group gathered in the backyard, a sad excuse for a rescue party. Blake, Joel, and Jezlem were bundled head to toe, but Bia sported nothing more than jeans and an off-the-shoulder maroon sweater.

"All right, we need to stay close," Jezlem said. "With Bia's help, we were able to pinpoint the last area that registered ethereal activity in the mountains, but Atlas isn't going to be waiting in the open. After we breach the surface, wait for my signal. Stay alert. There might be security measures in place." She placed her hands on her hips. "Ready?" It didn't sound like a question, but a command.

Blake inhaled sharply, readying himself to face the bottomless darkness once more. But this time, there was no black hole to teeter above and no warning. The ground suddenly gave way beneath his feet, opening to swallow him whole. Reacting on instinct, Blake threw out his hands, desperate to grab hold of something to keep from going under. His fingers clawed at the warm air as the small yard vanished from sight. Adrenaline pumped through Blake's body, but there was nowhere to run. The world was pulled away, and choking blackness welcomed him back as the smell of rich soil engulfed him.

His feet collided with the ground much faster this time. The earthen cage constricted around his body, rocky sand and dirt seizing the air as it filled in the gaps. Again, he couldn't move, couldn't inhale without losing more precious space. Dirt piled onto his shoulders, sealing him in.

He tried to take a calming breath. Where was Bia? Was something wrong?

Without thinking, he sucked in a lungful of oxygen. As he released the breath incrementally and his chest deflated, dirt slid over his jacket, against his mouth, into his nostrils. She said it would be easy this time. Panic overwhelmed him.

At last, a ripple bumped beneath his feet, pushing him up through the heavy layers of dirt. All Blake could do was shut his eyes and mouth while he rocketed to the surface. Icy wind ruffled his hair, greeting him to the mountains as the magic vomited him up.

Hurtling through the white sky, Blake couldn't tell which way was up until his back smacked against the ground, knocking the wind of out him. He lay there for several minutes while his vision spun, trying to reestablish his equilibrium. The whole world was white, as if he had been thrown into a snow globe. He rose to a sitting position and choked.

He was on the mountain and had been thrust into a powerful blizzard. The wind howled like a pack of wolves ready to hunt as it twisted and danced through towering boulders. Blake craned his neck, searching in every direction. He was alone.

"Hello!" he cried, but the wind muted his voice, laughing as it sped away with his words held hostage. He cupped his shaking hands around his mouth and tried again, louder. "Hello!" There was no response. No sign of life. "Joel! Bia! Jezlem! Anybody!"

The heavy snow continued to fall, a fine layer already coating Blake's legs. He had to move. He jumped to his feet, wincing as his sore body screamed in protest. He took several steps forward, his feet disappearing as the snow swallowed him up to his knees. He couldn't walk, not in snow that deep.

"Bia!"

The shrill wind echoed his cry. He could almost feel the mountain smiling. Another frozen body for its collection. Now Blake allowed himself to panic. There was nothing worse than being buried alive—except for freezing to death. How long could he hope to hold out? He stood atop the mountain in wet jeans and a coat. His shoulders shook violently as the bitter wind sliced through the pathetic layers. Already his fingers and ears tingled as the blood drew away, trying in vain to keep his heart beating for as long as possible.

Turning around, Blake trudged several feet to where he thought he'd landed. Snowflakes clung to his eyelashes and froze to his skin. He raised his arm to shield his face, but the swirling snow blinded still him. He could walk off the mountain and have no idea until his feet left the ground. The thought sent shivers up his spine, shredding the last bit of warmth his mind clung to. The toe of his shoe hit something, and he stumbled. Blake's heart lurched, and his hands shot out to catch himself, visions of the cliffside still fresh in his mind. Powdery snow slid between his fingers and climbed into his sleeves. The object wasn't hard like a rock as he'd expected.

"Joel!"

Dusting off as much snow as his numb hands allowed, Blake uncovered his friend, terrified of what state he would be in. Blue lips and glassy eyes dominated his thoughts. He hurried to dislodge the snow.

"Joel! Come on, man! Get up!"

Blake found Joel's head and wrenched him up by his shoulders. He was pale, and his eyes were closed, but his cheeks blazed a bright red. "Joel," Blake said, shaking his friend. Slowly, Joel came back to life.

His eyes peeled open, then blinked, trying to battle the accumulating snow. "Blake? What happened?"

Blake could barely hear him over the roar of the wind.

"I don't know. The girls are gone. I didn't even know you were here. Why didn't you get up?"

Joel shook his head, pressing a hand to his skull above his right ear. "I think I hurt my head." He pulled his hand away. Shining red blood pooled in the creases of his palm.

Blake groaned. "Oh, Christ."

Keeping a tight hold on Joel's jacket, Blake pulled them both to their feet. Spinning in a tight circle, he squinted through the endless snow.

"Do you see that?" he called, pointing to a shadowy outline a few yards away.

Joel didn't respond, but Blake could feel his entire frame shaking. Gritting his teeth, he guided them forward, one hand gripping Joel while the other waved back and forth before him, doing little to help him keep his balance as the wind surged even stronger. It was as if it were trying to blow them off the mountain.

Blake's fingers curled into icy claws, and his fingers shook with each step, but he kept going, praying that the convoluted shape was real. The swirling snow played tricks on his eyes, and it seemed as if they were getting farther away rather than closer, but rough stone grazed his searching fingertips twenty steps later, and Blake collapsed into the tiny alcove. Joel fell beside him, using his elbows to crawl up the snowy rock floor.

He was right. The shadowy outline was a curved boulder with a natural pocket that blocked the worst of the wind. Now that they were out of the wind and snow, Blake heard a furious chattering sound, only to realize it was his jaws clashing together with such force his teeth threatened to come loose.

"Blake!"

Blake tried to move his head toward the speaker, but his body was too cold. He didn't have any energy left. "B-B-Bia?" he whispered between his bouncing teeth.

"Oh my g-goddess. Jez, help me get them up here."

Blake frowned at her. She didn't even have goose bumps.

A pair of strong arms hooked beneath Blake's armpits and hauled him farther into the shelter. With some effort, Bia was able to maneuver Blake's legs.

She sat him down with his back pressed against cold rock. Suddenly, her face was inches away, her amber eyes clear and her cheeks glowing with a rosy hue.

"Give me y-your hands," she instructed, then wrapped his shaking fingers in her warm embrace. "This might hurt." A raspberry glow emanated from their joined hands, the only color in the stark white wasteland.

Blake's skin tingled, becoming painful as the blood flow switched directions, pulsing away from his heart to reclaim his extremities and fend off the threat of frostbite. Bit by bit, his teeth ceased chattering and he felt a bubble of warmth spread from within. He flexed his fingers inside Bia's grasp, amazed that the feeling had returned.

"Bia!" Jezlem shouted. "Hurry, Joel needs you!"

Bia dropped Blake's hands. "Better?"

Blake nodded, his mind able to focus on something besides the cold at last. "Yeah, go help him." He gestured to where Jezlem crouched over Joel.

Bia spun, her movements graceful over the snow. Craning his neck, Blake watched as she drove the cold out of Joel's body as well. She touched the wound on his head and set to work healing the gash.

A flash of light blue flickered in the corner of Blake's eye. Jezlem was at his side. Rising to meet her, he flexed his fingers, still unsure if the blood was flowing correctly. "What happened?" he asked. "You said this time would be easy."

Jezlem burrowed the tip of her nose in her coat as the wind screamed, hammering their small shelter. "Wards," she replied. "Atlas must have more security measures in place than I thought."

"What do you mean?"

Jezlem gestured with her arm, her fingers tucked into the sleeves of her coat. "All this, it's a protection spell to ensure anyone curious enough to seek out Atlas never reaches their destination. I assume most who try end up dead."

Blake frowned. "This? It's a blizzard. We're on a mountain."

Jezlem's teal eyes glared at him. "And yet you're traveling with a nymph who can control the earth. It's a spell. If you listen closely, you can hear the pattern in the wind."

As if on cue, the wind howled, reminding Blake of the wolf pack once more. "How do we stop it?"

Jezlem shrugged. "I have no idea. Kait's the aurai. If she were here, she might have some luck controlling the cyclones, but the best Bia can do is enlarge this overhang."

"So we wait? Or try to find Atlas through the snow?"

"It won't stop, and it's impossible to go any farther. There's no visibility. We'd end up pitching ourselves off the side of the mountain."

Blake nodded. "So we came for nothing?"

"No." Jezlem shook her snow-kissed curls. "There's still a chance Bia might be able to use the sensors in the earth to locate Atlas's hideout. If we're close enough, it might work."

"But what if the wards are too strong and block Bia's magic?" Blake asked, starting to understand the worried look in Jezlem's eyes.

"Best case? Bia's able to transport us back to Florida, but if the wards are too strong…hopefully we freeze fast."

"Awesome." Blake huddled down farther into his collar. Without Bia's touch, the cold had claimed him again, or perhaps it was the hopeless thoughts of survival piling atop him like the angry snow.

"Everyone all r-right?" Bia asked, her voice heavy with more worry than usual.

Blake glanced at the nymph. Her sweater left her shoulder and neck exposed, and every few seconds, the material would lift above her stomach, exposing the smooth skin beneath. Yet Bia acted as if she couldn't feel the cold.

"How are you doing that?"

Bia tilted her head. "Heal him? It's one of m-my talents. I mastered the ability to fix minor wounds decades ago, but I must admit, it's only been a few weeks since I learned how to alter heart rate and blood flow."

"No, he means, how can you stand there in a thin shirt and not freeze," Joel explained, looking much better than the frozen corpse Blake pulled out of the ground half an hour ago.

"Nymphs don't get c-cold. We register the change in temperature, but it does little to affect our bodies."

Blake turned to Jezlem. "So this must be——-"

"Horrible? Terrifying? Shocking?" Jezlem scowled. "All those and more. How do you stand this?" Her teeth vibrated in her skull. She turned to Bia, clearly not really looking for an answer. "Do you think you can get around the wards? Find a way out of this mess?"

Bia took a step closer to the black stones at their backs and placed her palm flat against the wall while the fingers on her other hand moved in a swift pattern. She sighed. "The wards are strong. Clearly, Atlas doesn't want to be f-found, but there *is* something here—a large concentration of activity—but I can't tap into it. I can get close, but then my magic is deflected."

Walking along the wall, Bia traced her fingertips in curving lines, almost as if she were searching for a chink or weak spot. She paused and turned, leaning the back of her head against the stones. A strained breath whistled out between her lips. Bia's shoulders were rigid with effort, and her temples creased with steely focus.

"The b-boulders are the problem. If I concentrate on the earth, then—oh!"

Bia's unexpected cry caught everyone's attention. Blake glanced up to see the nymph fall backward into the rock, swallowed by a menacing black mouth.

"No!" Jezlem lunged forward. She reached for her sister, but the hole was sealed and her fists slammed against solid rock instead. "Bia! No, no, no!"

"What happened?" Joel asked.

"She's gone, you idiot. She must have set off another ward." Tears painted her face, their tracks freezing instantly on her skin.

"We can open it again. Just push the hidden button." Joel bumped against the wall, hitting and kicking the rock, but the entrance did not reappear.

Jezlem sobbed. "I never should have let her come."

"What more can we do? Check the rocks for a crevice or something."

Joel and Blake ransacked the alcove, pressing, touching, kicking, and smashing the rough surface again and again. After a few minutes, Jezlem joined, unleashing her fury. The ward remained inactive.

Jezlem stopped, her breathing ragged.

"What is it? Are you okay?" Blake asked.

Fear leapt into Jezlem's glassy eyes. "Someone's coming."

⚡ 29 ⚡

"Get down!" Jezlem ordered, pressing her body against the wall. Blake and Joel followed suit.

"Is it Atlas?" Joel's voice echoed off the rocks.

"I'm not sure. Stay quiet," Jezlem said under her breath.

"But don't we want him to find us?"

Jezlem flinched as Joel's loud words surrounded them. The trio pressed themselves farther back into the alcove. An eerie feeling crept into Blake's frozen toes, tickling the back of his mind.

"Something's wrong," he whispered, but his words were still too loud. Before, they had to shout to hear themselves. Blake locked eyes with Jezlem, seeing her come to the same conclusion. "The wind…it's gone."

Chancing a peek away from the black wall, Blake shuffled closer to the entrance and choked in surprise. No longer did the blizzard rage. Instead, each snowflake hung suspended in the slate-gray sky, as if the world were holding its breath. Hypnotized, Blake stepped out, ignoring Jezlem's hushed warning. He raised his hand to touch one of the flakes, able to view its intricate design in perfect detail.

"Guys, check this out." His cold breath enveloped the snowflake. He watched the delicate edges wilt and water vapor cling to the numerous spokes.

"Pretty spectacular, isn't it?" a sweet voice called, shattering the silence.

Blake looked up. He was supposed to stay hidden, yet he had walked right out into the open, a sitting duck. Blake peeked over his shoulder, curious but terrified. The speaker was female, and her voice was familiar.

It was a nymph. She wore a sky-blue snowsuit, her long legs tapering down to a pair of thick white boots. Blake allowed his eyes to wander, drinking in the nymph's graceful silhouette. Her jacket hugged her petite frame, and her hood was up, obscuring her face. A gentle golden halo of light surrounded her, like a nightlight chasing away his bad dreams. Dark chocolate curls cascaded down the front of her coat in heavy ringlets.

"It's not polite to stare," the nymph said with a smile in her voice. She stopped a few feet away from Blake and glanced up, fixing him with her violet eyes as her hood fell away.

Kait.

"Oh my God. It's you." Blake blinked in surprise. "What are you doing here? We thought—we thought Zeus had you."

Kait's lips parted, and a high-pitched chuckle slipped out as her eyes roamed over him. She took a step closer, arching her toes to whisper in Blake's ear.

"This is my favorite part." Kait's lips brushed the exposed skin on Blake's neck.

"What is?" Blake asked, his mind woozy.

"Watching you fall."

"Who are you?" Jezlem called, her voice a serrated knife severing the spell.

Kait's lips slid into an enchanting grin, and she batted her eyelashes. "I'm whoever you want me to be."

Her voice was honey, dripping sweet venom across the frozen tundra, warming Blake from the inside out. The punctuating sound of boots disturbing the snow sounded until Jezlem stood beside him.

"This is a trick," she said.

"Are you sure? Maybe you've stumbled into a wonderful dream?"

"Or hell. You're not real."

"How can you be so sure?"

Kait abandoned Blake and stepped in front of Jezlem, coiling one of her long curls around her slender finger.

The sound of scraping metal created ripples in the peaceful moment, jarring him. Blake shook his head and turned. Jezlem now held a knife to Kait's throat.

"I'll rephrase my question: *what* are you?" Jezlem twisted the knife so that the edge of the blade kissed Kait's dark skin.

"Jezlem!" Blake shouted. "What are you doing? That's your sister."

"No, she's not!" Jezlem hissed.

Joel came to stand on the other side of Blake. "What's going on?"

"I'd be happy to explain, but the knife is getting a little uncomfortable." Kait cocked her head. Her long waves brushed Jezlem's forearm. "What do you say, *Jez*? Let me go?"

Jezlem hesitated. Confusion and longing mixed in her eyes as she regarded Kait. Slowly, she lowered the knife to her waist, but kept the blade at the ready.

Kait rolled her neck, exaggerating the movement as she arched her back. She pushed out her chest and ran her hand down the length of her torso, highlighting her willowy curves. Blake frowned, trying to remember the nymph he met last week. Before, she was standoffish, even nervous around him, but now she seemed confident and brazen. He continued to stare. All of Kait's features were present, but something was off.

Kait tossed her curls over her shoulder, her fingertips fluttering above her neck. "You're lucky you didn't cut me. He wouldn't have been pleased with you if you had."

"Who are you?" Jezlem asked again.

The same devilish grin dominated Kait's lips, transforming her features. A flicker passed over her, like a hologram lagging. "I can be whoever you want. I twist and contort, morphing my features to become the perfect snare." Her eyes traveled first to Joel and then to Blake, gleaming. "I am a mistake, but a lethal one."

Jezlem's jaw fell slack, and she took a step back. "Oh my goddess. You're an omodian." Her breath danced off her lips in a gentle puff of vapor.

"What is that?" Blake's eyes flickered back to Kait.

"I'm a shape changer—a true rarity among nymphs. I take the form of the one you want most. It's not until I reveal my true self that the mirage is shattered. But by then, well…" Kait smirked. "By then, it's too late. I'm in your head, under your skin. I can do whatever I want to you, because you want me too."

Her voice was smooth, lulling Blake into a sense of calm. He vaguely noticed that she had left her place in front of Jezlem and sidled up before him. Her movements were as fluid as water, curving and gliding so sensually she seemed to float above the snow.

"What is it you'd like me to do to you?" Kait whispered, walking her fingertips down the front of Blake's thigh as she rubbed his jaw with her cheek.

A loud thwack broke the spell. Blake shivered, wiping snow off his face. He blinked at Jezlem, who was readying another snowball.

"Oh, little mortal, you're starting to get on my nerves," Kait said through her teeth. "I just wanted to have a little fun."

"And once your fun was over, you'd leave him in the snow to freeze to death." Jezlem glared. "I know your games. I've heard the stories. Your kind are dangerous, dark nymphs created in the time of the Titans."

Kait waved her hand and rolled her eyes. "Spare me the history lesson."

Joel groaned. "Someone please tell me what's going on."

"This nymph is an omodian," Jezlem explained, her jaw clenched. "Her talent lies not with a single element, but with flesh and blood."

"And memories," the nymph added. "I can scramble your most precious thoughts, distort your past, and erase the faces of loved ones. I can make you a ghost."

"She changes her appearance to mimic the person who will make you the most vulnerable. I thought they were all dead." Jezlem's eyes slid to the nymph once more.

"Nope, still one left."

"So, what do you really look like?" Blake asked. Part of him was relieved that the nymph before him wasn't Kait. She was so different. He felt like a fool for not realizing it sooner. Yet, another part of him was terrified. He was meant to see the person who disarmed him the most. Was that Kait? Apart from their brief meeting, he didn't really know anything about her. What did it mean that he saw her? Maybe she assumed he desired Kait because he was there trying to save her. Blake put a hand to his head.

"I can show you." Kait whirled back to Blake. "Should I take my suit off for the full effect?"

"Just alter your facial features, please." Jezlem's lips were set in a firm line, but ghosts haunted her eyes.

"Have it your way." Her voice bubbled with seduction.

The nymph squared her shoulders and calmed her face to a neutral expression. Another series of flickers made her skin vibrate, and then the change began. The nymph's heavy curls shortened, flattening to ink-black wisps ending just below her shoulders. Kaitaini's dark skin paled to a smooth, ivory finish. She resembled a porcelain doll. The bright violet bleached from her eyes, leaving behind a color so translucent, her irises shown like frigid ice. Black slender eyebrows arched high on her forehead as her nose narrowed above a set of pink lips.

"Whoa," Blake and Joel breathed at the same time.

The nymph licked her lips and rolled her neck. "An improvement, I'm sure."

"What is your name?" Jezlem asked, still wary.

"Layla. Shall we head in?"

Blake looked around. "Head in where?"

Layla laughed. "You're here to see Atlas, correct? I can't think of any other godforsaken reason you'd come up here." Her voice was light and teasing, but Blake sensed a strong undercurrent of frustration as she gazed at them.

"Yes, we have a proposition for him," Jezlem said. "And I'd like to have my sister back."

Layla nodded. "She did cause some trouble when Atlas snagged her."

She waltzed past the trio, straight to the spot where Bia disappeared. A flash of silver spun in her hand—a knife, its tip sharp and serrated like a tooth of a shark. Before anyone could react, Layla drew the blade down her own palm until scarlet blood pulsed to the surface. The knife vanished into the cold air, and Layla pressed her bleeding palm to the snow-crusted stones.

A moment later, the ground shook as the hidden door slid open. The same gaping hole from earlier now waited for them. Layla turned, gesturing for the group to enter.

"Come on. Atlas doesn't like to wait."

Layla raised her palm in front of her face. Using her tongue, she licked the thin line of blood from the base of her hand up, grinning like a bathing cat. Blake cleared his throat and averted his eyes, shouldering past the others. With a dry swallow, he stepped inside the mountain.

The others joined him, their shuffling feet and warm breaths the only sound. It was pitch black inside. Blake put out his hands and was surprised when his knuckles scraped the wall. The hallway was narrow. Claustrophobia made his heart pound. He was inside a mountain, in an alley barely big enough to pass through. What if the walls started to cave in? What if the blackness never went away? Blake took several steadying breaths, forcing himself to count to three before exhaling so he didn't hyperventilate.

"You'll have to follow me," Layla sang in her high-pitched voice.

A chorus of grumbles echoed in the tunnel as Layla pushed to the front of the line.

Blake glanced over his shoulder, a small blossom of relief slowing his racing heart. Behind him, the light blue halo that surrounded Layla emitted a very dull light, but it was enough to force the choking darkness away. Her gaze found Blake's, and her smile widened as she pushed Jezlem into the wall.

"Sorry," Layla muttered, but her expression was far from it. "Hey, Blake, mind if I slip by you?"

Blake shook his head and pressed himself against the wall, trying to give her as much space as his large jacket would allow.

"Thanks." She slipped by, brushing her firm backside against the front of his jeans. "It's a tight fit," she whispered with a wink.

Blake's cheeks burned a dark red, and he was thankful for the dim lighting. Layla continued by. A longing sigh wrapped around his brain. He had to focus.

"How much farther?" Joel called from the back, his voice loud as a cannon.

"A few more twists," Layla said. "Stay close together. There are tunnels that branch off into different parts of the mountain. Believe me, you don't want to wander down the wrong one."

Images of giant spiders skirting the walls or bloodthirsty monsters moaning for his flesh flashed in Blake's mind. He shook his head to dislodge them and focused instead on the blue halo that surrounded Layla. When Blake first noticed Kait's golden shimmer, he'd thought his eyes were playing tricks on him, but as he looked closer at the nymph in front of him, he could see the way the pores in her skin shone like thousands of crushed diamonds. The effect was subtle, but incredible.

With a startled gasp, Blake realized Layla was standing still directly in front of him. He stopped short to avoid walking into her. Layla smiled, slow and lazy, as her arms wrapped around his neck in the dark.

"Keep staring. I love the feeling of your eyes on me." Her breath clung to his neck. "Maybe you'd like to put your hands on me too. It's been so long since I've had someone new to play with."

"We should keep moving," Jezlem called, causing Blake to jump. "We don't want to keep Atlas waiting. Isn't that right?" Her words were crisp, non-negotiable.

Layla moved away from Blake. "Of course."

He cleared his throat and followed after her. He hurried to keep up, increasing his pace as Layla danced through the tight turns. Several minutes later, he noticed another source of light illuminating the far end of the tunnel. Without a backward glance, Layla raced out of the dark, disappearing from view.

"Hey, wait up!" Blake called, scraping the back of his hand on the humped rocks jutting out unevenly from the walls.

"What's going on?" Jezlem called.

"Layla—she's gone. I see a light up ahead though."

With the additional light, he started to run and reached the break in the tunnel a few moments later. He rested one hand on the rough rock while he gazed into the light. His jaw fell slack, and his eyes widened in disbelief. The rhythm of slapping footsteps quieted to a shuffle as Jezlem and Joel reached his side.

Joel gasped, mirroring Blake's awe. "Whoa."

"Yeah, not what I was expecting." Blake took in the ornate room sprawled out in front of them.

No longer were they enclosed in a suffocating tunnel. Layla had led them into the center of the mountain. The room was very wide, with ceilings so high, the pinnacle was lost in the shadows. Blake's gaze wandered down to the eclectic array of furniture scattered atop the thick Persian rugs. Numerous chairs, couches, tables, and desks were arranged in small groupings. At the back, half a dozen stone pillars separated a large clearing from the rest of the room. Metal glinted from built-in shelves, winking menacingly. A massive bed with sheer white gossamer curtains decorating the towering posts sat along the right-hand wall. Bookshelves lined the stone walls, wrapping around the entire room, their dusty volumes casting a silent vigil over the newcomers.

There was so much to take in that Blake missed the angry man charging at them from the left. Too late, Blake turned, his eyebrows shooting up in surprise as a man with long white hair came to a stop in front of them. He crossed his arms, his muscles bulging.

"Mortals." He sneered, picking his teeth with his fingernail. "You're a sorry-looking bunch. Come, we don't have much time to prepare."

"Prepare for what?" Joel asked.

"For the only reason you'd seek me out. For the only reason any of us are here. Zeus."

⚡ 30 ⚡

"Keep your mouth shut and a smile on your face, understand?" Zeus growled in Kait's ear.

The blindfold slipped away, and she blinked against the unexpected brightness. They were no longer in the cave. Instead, the bustling streets of a busy city welcomed her. She inhaled deeply. The air was heavy with exotic smells and oblivious humans, each of their scents adding to the cacophony of flavors.

"Where are we?" Kait asked, unable to help herself.

"Paris." Zeus snaked his arm around her waist. Kait could feel the electricity pulsing from his skin. Two thin silver bracelets decorated her wrists. Carefully glamoured, the fiery manacles appeared to be nothing more than delicate jewelry, but they still hummed with power and debilitated Kait's magic.

"But—"

Zeus spun her body into his and crushed her lips with his own, silencing her question.

"I told you to keep your mouth shut, or I'll forgo this trip and kill all these lovely people enjoying the day."

Kait pushed off Zeus's chest. She closed her mouth, tasting him on her lips. A flurry of insults leapt to her mind, but she refrained. Instead, she spat a stream of saliva onto the sidewalk, narrowly missing the god's foot.

"I'm going to overlook that, but you'd be wise to heed my warning."

His arm flashed as he tightened his hold on her waist. Kait rolled her shoulders, twisting away from his touch as much as possible. Zeus shifted his weight and leaned into her, eradicating the thin space she had gained.

"None of that, my dear. I'm taking a great risk exposing you like this, though it seems the Council is still blind to my deeds. Didn't they listen to you at all?"

Kait seethed, anger at Zeus and the queen's resistance culminating together to make her blood ring in her ears. She had to get away from him, but she couldn't possibly run, not with her hands and magic rendered useless. Her violet eyes scanned the mortals walking alongside them. Some showed interest in them, but mostly, they were ignored.

"Why did you bother bringing me out, then? Even if the Council isn't searching for you, the queen's soldiers are."

Zeus guided her through a set of glass doors into an elegant boutique. The word *Chanel* was written on the white marble floor in elegant script.

He steered her through the endless racks of expensive silks and faux furs, his fingertips grazing each item. She noticed he was careful not to look at her. Zeus paused, holding up a slinky black dress. "This would look spectacular on you."

"You didn't answer my question."

Zeus waved his fingers in response. Kait's tongue felt like a dead sea slug shoved inside her mouth. He pulled her close and ran his mouth along her jaw, whispering into her ear. To any onlookers, they embraced like passionate lovers. If only they could hear the sweet nothings he told her.

"Another word leaves those pretty lips, and I'll slice them off. Understand?"

Kait nodded, unable to reply even if she wanted to.

Zeus sighed. He pulled away, but kept one hand on Kait's hips, his grip possessive. "Black is too sullen." He replaced the hanger on the rack and pushed her toward another row. He withdrew an even racier red dress. "What about this one?"

Zeus cocked his head, fixing her with a dazzling smile, but underneath, she caught a glimpse of the ugly creature prowling beneath his perfect exterior.

"Why don't we try this one on?" His deft fingers slid her straps off her shoulders.

Panic overwhelmed Kait. Craning her neck, she looked for an associate, but they were partially blocked by a large floral arrangement. Revulsion climbed her throat. She spun away and beat Zeus's chest with her fists, but before she could land one punch, he let the red dress puddle at their feet and shoved her against a black table displaying cashmere scarves. His fingers slipped beneath her dress, gripping her upper thigh.

"Go on, fight me off you. I'll have you right now and kill every mortal in here while you watch." His fingers stroked the soft skin between her legs, tapping her thin panties.

"Do you need help finding anything?" a hesitant salesperson asked, their words curling musically in French.

Zeus straightened, withdrawing his hand while his other arm remained snaked around Kait's waist. "Sorry. We're on our honeymoon, and I can't seem to keep my hands off my beautiful wife," Zeus replied in perfect French, his accent flawless.

"That's so sweet," the saleswoman chimed. "Can I help you find something for the special occasion?"

"No, we're fine, thank you. But I will be sure to let you know."

The woman gave a slight nod, her brown eyes raking Zeus appreciatively. If she only knew.

Zeus turned back to Kait, a playful smile on his lips—a stark contrast to the severity of his gaze. "I'm a god, and you are a nymph. The sooner you understand that you are mine to use as I like, the better this arrangement will be for both of us. You are a flaming star, burning through the cosmos, but every star must die."

Zeus shifted his shoulders and pulled out one last dress. A thin strap hooked around the hanger, and silk cascaded from it like a golden waterfall.

"I think this is the one," he said, his carefree mask slipping into place once more.

Kait pressed her lips into a thin line, still mute, but her eyes questioned the need for a new dress adequately enough.

"We've been invited to a little get together," Zeus told her. "And every woman needs a party dress."

Atlas collapsed into an armchair, pulling Layla down on top of his lap. "So how did you manage to incite a god? And not just any god, Zeus of all people." His booming laughter was unmistakably cruel.

Blake shrugged out of his jacket and sat on the arm of a nearby couch as Joel occupied the cushion. "It wasn't planned. It just happened."

Atlas shook his head and sat forward, wrapping his long hair in a bun with a rubber band from his wrist. "Hell of a day." He arched his eyebrows. "How did you know to seek me out? How did you find me?"

Before the conversation could continue, the lamps on the end tables surrounding them shook, then clattered to the floor in dozens of ceramic and glass shards. A large gash split the floor in two along the side of the wall. Numerous books leapt from the shelves.

"What's going on?" Joel looked up at the ceiling as if it might come crashing down.

An annoyed frown dominated Atlas's face. "That's not my doing."

A moment later, Bia appeared, brushing broken pebbles and dirt off her shoulders. "Thanks f-for the concern. You could have at least asked about me."

"We were getting to you," Jezlem replied, looking sheepish. "A lot was going on."

Bia sat down beside Joel. "Well, I'm fine, if you w-were wondering. As soon as I realized w-what happened, I merged with the earth to stay out of his grasp."

"We tried to find you outside," Joel offered, but Bia shot him a pointed look. "Let's get on w-with it."

"Are you going to fix that?" Atlas asked, gesturing to the huge crack in the floor.

"No."

Atlas hissed under his breath. "You came to me for help. I suggest you clean up your mess." His icelike eyes flashed, simmering with rage.

"Bia," Jezlem warned.

"Okay." Bia slunk out from under the Titan's fierce stare.

Once Bia began sealing the floor, Atlas cleared his throat, his anger simmering. Blake got the impression he had an explosive temper. "Back to wherever we were, then."

Blake sighed. "Long story short? I'm the only thing standing in the way of a captured nymph's freedom—a nymph Zeus seeks to rape and destroy. I need to defeat him; otherwise, he's going to kill the both of us. Can you help me find him?"

Atlas scoffed. "I don't think finding him will be the problem. Sounds to me like he wants to fight. If I were you, I'd start mastering the sword or at least do some push-ups." Atlas's gaze scanned Blake up and down, unimpressed. "There's some weaponry over in the far corner. Help yourself."

Blake nodded and glanced toward the back corner. He was surprised to see such a vast collection lining the chiseled cavern walls, ranging from medieval long swords, battle axes, and bows, to more modern-day weapons like throwing stars, grenades, and bayonets.

"There's one other thing," Jezlem said, hesitant.

Atlas and Layla peered at her, their eyebrows raised. "By all means," Atlas said, "as long as I'm granting wishes."

Jezlem's cheeks flushed pink, and she wrung her hands. "I'm not sure if it's possible or if it has ever been done before, but I was wondering if you knew how to possibly restore my elemental connection? Zeus... He..."

"You don't want to remain mortal?" Atlas guessed.

Layla hit his large bicep. "Can you blame her? I don't know, sweetheart." She frowned. "I've never heard of such a thing."

Jezlem bowed her head. "Okay, thank you anyway. I knew it was a long shot. I should have known."

Blake had to look away from the disappointment that claimed Jezlem's hopeful features. "There has to be something," he said.

"Layla's right." Atlas pursed his lips. "I've never come across an…antidote, if you will, for the effects of a god's touch, but have a look. Maybe these volumes hold the secret."

Jezlem glanced at the endless sea of tomes apprehensively but rose from the couch, wandering over to the towering shelves.

"I'll help you l-look." Bia shot a cool glance at Atlas as she returned from healing the floor.

Layla slid off Atlas's lap. "Me too."

"Really? You don't have to."

Layla shrugged. "It's not like I have anything better going on."

The three women started combing through the ancient texts, silently at first, and then Layla began asking probing questions that Blake pretended not to hear.

"How long has it been?"

"About four months," Jezlem replied, not meeting the nymph's gaze.

"How did he find you?"

Jezlem cleared her throat. "He used a disguise and tricked me into falling for him. When I confronted him, he had a piriol waiting. I couldn't get away."

"Did it hurt?"

"What?"

"Losing the connection. What did it feel like?"

"Oh, it…" She twisted her finger around a long curl, pulling the strand of hair tight. "It was terrible. Like I had been left with my wrists sliced, bleeding out every ounce of magic within me until I was nothing more than a shell. It took everything out of me. He took everything from me."

Layla was quiet for a minute and then slammed the book she was skimming with more force than necessary. "Sounds like an asshole to me." She grinned.

A small laugh hiccupped out of Jezlem. "Yes. Yes, he is."

"It's a good thing we're going to kill him them." Layla's strange eyes flickered like a snake's.

Blake swallowed roughly as he imagined Jezlem lying there broken and alone. He refused to let the same fate befall Kait. Atlas cleared his throat, drawing Blake's attention once again.

"Now, boy. Get to it."

Blake leapt to his feet and looked to Joel. "Come on."

The two boys headed for the weapons collection, though Blake had no idea what exactly they were supposed to do. This wasn't the fourteenth century. It wasn't like he already had a basic idea of swordplay and just needed to get warmed up. He knew how to throw a punch, but what chance did his fists stand against swords and whips?

Blake exhaled, picturing how pathetic the fight would be. He hadn't managed to do anything right. As always, life was tossing him around, laughing as he struggled to land on his feet. Frustration boiled inside. He grabbed a heavy axe from the stand and lifted it above his head, a sandbag his target. But the weight was too heavy, and the axe pulled him off balance. Both Blake and the weapon clattered to the stone floor.

Heavy footsteps echoed as Atlas joined them, tucking a piece of crumpled paper into the front pocket of his jeans.

"I hope Zeus decides to get drunk before your big battle. What was that?" He grabbed a long sword from one of the racks, wielded it over his head, and pointed to a nearby end table. "Pretend that's Zeus's skull." With a quick breath, he swung the sword down in a graceful arc, slicing through the thick wood easily.

Blake and Joel stared, their mouths hanging open.

"It's that easy, huh?" Blake said at last, climbing to his feet.

"If you know what you're doing."

Blake rolled his eyes. "Look, no offense, but this is a waste of time. I haven't spent the last hundred years working out, and there's no way I'll learn any game-changing moves before the time limit is up. I only have a day and a half left. This is a joke. I don't know why I agreed to this game in the first place." Blake kicked the handle of the axe and crossed his arms over his chest.

"We can always hit him with a grenade," Joel volunteered, scouring the shelves containing enough weapons to destroy a small country. "Why do you have these?"

Atlas strode to a polished table amidst the metal racks and set down the sword. "You never know what you'll run into. Even though I'm no longer immortal, I still have enemies. They come in all shapes and sizes too, so I like to be prepared. I've been collecting these since I was cast out of Olympus. As you can see, they span centuries. And for your information"—Atlas turned his eyes on Blake—"even immortals can be wounded. It's true you won't be able to kill him, but maiming...maiming is easy." Atlas picked up a silver throwing star and tossed it to Blake. He fumbled with the jagged points. "You need to use your imagination."

Understanding brightened in Blake's eyes, and he spun the lethal star around his index finger. "Why are you helping us?"

"I'm not helping you. I'm helping myself."

"What does that mean?"

Atlas picked up a crossbow and pulled the string taunt. "Zeus and I have an arrangement. He spared my life after the Titan War—exile in place of execution. He charged me with the burden of maintaining the veil that keeps Olympus and the ethereal realms from human observation. In exchange for my life, I offer him my mountain as a retreat whenever he needs a place to…escape the stress and limitations of Olympus. I swore an unbreakable oath upon my defeat after the Titan War. I promised to never kill another god, so you're going to do my dirty work for me." He grinned, running a hand through his white hair. "Once Zeus is dead, I can leave this miserable mountain and relinquish my duties. Keeping you humans ignorant will be someone else's problem."

"But I thought you said immortals can't be killed," Blake said.

"Weren't you listening? The soul can't be killed, but the body can. It's just a vessel. Once the connection is severed, his soul will be powerless, and I will be free."

Joel brandished a heavy gold whip. "Where do we start?"

Atlas squeezed the trigger, and the crossbow exploded with a powerful *thwang*. The metal arrow soared through the air, then buried itself into a wooden shield hanging off the wall. "Target practice."

⚡ 31 ⚡

Thunk, thunk, thunk.

Steel stars flipped through the air and bounced off the rock pillars that separated the armory from the rest of the room. The stars zinged past Blake's skin, narrowly missing the tip of his ear, his index finger, and his elbow. He tried not to flinch, but Atlas's smirk told him he had.

"Why are you the one throwing?" Blake called. "Shouldn't I be practicing?"

Atlas crossed the short distance between them, kicking one of the stars with the toe of his shoe. "First, you need to learn to control your emotions. Zeus is a shark; once he smells blood, he won't hesitate to tear you to pieces. Get your emotions in check, mask your fear, and then we move on to the actual fighting. Again," he ordered, stooping down to collect the fallen star.

Blake exhaled and wiped the sweat off his brow. Joel stood off to the side, fitting the crossbow with a sleek metal arrow. Atlas raised the first star and arched his eyebrows. Blake steeled himself, biting down hard on the inside of his cheek. He drew in a steadying breath.

Atlas raised his arm and flicked his wrist, his movements graceful. The star danced through the air, flashing once before it struck the pillar inches from Blake's head. He released the breath.

"Well done. A little closer this time, I think." Atlas drew back his hand again and let the second star fly. Blake set his eyes on a spot just above Atlas's head and forced his eyes to remain open. The star whooshed by, the small breeze tickling his nose. "Not bad." A wild gleam leapt into Atlas's eyes. "Last one."

His arm wound up and released. The star spun directly at Blake's chest. An alarm rang in the back of Blake's mind, and his eyes shifted down just in time to see the hurtling star's trajectory. Throwing his right arm around his torso, he pulled himself to the left seconds before the star bit into the center of the pillar rather than his rib cage.

"What the hell was that?" Joel cried. "You could have killed him."

Atlas fixed Joel with an indifferent stare. "Training is all about preparing for the unexpected. Do you really think Zeus is going to stand there and let you cut holes in him? No. He is going to try to kill you. The least you can do is make him work a little." Atlas stepped in front of Blake and gripped his chin, forcing his face up. "Always keep your eyes on your opponent. Look away and you're dead." He pushed Blake away, causing him to stumble.

"Let's go again," Blake said, regaining his footing. "One-on-one, me and you."

Atlas shrugged and spread his hands wide. "Fine. Which weapon?"

Blake shook his head. "No weapons. Let's try some hand-to-hand combat."

A throaty chuckle reverberated in Atlas's broad chest. "I'm not going to take it easy on you, boy." He took a step forward.

Blake replied by putting up his fists. He circled Atlas, positioning himself just outside his long reach. He took a steadying breath as muscle memory took over, his feet slipping into the familiar rhythm years of boxing ingrained in him. Atlas's lips twitched at the corner of his mouth, his confidence brimming. He obviously didn't take Blake seriously.

Atlas swung first, fast and accurate, catching Blake in the left cheek. The hit was powerful, and Blake shook his head to regain his focus. Atlas was there, taking advantage to close the gap. He smacked Blake's other cheek with an open palm, sending him reeling into a side table.

Blake stood up and licked his lip, tasting blood where his teeth cut it. He put his hands back up, and Atlas jabbed once more from the left, but Blake was ready. Ducking his head, he pulled his arms in tight to his body and spun on his heel. Completing the motion, he brought his left elbow up and smashed it into Atlas's nose.

The thin cartilage cracked under Blake's hit, catching Atlas off guard and unleashing a shallow gush of blood. Atlas grinned, ignoring the blood dripping onto his teeth. He took two long strides, then grabbed Blake by shoulder and punched him in the face, knocking him to the ground. Blake's skull cracked against the stone floor, but he rolled out of the way of Atlas's second punch.

Blake leapt to his feet, brought his fist up, and smacked Atlas in the ear one, two, three times before the Titan whirled, now wielding a double-sided axe. The glinting metal reached for Blake, catching the edge of his shirt with its razor-sharp teeth. He glanced down at the torn material where his stomach peeked through. The game had changed, but he couldn't give Atlas a reason to think he was weak.

Atlas swung again, backing Blake into the wall, cornering his prey. Blake lunged for a gold staff positioned on the bottom shelf, but Atlas hammered the axe down, cutting off Blake's reach and skimming his pinky. Blake pulled his hand in, inhaling as the cool wind burned his bleeding finger. If he was mutilated before he even found Zeus, he didn't stand a chance at saving Kait.

"Yield," Blake said. "I said no weapons."

"Yeah, lay off, man," Joel called.

Atlas regarded the boys like a wild animal, licking his lips, thirsty for more blood. "There are no rules in this game, boy." Blood still trickled down his lips and chin. "You think Zeus will fight fair? He'll cut your head off and stick it on a pike so fast, your tongue will still be wagging. You're a fool. I should just kill you now. Save you the humiliation. A corpse is a corpse, no matter who kills it."

"Atlas, what's going on?"

Blake's eyes wandered away from the Titan to Layla. Concern and confusion shone in her translucent eyes.

"Blake wanted a taste of the fight to come." Atlas spat blood down the front of his shirt. "I was obliging our guests."

"We're supposed to help them, not kill them." Layla's sharp reprimand lashed out like a whip. "Don't do this. It's our only chance. Do you understand? Drop the axe and cool down. You've been cooped up in here too long. Go outside and check the stratosphere levels or something." She turned away from Atlas, ignoring him as he pivoted on his heels and stalked into the tunnels, grumbling under his breath. Layla laid a cool hand on Blake's bleeding face. "Are you all right?"

Blake nodded, wiping the blood off his mouth with the back of his hand.

"Sorry about that. He gets tunnel vision. Doesn't know how to stop himself once he's gone over the edge."

"Does that happen often?" Joel joked, but Blake could tell he was shaken.

"Lately, he's been more ornery than usual. It's being trapped in here. There aren't many outlets for frustration."

Layla led them back to the couches, where Jezlem and Bia were camped out, scouring several thick volumes. Blake shuddered, remembering the way Atlas had looked at him moments before. Anyone on the other side of his fury didn't stand a chance.

"You say that like you're trapped here too," Joel said.

Layla sighed, pulling her hair over her left shoulder as she remained standing. "I am. I was one of Atlas's prisoners. The Titans collected all the omodians at the end, hoping to increase their strength against the Olympians by indulging in a vast amount of euphoria at once. I watched as he raped my sisters, then slit their throats once he absorbed their halos. Finally, it was my turn. He grabbed my hair and spread my legs, but before he could do anything more, Artemis shot an arrow through his back and the gods descended."

Jezlem gasped. "What? He tried to take you? What are you doing with him now?" She let the yellowed-paged book slip from her fingertips.

"Once the Olympians realized what I was and what I could do, they agreed to have me executed. You see, omodians weren't created by Gaia like the rest of the elemental nymphs. We were bred by one of the female Titanesses, Theia. She crafted the race of omodians using elements of the dark side of the moon and the beauty of the coming dawn. Omodians were meant to rival Gaia's creations. The Titans wanted to show the gods they could bring beauty into the world as well, but for all the power our race had, we lacked compassion and carried out the Titans' orders to trick and kill lesser beings without hesitation—a trait the gods didn't favor whilst trying to establish a new world."

"Why did they let you live?" Jezlem asked.

"I begged. I begged for a second chance. I told them I would do anything to make up for the crimes I'd been ordered to commit."

Bia's eyes widened. "They e-exiled you w-with Atlas."

"What?" Blake said with a jerk. "After what he almost did to you?"

Layla nodded. "They agreed to let me live, but they didn't trust me to stay in Olean, so Zeus banished me with Atlas and confined us to this mountain."

"But th-that was thousands of y-years ago."

"Yes. They stripped him of his powers but ensured he would live forever to maintain and carry the burden of the veil. As for me? They gave me immortality."

"That's cool," Joel said.

Layla fixed him with a frigid stare. "You're right. I should be grateful that beast can take me over and over again and my halo remains intact."

"Oh, sorry. I didn't think about that."

Jezlem shook her head. "But earlier, you two seemed happy, comfortable with one another."

Layla played with the ends of her hair. "A relationship born out of necessity. We only have each other for eternity. I figured my wretched existence would be a little less miserable if I didn't wallow in isolation. That's why it's such a treat when we have company. It makes me feel like I'm back with my sisters."

The group was quiet for a few minutes, each at a loss for what to say next. Blake was stunned. Layla's bold and confident personality had cloaked this fragile insecurity. It was almost as if they were peeking behind the curtain at who she really was—a tortured soul like the rest of them.

Jezlem narrowed her gaze. "When you have company. What does that mean—"

"Where did you learn to fight like that?" Layla asked, talking over Jezlem's question. "It's not easy to land a punch on Atlas."

Blake shrugged. "I learned how to box a few years ago."

"He was awesome." Joel's enthusiasm eased the awkward tension among the group. "He dropped this one guy like a sack of potatoes."

Layla eyed Blake's soft physique. "Why'd you stop?"

"We couldn't afford it." He rubbed the back of his neck.

"Well, that was very impressive. Want to spar against me?" Layla put up her fists.

Blake shook his head and scoffed. "No way. You'd kick my ass. That was the first time I've done that in a while. Besides, I think I've had enough practice for one day." Blake sunk into an unoccupied chair. His limbs felt as if they weighed fifty pounds each, and his eyes fought to stay open. When was the last time he'd slept?

Layla moved to stand behind Blake's chair. "Well, for what it's worth, I thought you were really good."

Bia and Jezlem wandered back to the pile of books, immersing themselves in the ancient texts once again, while Joel curled up and drifted off to sleep on the floor near the occupied couches.

"Thanks. But I doubt punching Zeus in the face a few times will result in victory."

Layla leaned down. "Leave that to me," she whispered. Her words tickled Blake's ear.

He glanced at the others, but they hadn't heard Layla. "What do you mean?" His mind grew fuzzy as he tried to fight off exhaustion.

"You'll see. I can help you even the odds, but you have to do something for me in return." She kept her voice so low, Blake wondered if he was imagining the conversation.

Blake's eyelids fluttered. "Do what?"

"Shh. Don't worry. Sleep now." She pulled away, her unique scent of cinnamon and clove wrapping around his senses.

Blake shifted his body and exhaled, giving in to his exhaustion.

"How long has it been since you all took a break?" Layla's voice cut in and out as Blake tried to remain conscious.

"A while," Bia admitted. "We c-could all use a good night's sleep."

"Then rest. I'll make sure Atlas doesn't slit your throats while you dream," Layla joked, but something in her tone sounded forced.

Blake frowned but didn't open his eyes. Sleep claimed him, spreading through his body like a welcomed drug.

"Sleep well," Layla whispered.

⚡

Blake was walking. His footsteps echoed eerily within the black tunnel. From somewhere up ahead, he heard the steady sound of flowing water. Had he wandered deeper into the mountain?

A throaty laugh surrounded him, twisting his gut as the feeling of being watched caused his skin to prickle.

"Who's there?" Blake called, feeling with his hands for any indication of where he was. His fingers came away wet, and the cool air turned stale and humid. Blake imagined himself standing in a great beast's mouth. He only hoped he'd be able to escape before it awoke and swallowed.

"So glad you could join us." The voice rang out in the tunnel as the words whispered inside Blake's mind at the same time. "I've been growing impatient."

A dim light flared to life, dully illuminating the small room Blake found himself in. He could make out wispy outlines and shifting silhouettes.

"Enough games, Zeus." A heavy weight materialized in Blake's hands. He ran his hand up the length of the powerful staff and felt the cold metal knives mounted to the tip. He took a steadying breath, his confidence growing a fraction now that he had a concrete weapon.

"Oh, but I have one more to play." It was impossible to pinpoint where Zeus's voice was coming from, especially when it repeated in Blake's mind, as if it were his own thought. "You're so close to the prize. All hail the conquering hero. All you have to do is find your nymph."

Blake gripped the staff tighter in his sweaty palms. "I know you won't let us leave. It's another trap. The only way out is to kill you."

Another dangerous laugh sounded to Blake's left, and he spun around, jabbing the darkness with the jagged blades.

"Quite right."

Blake slashed the space around him, straining his eyes to make out anything in the blackness.

"Oh, that was a close one. You're getting warmer."

Blake thought he saw a tall shadow shift up ahead. As quietly as he could, Blake closed the distance between him and the god, bouncing the staff in his palms as he readied to strike.

"Warmer," Zeus hissed, his voice an angry yellow jacket stinging Blake from the inside.

The shadow directly in front of him moved, and Blake didn't hesitate. Thrusting the staff forward, he buried it in the center of the shadow, plunging it in as hard as he could until he heard the satisfying sound of the blades severing flesh. Warm liquid pulsed down the length of the metal, pooling in the space between his thumb and forefinger.

Blake released his hold. The staff drooped but remained embedded in the god's stomach. He took a step forward, smelling blood, and smiled. "Gotcha."

An eruption of light and sound assailed him as a chorus of applause accompanied numerous floodlights. Blake shielded his eyes. Large black splotches danced behind his eyelids.

"Well done, well done! Marvelous effort!" Zeus exclaimed, his hand claps bursts of gunfire.

Blake opened his eyes against the harsh white light. Zeus was standing on the far right wall, a devilish smile on his lips and his piercing blue eyes alive with anticipation.

"Honestly, I don't think I could have done a better job myself." He gestured to the wall in front of Blake.

"But how?" Blake's gaze followed Zeus's directive. He sucked in his breath. All warmth and color drained from his body. Kait stood before him, his ugly staff buried in her chest. "No! You tricked me."

A scarlet bubble of blood popped on her lips, dribbling down her chin. Her violet eyes rolled into the back of her head. The blank whites gleamed accusingly at him.

Zeus's laughter enveloped Blake as Kait slouched forward, and her golden halo faded. Her lips parted, and she choked out one syllable as she fell:

"Blake."

Blake woke with a start, his eyes snapping open. There was blood, so much blood, because of him. He had killed Kait, watched the light drain from her eyes. He flinched when he caught sight of a body lying at his feet, but the macabre visions he had just escaped from faded, and he realized it was only Joel asleep on the floor. He let out a long breath and rubbed his eyes with the heels of his hand.

It was a dream, but even that realization wasn't comforting. Why would he dream about killing her? Was she already dead?

"Get a grip," Blake mouthed, knocking his head on the back of the chair to clear it.

"They've just returned." Atlas's quiet voice sounded several yards away. "Make sure her halo is still intact. As soon as the boy kills him, I want her to be ready."

"How charming," Layla said. "Should I hold her down for you as well?"

"You could join us if you'd like. I wouldn't mind watching you try to glean some euphoria for yourself."

"Please. The second he dies, the curse binding me here will shatter. I'm leaving and getting as far away from you as possible. How do you know he won't take her first and then fight the human?"

"He loves to humiliate and belittle. He'll give the boy a shot, let him think he might have a chance, and then deliver the fatal blow. Trust me, he loves an audience. He'll wait until the end to experience euphoria." Atlas paused. "Make sure you give those idiots the tonic. The plan won't work if he carves them up with the first strike."

"Yes, my lord." Layla's voice dripped sarcasm.

Joel mumbled loudly in his sleep, cutting off the hushed conversation. Blake wanted to kick him in the face. He pinched his eyes shut.

"Get them up," Atlas said. "He needs to practice, for all the good it'll do." His heavy footfalls made the nearby lamp vibrate in its place as he strode by.

Thoughts tumbled through Blake's mind: Who was back? What tonic?

Trying to appear calm and relaxed, he breathed deeply, feigning sleep. Layla's spicy scent grew in intensity as she advanced toward the couches where the girls were stretched out and deep asleep. Blake watched through his eyelashes, closing them fully before Layla stopped in front of him. A moment later, he felt her lips brush his neck as her hair tickled his ear.

"Time to wake up." She ran her fingers down his forearm while her legs knocked his knees apart.

Blake opened his eyes, faking a yawn. "Oh, man. What time is it? How long did I sleep?"

Layla shrugged, and the soft white strap of her shirt slipped down her smooth shoulder, revealing her collarbone. "A few hours. Atlas wants you to practice some more." Her full lips extended in a pout, as if she felt bad for waking him.

"Oh, right. Yeah, that's probably a good idea." Blake stretched out of his slumped position. He waited for Layla to step away, but she remained standing in front of him.

"Did you sleep well?" she asked, combing her ink-black hair with her fingers as she rolled her shoulder. The movement was innocent enough, but Blake noticed she'd pushed her chest closer to him, her neckline barely hiding the swell of her breasts.

He glanced at the floor. "Yeah, yeah, sure."

Layla cocked her head to the side. "Have you been up for a while? You seem...I don't know, anxious for some reason."

Blake frowned and shook his head, running his sweaty palms down the front of his jeans. "No, I just had a bad dream. I guess it shook me up a little." He met her frosty gaze for the first time.

"Oh dear, a bad dream? We can't have that." Layla climbed onto Blake's lap. She slipped her thighs onto either side of him, straddling his hips as she wrapped her arms around his neck.

Blake cleared his throat. "What are you doing?"

Before answering, Layla leaned forward, her heady scent overwhelming him as his resistance vanished. She slid farther up his lap, her backside stroking the front of his jeans. Brushing his temples with her lips, Layla kissed him, lingering much longer than necessary.

"I'm kissing the dark thoughts away. You need a clear head for what's coming." Her lips wandered lowered until she found Blake's and slipped her tongue into his mouth. Her breath was cool and tasted just like the cinnamon scent that surrounded her.

He couldn't think, couldn't breathe. Blake's hand snaked around Layla's neck and pulled her closer, deepening the kiss as his other arm encircled her thin waist. In the back of his mind, he knew he should stop, knew something was wrong, but Layla tasted so good. Blake was lost in her kiss, hypnotized and unable to stop.

"I brought this," she said against his lips. She pulled a clear glass vial out of her cleavage and held it up for him to see.

"What is it?" Blake took it from her.

"A tonic I brewed. I've had centuries to master potions."

Blake went rigid, alarm bells ringing in his mind. He sat up a little straighter. "What's it for?" He unscrewed the metal cap and sniffed, but the liquid was void of scent.

"Something to help you fight Zeus. It'll increase your strength and more importantly, make your body resilient to injuries. The effects are only temporary, but the properties within will allow your body to rapidly heal for the next several hours. There will be blood, but you can be confident you won't die—at least until the effects wear off. You have to be ready for anything, right?" Layla eyes shone in the dim light.

Blake looked at the vial skeptically. The private conversation between Layla and Atlas still swirled at the back of his mind.

"Come on, drink up." Layla reached out to help guide the vial between his parted lips.

"I'm all right. Maybe later." He turned his head away, earning a deep frown from Layla.

"What? Don't trust me?"

"No, it's not that, but if it only lasts a few hours, shouldn't I wait to take it closer to the fight?"

Layla's eyes flickered with unease, but her concern evaporated a moment later. "True, but remember what Atlas told you? Zeus won't fight fair. You should always be ready. Come on. Drink."

Blake's ire rose. "I said not now." He cupped the top of the vial with his hand and lowered it. "Please get off me."

A low hiss emanated from Layla's parted lips. "Fine, it's your mind."

Before Blake could respond, Layla gripped the crown of his head with her empty hand, digging her curved nails into his skin. He moved to throw her off his lap, but his vision blurred as the strangest sensation washed over him. His head bobbed back and forth while delicate wisps tickled his scalp. He couldn't concentrate, couldn't remember anything. Swirling in a fog of black smoke, he fell back into his dream, startling when images of Kait, her chest splayed open from his staff, flashed bright red against the darkness.

"No!" Blake cried, his eyes flying open. His chest heaved, and his stomach knotted. There was so much blood. Cool hands brushed the beads of sweat off his forehead as the heady scent of cinnamon calmed his rapid breaths.

"Shh, it's okay, Blake," Layla cooed. "You had a nightmare. Here, drink some water."

She pressed a curved glass against his lower lip, tipping the contents onto his tongue. Blake swallowed. The liquid had a slightly bitter taste.

He grimaced. "Are you sure that's water?"

"Mountain water. Different minerals." A coy smile played on Layla's lips as she wiped a rogue drop off his chin with the pad of her thumb. She was sitting on his lap, her hair tickling her collarbone.

"What are you doing?" Blake asked.

Layla smiled, slipping her hand under the edge of his shirt. "Don't you remember? You're hurting my feelings." She leaned down, planting fiery kisses down the length of his neck.

"Remember what?"

The same wispy feeling tickled his scalp. Memories of stolen glances between him and Layla swam behind his eyes, along with lingering touches since the moment they'd met. He licked his lips, the taste of cinnamon tingling his tongue. He grew hard as the memory of tracing Layla's curves blossomed in his mind.

Layla grinned, sensing his arousal. "That's better."

Her tongue parted his lips as her hips wiggled atop him. Her thighs held him in place. Blake groaned, caught up in the taste of her.

"Do you want me?" Layla asked.

"Yes."

Blake wanted nothing more than to slide her shirt down, cradle her breasts, but the yearning felt detached, hollow. He focused on his memories of her, but they felt wrong, as if they were dreams rather than his own lived experiences.

"Before I let you take me, can you promise me one little favor?" Her voice cast a spell, diminishing Blake's concerns. "After Zeus falls, kill Atlas."

Blake pulled away from her lips. "What?"

"Shh." Layla ran her fingers through his hair. She pressed her body closer, planting sensual kisses along his collarbone, nibbling her way up to his left ear. "It'll be easy. Just one stab through the heart," she whispered and squeezed Blake's skin over his own heart.

"Why? I thought you…"

"What? Loved him? No, Blake. I'm his prisoner."

"But if we kill Zeus, you'll both be free."

"Please, Blake. Atlas views me as his property. If I run, he'll hunt me down and drag me back. As long as he lives, my life will always be his."

"I don't know."

Layla sighed, sliding her hand into the front of his jeans. Blake inhaled sharply as her hand wrapped around him. "Set me free. Say you'll do it, and I'll give you what you want." She looked up from under her thick eyelashes as she squeezed him tighter.

Blake glanced up at the towering ceiling, trying to think about anything other than how good her hand felt.

"Please."

A flicker of movement caught his attention. Rather than Layla's inky black hair and ivory skin, chocolate curls cascaded down Kait's brown skin. His thoughts wandered back to the first time he saw Layla, when she was Kait standing before him. Layla had said it herself—she was a lethal mistake. This memory was clear and sharp compared to all the others. She was playing him, using him for her own means.

Blake withdrew the nymph's hand from his pants and shook his head. "I can't."

Layla tilted her head, running her pink tongue over her lips as her appearance shifted back. "How about rather than saying no, tell me you'll think about. In the meantime, we can play." Layla smiled, then kissed him harder.

"Stop. I don't want to do this," Blake said, gently unwrapping her fingers from his neck.

Layla giggled and licked his earlobe. "Atlas won't find out. He's too preoccupied to notice what I'm doing. From the moment I saw you, I wanted you, Blake. There's something about you I can't ignore." Her voice was a lullaby. "I know you want me too. It'll be so easy, and I promise, the pleasure will blow you away."

Layla tossed her hair again, inching even closer to Blake. He glanced over at his friends, who were still deep in slumber. An uneasy feeling gripped him, turning his stomach. He had to get away from her.

It felt as if a rubber band had snapped, bringing Blake back to reality. He shut his eyes against Layla's full lips, her warm body. She was willing to do whatever it took for her freedom. What if manipulating him was the first step?

"Stop." Blake pushed Layla off his lap.

She stumbled, just missing Joel's hand. "What's wrong?" Hurt shone in her pained eyes. "Don't you want me?"

Blake stood and wiped her taste off his lips. He fixed her with a hard stare. "I don't know what's going on, but I'm not interested in being your plaything. I came here to save Kait."

Layla licked her lips and brushed a tear from her eye. She looked so sad, so vulnerable. Blake's gaze hardened. It was all an act.

"I don't know what you're talking about. I thought you wanted me. I guess I misread the signs." She stepped back, squaring her shoulders. "I wonder how Atlas will feel about this." Her voice hardened to ice. "I wonder what he'll do when he hears how you forced yourself on me." A look of wide-eyed horror crossed her features. "You know, I think he may kill you." Her lips twitched. Gone was the pain and rejection. Now her eyes only held power, dominance.

"He won't believe you," Blake said. "I didn't do anything."

"Your denial won't matter." She fluttered her eyelashes. "When he hears my frightful tale of how you held me down and forced me to your will…" She uttered a broken sob, summoning shining tears. "Why, you're no better than Zeus."

Understanding hit Blake in the chest. He was trapped no matter what he said. Atlas would never believe the truth. Even if he did, Layla's scent was all over him, woven into every skin cell, every hair. He licked his lips. Her lingering flavor still coated his mouth. Blake looked up at her in alarm as she neared the curved entrance to the twisting tunnels.

"Ta!" Layla said with a wink and a wave.

Blake's heart sunk. He turned, debating whether or not he should wake his friends. It would be reassuring to have someone by his side, but there wasn't time to explain. Cursing under his breath, he raced after Layla, stepping into the shadows.

Darkness consumed him, and his breathing hitched as he envisioned a thousand horrors waiting for him. Chasing after Layla was stupid. He had no idea where to go. Once Atlas returned, he could explain everything.

Another image entered his mind, this one depicting Atlas hurling the throwing stars at his head. All three hit their mark, tearing through his flesh and bone to the soft brain tissue beneath. Atlas would act first and then let his corpse explain. He had to find Layla.

Drumming his knuckles on the rough stone, Blake thought back to their trip into the mountain. They had come from the right. Layla must have disappeared somewhere to the left of the large cavern. Swallowing his fear, Blake ran down the left tunnel, doing his best to follow the uneven wall with his hand so he didn't fall flat on his face. He wasn't sure how far he ran before he slowed his pace to a walk. As far as he knew, the tunnel had yet to deviate or branch.

Shivers gripped him, along with thoughts of his dream of wandering aimlessly in the dark. Blake's breathing rasped in his ears. A deep snarl echoed off the walls.

Straightening, Blake whipped around, trying to identify which direction the sound originated, but only silence greeted him. The blackness was unnerving. He pressed his back against the wall and exhaled through his mouth, feeling his heart pound against his rib cage. Another minute went by, and the sound didn't return.

Blake shook his head. "It's all in your head," he said aloud, trying to dispel his fear.

Just then, scuttling legs brushed his neck, and Blake screamed, leaping away from the wall. He smacked his hand against his neck, terrified he might have only managed to knock the insect down his shirt. His fingers brushed a hard, beetle-like shell.

"Christ!" Blake ran his hands down his entire frame. He could still feel the delicate legs on his skin.

A feral roar sounded, and the pebbles under Blake's feet vibrated. The sound of sharp claws raking stone was unmistakable as something edged closer. Blake stood frozen, terrified. He wanted to run, but he was all turned around. If he wasn't careful, he'd run smack into whatever monster was lurking in the tunnels.

Blake tried not to breathe, tried to make himself as small as possible. A moment later, a foul smell washed over him, like rust and rotting meat. Blake's eyes searched back and forth, but the blackness was crippling. He took a step back, praying it was in the right direction. Another furious snarl exploded, and Blake jumped in fright. It was too late to escape.

A deep grumbling reverberated in the creature's throat. Blake could feel the heat of the animal. It was so close, but he stood still, too frightened to move. A pair of glowing golden eyes erupted before him at shoulder height, illuminating the top half of the creature's face, along with the daggerlike fangs reaching for him.

Blake dropped to the floor and rolled over his shoulder out of the beast's reach. When he regained his footing, he ran in an unknown direction. His sneakers slapped against the hard floor until a piercing pain struck him in the left calf. Blake gasped and hobbled to the side, throwing his body against the wall. With a shaking hand, he found a thick stick protruding from his leg. He had to move; the creature was almost on top of him. He took a step, but a strange numbness seized his muscles, and he fell to his knees. He couldn't walk, couldn't escape.

Another wave of the foul stench permeated the air, and Blake glanced up to find the golden eyes glaring at him, its black pupils thin horizontal slits. He took a shaky breath, and the animal lunged. Five claws fanned out, then struck his temple. He fell, already unconscious from the blow. He didn't feel the teeth.

⚡ 32 ⚡

The deadline was fast approaching. Blake had yet to find Kait, and with each passing hour, Zeus grew more agitated. Kait observed silently, drawing as little attention to herself as possible. One more day lingered before his promise not to take her elapsed, but she worried he wasn't going to last that long.

He sent numerous messages, each one scrawled more hastily than the last and burned in his palm, a spell carrying it to whoever was waiting on the other end. He was antsy. They had returned from Paris late last night, and Zeus had forgone chaining her back up, trusting the bracelets to do the job instead. In fact, he hadn't so much as spared her a glance. Maybe the wheel was beginning to turn and luck was spinning her way.

An hour after they came back, Zeus left her alone in the cave. She didn't waste time, sprinting down the single corridor only to end up on the other side of the bedroom. She tried again, this time searching for a hidden seam or ripple magic always left behind, but her fingers found nothing but damp stone and muddy soil.

Dejected, Kait had wandered back to her prison, slumping onto the bed. Of course Zeus sealed the exit. No matter how distracted or agitated he became, he wasn't careless.

Now, a few hours later, she lay on the mussed sheets, studying the unremarkable bracelets. While she was no longer chained to the bedframe, the jewelry continued to inhibit her powers and ethereal connection. She may have reign of the cave, but Zeus's message was clear: without her magic, she was defenseless.

"Cheer up, darling," Zeus said, appearing at the foot of the bed. The paper he held crackled and curled. The hungry orange flames hovered above his palm, devouring the paper in seconds. Thin wisps of smoke danced toward the low ceiling. "You'll be with little Blakey soon."

She didn't flinch at the god's sudden presence. Even when he left her, she still sensed his eyes on her. "I thought you were taking me to some immortal gathering."

"*Immortal* is a strong word. I know of a couple that will be present, myself included, but the rest of the company will be a bit more…vulnerable."

Kait narrowed her eyes. Zeus wasn't going to wait for Blake to find her. They were going to him. She rose to her feet. "How do you know he'll even fight you? What if he doesn't care?"

"Please." Zeus fixed her with a pointed stare. "He's already come this far. Why would he stop now? He won't be able to help himself, especially once he sees you." Zeus tossed her the gold dress purchased from the store in Paris. "Here, it's time to put this on."

Kait caught it. The gentle silk kissed her skin as the material draped over her hands. She considered refusing, but it wouldn't matter. Besides, the dress offered more coverage than her current garment.

Kait disappeared behind the crude bathroom door she'd fashioned by inserting the ends of a torn blanket into two crevices on either side of the stone alcove. The new dress felt wonderful as it slipped over her shoulders, but Kait frowned at the beautiful fabric. It was another part of the game. She was supposed to be the unattainable prize. To Zeus, she was nothing more than an object.

Kait stared at her reflection in the spotty mirror. Her hair was a mess, greasy and sticking up in odd places. Dried mud clung to the creases in her neck, and her fingernails were black with grime. Apart from the little sink and thin washcloth, Kait hadn't been able to properly wash since Zeus captured her. Her violet eyes raked the dress from top to bottom. It was enchanting, but it was a shallow beauty, unable to disguise the truth that lay beneath.

"You have to kill him," Kait said to her reflection.

She brushed her matted curls over her shoulder and reached up to uncoil the thin black cord wrapped around the top of her left ear. It wasn't anything special, a bit of wire she'd stripped off a security device on a designer purse at the store. She wasn't strong enough to kill Zeus. Even if he weren't immortal, she doubted she'd be able to inflict any lasting damage. If she managed to apply the right pressure to his windpipe, however, he might pass out long enough for her to escape the bracelets and get out of there—but not before taking his manhood with her. Fluffing her hair back into place, she squeezed her left fist shut, the cord tucked inside.

Kait stepped back into the bedroom. Zeus was facing away from her, poring over the notes he had received in the short time they'd been together.

"Satisfied?" Kait waved a hand down the length of her body. The dress was an asymmetrical cut that ended at her knees while the other side trailed higher, exposing her inner thigh.

Zeus turned, his gaze starting at her toes until his blue eyes locked on hers. "You're beautiful," he said. "As if it were made for you."

Zeus crossed the space between them in two long strides. He brushed her hair away from her temple. His hand twirled down her bare skin, caressing, marking her as his property. Kait refrained from grinding her teeth, enduring his inspection in silence. Her moment would come.

"I especially love this part." Zeus trailed the tips of his fingers over to the center of her chest. "The way the fabric falls in a little V makes me want to see more." His fingers stroked her skin, dipping below the rippling fabric. "It's a shame your mortal won't see you like this."

Kait staggered, his words catching her off guard. "What do you mean? I thought we were going to him?"

"And we are, my pet." Zeus nodded, running his other hand up the inside of her leg, pushing the dress's slit to the side. "The nymph your Blake will see won't have your beauty, your grace, or your strength. First, I'm going to take it all away and reduce you to a feeble shell of the great aurai you once were." Zeus smiled, his eyes blazing with lust and aggression.

Kait's jaw fell slack, and she took a nervous step backward, but then her fingers curled around the hidden wire—a small token to remind her she wasn't weak.

Zeus chuckled, misreading her calculating gaze for one of fear. "I know I promised Blake he could watch, but plans change."

His lips twitched and he lunged, grabbing Kait by the waist. He lifted her off the floor with ease and threw her against the stone wall.

Kait's shoulder collided with the unyielding rock as she tried to shield her head. Landing on her elbow, a fierce burst of pain exploded behind her eyes as it continued up her neck. Zeus loomed over her, hungry and crazed. He brought back his fist and punched her, again and again, until her vision blurred. She tried to crawl away, but he stood on the flowing fabric of her dress and wrenched her back.

With a swift tug, he ripped the bottom of the dress and grabbed her backside in both hands, his fingers rough as they tore away her undergarment. Kait cried out and unclenched her fist, snaking the cord around the god's neck as he hauled her back up and slammed her back into the wall.

A quick flash of surprise sparked in Zeus's eyes as the wire bit into his flesh and cinched his windpipe shut. His skin flushed a deep red, then purple. His hands fluttered against her back, his fingers curling around her hair. Kait clenched her teeth and tightened her grip, ignoring the horrible gasping sound coming from Zeus's choked lips.

"How do you like that, Zeus? You really thought I'd just let you take me?" Kait growled. "You're a monster, and I won't stop until you're dead and cold at my feet."

She tightened her grip again, her gaze unflinching as she stared into Zeus's desperate eyes. Something pulled at the back of her mind—this seemed too easy.

Zeus's fingers wove deeper into her hair, the strands becoming entangled around his knuckles. He gave a shuddering gasp as his eyes rolled into the back of his head and he ceased fighting. Kait wasn't convinced and kept hold of the wire, yanking it even tighter. Then a deep chuckle sounded. Zeus raised his head and smiled, the immense pressure to his throat seemingly a forgotten memory.

"Want to know a secret?" he whispered. "Immortals don't breathe."

Zeus bashed Kait's head into the jagged stones behind her. Her grip fell slack, and her body slumped forward as her head swam with pain. He ripped the cord off his neck and tossed it to the ground.

"You put up more of a fight than I predicted. I must say, I'm impressed with your determination, but it doesn't change anything. I'm a god, and you're a nymph. The only thing you've done is make me desire you more, and now, I get to teach you a lesson."

His eyes flickered with frenzied hunger as he hefted Kait up. He threw her onto the bed and slapped her face.

"Here comes the best part."

Fear gripped Kait's heart. "No, don't touch me."

Her hand shot out, and the heel of her palm caught Zeus beneath his chin. She heard his teeth clack together as his head snapped back. In response, a jab connected with her jaw. Kait's blood splattered the sheets. Her ears rang, and the room swayed as her brain rattled around inside her skull. She had to stay conscious, had to keep fighting.

But already the black edges of her vision threatened to converge.

A cold hand squeezed Kait's thigh, and a tearing sound reverberated off the cavern walls as Zeus ripped the beautiful gown to rags. She climbed out of her fuzzy thoughts, kicking her legs, trying to reach the edge of the bed. More mocking laughter surrounded her as Zeus's other hand wrapped around her neck and lifted her into the air. He brought her closer, inhaling her scent. He cupped her breasts, forced her legs apart.

"You wanted a monster," Zeus spat. "Here I am."

A bitter odor assailed Blake's nose, waking him from the endless black. His eyelids flickered, revealing a small room with a flat ceiling. A large fire blazed several feet to his right, casting strange dancers across the walls, stretching and twisting as the flames crackled. Pushing himself onto his elbows, he surveyed the stiff couch supporting him as well as the quiet room. Apart from a few dark bottles on an overhead shelf across the room, he was alone.

He tried to stand, but searing pain seized his leg. Glancing down, Blake saw his left pant leg was crusted in blood. He struggled to sit, gritting his teeth as he rolled the bottom of his jeans up. He froze at the sight. A large hole the size of a quarter stared back at him. Angry pink tissue shone in the firelight, but Blake felt none of its warmth.

He touched his fingertip to the gruesome wound, shrinking back from the pain the gentle touch ignited. He steeled himself and tried again, but sharp barbs of pain prickled down to his feet. His leg hair was mattered to the skin. He glanced away from the wound. Where was everyone?

He tried to remember what happened before the blackness. Layla's bewitching eyes, the fevered chase through the tunnels, and the terrible pain as claws shredded his skin.

Blake reached up. If he ignored the pain in his leg, the pounding in his head rose, not to be forgotten. Several deep gouges lined his face, cutting across his eye all the way down his neck. A coagulated puddle of blood clung to his shirt. Surely he looked the part of a horror victim left for dead. His left eye twitched as fresh blood began to flow from the cut just above his eyebrow. Now that his heart rate had increased, a new wave of pain seized him, as though a giant fist was trying to wring out the last few drops.

A high-pitched chirping sounded behind Blake. Doing his best to maneuver on the hard couch, Blake spotted a pile of white fur decorated in strange markings lying on the floor. Following the odd lump with his eyes, Blake gasped when a set of familiar golden eyes opened, drinking him in with an intelligence an animal shouldn't possess.

It was the creature from the tunnels—nothing but teeth and blood and heat. It stared at him, watching, waiting for him to move. Yet, instead of the terrifying bloodlust it attacked with before, the large animal now gazed at him with indifference.

After a few tense minutes, Blake relaxed, confident the creature wasn't interested in spilling more of his blood at the moment. The animal yawned and stretched, laying its massive head on its crossed paws. Blake frowned. It looked like a big cat. His eyes traveled down its muscular body. Even in its state of rest, the animal was menacing.

Thick silver claws flexed, catching the firelight. A heavy tail curled around its body, the tip glowing faint blue. A quiet rustling sound drew Blake's attention to the cat's back. Rather than fur, two dozen gray spikelike objects protruded from its skin. They lay dormant for the moment, but the idea of what the creature looked like on the offensive caused the gash in his calf to burn once again.

Blake groaned as the pain gave way to fierce itching. The desire to scratch the raw skin around the wound was all consuming. He closed his eyes, breathing deeply as a strange sensation flooded him. Opening one eye, he gasped. His skin moved on its own, slowly knitting itself back together until the muscles and blood disappeared, leaving a smooth scar behind.

"No way." He pulled his leg up, bending it at the knee to run his hands over it. He felt no pain. Curious, he reached up to feel his face. Gone were the rough slashes, the pounding headache. A fuzzy image of a glass vial popped into his head. What had Layla given him?

The gravity of the situation made Blake's eyes bug. Where was she? What lies had she told Atlas? Did he make the animal attack him?

Out of the corner of his eye, Blake regarded the great cat. It wasn't paying him any attention. Instead, it was focused on cleaning its paws.

"Are you here to kill me?" Blake asked, but the animal ignored him. He rubbed a hand along his healed scalp.

A loud rattling erupted behind the couch, and the cat leapt to its feet. It slunk toward Blake, staring at him, its powerful jaws level with his throat. Swallowing, he froze, pushing his body into the worn fabric of the couch. The cat bared its fangs and growled. Its yellow eyes didn't blink, daring him to look away.

Blake's heart raced as he looked death in the face. This time, he didn't have the luxury of falling unconscious. This time, he would feel the teeth.

"Uh-oh," Atlas called. "What do we have here?"

Blake snapped his neck and looked straight ahead. The Titan stood in the doorway, a woven basket in his hands. He took two steps forward and dropped it on the couch by Blake's sneakers. An angry snarl erupted, capturing Blake's attention once more as the cat swatted him with his paw. He clenched his eyes shut, terrified the animal would carve his gut with its claws.

"Now, now, Kaf. Settle down." Atlas waved the cat away. "I'm sure you'll get your chance."

The creature huffed in defiance but backed away, settling in front of the fire.

"Good to see you're awake. Kaf's venom is strong. Being mortal, I expected you to die."

"Lucky me," Blake replied.

Atlas walked toward the high shelf on the other side of the room. Humming, he began rifling through dark brown bottles perched precariously on the shelf. He withdrew an unmarked glass bottle and unscrewed the lid. "Have some of this." He passed it to Blake.

Blake tipped the contents of the bottle into the back of his throat, wincing as the liquid scalded the lining of his esophagus. "What is this?"

"Scotch," Atlas replied, taking it back. He drained the rest, then sighed and smiled. "I keep some stashed all over. Lay doesn't like when I drink, says I get mean." His slate eyes gleamed. His words sounded like a promise.

Blake cleared his throat, trying to erase the burn. He gestured to the sleeping cat. "What is that thing? How did it get in here?"

"It's a piriol," Atlas said, his eyes on the dying fire. "Bonded with a single god, they are unstoppable killing machines. Titans used them for eons. They're fiercely loyal and protective."

"Is it your pet?"

Atlas narrowed his eyes, swirling the liquor at the bottom of the bottle. "Don't mock them, boy. A piriol is an incredible hunter, designed to track over hundreds of miles and across realms. It never slows, never gives up on a quarry. That's why we created them to hunt nymphs."

Blake cocked his head. "What do you mean?"

Atlas's eyes shifted, as if he'd said too much. He leaned against the wall to the left of the fireplace, staring into the flames. "Immortals are like piriols. Once we catch the scent of a nymph we desire, there is no snuffing out our lust. We don't stop. However, our quarry developed defensive techniques to keep us at bay. Piriols changed that. Gave us back the advantage."

Blake frowned, narrowing his eyes. Atlas sounded envious and excited. "That's disgusting. These are people you're talking about." He sat up straighter. "Are you still hunting them?"

Atlas scoffed. "Calm down, boy. This was thousands of years ago. The piriol isn't mine. I harbor him for your friend, Zeus—another stipulation of our arrangement. He used to employ the animal more frequently for his hunts, but your little nymph put a stop to that a century ago. The playboy had to get smart. He couldn't just hunt anymore. He had to adapt his strategy, become coy and charming to trick the nymphs into sleeping with him to avoid detection. That's why your Kait has him so riled. She figured out his game of dress-up. After Kaf caught her, Zeus sent him back here. My mountain cloaks his existence from Olympus. Like Layla and I, he shouldn't be alive. The piriols were all slain after the Titan War."

"Why does Zeus have one? How does he get away with this?"

Atlas cocked his head. "He's king of the gods. As long as the Council is kept in the dark, he can do whatever the hell he wants."

Blake shifted on the couch and placed his feet on the floor. He wrung his hands together, seething with rage. "It's wrong. No one has the right to exert such force and control over another person like that. It's despicable."

"That's why we're going to kill him, remember? We should slit Kaf's throat before he arrives. Bastard cat will put up one hell of a fight when his master comes calling."

"Kill him? You can't murder an innocent animal."

"Innocent? Do you know how many lives those jaws have taken? How many hearts those quills have penetrated?"

"Quills?"

Atlas pointed to the gray spikes on the creature's back. "They're laced with a neurotoxin that inhibits a nymph from accessing their magic. During a hunt, they shoot the quills from their back." Atlas fixed his eyes on Blake. The left side of his face reflected the flames, like a shifting mask. "That's what drilled through your leg."

"Oh." Blake's palms began to sweat, and he cracked his fingers to relieve the pressure. His anxiety to rejoin the group mounted. He wasn't sure if it was the large cat or Atlas's story, but the god's smile unnerved him. He cleared his throat.

The Titan set the empty bottle on the edge of the mantel. "Let's get you fixed up. You're not much good to me lying there like a cripple."

"Actually, I'm good." He lifted his leg for Atlas to inspect.

Atlas crossed the short distance and grabbed hold of Blake's foot. He extracted a damp cloth from the basket. Blake waited, watching as he wiped the blood away to reveal the healed wound.

"That's not possible," Atlas whispered, lowering his leg. "Lean forward." Applying the same cloth to his head, Atlas cleaned Blake's face from his hairline to his chin. The once deep scratches were gone. "How?"

Blake licked his lips. "Layla gave me something. I think she said it'll make me stronger."

Atlas fixed Blake with a hard stare. "Oh, did she? Well, how about that. Seems she's taken quite a shine to you."

"No," Blake answered too quickly. "She wants me to kill…Zeus."

Atlas didn't answer. He replaced the bloodied cloth on top of a roll of gauze and a bottle of unmarked white ointment. "Layla has always had a soft spot for defenseless creatures. What were you doing down here, anyway?" Atlas pinned Blake with his gaze once more.

"I was looking for Layla before she told you—" He bit his tongue as he realized what he was about to say. Obviously, Atlas didn't know; otherwise, Blake wouldn't be breathing.

Atlas's brow furrowed. "Before she told me what?"

Blake rose to his feet, grateful the movement remained void of pain. "You know, the details. Told you the details before—before the girls went over their plan." He grasped at straws. "But I shouldn't tell you. Let's go back, and they can explain it for everyone at the same time." He inched toward the exit.

Atlas stood still, his expression a thundercloud as he watched Blake edge farther and farther away. "Don't lie to me. I'm going to ask you one more time, and if anything but the truth comes out of your mouth, I'm going to sew it shut and bury you right here at the bottom of this miserable mountain. What happened with Layla?"

"Um…" Blake didn't doubt Atlas's threat. If he didn't choose his next words carefully, he'd be dead in minutes. "She—she came on to me a little bit," he admitted, then backed closer to the dark tunnels. A chill slithered up his spine. The madness in Atlas's eyes seeped every ounce of warmth from his body.

"Is that right?" Atlas stepped back in front of the fire, withdrawing the empty bottle from the mantel. He clucked his tongue, tapping the glass. Blake flinched at the high-pitched sound. "Did she kiss you? Ask to pleasure you?"

Blake licked his lips, trying to gauge the length of the tunnel out of the corner of his eye. If he could find his way back to the cavern, back to the others, he might have a chance.

"Uh, yes—I mean no. No. She kissed me, but that's it."

"I see." Atlas glanced down at the bottle in his hands. "You think you can come in here and steal my nymph?" The bottle shattered as Atlas squeezed it. Blood coursed down his fingers, staining his hand crimson. "I take you in, offer to help, and this is how you repay me? Jumping on my nymph as soon as my back is turned?" Atlas opened his fist, dropping the bloody shards to the floor.

Alarms bells exploded in Blake's mind. "No, no, please, it wasn't like that." Blake held up his hands. "I stopped her before we—"

"Before you what? Let her undress? Let her dance for you? Did she touch you? Did it feel good?"

"No, no. I didn't want her. I told her to stop."

The god cocked his head as he followed Blake out. They were both in the tunnels now. Blackness surrounded them, creeping in like a venomous fog. Blake glanced behind him. He couldn't see anything. When he turned back around to face Atlas, the god's eyes were shining with hate.

"And why is that? Layla's not good enough for you? Not as beautiful as the nymph whore Zeus scooped up?"

Blake felt around blindly with his hands for any kind of crude weapon. "No, that's not what I meant. She was very good."

"So you did enjoy her. I hope you enjoy spitting out your teeth just as much." Without warning, Atlas lunged, and his fist connected with Blake's face.

Slamming against the wall, Blake felt a torrent of blood gush from his nose. Atlas cried, lunging again. On instinct, Blake ducked and rolled onto the floor, disappearing into the dark. He heard Atlas's fist crack against the granite wall.

"Where are you, boy? You think you can run, but this is my mountain. I'll kill you. I swear I'll kill every last one of you!"

Blake backed away, scuttling on his hands. A jagged piece of rock sliced into his palm, and before he could stop it, a sharp gasp whistled between his teeth. Rough hands grabbed his legs, hauling him across the cave floor and back into the dull light of the dying fire. Atlas threw him in the air and pinned him against the wall. Blake stretched his legs, trying to get his feet on the floor, but empty air surrounded him.

"Was this worth kissing my nymph? Is your life worth her touch?" Atlas chuckled, grinding his teeth. "You're going to wish Zeus got you first. The things that I'm going to do to you will make his plans seem kind." Atlas slammed Blake against the wall again, his skull audibly cracking against the surface. He let Blake sag to the ground, delivering another blow to his head with his knee.

Blake slumped. He couldn't see, couldn't hear. Atlas's words were thick bells clanging together. He inhaled, his breath rattling as his brain tried to focus. Shifting shadows elongated and twirled, making him dizzy. Atlas was still talking, but his speech fell on deaf ears. The only thing Blake was aware of was the thin layer of gritty sand biting into his wounded hand.

Calloused fingers ripped his head up, forcing his gaze back to the god's cruel eyes. Atlas's lips moved, but all Blake could hear was muted ringing. His fingers closed around the sand, his palm stinging as the tiny particles slipped underneath the sliced skin. Atlas pulled back his arm, his serrated knuckles shining with blood. Blake didn't think; he just raised his own arm instinctually, but rather than blocking the coming blow with his fist, he opened his hand, flinging the small pile of sand into Atlas's eyes.

Atlas roared and spun away, trying to clear the obstruction marring his sight. Blake's hearing came rushing back like an opened dam.

"Oh, wasn't that a clever trick," Atlas growled. "For that, I'll slice off your eyelids so you can't look away when I force open your nymph's legs. She's used goods at this point, but I'm sure she'll still taste fine." Atlas swung his massive fists, scraping the skin off his knuckles against the stone walls while the tiny grains of sand continued to burrow deeper into his eyes. He screamed. "Kaf! *Ut pueri!*"

Fear clenched Blake's gut. The moment his equilibrium returned, he sprinted as fast as he could deeper into the tunnels, keeping his hand on the stone wall as a guide. His breathing was ragged, falling in and out of his mouth in short gasps. He imagined the cat sneaking up behind him, wrapping its vicious jaws around his neck as it dragged him back to Atlas. Maybe the piriol would kill him. It would certainly be a kinder death than what the god had in store. Blake strained his ears, hearing nothing. Maybe the piriol wasn't chasing him after all. Or maybe it knew how to hunt without making a sound.

"Get back here!" Atlas cried.

Blake's head snapped forward, and he pushed his legs faster. Up ahead, the darkness receded to a dark gray. Had he found the cavern? Images of a dead end or locked door flooded his thoughts, while a surge of adrenaline kicked in. He had to keep going.

The tunnel was brightening. Blake strained his ears to hear around his raspy breaths. Voices. He could hear voices. His head throbbed as his brain sloshed from side to side. Just a few more steps.

Blake panted, relishing the tonic once again as it increased his endurance tenfold. The stone wall curved, opening into the magnificent cavern. A sea of couches and tables greeted Blake's exhausted gaze as he rounded the corner. He stumbled across the threshold, a small smile breaking on his lips.

Sharp nails gripped his ankle, wrenching his leg out from under him. Blake slammed down, his chin bouncing off the floor. His teeth rattled. Several sunk into the fleshy sides of his tongue. Coughing, he spat out a sticky stream of blood. He kicked his legs, but Atlas's hold was unbreakable.

"I've got you now." Atlas yanked Blake back into the tunnel like a lion dragging its kill. He pulled him along the unforgiving stone, rubbing his cheek raw with the effort.

"Help!" Blake cried. "Help!" He prayed the group could hear him, could save him. His hands reached out, trying to find something to slow his momentum, but Atlas was too strong, too savage.

Several hands wrapped around Blake's wrists and forearms. Blake arched his neck. Jezlem and Joel stood above him, straining to break the god's hold, but they were no match for his rage.

"Forget it." Jezlem surrendered her hold on Blake's right hand, so Joel now held both. Without another word, she disappeared. Blake's heart sunk.

"Hurry up!" Joel cried. His sneakers slipped on the stone, and he fell onto his back, letting one of Blake's wrists go.

Blake tried to claw his way back to Joel, but a shrill cry of pain broke out behind him. Atlas dropped his legs, his furious curses echoing off the walls. Blake glanced back and saw Jezlem wrapped around Atlas's thick neck, her white teeth smeared with blood as she spat out the top of his ear.

Blood pulsed down Jezlem's chin and Atlas's neck. Reaching up, he grabbed Jezlem by her hair and slammed her to the ground with a piercing cry. A soft whoosh of air puffed out of Jezlem's lips, but she managed to pull her limbs in and roll out from beneath Atlas.

"I'll make you pay for that, little whore." Atlas cupped his maimed ear with his hand.

Joel pulled Blake to his feet, and Jezlem hobbled toward them. Together, they backed out of the tunnels into the cavern. Atlas stalked forward, his glare murderous.

⚡ 33 ⚡

"What's g-going on? Blake?" Bia called from the side of the room. A blur of red flashed in the corner of Blake's eye followed by a cool touch to his shredded forehead. "They made me stay behind. Where have you been? What happened?" Her worried amber eyes took in the dried blood on Blake's head and Jezlem's ruby-stained chin.

"Get back," Blake ordered, turning her around.

He ran after Joel and Jezlem, pulling Bia along as they raced to the shelves of weapons. Blake stumbled, nearly impaling himself on a long dagger protruding off one of the tables. His clumsy hands closed around the hilt of a long sword. Joel grabbed the crossbow, and Jezlem armed herself with two silver throwing disks.

"What's g-going on?"

Jezlem gestured with a deadly-looking mace. "Make another crack in the floor. Right there. Do it now."

Bia nodded, needing no further instruction. With her back against the farthest pillar from the cavern entrance, she raised her arms. Red sparks sizzled along her fingertips. A crack like that of gunfire exploded as the stone floor shattered, cutting them and the weapons off from the rest of the room by a six-foot gap.

Layla materialized out of the air beside them. "What's going on?"

"Where've you been?" Jezlem's voice was hard, accusing.

"I was making another tonic." She presented a glass vial in her hand.

"Another tonic? What do you mean?"

"I brewed one for Blake earlier. Goddess, I'm sorry. I didn't even think to make one for you, but you look like you can handle a sword. I hoped it would give the boys a fighting chance against Zeus." She looked at Blake for the first time. "You didn't tell them?"

Blake gritted his teeth, frowning at her twisted game. "There wasn't time."

"Did it work?"

"Did what work?"

"The tonic. Your pant leg is covered in blood, but you don't seem to be in any pain."

"What is she talking about, Blake?" Joel asked.

"Yes, it worked. While you guys were sleeping, I went into the tunnels, and Atlas's pet attacked me. It put a hole through my calf and scratched up my face, but whatever Layla gave me…healed everything." Blake displayed his left leg, showing them the large hole in the material against his unmarred skin.

"Really? Dude, you're like Wolverine! And that's for me?" Joel strode forward, shouldering his crossbow.

Layla nodded, handing him the vial.

"Joel, wait, we don't—" Jezlem began, but Joel didn't hesitate.

He unscrewed the lid and tossed the contents into the back of his throat. "Will it give me any other cool powers?"

"Your strength will improve, but all the effects are temporary," Layla said.

"Well, thank you." Jezlem offered Layla half a smile. "I wasn't looking forward to watching them die. Maybe now I won't have to."

"Of course. I wish there were more I could do." Layla inclined her head to the entrance of the tunnels, then to the weapons held tightly in their grasps. "What's going on? Is it Zeus?"

"Not exactly," Blake replied.

Joel repositioned his crossbow. "Atlas went a little nuts."

Blake's gaze locked with Layla's. The nymph's eyes grew wide with understanding, but the smugness he expected was nowhere to be found. Instead, she regarded him nervously, fear flickering in her pale eyes as the sound of heavy footsteps boomed.

Atlas strode out of the tunnels, his towering presence dominating the room.

"Darling?" Layla tried. "Is everything all right?"

Atlas fixed his hungry eyes on Blake. "Seems the mortal has bigger balls than I thought. One nymph isn't enough for him."

Jezlem shot Blake a quick glance. "Blake, what's he talking about?"

"Atlas, don't do this," Layla said.

"Shut up, slut. I know you sought him out. I know you detest me—always have. You made them invincible so I can't kill them, but guess what, sweetheart? If I can kill Zeus's body, I can sure as hell kill yours."

"You're wrong, Atlas. There's another—"

"The time for discussion is past. You always were uncomfortable with bloodshed, but this time, you'll see up close the consequences of your tricks and lies."

Atlas withdrew a huge golden broadsword from behind his back. Blake's eyes bulged as he looked at his own. It made his weapon look like a child's toy.

"What did you do?" Jezlem looked from Blake to Layla.

"Nothing. She kissed me, but I pushed her off."

"It doesn't matter that you didn't have the balls to finish the deed, boy. No one touches my nymph. She is my property—a lesson you will learn slowly as I dismember your pathetic frame piece by piece." Atlas rushed forward, his white hair flying behind him as the rubber band snapped.

Layla appeared on the other side of the chasm and stood in Atlas's path. "Atlas, please. Let's talk about this. We don't want to do anything rash to jeopardize—"

Atlas barreled past, tossing her violently aside.

Layla caught herself on the arm of a nearby couch and stepped in front of him once again. "Atlas, it didn't mean anything. I'm sorry. Please, we can't just throw away everything Zeus promised!"

Atlas swung his sword, barely missing the top of Layla's head. "I don't care if that bastard grants me immortality. Do you think a prize will make me forget that you chose a mortal over me? I'd rather die in this wretched mountain than see you beneath another man. You're mine. Bound to me."

"I've been loyal to you for three thousand years. Yes, I strayed, but look at the life your actions condemned me to. Before the war, all my life consisted of was death and deception. Then, I finally got a chance to break away from that horrid existence, and the gods labeled me an abomination. Zeus granted me immortality, but only so that I could remain your slave forever, your plaything to use at your every whim."

Angry tears fell from Layla's eyes, but her voice didn't waver. "I thought when Zeus kidnapped those other nymphs and brought them here that I might figure out a way to escape. When I escorted them down the mountain after he absorbed their halos, I planned to run. But no. He saw to it that I used my talent to wipe their memories and then sealed me back into this tomb with you and your jealousy."

"Jealousy? I don't envy that peacock."

Layla slapped her palms against Atlas's broad chest. "Don't lie to me. Ever since he stripped you of your powers, you've been emasculated, which was only perpetuated by the fact that you can't attain euphoria with me. But did that stop you from trying? Did that stop you from beating me? From forcing yourself on me until I bled? You laughed when Zeus raped me, satisfied when I couldn't give him euphoria either."

Layla wiped her wet cheeks, discarding her tears as fury replaced them. "I fooled myself into thinking you cared about me after all these years stranded together, but I was wrong. You don't see me as a true being. I'm just another reminder of how insignificant you've become. I hate Zeus, but I hate you more." Layla's words were a whip. Her lips pulled back in a snarl, and she threw her arm behind her, gesturing to the statue-still group. "I tried to seduce Blake so that maybe I could feel some sort of connection with another person before my miserable life ends. I gave them a tonic of my own creation to help them kill Zeus and, gods willing, you too."

"Stop talking, darling, before I do something you're going to regret."

Layla shook her dark head. "You will never tell me what to do again."

Atlas roared. He thrust his golden sword forward, stabbing the gleaming blade through Layla's chest. The sharp edge plunged into her heart and exited between her shoulder blades. Blake's jaw dropped. Beside him, Jezlem gasped. He squeezed his eyes shut. It was a dream. He was dreaming again.

With a sickening squelch, Atlas withdrew the sword from Layla's body. Thick, scarlet ribbons danced down the length of the blade and dripped onto the carpet. Atlas watched the blood, his eyes alert and shining.

Layla remained standing, swaying on the balls of her feet. Instantly, her grievous wound began stitching back together. An acidic bark fell from Layla's lips as she strode forward. She spat blood on Atlas's chest. "You're going to have to do better than that, *baby*."

The long sword sliced through the air, arcing gracefully. Atlas carved Layla's body with the gleaming blade. She looked ghastly, like a walking corpse brought back from the dead. Deep cuts zigzagged over her chest, face, and thighs. Her white shirt absorbed the blood, scarlet blooms erupting in macabre designs across the fabric. Her hollow laugh echoed eerily around the cavern.

"Keep going, Atlas. Cut me into tiny pieces. I'll never leave. I'll haunt you forever. I'm immortal—the one thing you'll never be."

Atlas's face darkened with rage. "Remember what I said, darling: maiming is easy. Death would be too sweet a sentence for you. You think this mountain is hell? Wait until Hades throws your soul into Tartarus for eternity."

Without another word, Atlas attacked, undeterred by Layla's healed injuries. Blake took a step forward, alarmed by the fury in the Titan's eyes.

Joel ripped him back, pointing to the deep chasm at their feet. "Dude, we can't help."

Blake's eyes flashed to Bia. "Can you do something? Anything to help her?"

Bia shook her head, her hands flapping madly by her sides. "They're too c-close together. I might hit her."

Blake turned back to the horror unfolding before him. He was transported back to when he was eleven years old, watching his father beat his mother. "We have to help."

But his friends remined silent.

Atlas laughed, brandishing the sword over his head. Blake's gut clenched, unable to look away. With the back of his hand, Atlas struck Layla across the face, sending her staggering backward. He pursued, slashing the sword in a wild X across the nymph's chest. Fresh blood pooled down the front of her shirt. Her tattered flesh was visible through the severed material. Atlas wasn't done. In a golden blur, the sword tore into Layla's neck, biting and biting and biting as Atlas hacked away at the thin muscle.

Bia wailed, her hands slapping her thighs as she curled against Jezlem's chest. Joel wretched behind them, but Blake and Jezlem watched in shock. But she was immortal, she couldn't die. She would heal again.

Layla's head rolled to the right, the tendons unable to support the weight any longer. Her gaze caught Blake as she fell to her knees. The bright red blood looked alien as it burst on her lips and dribbled down her chin. Her head tilted back, her eyes growing cloudy with death. She reached a shaking hand toward him, her strangled gasp the only sound as he continued to watch with bated breath.

Layla's eyes rolled into the back of her head, and her body swayed before collapsing to the floor. Her head collided with a small coffee table, cracking through the glass. Shards rained down onto her face, slicing across her forehead, her cheeks. Her momentum rolled her onto her back. Her glassy eyes stared up at the mounting shadows hidden in the ceiling. The impact ripped through the last remaining flesh keeping her body together. Her head rolled a few inches away, decapitated from the stump above her collarbone. The blue halo surrounding her body dulled and extinguished as her soul fled, her body nothing more than a hollow pile of bones and skin and blood.

Atlas looked down at the crumpled vessel, a wide grin on his face as he gripped the blood-covered sword tighter. He raised his gaze to Blake's. "Your turn."

Jezlem shuffled toward the lip of the fissure, her teal eyes brimming with tears. "What have you done?"

Atlas licked his lips. "I warned her to stop."

Jezlem untangled herself from Bia's grip. "You're a monster."

Atlas shrugged the accusation away, his eyes only for Blake. "If you think I'm a monster now, you better hide before the real demons emerge."

At last, Blake remembered to breathe. He couldn't pull his eyes from the dead nymph, absorbed by the sight of the red blood pooling beneath her body. "How could you do that?"

Atlas clicked his teeth together. "There's plenty more nymph where she came from. I'm not going to mourn the loss of that one. In a few minutes, I'll have quite the selection before me once Zeus arrives."

"What are you talking about?"

Bia rushed to Jezlem's side and whispered in her sister's ear. Jezlem's head snapped up, alarm screaming in her eyes.

Atlas threw back his head, laughing. "You're such a fool. Haven't you figured it out yet? There was never any game. Zeus isn't waiting for you. He's been waiting for me." He walked forward, dragging the tip of the blade along the floor.

Blake narrowed his eyes. "What do you mean?"

"He's been here this whole time, hidden away in another part of the mountain. You ran right past his chambers. If you weren't so concerned with saving your own skin, you probably would have heard her screams." Atlas's arched his eyebrows. "It sounded like she was in a lot of pain too."

Jezlem shook her head. "But how could you have known we would seek you out?"

Atlas smiled, sucking his teeth. "Didn't any part of you find it strange that a mortal would have any knowledge about me or my whereabouts once she lost her connection? You didn't find me by accident. Zeus told me his plans and gifted you my location. Gave you little sparks of hope that maybe you'd be able to rejoin the ethereal realm too."

"What?" Jezlem's brows drew together. "That isn't possible."

"I doubt it was hard for Zeus to paint the idea in your mind. A few hushed whispers while you dreamed, some fabricated texts set down within your reach. Use your imagination."

"It was all a trap. Everything, just to fuel his sick fantasy." Jezlem covered her face with her hands. "I'm so sorry."

Heat rolled through Blake, followed by embarrassment and stupidity. For once, he'd wanted to do something right, to save someone before it was too late, but it was impossible when all the pieces were fixed. "What about Kait?" he asked. "I still have to save her."

Atlas swung the sword, slicing the air with a whoosh. "Save her all you like." He snorted. "She's mine once Zeus is finished with her. No doubt she's already given him euphoria, but that won't stop him from raping her again for you to watch." His deep laugh filled the room, echoing like a thunderclap.

Blake's jaw clenched as rage raced through his veins. "You won't touch her."

"You might think that, but in a few minutes, you'll be a cooling corpse on the floor. You won't be able to stop me."

Behind Atlas, a white shadow slunk along the wall. Blake followed the piriol with his eyes. It appeared relaxed as it maneuvered around the furniture, but Blake knew how quickly that could change. Circling back, the animal padded over to Atlas's side. It stood alert, its large head level with the Titan's torso. The cat opened its mouth, tasting the air as its golden eyes zeroed in on Bia.

Blake heard a sharp intake of breath. Frozen in place, Bia stared back at the beast. A deep rumble sounded in the piriol's throat, and the quills on its spine rustled to life.

"Easy, Kaf," Atlas said. "You'll get her soon."

"What is that thing?" Joel asked under his breath.

Blake kept his eyes trained on Atlas. "It's called a piriol."

"Can you give me a little more than that?"

Blake gripped his sword tighter, ready for the creature to pounce. "They hunt nymphs."

"Shit, look at those teeth. Are those needles on its back?"

"Something like that."

Atlas glanced away from the piriol, a mad gleam in his eyes as he took in the pathetic group before him. He swung the golden sword, the muscles between the bones of his hand standing out. "I should wait for Zeus; he's just finishing up. He'll be disappointed, but…I want the pleasure of killing you." Atlas sauntered forward. The piriol stayed rooted in place.

Blake licked his lips. They needed a plan.

"Won't he be angry?" he asked, trying to stall. "You said yourself, he needs me alive. He wants me to watch him take her." Blake swallowed his revulsion. "What do you think he'll do to you when his elaborate play is ruined?"

Atlas grinned. "Nice try. Zeus already has his prize. I'm sure he'll get over losing his audience."

"How g-good will immortality f-feel with Layla's blood on your hands?" Bia asked. Her stutter was prominent, but her voice was strong.

A flicker of uncertainty passed over the Titan's face, but it vanished in the next moment. "It will be better than I remember. Once I'm immortal again, I will be an unstoppable force. Even the great Zeus will bow to me. I've slaughtered hundreds of nymphs. What's one more?"

"You'd condemn Layla to the Underworld that easily? After she stayed by your side all those years?" Jezlem asked.

Atlas rolled his eyes. "You act as if she were a saint. Layla would have done the same given the chance. I had no illusions that she loved me. Our relationship was born of necessity; otherwise, isolation would have driven us both insane. The goal of this partnership with Zeus was never about protecting Layla. My only motivation in working with that bastard was to restore my powers. But how about you, love?" He arched his eyebrows in Bia's direction. "You'll do nicely beneath me now that Layla's gone."

Joel aimed the crossbow. "Leave her alone."

"Or what? You'll put a little hole in me? Be my guest, boy. My sword will be slick with your blood before you manage to nock one arrow."

Jezlem flicked her wrists, revealing two silver throwing disks clutched in each hand. "What about all of us? Think you'll survive his arrow, my chakram, Bia's magic, and Blake's sword?"

Atlas gripped his sword. "Let's find out."

⚡ 34 ⚡

Without warning, Jezlem lunged, propelling herself over the gap with the grace of a crane, her long legs soaring over the precipice. She landed on her knees, sliding across the smooth stone floor in front of the great Titan. Slicing upward toward Atlas's unprotected stomach, the discs sang, biting flesh. She leapt to her feet, spinning in a tight circle, and delivered two more slashes to his torso. A thin red line bloomed across his shirt, but his reaction was swift. With an annoyed growl, Atlas knocked the blades away before they could penetrate any farther.

"Stupid girl," Atlas barked, swinging his sword. The metal sliced into the soft skin of Jezlem's shoulder. A startled cry fell from her lips; pain blossomed in her eyes. She stumbled away, out of Atlas's reach. Crimson blood seeped into her shirt, down her arm.

"No!" Joel cried. "We have to get over there!"

Blake looked from Joel to the gap in the floor. "But how? I can't jump that."

"Leap. I'll d-do the rest," Bia said. "Go!"

Reacting simultaneously, the boys sprinted to the lip of the cliff and pushed off with the soles of their sneakers. With one hand holding his sword, Blake's other arm pinwheeled as they sailed through the air, the black hole gaping beneath them. His heart dropped. They weren't going to make it.

Blake felt his momentum slow. His feet were still several inches from the opposite ledge as his body fell. His throat swelled with fear, but a solid smack roused him from his terror. Beneath his feet, a flat rock hovered, keeping the blackness at bay. He glanced at Joel. He, too, balanced on a suspended rock.

"Hurry up!" Bia screamed. She held both hands out in front of her, her fingers bending and twisting as her magic started to drain.

Blake jumped to the other side with Joel beside him. He shot his friend a knowing look. Wielding his sword behind his shoulders like a bat, Blake cried, sprinting the short distance separating them from the Titan. An excited grin took over Atlas's features.

Blake's sword collided with Atlas's, the blade shuddering as Atlas parried it. Blake heaved his sword again, feeling the strength in his muscles expand as the tonic activated. The sword now felt light in his grasp, and he was amazed to discover that his limbs seemed to know what to do and how to move.

Thank you, Layla.

Letting his anger flow freely, Blake gritted his teeth, refusing to go down without a fight. Metal clanged, but the Titan was ready, blocking Blake's attack with an absentminded wave of his hand.

"Is this the best you've got?" Atlas yawned. "Maybe I'll cut off my hand to make this pathetic excuse for a fight last a little longer."

Atlas brought his sword down hard, hammering the long blade inches from Blake's fingers. Blake's arm vibrated, and he dropped his sword as his fingers tingled, unable to maintain their grip.

A whistle whispered past Blake's ear, followed by a solid thunk. Blake glanced around, trying to identify the source when Joel shouted on the other side of Atlas.

"Keep going, Blake! I've got your back!" Joel let loose another arrow. He stood atop a table, papers and books strewn about the floor to make room for his feet.

Blake ducked, swiping his sword off the floor as Atlas swung wide, just missing his neck. Without stopping, Blake spun once more and raised his sword to block another attack as Atlas's blade dove at his chest. A silver arrow jutted out of Atlas's thigh, another through his bicep.

Chancing a look around the room, Blake's eyes flashed away from Atlas. Jezlem and Bia were nowhere in sight. He hoped Bia was able to heal Jezlem as easily as she had fixed them.

A loud growl shook him from his thoughts, and he snapped back to the fight just as Atlas sliced his sword an inch away from his right leg. He escaped the blade, but he was too slow for Atlas's curled fist. The blow smashed into Blake's eye, rattling his teeth. Blake tripped, catching a small end table in the gut. A weak whoosh of air was knocked out of him as his forehead bounced off the light wood.

Before he could right himself, Atlas pulled Blake up by the front of his shirt, brought his fist back, and released, punching him square in the nose. The brittle cartilage buckled. Blood poured forth over his lips.

The Titan dropped him back to the floor, laughing. Blake's head pounded. Hopefully the tonic's healing properties would kick in soon. His sword tumbled from his grasp and clattered to the floor, but the missing weapon barely registered as his eyes closed.

"Blake! Get up!" Jezlem shouted, her voice clear and bright.

Blake's eyelids flew open, his headache softening. Jezlem stood over him with two long knives in her hands. Dancing away, she jabbed and pivoted, stabbing and slicing through the air like an assassin. Blood still covered her shirt, but Blake was relieved to spy smooth skin beneath the fluttering fabric.

Atlas smiled as he knocked Jezlem's attempts away, but she didn't relent. Her movements became faster, her arms weaving like a ribbon, the knives drawing jagged lines across his skin. His smile fell away, and a deep divot appeared in the middle of the Titan's forehead as he concentrated, working hard to defend himself.

Blake scrambled to his feet, an idea forming as Jezlem's movements blurred. She was fast and lethal. All she needed was a moment.

"Hey, Atlas!" Blake shouted.

Atlas's gaze met Blake's, but Jezlem didn't stop. She spun, a whirl of colors, and punched both daggers into Atlas's chest with a wild cry. Within the same second that the serrated blades kissed the Titan's skin, a spark of lightning exploded amidst the fight. Billowing fog poured forth from the small crater the strike created, obscuring the entire room.

Acrid smoke filled his nose, and his lungs seized as they fought for oxygen around the thick fumes. Teary-eyed, Blake gazed through the dissipating smoke. Atlas's form sharpened into focus, but something was wrong. The Titan's chest was intact, unmarred by the daggers or their bloody kiss.

A deep chuckle reverberated off the walls.

"Well now, old friend, what do we have here?"

⚡ 35 ⚡

"Looks like you're having quite the party…except for her." Zeus laughed, gesturing to Layla's lifeless form. "She was a pretty one, Atlas. Great body. What a waste, but I don't doubt you had your reasons. You always do."

Atlas dropped his sword, his bloodlust for Jezlem seemingly extinguished in Zeus's presence.

"Don't talk about her," Jezlem barked.

Zeus paused his assessment of the room, interest sparking in his deep blue eyes. "Oh, I know that voice. Hello, darling." He took a step closer to Jezlem. "It's been a while."

A low hiss escaped Jezlem's teeth as she jerked away from his touch.

A dark smile crawled across Zeus's perfect face while his hand remained suspended in the air. "I forgot how beautiful you are. But then, I've always had a weakness for blondes." He shrugged. "I'm making do though. This new treat I have is quite delicious."

A quiet zing rent the air as a steel arrow flew past Zeus's shoulder, skittering off the stone floor behind him.

"Keep talking like that and the next one is going down your throat," Joel said, steadying the crossbow.

Zeus raised his eyebrows. "Put that toy away before you hurt yourself, boy. Where's the other little hero? Is he dead too?"

Atlas glanced around the wreckage and pointed to where Blake crouched on his knees. "He's still alive, as promised."

Zeus pivoted, his eyes full of amusement as they took in Blake's battered face. "Ah, there you are. I was worried for a minute."

Blake's eyes hardened. He climbed to his feet. "Where's Kait?"

Zeus clicked his tongue. "Not yet. I'm hesitant to part with my prize. You have to earn her, remember?"

"If you've hurt her—"

"Hurt?" Zeus scoffed, shaking his golden hair with a laugh. "Maybe I misinterpreted her when she told me to go *faster, harder*—my mistake." His smile was venomous, transforming his handsome features into a vicious snarl.

"Somewhere around here is another pure one, never been touched." Atlas's steel eyes glistened. "We could share. I am anxious to experience euphoria once you restore my powers."

Zeus lifted a slender eyebrow. "I'm fine, old friend, but thank you for the offer. I'm enjoying the little nymph I have now…so feisty."

Jezlem emitted a disgusted growl, slipping a hidden knife from her waistband. "Stop your filthy lies."

"Or what? You'll run me through?"

Without warning, Zeus's hand flicked out. His long fingers wrapped around Jezlem's wrist to pull her closer. He melded her body to his lean frame. The blade she gripped pressed against the vulnerable flesh beneath his chin. Unlike Blake's first encounter with the god on the beach, Zeus was no longer vapor; he was tangible, and the knife cut him.

Golden red blood bloomed to the surface and ran down Zeus's neck in a thin rivulet, but his calm features reflected no pain. He buried his face in Jezlem's hair and inhaled. When he leaned back, there was a serene smile on his lips. "Oh, that brings back memories."

Jezlem squirmed in his arms. "You're a snake," she spat, her words acid.

"Didn't stop you from crying out my name before, love."

He pushed Jezlem away, her knife now balanced in his hand. She stumbled, managing to catch herself before she fell to the debris-covered floor. Zeus twirled the knife between his fingers as his blood evaporated, lifting from his skin in a fine red mist.

Blake took a step closer. If Zeus was tangible, maybe he would be able to harm him after all. The lethal blade flashed in the light of a nearby bulb. Blake's steps faltered. Confidence rolled off Zeus, a perfect warrior. Blake didn't stand a chance, but that didn't matter.

"Let's get this over with, Zeus," Blake called.

Zeus glanced over his shoulder, then turned to address Blake head-on. "Brave for a mortal. Is your life worth so little that you'd throw it away this easily? I gave you a chance to leave our world, leave the nymph behind, but here you are, practically begging for death."

In response, Blake took another step. The last remnants of pain in his head lifted, leaving him renewed and refreshed. "I promised I would fight for her. If I defeat you, then I'll go home, once she's safe from you."

Atlas laughed. "Stupid boy doesn't know when to quit."

"No. This is perfect—exactly what I wanted. How shall you die, Blake? Would you like to bleed out, or do you prefer electrocution?" Zeus spread his hands, blue flames crackling on the tips of his fingers.

"Release Kait first." Blake edged closer. "You promised you wouldn't hurt her."

The god held up his pointer finger and smirked. "Technically, I promised I wouldn't rape her before you showed up. Our deal said nothing about harming her. Plus, you haven't defeated me yet."

"Let me help you, Zeus," Atlas offered. "Restore my powers. I've kept this haven among the human realm a secret for you for eons. I've harbored your piri-ol from the eyes of the Council and disposed of your nymphs once you were through with them. Give me back my powers."

Zeus nodded, his bare feet carrying him across the dark carpet. Clapping Atlas on his large bicep, he smiled, flashing too many teeth. "I suppose you're right, old friend. You have upheld your part of the agreement. After all these years, you are finally worthy of resuming your place among the gods."

Atlas's worried expression relaxed. He exhaled a heavy breath. "Thank you. I've dreamed of this day from the moment you chained me to this mountain." The Titan's tone was smooth, but fury glowed in his eyes.

"Ironic that murder earns you a place in the heavens," Jezlem said. "I didn't realize killing innocents was a worthy characteristic."

Atlas scowled at her. "No one is innocent. I'd like to see how long your list of friends to sacrifice would be if you were offered the same."

"I'd rather die than risk the lives of those I love—a lesson you clearly haven't grasped." She gestured to Layla's still form.

"She betrayed me. The minute she let him put his hands on her, she was dead to me. I just finished the job."

"Oh, oh?" Zeus's voice rose, his interest clearly piqued. "Seems you've been naughty too, eh, Blake? I completely understand. Want to test warmer waters before you pledge yourself to one woman. I think it's grand, but how will your nymph take it, I wonder?"

Blake's fingers tightened around the hilt of his sword. "It wasn't like that."

Atlas grabbed Zeus by the shoulder and redirected his attention. "Come. Restore my powers and we can kill them all and get on with our lives."

Zeus took a step away, his expression unreadable, but Blake saw the way his shoulders stiffened, saw his nostrils flare. A silent moment passed, then he clapped his hands, his charming smile back in place. "I can perform it right now, old friend. Then we'll finish these children off and head up to Olympus! Won't the Council be surprised to see you?"

Atlas grinned and fell into step with Zeus as he led him toward the center of the room. "It will be nice to step inside those gates again." He sighed. His fierce aggression was gone, replaced with an eagerness to please.

Jezlem snuck to Blake's side. "We need to do something before we have to face two immortals."

Blake nodded, a raspy breath catching in his throat. "We should focus on Atlas. Kill him before he transforms." He eyed a blade on the other side of a couch. His palms began to sweat at the thought of retrieving it. Who was he kidding? Even with Layla's tonic knitting his wounds, he was still up against two impervious gods.

"Yes," Zeus said. "Though I believe the gates you'll be entering through will look a little different." His voice dropped to a threatening baritone.

Blake turned away from Jezlem. Something was wrong.

Atlas's brow creased. "What do you mean?"

Atlas gasped, his breath whistling between his teeth as his body began to shake. Zeus stood beside him, a serene smile on his lips. Blake scoured the scene, trying to make sense of it. The smell of burning flesh permeated the air, and the full image formed.

"Never touch me again," Zeus said, punctuating every word.

Atlas glanced down, confusion shining in his eyes as he recognized the glowing golden sword punched through his chest. He touched the long blade, as if trying to comprehend how it came to be protruding from his skin.

A trickle of scarlet blood blossomed around the wound, then exploded in a rushing torrent as his skin began to peel away, exposing sundered muscles and sinew beneath. "No! Please!" Atlas choked, unmasked fear in his gray eyes. He collapsed to his knees and clutched the edge of the sword in an attempt to free it from his body. He screamed. His calloused skin sizzled to dust as it evaporated upward, filling the air with macabre snowflakes.

A pool of blood encircled Atlas, sloshing against his knees as the outer layer of skin peeled off his body. Blake couldn't look away. Out of the corner of his eye, he saw Jezlem staring, hypnotized by the grotesque sight as well.

Zeus stepped closer to Atlas, careful to sweep his long navy robe out of the blood's reach. "Did you really think I'd restore your immortality? You're more gullible than the mortals."

"I was l-l-loyal." Bright red blood bubbled over Atlas's white lips and down his shaking chin. "I have been your man for centuries. Harboring nymphs and seeking mortals to warm your bed. I have endured this hell you sentenced me t-to." Blood gurgled in his throat.

The thin skin on Atlas's face curled, peeling and ripping up to his scalp until he resembled a terrifying Halloween mask. He gasped, then crashed to the blood-soaked floor. His weight splashed into the deepening pool, peppering everything nearby with large red drops. Blake flinched as warm liquid splattered his neck and face.

Zeus unleashed a hideous laugh, his dark blue eyes hard and unyielding as stones. "You will never be welcomed back into Olympus, not after what you've done. You are nothing more than a slimy, groveling dog who has worn out his usefulness. I should have killed you eons ago. I wanted to make your death as painful as possible. How did I do?"

Blake was transfixed by the hideous figure that used to be Atlas. The Titan was no longer trying to fight for breath. Apart from a few sporadic twitches, Atlas was still, his mouth frozen in a painful howl.

Zeus paced around the fallen Titan, fluffing his robe like a vulture preparing to feed. The blood seeped across the floor, and Blake shifted to avoid it, bringing himself closer to Zeus.

At last, Blake tore his gaze away and locked eyes with Jezlem. If they could reach the weapons, they could catch him while he was distracted. Jezlem cocked her head and began to move, but Zeus chuckled, freezing them in their tracks.

"Trying to catch me by surprise? You should know better." He gave them a disapproving look. "Don't worry, I have other plans for all of you—especially you, Jez." His tongue flickered out, licking his lower lip. "Don't you have another sister here as well? I'd love to meet her."

"Touch her and you're dead," Jezlem snarled. She stepped back toward the large crevice separating them from the rest of the weapons.

Zeus sighed. "I've missed that. Kait has fire, but she's not as sweet as you."

Blake shook his head. "You said you wouldn't touch her."

Zeus groaned, looking bored. "When you grow up, you'll realize there are other ways to enjoy a woman. No, I haven't taken her yet, but I've tasted—oh, have I tasted."

"You're deplorable," Blake spat. "Why agree to my wager when you were just going to put your hands on her anyway?"

The god was quiet as he bent down to withdraw the golden sword from Atlas's stiff chest. The blade slid out of his congealing blood with a wet sucking sound. Zeus held it out, and with a simple wave, its scarlet coating disappeared. He didn't sheath it.

"Answer me!" Blake cried.

"For that," Zeus replied. "That reaction right there. It was too good to pass up, and it gave me more time with the nymph. Typically, they only entertain me for a few hours, but Kait—well, she just doesn't stop." He chuckled.

"You're lying," Blake shook his head.

"Lying? Why would I do that? I may be a bastard, but I'm an honest one." He took in Blake's doubtful expression. "Fine, ask her yourself." Zeus spun the golden sword, and a crackle of lightning flashed, illuminating the dim cavern.

Blake shielded his eyes from the bright light and held his breath, anticipating more smoke. After a few seconds, he was able to look, and his eyes fixed on a dark object.

Bruised legs tapered down from tattered golden fabric, and matted dark curls topped the vision. White spots danced across Blake's eyesight, and he fought to focus. Then the image sharpened, and his vision cleared.

Kait.

Relief warmed him. He didn't even realize he was moving toward her. His feet acted of their own volition. Too late, he saw the excitement in Zeus's eyes, the sinister smile spreading on his lips.

Kait stood before Blake, bruised and hunched, but when she caught sight of him, her eyes lit up, though not with joy, but fear. She reached for him, a small wrinkle forming between her eyebrows.

Alarm bells rang in Blake's mind. What had Zeus done to her? Why couldn't she speak?

Numerous thoughts swirled in his head, but he kept going. His sneakers slapped the stone, the tonic surging through his veins, increasing his speed. She was only a few feet away and—*crack*! Blake collided with a brick wall.

He bounced backward, sprawling to the floor. Yet another eruption of pain made him cry out. He didn't need to feel for damage. Blood spouted from his broken nose and gushed down his face and shirt anew.

Laughter rained down, punching sharp staccatos in Blake's ringing ears. "I could watch that all day." Zeus sighed. "I underestimated you. Mortals are quite entertaining."

Jezlem came to Blake's side. "Are you all right?"

He groaned. "Yeah. What did I hit?" He shifted his gaze from the ceiling back to Kait. She was furious, her rage evident as she shouted mutely at Zeus.

"What, my dear?" Zeus cupped his ear. "Try to speak up." He grinned.

She slammed her fists against the air, and her hands stopped abruptly, re-bounding off something. Understanding tugged at the back of Blake's mind. She was locked inside an invisible chamber.

"Let her out of there." Blake's tongue swirled inside his mouth, tasting fresh blood. Growling in the back of his throat, he spat a short stream of coppery blood at the god's feet.

Zeus rolled his eyes and scratched the bridge of his nose. "She's fine. She'll come out in a minute. You're so serious, suck the fun right out. I take back what I said before."

"I'm not here to have fun. I'm done stalling. Let her go and we can end this."

Zeus fixed Blake with a pointed stare, fire sparking in his eyes. "Fine, if you're so eager for death…" His smile transformed into a grim line. "Who am I to object? Kaf, *occidere eos*!"

The god threw his arms to the side. The palms of his hands glowed a fierce blue. Pulling his right arm back, Zeus moved as if throwing a pitch. A fiery sphere left his hand in a glorious blaze. The air sizzled as the fireball roared to-ward Blake's chest. A sharp tug ripped him sideways, just as the fire smashed into a chair behind him.

Blake rolled onto his stomach, and Jezlem leapt out of the way, landing on her side. Blake didn't look back at Zeus. Instead, he dug his elbows into the car-pet and crawled to Jezlem as another fireball missed the heel of his shoe.

"You okay?" Blake yelled.

"We have to move!"

Together, they sprung to their feet, dodging and spinning out of the path of two more fireballs. The one meant for Blake skimmed his ear, crackling hungrily as it sailed past. More flames landed with a hushed thuds, scorching the Persian carpets behind them to fine ash.

A gold shimmer sparkled beneath a love seat several yards away. Blake ducked as a fireball soared overhead. He rushed in the direction of Atlas's forgotten weapon, but Zeus was faster.

A blue ball of fire seared across Blake's shoulder, shredding his thin T-shirt to lick the vulnerable skin beneath. The blue flames engulfed his flesh, weaving a trail of scorching bites. The scent of burning hair filled Blake's nose as the hellfire latched on, devouring the length of his arm and wrapping around the back of his neck.

"Blake!"

Distantly, Blake heard his name, but he didn't look away from the fire. He was burning alive.

He smacked his arm in a vain attempt to smother the flames, but the fire burned brighter, leaping to his other hand. His flesh bubbled as the fire engulfed him. It was as if the flames were seeking vengeance, growing stronger with his screams.

Jezlem screamed, imprisoned in Zeus's arms as the god careened with laughter. Blake buckled to the ground. His eyes watched the fire. He didn't recognize the morphed skin peeking back at him. A prayer for death danced on his lips. There was no way the tonic could conquer that.

Zeus raised his hand, his fingertips glowing, prepping for another attack. Jezlem threw her head back, smashing her skull into the god's teeth. Zeus spat out a stream of sticky blood as Jezlem slipped from his hold.

"Don't make me chase you. You're not going to like what happens."

Jezlem ignored Zeus's taunt. "Help him!"

Blake frowned, struggling to stay conscious amidst the pain. Who was Jezlem talking to?

"Blake!" Joel's voice echoed.

A heavy weight hit Blake, knocking the last shred of breath from his lips. Furious blows peppered his body. He tried to pull in his limbs in self-preservation, but Blake couldn't hold on, couldn't fight back. The fire raged around the harsh kicks. He closed his eyes. All he could do was endure until death intervened.

"It's over, man. It's out." Joel gasped close to Blake's ear. "Christ, your skin…"

"Joel?" Blake's voice grated, rougher than sandpaper.

"I'm here. Sorry. The piriol cornered me. Clawed me good, see?" Joel pointed to his shredded shirt and the newly healed skin beneath the tatters. "Bia did something to the ground and trapped its paws so we could get away. Man, I would have been dead already if it weren't for that tonic Layla gave us."

Careful not to touch Blake's raw flesh, Joel slipped his hands underneath his arms. He dragged Blake backward, grimacing as a large flap of blackened skin flaked off the back of his hand. "Damn, man. Aren't you supposed to be winning?"

A low, painful sigh whistled out between Blake's teeth. He tried not to look at his skin, tried to dispel the scent of his body burning, but it was everywhere. He licked his charred lips and tasted blood and ash. "Working on it," he rasped. "Where's Bia?"

"Grabbing weapons so we can kill this asshole."

"Leave me. Help Jez."

"No. It'll take all of us to bring him down. Besides, you'll be good in a minute."

Blake glanced at his arms, shocked to see the dead and blackened flesh was now shiny and pink. He tested other parts of his burned body and found the skin healed all over. The crippling pain had fled as well. "Help me stand," he said. Joel obliged, helping him to his feet.

Bia appeared before them, blooming from a tangle of thick vines snaking across the floor. Her arms were laden with an array of swords, a whip, a staff, and a pair of axes. She dropped the weaponry in a heap, her hands still, her eyes clear and focused. "Keep him b-busy. I'm g-going to work on f-freeing Kait. See if I c-can get around the s-spell."

The boys nodded, grabbing the first weapon nearest them: a whip for Joel and a staff for Blake.

A startled cry alerted Blake. Zeus wielded a rope of white flame. With the crack of his wrist, the rope lashed out, wrapping around Jezlem's waist. It halted her momentum, spinning her back to where Zeus stood waiting with open arms. Angry red welts scarred her stomach, but the god only made the flames burn brighter. Tears welled in Jezlem's eyes, but the god was blind to her pain. Instead, his attention zeroed in on Blake.

"Seems you've been resurrected. What magic is this?"

"A little something to even the odds," Blake replied, pleased by the scowl on Zeus's face.

"I see. But now it's two against one. Hardly seems like a fair fight." Another blue fireball danced in his hand.

Joel cocked his head. "Fair? What about this is fair? You're an all-powerful god and can throw balls of fire. Though for some reason, you're using Jez like a human shield."

Zeus's eyes narrowed. "Fine, I'll let her go, but not in one piece."

Zeus pushed Jezlem toward the boys. A glint of silver smiled as his hand flashed, his movements a blur. He grabbed the hilt of a falling knife and slashed Jezlem's calves, exposing the pink tissue.

Jezlem's eyes bulged as her scream rent the air. She collapsed in a heap, squeezing her eyes shut against the pain.

"Jez!" Joel cried, catching her before her head hit the ground.

"What is wrong with you?" Blake shouted.

"Just wanted to be sure I had your attention." Zeus shrugged.

Blake spun away. He slid his arms under Jezlem's legs and helped Joel carry her away from the fight. They laid Jezlem down, and Joel brushed her tears away, cradling her face.

"I'm sorry I can't heal you. Rest. We'll take care of him," Joel whispered.

Jezlem raised her shaking hand and interlaced her fingers with Joel's. "Thank you."

Joel didn't pull away, and Blake noticed the lingering way their eyes held one another.

Zeus cleared his throat. "How touching." He threw the knife, burying the tip into the carpet, and opened his arms, exposing his chest. "No magic, no shields. Just me. Ready?"

Blake glanced at Jezlem, fury rolling through him. Zeus had taken so much from her. His gaze swept the large cavern, alighting on Kait, who was still trapped within her unbreachable prison. Dark bruises covered her face and neck. Her fists continued to beat the air.

"Hell yes," the boys answered in unison.

"Excellent." Zeus's laughter reverberated around the room as he disappeared in a crack of lightning, only to reappear inches away from Blake. "Pick up the staff. Make me bleed. Then we'll have our fight."

Blake stared at the god, trying to read his stoic features. Was this a trick? Blake gripped the staff, leveling it with Zeus's chest.

"No, let me," Joel called.

Blake opened his mouth to argue, but the cold look in Joel's eyes silenced him. Joel sauntered up to the god with the golden whip at his side. Rather than using the weapon though, Joel pulled back his right arm and smashed his fist into Zeus's jaw. Blake heard several of his tiny bones snap on impact, but the look on the god's face was priceless.

Joel cursed and cradled his hand. "Don't ever touch Jez again."

Zeus lifted his hand to his reddening jaw. "I wasn't expecting that," he admitted. His mouth twitched from side to side. "My turn."

⚡ 36 ⚡

Before either could react, Zeus flipped his wrists, aiming his palms at Blake. Rather than blue fire, white lightning exploded from the center of his hands. The force of the attack surged through Blake, picking him up and catapulting him forward in a sailing arch. His arms flailed, trying to slow his momentum, but there was nothing to impede his progression, save for the exposed rock floor he hurtled toward.

"Blake!" Joel shouted, but Zeus directed the crackling lightning at him as well.

The stone floor loomed as gravity took over and yanked Blake from the air. He tried to position his hands beneath his body to cushion the fall, but they did little to soften the impact. His forehead bounced off the ground. Blood welled in his mouth as his teeth sliced through the sides of his tongue. Everything hurt—every bone, every muscle, every cell.

"Kaf!" Zeus sang.

Waiting like a poised spring, the piriol leapt forward, bounding across the room. A terrifying snarl echoed off the stone walls. Just like its master, the cat desired blood.

The piriol swiped at Joel, claws reaching out like curved daggers. Joel yelped in surprise and fell back. With shaking hands, his fingers fumbled for the bow he dropped earlier. He notched an arrow. The trigger released, and a furious snarl resounded as the needle-sharp tip pierced the piriol's eye.

Joel nodded at Blake, leaping onto a nearby dining table. "I've got this. Go!"

Bellowing, the piriol retreated, swatting at the arrow with its paws. Blake stared in disbelief as the cat abandoned its attempt to dislodge the shaft and arched its back, prompting the quills there to leap to attention. Without pause, it unleashed three lethal spikes at Joel.

Joel tucked his arms in and tried to roll off the tabletop. The first two quills buried into the polished wood with resounding thuds, but the third caught him in the thigh. Crying in pain, he fell to the floor, dropping the bow. The cat roared and bared its fangs, preparing to fire more quills.

Blake doubled back to help Joel. He raised the staff like a baseball bat, preparing to bash the animal in the head. He raced over, but a sizzle of lightning erupted between him and the piriol. A loud slap cracked him in the side of the head, sending him flying backward.

Zeus chortled with laughter. "Gods that felt good!"

Joel screamed, his terror tangible. The piriol was on the table, looming over the edge. The wood groaned under the cat's weight, threatening to snap. Gnashing its teeth, the cat swiped downward. Joel struggled on the floor with the large paw as it cut through the flesh on his forearm. Bright red blood swelled. The piriol sniffed, encouraged by the metallic scent.

Blake dragged himself to his knees.

A scream bellowed, followed by a metallic bark.

Blake squinted through the blood dripping into his eye to see Jezlem. The bottoms of her pant legs were torn up to her thighs, and the uneven fabric was wrapped around her wounds like tourniquets. She was a fierce savage, swinging her arms in wide circles, the silver discs clutched in her hands once more.

Zeus ducked Jezlem's attack, sidestepping around her as her momentum carried her past him. His arm shot out and grabbed her by her curls, yanking her backward with a grunt. Jezlem hit his body hard, trapped as his white electricity hissed, forcing her arms down at her sides.

Zeus trailed the tip of his nose down her rigid jawline. "Why do you fight me so? I know you enjoyed it—my touch. I could give you so much more."

"I will never want you. You took everything from me."

"So determined. That's what drew me to you in the first place." Zeus nibbled her earlobe between his teeth. "How about we take a break from all this hostility?" His hands slipped inside the top of Jezlem's bloody white shirt, caressing her breasts. Her body stiffened, like a deer in a hunter's scope.

"Let her g-go!"

Blake's attention was pulled to the left, where Bia stood several feet away.

Zeus glanced toward her with a mix of annoyance and interest. "Well, well. What a pretty little thing you are. You must be the last sister. All so different, all so delic—"

The god didn't get the chance to finish his sentence. Bia crouched low and moved as if scooping up a great weight. In response, the cavern shook. The stalactites above rattled, threatening to break away, and the heavy books vibrated, shaking off the dusty shelves. Blake hunched his shoulders, trying to avoid the falling objects as he scrambled to his feet.

The ground below his shoes quaked, laughing as it split, preparing to crumble. Jagged peaks pushed through the smooth floor. Seizing the opportunity, Jezlem rolled out of Zeus's distracted hold.

The god's fingers curled around empty air. Jezlem slid down a natural hill as the floor continued to rise. Zeus stumbled, his perfect features creasing. Higher and higher the mountains rose, transforming the room. Blake scanned the uneven rocks from his new vantage point for Joel. He spied the now crooked table, but the piriol and his friend were gone.

"Blake!" Joel emerged from behind a jagged peak. He held his injured hand to his chest, but his attention was drawn to something farther away. "Kait!"

Fear filled Blake's throat. Was she still stuck in her prison or had the eroding floor buried her beneath?

"Down there!" Joel pointed to a small valley on the other side of a precariously balanced couch. Still encased in the glass box stood Kait, worry in her violet eyes. Blake followed her gaze and saw Bia stagger, her magic weakening as the rocks quieted.

"Joel," Blake yelled. "Get Bia. I'm after Kait!"

Joel's head snapped in her direction as the shifting floor stilled. Bia slumped to her knees beside a broken lamp. Joel scooped her into his good arm and maneuvered down the challenging terrain to level ground. Blake sighed in relief. Bia was safe for the moment; now he needed to figure out how to get down to Kait.

"Blake!" Jezlem was now thirty feet in the air holding on to a rough pillar of stone with terror in her eyes. "Watch out!"

Blake turned, but his view was blocked by a towering rock. He placed his hands on the rough peak, ready to pull himself over when a heavy paw swatted him, the claws raking the skin of his fingers all the way down to the knuckles.

Blake cried out and lost his grip. His feet weren't quick enough, and he fell into a tight crevice. "Shit!"

A low rumble of thunder resounded off the rocks. Blake scanned the area in front of him for the piriol when a rasping snarl exploded beside his head. The giant piriol bared its saber-like fangs, hatred burning in its remaining eye. Without pause, the large creature lunged, wrapping its powerful arms around Blake's shoulders as its teeth snapped toward his neck.

Blake allowed it to overtake him and used the piriol's momentum to pull him out of the crevice and down the uneven mountain. The pair smashed against the rocks, and Blake was knocked out of the animal's grasp. Scrambling up, Blake rolled away just as one of the long claws sliced the gray stone, leaving a deep gouge behind.

"Throw me a knife, a sword! Anything!"

He surveyed the room, but his friends were nowhere to be found. Blake shimmied through a tight opening and crawled out the other side, then pulled himself up the next jagged plateau. The piriol snarled, but based on the sound of its claws, it was struggling to follow. The cat hissed. Blake had evaded it for now.

Blake slid down a vertical slope. His feet hit the floor with a muted thud. The shelves of weapons had collapsed.

"Hey." Joel appeared in front of Blake. A few shallow cuts decorated his hands, and one side of his face was covered in blood and grit, as if he'd dragged it down the rocks.

"You okay? Where's Bia?" Blake dropped to his knees, searching through the mangled assortment of sharp objects. He needed a weapon before the piriol or Zeus resurfaced.

"Fine. Or will be in a second. She's trying to help Jezlem down, but unless she's got a grappling hook hidden in her dress, I don't see how she can. Did you see how high up she is?" he asked with a tremor in his voice. "What happened to Zeus?"

"I don't know." Blake shook his head. "I lost him. But the piriol found me." He held up his injured hand. The flayed skin was in the process of neatly knitting itself back together. Joel winced.

Blake chose two small daggers and slipped them into the back of his waistband. A curved sword claimed his attention, and he reached out to test the gleaming edge. The blade nicked his skin, drawing a bead of blood.

"Where is it now?" Joel glanced behind him.

"Close. It almost had me, but it couldn't fit though that space." Blake pointed.

Joel gripped a three-pronged knife, along with a deadly-looking mace. "Oh, I like this." He bounced the mace's handle in his hand.

"As long as it works." Blake jumped to his feet. The air above his head surged as shocks of sizzling lighting roared.

"Come out, come out, boys," Zeus called from his perch on one of the elevated plateaus.

Straightening out of his hunch, Blake's gaze connected with Joel's. He looked exhausted, and worry shone in his dark eyes.

"Ready?" Blake asked.

"Not at all," Joel admitted. "But it's fight or die, right?"

Blake nodded, giving his friend a weak smile. There was so much he wanted to say, but there wasn't time. "Sorry I dragged you into this."

Joel sighed. "There's nowhere I'd rather be. Well, actually that's a lie, but you get it."

"Thanks, man."

"Let's end the bastard."

⚡ 37 ⚡

Together, they advanced, staying close to the rocks to take advantage of the cover for as long as possible. Once Jez descended, hopefully the girls would know to flank the god. Blake couldn't wait to wipe the cocky grin off his face.

Another stream of lightning erupted from the god's palms, scorching the warped carpet at his feet to ashes.

"So much for fair." Joel readjusted his hold on the mace. "What happened to man-to-man?"

Zeus's jaw clicked in agitation. The god wanted to make short work of them, but Joel was doing a good job of undermining his pride and masculinity. Zeus's hands dulled, and the crackling energy diminished.

"Fine." Zeus reached behind his back, his hands hidden by his heavy robe. "Remember, you asked for this. For pain." He smiled and unleashed his hands, brandishing two giant golden swords, each longer than Blake's leg.

"Damn," Joel said. "Pull those out of your ass? No wonder you're such a prick."

Zeus's blue eyes narrowed. "You'll die first. Kaf, *occidere eum.*"

Blake's head snapped to the left as the white piriol launched off the rock wall. With a loud smack, it collided with Joel, knocking him to the floor.

"No!" Blake rushed to his friend's aid, but before he could even take two steps, a blade swung in front of his face, slicing the air with a *thwang.*

"He can handle himself, but I have serious doubts about you." Without pause, Zeus whipped the other blade over his head in a severe arc toward Blake's neck.

Blake wielded his own blade, knocking the blow aside with a metallic scream. Zeus didn't hesitate, handling the golden swords as easily as if they were extensions of his own arms. Again, he hammered Blake, swinging both swords over his head and sideways simultaneously. Exhausted breaths rattled in Blake's chest as he barely managed to parry each strike. After several minutes, he got the uneasy feeling that the god was taking it easy on him. The corner of Zeus's mouth twitched in a repressed smile, confirming his fear.

Beads of sweat rolled down Blake's face and neck as the tonic surged through his veins, trying to keep up. Zeus's onslaught was never-ending. He never tired, never showed signs of being winded. He beat Blake back farther and farther, his attacks growing sharper and closer with every weakening breath Blake drew. It was as if Zeus were inhaling Blake's waning energy, each swallow empowering his own stride.

Holding his sword with both hands, Blake swung the sharp blade across his body like a bat, using the last of his strength. Zeus didn't flinch. His hands were a blur as he caught the sword with both of his blades. Blake's momentum rebounded, sending waves of shock up to his shoulders.

Blake's jaw fell slack with surprise. Zeus arched his brow and used the swords to push him back, crisscrossing the blades together in a menacing X. Blake stumbled against a wall behind him. Zeus didn't relent, victory shining in his blue eyes. He charged, the points of the blades gleaming. Blake lashed out. His sword kissed one of Zeus's, managing to knock it off course, but the other buried into its mark.

A brilliant slash of pain bloomed like a scarlet flower just above Blake's heart as the golden sword tore into his flesh. A scream exploded from his lips. His sword slid from his clammy fingertips, clattering to the rock floor as Zeus held him up, pinning him against the stone wall.

Desperate, Blake wrapped his hands around the blade, attempting to draw it from his chest, but it was solid and unyielding. He dropped his hands away. His palms had split from end to end from the effort. His heart gave a weak flutter.

He tried to stay calm, keep his breathing even. The tonic would fix it just like all the other wounds, but he didn't know how close the blade was to his heart. If his adrenaline heightened, he would bleed out in seconds—if he didn't go into cardiac arrest first.

"Blake! Hang on!" Joel cried.

Tears pooled in Blake's lower eyelids, distorting the scene behind Zeus. Joel danced around the piriol as it shot quill after quill, striking him in the shin and bicep. Blake couldn't be sure, but it looked as if the cat's good eye was caked in blood to match its earlier wound. The piriol let out a frustrated snarl and bounded forward, relying on its massive claws instead of its damaged eyesight. The creature was fast, and Joel stumbled as the numbing toxin spread. Before Blake could utter a sound, the big cat raked its claws down Joel's back, shredding his shirt to crimson ribbons. He stared, horrified as his friend fell, his face pale, his features slack.

Blake gasped. "Joel." He struggled against the sword's hold.

His eyelids fluttered as blackness creeped in around the edge of his vision. Vaguely, he was aware of heat spreading down his stomach, followed by a steady dripping. It took him a minute to realize it was his blood pooling on the floor.

Zeus's cool voice sounded in his ear. "Is she worth it now? Is a nymph worth your life, your friend's life?" He leaned on the hilt of the sword, digging it in, twisting it deeper.

Blake screamed. Again, his hands clawed at the blade. Hot, red blood trickled down his fingers, running down to his elbows.

"You know she isn't," Zeus continued. "Right now, you're thinking about your cozy little life before you met her, before this knife pierced you. I can see it in your eyes. You'd give anything to go back, wouldn't you?"

Blake's eyes zeroed in on Zeus's face, just inches from his own. He could feel the power radiating off him. His heart was racing too fast, working too hard to compensate for all the blood leaking out of his wound.

"Just look at her. She's nothing special."

Kait was suddenly before him, still encased. Her dark curls were in a wild heap atop her head, and the transparent box was covered in rusty streaks. Blake's flickering gaze found her, watching as she threw herself again and again at the solid walls. Her eyes radiated fury as her lips spat muted curses. His gaze slid down the length of her, ending at her fingertips. Her nails were ragged and torn, blood crusting in her cuticles as if she had been trying to pry something open. The rusty streaks covering her cage—Kait had been trying to claw her way out, desperate to help them, to help him.

Blake's attention rolled back to Zeus, where he stood confident with victory. At this point, Blake could hardly disagree.

Over Zeus's shoulder, Joel lay on the ground, unmoving, but he wasn't alone. Bia and Jezlem were by his side, spearing and slashing at the blinded piriol with weapons of their own. Quills fired wildly, but without its sight, the piriol had lost its accuracy, enabling the girls to dodge the blows easily. Jezlem wielded a whip, while Bia fired magic like tangible knives, their combined attack decimating the cat's resolve.

Zeus glanced at the piriol, his expression conflicted, distracted. A beautiful thought entered Blake's mind.

Knives.

He pressed his lower back against the wall, and two solid objects kissed his skin. The hilts of the daggers still peeked out of the waistband of his jeans. Blake almost cried with relief. He'd forgotten them. Peering down at his chest, he felt a tightening, terrified his heart was finally giving up. Instead, he watched as the blood stopped flowing. The same tightening gripped him again. He realized in amazement that the tonic was attempting to force the blade out while new layers of skin formed.

New energy rushed through his veins. He wound his arm behind him. His fingers brushed the hilt of the one on the right, but with half his body pinned, there was no way he could throw effectively. He would have to make Zeus come closer. Releasing the dagger, he let his arm hang at his side once more, waiting for the perfect moment.

Zeus turned and gave him a pitying look. "Shame you stumbled into this. This isn't your fight. Isn't your world."

Blake grunted. "You made it my fight when you threatened her."

"Aw, how touching. What a hero."

"I'm not a hero."

Behind him, Jezlem's whip tightened around the cat's front legs. With a strong tug, she yanked the coil, and the piriol crashed to the ground. Bia spun through the air, her arms a blur as a silver spear materialized in her hands. The piriol hissed and struggled to get up, but Bia drove the spear into its thick neck. The cat went limp, and the few remaining quills on its back detached and collapsed to the floor.

Zeus stuttered, as if Bia's spear had sliced his flesh instead. He pressed a hand over his heart, then ripped the sword from Blake's chest as a ragged breath slipped between his lips. His calm gaze became crazed as he turned to the scene behind him.

"What have you done?" Zeus bellowed, his eyes settling on the conquered piriol. "You stupid nymphs. You couldn't leave well enough alone!" Zeus's anger raged. He raised the sword and launched it like a javelin. It smashed against the opposite wall nearly one hundred yards away. His handsome features twisted, transforming his beauty into a terrifying caricature.

Raising his arms, he opened his mouth and screamed until the sound of furious thunder drowned him out. His eyes strained, blood vessels popping as he continued to cry out, commanding the storm. The cavern shook, worse than before, but rather than disrupting the floor, Zeus's aim was higher. An ear-splitting crack fired as a large piece of the stone ceiling broke free and careened to the ground, directly above the girls and Joel. There was no time for them to move, no time to escape the heavy rocks. Blake watched as the ceiling smashed into the jagged floor, his friends disappearing in a splash of scarlet blood.

"No!"

Zeus cackled like a satisfied hyena, his blue eyes shot through with eerie red streaks. His laughter was insane, ricocheting like excited bullets. "I don't know why I didn't do that in the first place!" He danced on his toes. "Did you see all that blood? Pow!" Zeus slapped his palms together.

Tears filled Blake's eyes as he sunk to his knees. Joel, his best friend, was dead. Jezlem and Bia, gone.

A shrieking wail drew Blake's blurry gaze. The invisible box caging Kait vanished, and her cries were no longer muted. She lay on her stomach over the uneven rocks, her face in her hands. "No, please! No! Goddess, no!"

"Come now, dear." An expression of faux pity took over Zeus's face. "I know you've been dying to get out of there. Come on. Come, come, come." He gripped her by the shoulder and yanked her off the floor.

"Don't touch me! Don't touch me!"

Kait screamed and struggled against him, but he was quick to produce a crescent blade, the tip grazing the soft skin beneath her jaw. Kait's frenzied movements stilled. The blade twirled against her skin as her tears continued to fall.

"Darling, I believe you know Blake. He's been waiting so patiently for you. Why don't you give him a little kiss before I finish you off?" Zeus nudged her forward to where Blake swayed against the wall.

Blake ignored Zeus. His eyes hovered over the boulders, searching for Joel. Maybe they got out from under it. Maybe Bia saved them.

Numerous possibilities filtered through his mind, but in his heart, he knew they were all lies.

"I know what's in your heart. I'm going to fulfill your wish to escape all of this," Zeus said.

Blake frowned. It didn't matter what Zeus was going to go to him. Death was the only way he was going to leave the mountain—but he wasn't ready yet.

"I won't give up." Staggering to his feet, Blake felt the tonic surge, empowering his limbs to keep fighting, even with a quarter-sized hole in his chest. With a shaky breath, he lifted his fists.

Zeus cocked his head to the side. His smile faded, annoyance taking its place. He stepped closer, dragging Kait with him. The blade stopped twirling and bit into her skin until blood ran down the length of it. Kait drew in a sharp breath.

"Watch that tone, or you won't get your parting gift," Zeus warned Blake.

"Stop hurting her!"

"Should I hurt you instead?"

White lightning surged forward, striking Blake directly in the spot the sword had torn asunder. The bolt ripped the fresh sinew and muscle to shreds, dropping him to the floor.

Shrieking in pain, Blake withered back and forth.

Zeus grinned as the crescent blade twitched, licking another shallow cut along the side of Kait's neck. "But you need a goodbye kiss!" Zeus licked his lips. "What kind of gracious immortal would I be if I didn't honor the hero? After all, he's worked so hard." The god's eyes flashed, feral and wild as Blake whimpered in pain.

"Let him go, Zeus. Take me. Take me over and over again. Throw me at Hera's feet to serve for eternity. I won't fight you any longer. Just let him go," Kait begged.

Zeus dropped the blade and wrapped his fist around Kait's throat. Blood welled over his fingers as he squeezed. "Isn't that sweet? Two lovers willing to die for one another. Shame your generosity will be going to waste. No one is leaving unless they have a blade through their skull."

Kait's face purpled as Zeus tightened his grip on her windpipe, crushing, crushing, crushing, a haunting look in his eyes. "This is how I've been waiting to take you, weak and hopeless in front of the would-be hero. Then I'll send you to the Underworld with the rest of them, where your pretty lips can rot in the River Styx."

Blake watched helplessly as Zeus crushed his lips to Kait's, his hands working with a fever, pulling and tearing what was left of her dress. Gripping her head, he shoved his tongue inside her mouth.

Blake frowned as Kait smiled, exposing her teeth. What was she doing?

In the next moment, the scene changed from one of passion to horror. Kait bit down, her teeth colliding with a snap as her incisors sliced through the god's tongue. Zeus staggered back, his hands fluttering uselessly over his mouth. Kait spat his tongue in his face, splattering him with blood.

Vomit climbed Blake's throat, but he was distracted by a flicker of movement in the corner of his eye. He pulled his gaze away from Kait to check behind him but found nothing. A prickling feeling remained, but his pain began to recede as the tonic furiously set to work trying to mend his torn flesh again, and the relief canceled out his suspicion.

Blood pulsed down Kait's chin as she stared at Zeus, revenge dancing in her eyes. Her palms slammed together, and from them, powerful torrents of wind blew forward, knocking the god off his feet. Before Zeus could land, her fingers twisted and bent, casting more magic. Furious tornados wielding rock and splintered wood materialized, billowing around his tall frame.

Zeus was pulverized with the flying objects, his skin becoming red and raw. Another flicker of movement appeared in Blake's periphery, seizing his heart. Was the piriol still alive?

Pushing himself into a sitting position, Blake moved to stand, then doubled over in pain, clutching the wound. He had to warn Kait.

His body pleaded for rest, but he forced himself up, clinging to the rough walls for balance. He took a few shaky steps toward the wind nymph, flinching at the dark look illuminating her face. Part of him was tempted to stay back. Truthfully, she was menacing. Then, he envisioned the piriol slinking behind her, ripping into her with its bloodied fangs.

He swallowed his anxiety and continued ahead, letting go of the wall as the tonic crested, shooting strength through his veins. Another blur of color shimmered, but rather than the white fur he expected, a different figure snuck into view.

Blake's eyes were betraying him. She had to be a mirage or a vision, conjured up by exhaustion and blood loss. But the longer he stared, the more real Jezlem became. Her hair was greasy and matted to one side of her head, the color dulled to a rusty brown thanks to a large gash on her scalp. She hobbled, but her eyes were focused, intent on Zeus's back. A large bruise covered the majority of her face, and her shirt was in tatters. Blake gaped in astonishment. If she had survived the rock fall, maybe the others did too.

Kait's eyes flickered in Jezlem's direction, reading her sister's intentions. Commanding the wind, she pulled Zeus in and gripped both sides of his face with her broken nails. This time, the god's magic couldn't subdue her wrath. He was far too weak to even try.

"I warned you not to touch me," she said. "Since Hermes, I've chanted a mantra every day that if I had only been smarter, wiser, that I would have seen his treachery before it was too late. I thought I was to blame. For one hundred years, I wallowed in guilt, terrified that if I dropped my guard even for a moment, someone else's death would be on my hands. I couldn't save Willow, but I realize now that it wasn't my fault."

Jezlem stalked closer to Zeus, a long slender object in her hands. It looked like a large stick. Zeus tried to reply, but the stump of his tongue flopped uselessly behind his teeth. Blake inched closer, palming both dagger handles in his sweating palms. He had no idea what Kait's next move was going to be, but he knew it was drawing near.

"Hermes, you, and all the other immortals think you can simply take whatever pleases you. That entitlement ends today. I should force my winds down your throat until your lungs burst. You're a despicable creature that deserves far worse, but your life isn't mine to take." Without another word, Kait melted into the wind, leaving Zeus swaying on the balls of his feet alone and exposed.

That's when Blake realized Jezlem wasn't holding a stick, but a discarded quill.

She didn't hesitate. Jezlem lunged forward and jammed the tip of the quill into the base of Zeus's skull. A strained grunt erupted deep within her chest as she pushed the weapon with all her might. She gripped it tighter in her palms and thrust once more, this time penetrating his skull with a crunch.

Zeus's eyes dulled, and his mouth gaped open, stunned. A strangled breath rattled from his lips as golden red blood poured out of his nostrils and down his lips and chin like a powerful faucet. Dazed, he stumbled, nearly knocking into where Blake stood frozen.

Zeus flexed his fingers, searching for something to hold on to as his damaged brain stuttered.

It was almost over. One more blow. For Joel.

Blake inhaled and wrenched his hands from behind him, his fingers wrapped securely around the hilts of the daggers. The blades gleamed, smiling as they arced through the air. Zeus shuffled toward him, unaware of the impending attack.

Mustering all the energy he could, Blake sunk the serrated tips of the daggers into the god's jellylike eyes with a sickening squish, scraping the back of his skull.

Another torrent of golden blood squirted from Zeus's punctured eye sockets, spraying Blake. With three blades buried in his brain, Zeus's searching arms fell against his sides, and his neck slumped forward, bouncing off his chest.

An exhausted sigh slipped from Jezlem's lips as she withdrew the quill and let it clatter to the floor. She slid forward, submerging her foot directly in a pool of glimmering blood. Her arms snaked around Zeus's body, catching him as he began to collapse. Tiny droplets of blood splattered as she brought her feet together, shouldering the god's weight. Cradling Zeus's chin in her hands, she pressed her blood-covered lips to his clammy cheek. "That's from me, baby."

Zeus's upper lip twitched, but aside from that, he was motionless. Grunting, Jezlem gave his stiffening body a light push to the left, sending him crashing against a broken table. One of the daggers in his eye hit the tabletop at a sharp angle, carving his eyeball further. The once bright golden halo radiating from the god dimmed to a sickly yellow until the light vanished all together, leaving behind cooling flesh.

Blake gagged at the sight. Watery vomit coughed over his lips as Zeus's blood flowed, puddling against his sneakers. He shook his head as the adrenaline wore off and he succumbed to the horror of the earlier attack. He collapsed to the ground. The god's butchered eyes stared back at him. He couldn't stomach the sight another second.

"Jez." The word was no more than a wheezing puff of air.

Jezlem looked away from Zeus's cold form, a fierceness Blake hadn't seen before dominating her expression. He choked on the little breath he had, her wildness catching him off guard. The way she stared at the body, Blake half expected her to start devouring it.

Jezlem began to back away just as Kait materialized in front of him, her violet eyes a steadying beacon. "Blake, hold on."

His head throbbed, and his vision blurred. Gone was the comforting feeling of the tonic, gone was the adrenaline that had carried him this far. All he felt was blood slipping out of him from the hole above his heart. He tilted his face, trying to find Kait, but his eyes rolled into the back of his head.

⚡ 38 ⚡

"Jez!" Kait shouted, calling her sister away from Zeus's corpse. "Help me. We need to stop the bleeding." Kait's hands scoured Blake's body, searching for all of his wounds as Jezlem knelt by his shoulder. "Use this." She ripped off a strip of her dress. "Clean the blood off as best you can so we know the severity of his injuries."

It was quiet for a moment as the sisters worked, both unsure what to say after so many months apart. Kait's throat grew thick as she glanced at Jezlem. "I can't believe you're alive. When I saw the ceiling collapse I…I… What about Bia?"

"I'm here." Bia's soft voice was music to Kait's ears. "Joel is alive too. I've already started healing the internal bleeding. I need to get back to mend his broken bones before they set, but I needed to see you…" Her stutter was barely noticeable as she took in Zeus's mutilated body. Then her eyes slid over to Blake. "Is he…?"

Kait was silent for a minute, her fingers weaving back and forth as she applied pressure to the large gash above his heart. Her breathing hitched as she regarded the broken boy before her. Covered in blood, he lay unmoving. She wished she could remember the exact color green of his eyes. If only she could get them open again. This time, she wouldn't forget.

At last, she answered: "I don't know. Bia, please, you have to help him. He only has minutes left. If we can't stop this bleeding…" She sighed, unable to finish her sentence. "Why didn't he stop? Why did he continue to fight with all those injuries? How was he still standing?"

"Layla prepared a temporary tonic for both of them to heal their wounds, but despite that, Blake never would have given up." Jezlem's lips pulled into a sad smile.

Bia crouched beside Kait and wrapped her arms around her in a soft embrace. The gentle gesture caused Kait's eyes to tear. Bia disliked physical comfort, yet here she was initiating it. Kait yearned to hold her tighter, but Blake's wounds were too critical to pause for even a moment. She wiped the pooling tears from her eyes as she moved out of way, making room for Bia to work over him.

"Thank you," she whispered, removing her hands as Bia's fingers began twitching, casting her magic to revert the flow of blood back into his body.

Kait's eyes connected with Jezlem. This was their first meeting since Zeus had taken her halo. Jezlem stood, looking fierce and powerful after surviving the fight. Kait didn't think, only acted. She threw her arms around her sister's neck and held her, burying her face in her hair. "Thank you for coming after me. You saved me, even when I couldn't save you."

"No. Look at you. Your halo is still intact. You were alone with the most powerful god for two days, and you held him off. I had nothing to do with that. You're a warrior, Kait." With the pad of her thumb, Jezlem wiped tears from Kait's cheeks.

Kait shook her head, nestling into the warmth of her sister's hand. "What happened? I saw the ceiling collapse on you."

Bia was so practiced at healing the physical form that her spells wove one after another in perfect synchrony. The bleeding had stopped, and Kait could detect the faint beat of Blake's heart. Her pulse jumped. He was still alive.

"I knew we couldn't outrun the rocks," Bia said, "so I enlarged a narrow crevice and threw us inside. It took a while to climb back out. Jez clawed her way to the surface first. She wasn't going to leave you."

"But there was so much blood." Fresh tears gathered in Kait's eyes as the crimson blood splashed across her mind. "I thought I had lost you both."

"Shh." Jezlem stroked Kait's hair. "It's all right. It was the piriol's blood. The rocks crushed its body, but we're okay. We're all going to be okay."

Kait sniffed, too overwhelmed to respond. She crushed herself against Jezlem's torso, burying her face in her sister's sweat-matted curls. She smelled like blood and steel, but Kait didn't care. The guilt-riddled hole in her chest shrunk the tighter she held her.

Zeus was gone. The piriol was gone, yet somehow they were still alive. For all their struggles in the past, her sisters sacrificed everything to come to her aid. Kait always thought love made you weak, but she was wrong. Love was the strongest armor of all.

Blake veered in and out of consciousness, toeing the blurry line between life and death. He felt his body being prodded, pulled, and rolled as Bia worked to put him back together. He stopped listening to the girls' muted conversation almost as soon as it began. He couldn't understand the simple syllables. After so much fighting, it felt wonderful to turn everything off and hover above the black void threatening closer. He frowned as he felt death's grip tighten. At least he would see Joel soon. He pictured him leaning against the pearly gates, a cigarette hanging from his lips.

"Don't you give up now," a soft voice commanded in his ear.

Blake struggled against the blackness. He wanted to stay, knew he should try harder to remain conscious, but it was so much easier to slip away. He reached out, trying to settle back into his body, but it felt wrong, like a size too small; he couldn't fit the pieces in place.

"Jez, find some teardra. If I can administer it to him, it will act as a beacon and anchor his soul."

"Teardra?"

"Yes. Find it. I can save him. I can bring him back," Bia said. "He's still here. I can feel him."

Blake watched from above as Jezlem left Bia's side while she continued to work, healing and stitching, never stopping. Kait kneeled by his head, stroking his hair. Worry plagued him. Why couldn't he feel her touch?

"Oh my God," Joel whispered.

Bia shot a quick glance over her shoulder. Blake frowned as his soul hovered above. Joel looked rough. Ugly bruises covered his jaw, and dried blood crusted the collar of his shirt, but he was standing and coherent.

"Is he dead?" Joel asked, his voice thick with emotion.

Bia shook her head, but Blake saw the way she gnawed on her lower lip. "His body is healed, but his soul…it's drifting."

Kait stared at her sister with wide eyes. "What does that mean?"

Bia cleared her throat, refusing to meet Kait's gaze. "Layla had a talent for potions. If Jez can find some teardra, I can use it to reunite Blake's soul with his body, but…we're running out of time."

Blake watched as Kait's face drained of color, coming to the same conclusion she did. If Bia couldn't reunite his soul with his physical body, he would never wake. If he were connected to his body, his heart would be racing, and he'd be racked with nausea, but instead, he floated, feeling the invisible strings tethering him to his body loosen.

"Jez!" Kait shouted, her voice breaking.

The sound of sprinting feet echoed as Jezlem rounded a charred boulder. Her hair flew behind her, her expression tight, but her hands clutched a clear vial. "I found some in a room farther out. It must have been Layla's supply. There's not much left." She handed it to Bia.

"That's fine, fine." Bia grabbed the vial and removed the metal cap from the narrow mouth. A tiny pop echoed in the cavern, the only sound as everyone looked on. Bia rested the glass vial against Blake's chapped lips and tipped the contents into his mouth. The teardra splashed against his molars, running down his tongue, coating the back of his throat. She shuffled back, her eyes unblinking, but nothing happened.

Kait cradled Blake's head. "It's not working."

"Hush. Give it a minute."

Inch by inch, the liquid dripped into Blake's stomach until a small amount pooled, creating an anchor. Blake's spine arched violently. Kait and Joel cried out in unison as his body slammed back to the ground, but Bia grinned. It was working. Another surge ignited, shooting through Blake's veins like a firecracker. His body thumped again. With every pulse, the teardra escaped from his body as a translucent vapor, sending out an electromagnetic field to recover his soul.

"Come on, Blake." Kait bent down and kissed his forehead. "Breathe."

Blake's body reacted again. A choking gasp gargled in the back of his throat, and his eyelids peeled open as his chest rose and fell. The changes were subtle at first as remnants of the teardra swirled through Blake's bloodstream, the mixture spreading along his body with each new breath. The cold began to withdraw from his body, and he felt warmth. His fingers and feet twitched as his soul settled at last, wrapping around his vertebra and weaving its fingers into every cell and fiber.

"What's happening? How?" But Joel's questions went unanswered as everyone held their breath.

Another minute ticked by. Then, like the commanding beat of a drum, Blake's heart pumped, once, twice, three times, falling back into a steady rhythm.

Another minute.

Blake's green eyes flashed, and he inhaled sharply, his back rising off the floor as his lungs buoyed him up.

"Whoa," Blake rasped. "That was…strange."

"Oh my God, man. You're back!" Joel leaned down and pressed his cheek to Blake's chest, releasing a few relieved sobs as he held onto him. "You were dead!"

"Blake! You're okay!" Kait wrapped his head in her arms.

Bia sighed. "We weren't too late." A large smile split her lips—the first true smile Blake had ever seen her wear. The motion transformed her face, joy radiating from every pore.

"Let me help you up." Joel snaked one arm around Blake's waist and pulled him to his feet. "You are one lucky bastard!"

Blake chuckled while Joel tousled his hair. A warm touch alerted him as Kait slipped her hand into his. He turned, surprised. She stared up at him as if he were the sun. He mirrored her grip and wrapped his other arm around her.

Cheers roared as everyone patted Blake on the back. Reluctantly, he tore his gaze away from Kait's beautiful smile to face the others.

"You fought so bravely. Thank you both for saving my sister," Bia said.

Blake shrugged, looking confused. "It wasn't me. It was Jezlem. She killed Zeus. I just…made sure." His eyes roamed the blood-stained room, finding Zeus's pale form several yards away. "Is he really dead?"

Jezlem shook her head. "He's immortal. No matter what we do, it won't be enough. For now, this body has been destroyed beyond the point any magic can heal. I imagine his soul is at Hades's door right now, begging for a new body. We haven't rid the realms of Zeus, but maybe he'll think twice before hunting nymphs again." She looked at the broken god. Disgust colored her gaze, but Blake also caught her features softening.

"I'm sorry you couldn't get your powers back," he told her.

Jezlem sighed, brushing her hair over her ear. "Thanks, but I don't need my ethereal connection to be happy anymore. I proved that I was better than Zeus, better than what he did to me. I am strong."

Kait hugged Jezlem. "The strongest woman I know."

"What about Atlas?" Blake asked.

"He's dead," Bia said. "He will never come back."

"So…it's over then?"

"Yes." Bia smiled.

"What do we do now?" Joel asked.

"We go home." Jezlem slipped her hand into his. "To whatever future we decide to make. I'm not scared of being mortal anymore. I'm still me."

"Life can still be an adventure." Joel planted a quick kiss on her lips, clearly catching her off guard. "Let's get out of here." He turned to face the intimidating rock path ahead. "Bia, do you think you could take care of this?"

Bia raised her palms, stacking her fingers in intricate shapes, and commanded the peaks to recede.

⚡

Kait tugged Blake's hand, holding him back as the rest of the small group began navigating the uneven terrain. She licked her lips, nervous and anxious and relieved all at the same time. Her body felt too small to hold all her emotions at once. Blake waited, grinning, seeming content just to hold her.

A small chuckle fell from Kait's lips. "I promised myself something when you woke up."

"What's that?" Blake whispered.

Reaching up, Kait placed her hands on either side of his temples, sliding her fingers through his hair. Her heart raced as she met his gaze. His eyes were emerald green, flecked through with hazel specks. An amber ring encircled each of his pupils.

"I promised that I would never again forget the exact shade of your eyes."

Blake's skin flushed under her touch. "They're just green."

"No." Kait shook her head. "Like you, there's so much more to them. Thank you for what you did, for challenging Zeus."

Blake's fingers brushed Kait's cheekbones, tracing the purple and yellow bruises that surely marred her skin. "He still hurt you. I'm sorry I failed." His hand descended lower, gingerly touching the four identical scars on her neck.

Kait nuzzled his hand, then lifted his chin to move his stare from her injuries to her eyes. "You didn't fail. Blake, you saved me. All this time, I thought I had to defeat Zeus by myself. It was my punishment for the mistakes in my past. I made Bia stay behind when she tried to assist me; I thought I alone could protect Jezlem when she confronted Zeus; I ran from your kindness. I didn't think I needed friends, didn't think I deserved them, but seeing you, watching how all of you worked together to rescue me…"

Her words trailed off as rivulets of tears trickled down her chin.

"Relying on others isn't a weakness; it's a privilege." Kait wiped her face with the back of her hand. "If only I had realized that sooner, we could have avoided all of this." She released an uneasy laugh.

Blake gave her a crooked grin. "Sure, my week would have been a little easier, but then I never would have met you or discovered this incredible world. My body might be scarred, but I'll count each one as a permanent reminder of what I went through and why."

A coy smile pulled at Kait's lips. "And why did you battle a crazed god and a vengeful Titan?" She peeled open Blake's shredded shirt, slipping her fingers inside the gaping fabric. Her fingertips traced the knotted flesh where Zeus's sword pierced him.

"So that I would be worthy of doing this." Blake guided her face to his.

He paused, his lips hovering an inch over hers, waiting, offering her the chance to pull away. She didn't hesitate. Pushing onto her toes, she pressed her lips to his. Her posture softened as his arms enveloped her. The same flutter of warmth she felt during their first meeting came flooding back, seeping through her limbs like honey, weighing down her thoughts so she could exist wholly in this single, perfect moment with Blake.

He was mortal and she belonged to the ethereal realm, but none of that mattered as their lips moved together, sinking as one into the unknown world of tomorrow.

Someone cleared their throat, shifting them back to reality. Kait bit her lower lip as she settled back on her heels, but she didn't pull away.

Blake angled his head, smiling. "Do you think maybe we could hang out when we get back?"

She reached up and brushed one last sweet kiss across his jaw. "I'd like that." An electric tingle coursed through her as he hugged her tighter to his chest.

"Come on, guys," Jezlem called.

A laugh fell from Kait's lips as she spun to face the group, wrapping her arm around Blake's waist. "Ready?" she asked him.

"For anything," he replied.

They crossed the broken floor, Blake matching Kait's graceful stride. She had no idea what tomorrow would be like—or life in general now that Blake was a part of her world. Deep bruises throttled her neck, chaffed skin encircled her wrists, and blood splattered her dress, but she was breathing, with magic coursing through her fingertips—because of him. Joy buoyed her steps.

They couldn't have been more different—a nymph and a mortal from two separate worlds—yet somehow, a spark had ignited between them, interweaving their fates, connecting them through a common bond. Blake squeezed her hand. A thrill ran through her as she returned his touch and realized she had fallen for him completely.

Kait grinned, imagining all the ways her life was going to change with Blake by her side. The heavy layer of guilt she wore for Willow slid farther off her shoulders with every step out of the mountain. Maybe at last she'd allow herself to feel happiness, to stop running long enough to appreciate the beauty of everyday life.

She inhaled. Mistakes were going to happen, but now there would always be a steady hand to pull her up. She strode toward the future, brimming with hope. Only time would tell if she was ready for it.

⚡ EPILOGUE ⚡

"There, darling. He'll be home soon." Hera stroked the scaly head of her sleeping python. Its thick body lay coiled around her shoulders, elegantly draped as it slumbered.

The goddess leaned back against the soft cushions of the lounge chair and wrapped her lips around a delicate china cup. She inhaled the sweet fragrance of the hazelberry tea, closing her eyes as the hot liquid cascaded down the back of her throat.

A warm breeze teased the ends of her hair and rustled the white flowers decorating the surrounding dogwood trees. Apart from the wind, the private garden where she reclined was silent. It was a perfect summer's day on Olympus. She took another sip, delighting in the calming flavor. In the distance, a melancholy cry wafted through her sanctuary as her albino peacock mourned. Hera frowned, disturbed by the chilling sound.

Alarm seized her heart. "What did you see?"

Hera rose and crossed the marble terrace, her long skirts whispering as she moved. The rustling resembled voices, and the sound set her teeth on edge. She settled atop a waist-high column, the middle of which was hollowed out to resemble a well. The Skyglass awaited her command, peering down into the endless blue sky below Olympus. A wedding gift from Zeus, the Skyglass allowed Hera to view anyone or anything in all the realms with only a whisper.

Hera leaned over. Her teacup rattled on its saucer. "Show me my beloved."

The Skyglass responded. The cerulean sky clouded, swirling with vivid color.

The peacock's piercing cry echoed eerily once more as a wave of blood splattered visions transformed the tranquil view. Hera's cup tumbled to the ground, and the fragile ceramic shattered into a dozen shards. Black stone walls loomed, but she only saw Zeus.

"No," she whispered, but her plea did nothing to stop the knives. The blond mortal plunged a lethal quill into the base of Zeus's skull before steel points carved out his eyes. Hera couldn't look away, transfixed by the horrible images.

The python lifted its head, sensing its mistress's distress. It slithered down her arm. Flicking its tongue, it surveyed the garden beyond the terrace for danger, but the great snake was powerless to protect the goddess from the visions below.

Hera gasped as she watched Zeus fall. His glorious body collapsed in a pile of disjointed limbs. Golden red ichor puddled around his graying flesh. The glow of his halo diminished until there was nothing left but a stiff corpse. Silent tears coursed down Hera's cheeks as she stared ahead, unable to accept the truth that played out before her eyes.

She'd warned him to stay away from Atlas. He was dangerous, reckless, and bitter. Ever since his banishment, the seed of darkness within him had festered into cruelty. And that whore of an omodian he kept—Hera never trusted her. She was always throwing herself at Zeus after he finished with his latest hunt, but she had nothing to offer him, no euphoria to taste.

Hera spat. She detested the whole nymphian race—demons crafted in the goddesses' beautiful image to bring beauty to Earth. They were no more than devilish vixens that enjoyed teasing gods with hushed whispers and demure touches.

A heavy thud rattled Hera from her thoughts. Zee Zee, her python, had dropped to the cool marble and coiled around her calf. The python's tongue tickled her inner thigh as it held on tight, but Hera barely felt the pressure. Instead, she watched the nymph—the one with the dark hair, the one that Zeus abandoned her for. The aurai bent over the mortal Hera herself sought to kill at the hospital. He was lifeless after Zeus carved him like a bird for a feast. She hoped he died painfully.

Hera's eyes roamed farther. Hauling another broken boy out from under a mountain of rocks, the aurai's sisters struggled. She ignored the blonde. Because she was mortal, Hera was forbidden to harm her—a law that had landed her in hot water with the Council when word of the poisoned male reached them. Her punishment was insignificant though. Six months of probation was hardly a slap on the wrist.

Her eyes alighted on the redhead at last. Her heart rate quickened as an exhilarating idea formed. She studied the nymph's ruby glow, the way her chest rose and fell. Hera's lips curled.

"Breathe while you can, nymph."

ACKNOWLEDGMENTS

Thank you to all my readers! The journey that this book has endured has been exciting but excruciating at the same time! I wrote the first draft of *Among the Hunted* in 2009 and at long last it is here in your hands. I hope Kait's and Blake's stories resonated with you and I'm sorry if some moments were difficult to read. As someone whose life has been touched by addiction and has personal experience with sexual assault, I pray that we are all able to conquer the haunting thoughts and regrets and rise up.

I want to give a huge thank you to Vern and Joni at BHC Press for all their hard work on this book and for believing in me. Also, to my editor, Chelsea, you are beyond amazing for helping me unearth the true story buried beneath my doubts and for shaping me into a stronger writer.

Thank you, Bailey, you were a fantastic sensitivity reader in the early stages of this project and gave me great insight that I will always carry.

To Dale Reynolds, my high school friend. You read the first version of this novel and loved it even with all its flaws. Hopefully, this edition will blow your socks off!

To my husband, Daniel. Thank you for letting me try out battle moves on you! You're the best stunt double any author could ask for! Thank you to my babies, Jack and Joanna, for letting mama write in-between frisbee throws! I hope one day you will read this and be proud.

And lastly, a final thank you to my sister, Mercedes. She was there eleven years ago at the inception of this book and never gave up on me or the idea, though she may have wanted to throw it out the nearest window at times. I hope I wrote in enough romance for you!

ABOUT THE AUTHOR

Caytlyn Brooke is the author of *Dark Flowers*, *Wired*, and the Skyglass series.

She holds a degree in psychology from UAlbany where she studied fear and human behavior, which fueled her love of people watching. A lover of fantasy worlds, horror, orange cats, and Earl Grey tea, Caytlyn lives in Elmira, New York with her husband Daniel, her two children, and her orange tabby cat.

Lightning Source UK Ltd.
Milton Keynes UK
UKHW011930160821
388964UK00001B/14